"DID HE HURT YOU?"

"I—I'm all right," I replied shakily.

"I don't think he'll trouble you again."

"No. Thank you, Mr. Rockwell, for coming by when you did and . . ."

Abruptly he turned, and his eyes burned into mine. And then suddenly all of his usual reserve left him. He reached out and crushed me against him, his head bent, fingers entangled in my tumbled hair. My lips parted under the exquisite pressure of his; the taste and feel of him flooded my senses. I clung to him, his heart thundering against mine, my body responding to the desperate passion in him, and prompting it to inflame even further.

But though there was a fierce delight, a wild joy, in our embrace, I found it a torment as well. And somehow there were tears in my eyes. For there could be no happy ending . . .

ROMANTIC SUSPENSE WITH ZEBRA'S GOTHICS

THE SWIRLING MISTS OF CORNWALL   (2924, $3.95)
by Patricia Werner

Rhionna Fowley ignored her dying father's plea that she never return to his ancestral homeland of Cornwall. Yet as her ship faltered off the rugged Cornish coast, she wondered if her journey would indeed be cursed.

Shipwrecked and delirious, Rhionna found herself in a castle high above the roiling sea—and in thrall to the handsome and mysterious Lord Geoffrey Rhyweth. But fear and suspicion were all around: Geoffrey's midnight prowling, the hushed whispers of the townspeople, women disappearing from the village. She knew she had to flee, for soon it would be too late.

THE STOLEN BRIDE OF GLENGARRA CASTLE   (3125, $3.95)
by Anne Knoll

Returning home after being in care of her aunt, Elly Kincaid found herself a stranger in her own home. Her father was a ghost of himself after the death of Elly's mother, her brother was bitter and violent, her childhood sweetheart suddenly hostile.

Elly agreed to meet the man her brother Hugh wanted her to marry. While drawn to the brooding, intense Gavan Mitchell, Elly was determined to ignore his whispered threats of ghosts and banshees. But she could *not* ignore the wailing sounds from the tower. Someone was trying to terrify her, to sap her strength, to draw her into the strange nightmare.

THE LOST DUCHESS OF GREYDEN CASTLE   (3046, $3.95)
by Nina Coombs Pykare

Vanessa never thought she'd be a duchess; only in her dreams could she be the wife of Richard, Duke of Greyden, the man who married her headstrong sister, Caroline. But one year after Caroline's violent and mysterious death, Richard proposed and took her to his castle in Cornwall.

Her dreams had come true, but they quickly turned to *nightmares*. Why had Richard never told her he had a twin brother who hated him? Why did Richard's sister shun her? Why was she not allowed to go to the North Tower? Soon the truth became clear: everyone there had reason to kill Caroline, and now someone was after *her*. But which one?

MICHELE YOUNT THOMAS
THE SHIFTING SHADOWS OF MOONGATE

ZEBRA BOOKS
KENSINGTON PUBLISHING CORP.

for Noel

ZEBRA BOOKS

are published by

Kensington Publishing Corp.
475 Park Avenue South
New York, NY 10016

First printing: May, 1991

Printed in the United States of America

Author's Note

In this story, Copper Beeches is based on Chateau-sur, one of the mansions maintained by the Preservation Society of Newport County. I encourage my readers to visit this fascinating house and roam the grounds where they may find for themselves the Chinese Moongate in the stone wall, as well as the magnificent weeping beeches.

I am indebted to the Newport Historical Society for their excellent and comprehensive exhibit, "Newport in the Gilded Age," from which point I began my research.

I would also like to thank my own little girl, Colette, for sharing with me her books on fairies and elves.

". . . the weak members of civilised society propagate their kind . . . this must be highly injurious to the race of man."

Charles Darwin

"For if the unworthy are helped to increase . . . the effect is to produce, generation after generation, a greater unworthiness."

"The whole effect of nature is to get rid of such, to clear the world of them, and make room for better."

Herbert Spencer, Social Darwinist

". . . if we do not like the survival of the fittest, we have only one possible alternative, and that is survival of the unfittest . . . the latter carries society downwards and favors its worst members."

"The millionaires are a product of natural selection . . ."

William Graham Sumner,
Social Darwinist

Chapter One

We do not spend our summers in Newport. The rest of the year there is no place we would rather be, but the summers there are not for us. It is not that in those months the past comes hurling back with its stinging memories, though one might expect that. Nor do we fear that others will clutch those memories in feverish attempts to ward off boredom, the society matrons reminding one another gloatingly of what happened at Copper Beeches. ("Now how many years ago was it? They still do not dare show their faces.") No, even for them the shocking past fades and dwindles in the light of new scandals and tragedies to relish.

It is simply this: to Drew his home is not his in July or August. The character of the old seaport town becomes so greatly altered in those eight weeks that years ago we elected to spend the summers elsewhere. Newport, dignified, stately, but always with that forlorn air of decay, its splendor and prosperity left in the last century, is ill-suited to its eight-week role as host to the members of New York's Four Hundred. This sleepy wooden town with its old docks and weather-beaten houses, still noble, still genteel, becomes rapidly overwhelmed at the first signs of the summer invasion when the Fall River steamboats and elegant yachts discharge their gilded passengers, girded up for another campaign of determined enjoyment and lavish spectacle.

The quaint narrow streets which slope to the harbor, lined with colonial houses and churches, become nothing more than a watercolor setting, a washed-out backdrop which pales and recedes before the elaborate stage world and its glittering players in their summer palaces on the rise above the town.

We retreat across the sea to England where we lease an ancient stone house in the Cotswolds, one with a rambling garden where our children run and play and I sit with a canvas before me and a brush in my hand, where we savor a tranquility, an effortless carefree existence wholly foreign to the summer colonists who quit their mansions on 5th Avenue for those on the Rhode Island coast.

We take simple picnics, vastly different from the sumptuous, perfectly detailed and executed ones in Newport. Drew drives us himself in a slightly shabby trap, while across the Atlantic others are driven in glossy coaches by footmen in livery. We give small weekend house parties and discuss the arts or politics around a farmhouse table while hundreds of miles away others sit down to long silent dinners served on gold plates where only the crystal sparkles. In the dew-scented mornings I cut hollyhocks and larkspur, deliciously untidy and vivid, while in other rooms far away exotic flowers from the Nile stand statically in ornate vases, their authenticity somehow lost on the journey.

For two months we live as ex-patriates, delighting in our adopted land but never tempted to remain longer. In September we return to Newport when the salt-laced air fizzes like champagne, when the golden days mellow and shorten, when the rosehips blush crimson in the hedgerow. The flurried activity of the brief summer over, the dust settles about the old town once more and it resumes its dignified repose.

It was not always so for Drew. Cordelia would not have missed a single summer in Newport, not a single ball or dinner party. In the brilliant social scene, in its rituals and dogma, she found her raison d'etre, and Drew his prison.

It was that world which killed her, and which nearly destroyed Drew as well.

My father, Lancelot Morrow, was a great painter in his day. Recently he has become out of fashion, as it is the inevitability of all art styles, no matter how popular, to one day step aside to make way for the new. It will happen to me as well one day. One or two art critics have of late written disparagingly of Lancelot Morrow, dismissing him as merely an accomplished technician who catered to the wealthy and the powerful. But as few great artists have not sought out patrons, and as few great men have not desired some degree of permanence, my father and his clients were well-matched.

His particular brilliance lay in portraiture, rather than in landscape or genre painting. And it is the rich who award commissions to have their likenesses put on canvas. Having one's portrait painted by Lancelot Morrow was once a requirement of fashionable life on both sides of the Atlantic.

As a very young man he had left his native Philadelphia to study at the Ecole des Beaux-Arts in Paris. Later he submitted paintings to the Paris Salon where he received honorable mentions, and he began to receive his first commissions to paint the wives and daughters of Americans traveling abroad.

That is how he met my mother. She was making the Grand Tour in the company of the family of a school friend. While in Paris, they made the ac-

11

quaintance of the handsome young artist. The father of my mother's friend saw a sample of his work and liked it well enough to ask him to paint his own daughter. By the time the portrait was finished, my parents had revealed their love for one another and run off together. I always think that is such a peculiar phrase, "run off." In actuality I imagine they went in search of a Protestant minister, no small task in that Catholic country, and married quietly.

It was the terrible scourge of my grandparents' lives that they had allowed their daughter to go abroad, and they wore it like a hairshirt. Never for one moment did they stop deploring the past and the mistake they had made in permitting their only child to accompany the family from New York City to Europe. My mother's name was never spoken in their house, but not for one instant was it out of their minds. Yet it was not with longing that they thought of her, but with bitterness and fury that stiffened and hardened them until there was nothing else.

My grandparents made it clear that they never wanted to hear from their daughter again. Perhaps relieved, my parents moved to London where they were befriended by the aesthetes whose credo was: "art for art's sake." James McNeill Whistler and Edward Coley Burne-Jones were two close friends. If my father's London studio was similar to the one I knew years later on Tenth Street in New York, then it was a sociable place with fellow artists or members of the literati milling about or playing music while he worked.

I was born in London but I remember nothing of my short childhood there. When I was two years old my mother contracted typhoid fever and died. My father, having no family of his own, wrote to my mother's parents to inform them of her death, and to announce the existence of a small daughter.

I have no illusions about him. Had he felt inclined to keep me himself, he would not have done so; there had been no communication between them since the wedding. In writing to them three years later, he must have hoped or expected that they would ask that I be sent to live with them in New York, which indeed they did. They did not come themselves; my grandparents never traveled outside Dutchess County. Instead they sent an indigent relative across the Atlantic to fetch me and bring me back to their estate in the rolling farm country of the Hudson Valley.

That is why I have no memory of London, or of my mother, and no early memories of my father.

Evidently my grandmother decided (for I had realized at an early age that it was my grandmother who decided everything) that the indigent relative who had brought me from England would be the ideal person to look after me and act as my nurse, not because she got on particularly well with children, but because, as a poor spinster, she had no purpose in life in my grandmother's eyes but to live at Starlings and do whatever my grandmother wished for the privilege of calling her 'cousin.'

Cousin Martha was a weak, dried-up-looking woman who was terrified of my grandmother and burdened by migraines and rheumatism. She did not dislike me, for I was the reason for her sudden usefulness and my grandmother's burst of charity, but she never once attempted to enter my world or to speak to me with that exasperated weary tone absent from her voice. When I wanted comfort or kind words, I would go to the kitchen where there were gingersnaps and where Bessie let me rock in her big rocker by the fire.

My grandparents were both from very old Dutch families who had settled in the area in the late seventeenth century. They had more land than money and more pride than land. When their daughter, whom they had regrettably sent to finishing school in New York City, had eloped with a painter she had met in Paris, they took her shame and disgrace upon themselves and retired within the confines of their farmhouse. My father was still unknown in his own country when I was a small child. But had he been famous, exalted, it would have made no difference. That was not the match they wanted for her. Her betrayal of them, of her aristocratic Dutch heritage, damned her in their eyes forever.

The house, Starlings, was beautiful. It was built in the first half of the eighteenth century with all the handsome features one looks for in Dutch colonial houses. All the fireplaces were framed with lovely Delft tiles, some depicting pastoral scenes, some parables from the Bible. Throughout the house the raised paneling was magnificent, painted in bayberry or bright blue. There was an enormous fireplace in the kitchen with a beehive oven, and there were Dutch doors to the outside with their original iron latches still in use. In the dining room were two built-in corner cupboards. All the furniture was very old and nearly black.

In the upstairs landing stood an enormous *kas* where the linens were stored, the wood very dark and highly polished. I was not allowed to put my grubby fingers on it.

My grandmother held out against gas lighting, claiming it was dirty and smelly, and so at night we burned candles. I remember being frightened in the night by the looming shadows created by the one guttering candle I was permitted. Surprisingly in those times Cousin Martha was a solace to me, even if only because my grandmother would have been disturbed by my whimperings and blamed her. So she would sit with me until I fell asleep.

14

I have an early memory of just one of those nights, lying in bed, too thoughtful for sleep.

"Cousin Martha," I asked her, "whose child is that boy, Jeremy?"

"Why, Ariel, you know very well that Jeremy is Bob Hachard's boy. Don't be foolish."

"Then—then he has a father?"

"Of course he has a father. And a mother too. Whatever can you be thinking of? Go to sleep."

"I knew he had a mother and a father. Where are my mother and my father, Cousin Martha?"

There was a silence. But it was a not a true silence. The shadows on the walls, the gloomy corners of the room, the flickering light all whispered my question over and over. In the hushed murkiness was a secret.

"I must have parents," I went on, "all children do. Where are mine?"

When Cousin Martha spoke, her voice was sharp. But there was something else in it as well—dismay, even fear.

"Ariel, you are the most ungrateful child! Do you know how fortunate you are to live in this fine house, to have a grandmother and grandfather taking care of you, giving you everything a child needs? You might be living in—in squalor, in the very worse of degradations, but here you are at Starlings, a very fortunate little girl. Do not anger your grandmother by your ingratitude. I will not inform her of your cruel persistent questions if you promise never to ask them again. Promise me!"

I did not ask again for a very long time.

Every morning I joined my grandparents and Cousin Martha in the parlor to listen to my grandfather read from the huge old Bible. The verses were inevitably the dark, sinister-sounding passages with promises of our sins being met with well-deserved misfortune. Sometimes Grandmother would look hard at me when Grandfather read; I knew she was thinking of the ways I had fallen short the day before.

I have often wondered what my mother's life was like before she went away to school and then to the Continent. Had her defection so altered them that the people I knew were entirely different from the parents she had known? I did not think so. Surely she would not have been so willing to settle in London and turn her back on her former life had she been able to coax them round to her way of thinking, or even desirous of doing so. But the very idea of anyone coaxing my grandparents to change their views was so absurd that I was certain her childhood must have been very like mine. My mother must have told my father what her early life had been like, but still he had sent me to them.

The grounds of the estate were lovely and sprawling. From the road there was a very long driveway which passed through an apple orchard and then through wooded areas of maples, spruces, and dogwoods. Before the break-up of the patroon system, my grandfather's family had owned land ten miles in two directions, but they had been forced to relinquish most of it to the tenant farmers who had worked the land yet given much of their produce and earnings to the owner of the estate, the patroon. When that outmoded feudal way of life was declared illegal, my grandfather was no longer heir to a prosperous kingdom.

Starlings stood on a bluff high above the Hudson River and I liked nothing better than to sit on the back lawn, drinking in the peace and beauty of the view whose moods and colors changed almost daily. I did not know then that years before, in the middle of the century, a group of artists had extolled its virtues,

16

painting those glorious vistas so like our view from Starlings. I only knew that in the dense greenness of the rolling hills with the Catskills shimmering violet in the background, or in the blazing autumn shrubs and trees warming the blue currents below, I sought and found the solace and contentment which was sorely needed in my life. I loved to watch the riverboats steaming their way up to Albany or down to New York, and I would listen for the sound of their horns.

On Sundays we would drive into Rhinebeck to attend church, and that was as much of the world as I saw. My grandmother always wore black; I, too, was dressed in dark dresses and white pinafores, black stockings and boots. My grandmother's hair was gray, but she had no wrinkles on her broad ruddy face. Bessie, the cook, said no wrinkles would dare to appear there. Grandmother wore a bunch of keys pinned to her waist like some medieval chatelaine. Several times a day she would unlock the drawers of the silver chest and *kas* for the maid, Janet, and instruct her in what to take out. That way, I suppose, Janet could not steal from her — or so she reckoned. Janet, I'm certain, never felt the slightest inclination to take my grandmother's things.

My grandmother had very little to say to me as a young child aside from, "Sit still," or "Stop that at once." I was as frightened of her as Cousin Martha was, and I attempted to keep out of her notice as often as possible.

At mealtimes she and my grandfather rarely spoke; when we rode into town in the carriage, silence was the norm as well. Occasionally my grandmother would chide Cousin Martha for what she regarded as a failing on my part. When I picked up my grandfather's pocket watch to listen to it and accidentally dropped it, I was confined to my room for two days and fed only bread and water. I was four years old.

Such qualities as I had revealed in myself had to be stamped out early in a child. Joy was alien to their lives; forgiveness was a foreign word with a meaning they could not translate.

As far back as I can recall, I loved to draw, to sketch: any activity where I clutched some instrument in my hand which made its mark on a surface. I would scribble on my slate long before I learned to read and write, drawing people, animals, houses, clouds, boats on the river, whatever took my fancy. No one ever took any notice of this. But later, when I was six, and given paper, and taught to use an ink pen in order to form my letters, suddenly my favorite indoor pastime caused a furor which baffled and devastated me.

I was sitting at the table in the schoolroom one day. Cousin Martha was checking several of my lessons, and I was sketching as I often did when there was no other task set before me.

My grandmother rarely visited the schoolroom, but that afternoon for some reason she took it into her head to do just that.

We heard her steps outside in the hall, and then the door opened. Immediately I set down my pen and sat up straight in my chair; I could sense, rather than see, Cousin Martha also tensing, her scrawny body stiffening.

Whether she began to speak before her eyes alighted on the opened notebook before me, I do not recall. Suddenly it was snatched up from the table with an abrupt jerkiness, and I glanced up, startled and alarmed.

"What is the meaning of this?" said my grandmother in a shrill strangled voice. She never raised her voice.

I was by then truly frightened. Somehow again I

had offended, and even worse than the affair of the pocket watch.

"The child has completed her lessons, C-Cousin," stammered Cousin Martha, as bewildered and terrified as I.

"I ask you, why—why are you permitting this child to—to *draw?*" She spat out the last word, almost unrecognizable in her fury.

Cousin Martha blanched. "I—I—she sometimes—she is fond—"

"Fond! You dare to tell me that to my face! Have you no sense at all, woman? Permitting the child to draw!" Again the last word was treated as something unmentionable.

"I—I'm sorry, Cousin. I see now. Of course I see now. You are right; I—I have been very foolish. Please forgive me. It will not happen again, I promise you that."

"You can be certain that it won't, or you will find yourself without a roof over your head! I cannot believe my eyes. It never occurred to me that I would have to specifically forbid such a pastime. And if I had not come in today, I would not have known. I suppose it has been going on for years!"

Cousin Martha was quaking, her washed-out blue eye fading in color even more.

Walking over to the fireplace, my grandmother tossed in my sketchbook with a distasteful flick of her wrist. This was too much for even me.

I burst out, "Were my drawings not good enough? I'm sorry, Grandmother. I'll practice. I'll do better."

"Silence! And stop those tears at once. You are *never*—I repeat—*never* to draw or to sketch again, Ariel. Is that understood?" she thundered, her heavy broad face red, her large body a formidable tower. "Never again! You will be severely punished if I ever catch you making pictures again!"

19

Never had I seen her so angry. Trembling, I whispered, "Yes, Grandmother."

When she had gone, Cousin Martha said to me sharply, "You heard what she said. I—I was a stupid woman not to have realized. I should have stopped you years ago."

Shattered, I did not ask why. My sketching must have been very poor, I thought miserably, too poor to ever improve.

For a long time after that I did not disobey my grandmother by attempting to capture a likeness or image on paper again. But the love of it was within me, and could not be repressed forever.

When I was eight years old, Cousin Martha died. She died quietly, in her sleep, doubtless so as not to be a bother to anyone. Only it was a bother for Grandmother because who would see to my care and education? There was no other poor relation to call on, or not one who would agree to being Grandmother's unpaid servant.

About a week or so after the funeral, Grandmother sent for me to come to the parlor where she and Grandfather sat in the old caned chairs with high straight backs and turned knobs.

"We have come to a decision, Ariel," said my grandmother, meaning, of course, that she had come to a decision. "You are to go to school."

School! If she had said I was to go to the moon I could not have been any more astonished.

"The fees charged today by private tutors are exorbitant. Your grandfather and I have decided that the Rhinebeck school will be suitable, at least for the present."

I was thrilled. However, I was careful not to show it. If she realized how much the idea appealed to me, she might reconsider.

"You will begin tomorrow. I have already written

to the teacher informing her of your placement. Bob will take you in the carriage in the mornings and be waiting for you when classes are over. You are never to dally in the schoolyard. Bessie will prepare a lunch for you to take every day. You are to conduct yourself at all times as befits our granddaughter. I will not have you acquiring the bad habits or unruly behavior of the village children."

"Yes, Grandmother," I said meekly, all the while thinking—*school!* I was nearly beside myself with excitement. To be away from Starlings for hours every day!

The next morning I hurried down to the kitchen when I was ready, but was too excited to eat my usual bowl of oatmeal. "Is it time to go?" I asked Bessie more than once, and my heart leaped into my mouth when she said it was.

She handed me my lunch in a sack, saying, "This is a big day for you, Ariel. And a lot more natural, if you ask me, than to be cooped up under the attic. Don't be frightened now."

Frightened! What on earth was there to be frightened of? After all, I was leaving Grandmother here. "See you this afternoon, Bessie," I said.

I climbed in the carriage while she stood at the Dutch door opened at the top and waved. Bob, who was also the gardener and man-of-all-work, told me the teacher's name was Miss Kelly and she was young and pretty. I suppose he was comparing her with Cousin Martha.

When he stopped the carriage to let me out in front of the white schoolhouse, a wave of nervousness came over me. I felt suddenly shy and awkward. The children were filing in from the schoolyard; a few of them turned to stare at me. The bell was ringing.

Climbing down from the carriage, I smiled weakly at Bob, clutching my pencil box in one hand and my

21

lunch in the other. A lady in a pale blue gown stood on the steps and she smiled at me as I came forward.

"Good morning," she said. "You must be our new pupil, Ariel."

"Yes, miss."

"Your grandmother wrote me about you. I am Miss Kelly. You may take that desk over there, Ariel."

I sat down as she directed next to a boy with dark hair and behind a girl with blond ringlets. I thought how pretty they looked falling on her shoulders. My own straight auburn hair had always been plaited. Cousin Martha or Bessie had seen to it every morning. The children looked at me, whispering, until Miss Kelly called their attention.

"Good morning, class."

"Good morning, Miss Kelly."

"We will now sing 'America the Beautiful.'"

The children stood up, pushing their chairs up to their desks. I did as well, biting my lip. "America the Beautiful"—what was that? Cousin Martha and Grandmother had never taught me any songs.

Miss Kelly began to sing and the class joined in. I felt incredibly foolish. Desperately I pretended to mouth the words but it was evident to those around me who were regarding me with that faintly hostile air peculiar to children that I did not know the song. One boy sniggered behind his hand.

At the end the girl with the blond ringlets I had so admired turned around. "Didn't you learn to sing that at your old school?"

"I—I've never been to school. I used to have lessons at home."

She had no time to respond for Miss Kelly had begun to call out the names of the students. When a child's name was called, he or she said, "present," and sat down.

I was scarcely paying attention, so embarrassed was I about not knowing "America the Beautiful." Also I was now noticing other things which made me stand out from the rest of the children. The girls wore dresses and pinafores as I did, but in pretty cheerful colors and designs such as checks or tiny wildflowers, and many of the pinafores were coordinated in color. My own dress was black and my pinafore white. I did not look like any of the other girls.

"Ariel Morrow," said Miss Kelly.

So there was another Ariel, I thought, diverted. I glanced about the classroom, eager to see the girl with whom I shared a name. Perhaps I wasn't so different after all.

It was then that I realized that all the children were staring at me. Startled, confused, I looked up at Miss Kelly. She was regarding me too.

"Ariel?"

"Y—yes, Miss Kelly?"

"You must say 'present' when your name is called, as you heard the other children do."

"My name? I thought you said . . . did you call my name?"

Several of the children giggled.

"You must pay better attention, Ariel. I called your name several times."

"But you said, 'Ariel . . . something. I'm Ariel Van Horn."

She frowned. "I was informed that my new pupil would be Ariel Morrow, age eight. From Starlings?"

I nodded anxiously.

"She doesn't even know her own name," said the boy next to me and they all laughed. I colored hotly.

"That's enough, class," said Miss Kelly sharply. "I'm certain there's a very simple explanation for the confusion. But since your grandmother wrote me that Ariel Morrow would be starting school today, we

23

will take her word for it. Now class . . ."

For the rest of the morning I sat in a terrible daze, staring at the book before me but not seeing it. I had humiliated myself before the class and before Miss Kelly, and I did not understand how it had happened. Ariel *Morrow.* Who was she? Never had I heard that name before. Why had Grandmother written it in her letter to Miss Kelly? How could she have made such a mistake? The children had rapidly come to the conclusion that I was an idiot. I couldn't even answer when my own name was called. But I had always thought that my last name was Van Horn, as my grandparents' was. And, when occasionally I had written it down, no one had bothered to correct me.

Sitting there that morning I began to hate my grandmother. I had never hated her before; I had been afraid of her and I did not like her. But that morning the tight knot in my chest and the tears pricking at the back of my eyes gathered into an intense feeling against my grandmother. She was the cause of my failure, my disgrace, on my first day of school. I had a name that I had never heard before. She had even kept it from me on the day I would need it the most.

At noon we were dismissed but I could not have eaten a bite. My stomach felt sick and my head ached. Slowly I followed the rest of the children out into the schoolyard.

"The new girl is so dumb! She can't even remember her own name," said someone.

"And she can't sing!" said the girl with the blond ringlets.

They laughed and I turned around and hurried back into the school so they would not see me cry. The cool gloom folded comfortably around me and I could not keep the tears back any longer. They fell hot and thick down my cheeks. Stumbling over to my desk, I sat down and rested my head on my arm.

Soft fingers touched the back of my neck. "Don't cry, Ariel. The first day is always the hardest in a new school. It will get better, I promise you." Miss Kelly patted my head and made me sit up. She handed me a handkerchief.

"I didn't know my name was Ariel Morrow!" I wailed, "and now they all think I'm stupid!"

"Yes, that is perplexing, about your name, I mean," said Miss Kelly, a pucker in her brow. "I'll make inquiries about that. Do you feel like eating lunch?"

I shook my head forlornly.

"All right, then. Let's see where you are in your studies, shall we?"

Nodding, I wiped my face and blew my nose. Miss Kelly's handkerchief smelled of lavender.

Later she said, "No, my dear, you are most definitely not stupid. Your reading ability is above your age. Do you like books?"

"I haven't read very many."

"Well, I have some I can lend you. Have you ever read any stories by Washington Irving? He wrote about about our area—the Hudson Valley. The folklore. I think you'll enjoy him."

The story was "Rip Van Winkle". "Thank you, Miss Kelly." On the cover was a picture of an old man with a long white beard and a walking stick in his hand.

"Do you like magical stories, Ariel? Fairy tales?"

I must have looked blank because she said, "Never mind. You read this and then write a composition about what you think of it. Then I'll give you other things to read—poetry and more stories. All right? Your knowledge of history needs improving but we'll work on that. I'm going to ring the bell now to sum-

25

mon the class inside. Would you like to help me?"

At dinner that night I sat for a while, staring down at my plate, before finally summoning up the courage to ask, "What is my last name, Grandmother? The schoolteacher, Miss Kelly, said it was Morrow. I've never heard that name before." There had been no curiosity displayed by either of my grandparents on my first day out in the world, if the Rhinebeck schoolhouse could be considered the world. But the anger I still felt toward them prompted me to break the silence.

Grandmother and Grandfather looked at one another. Grandmother's mouth and jaw took on a set dogged look. "You proper surname is Morrow, Ariel."

So there was no mistake! The hard knot within me grew tighter and more swollen. "But you never told me. I thought my name was Van Horn, like yours."

"Your mother's name was Van Horn. When she married your father, her name changed. Your last name is Morrow like your father's." Her voice was expressionless.

"Where is my father? Where is my mother? Are they—are they dead?"

"Your mother is certainly dead, because she was a foolish, headstrong, irresponsible girl. Where your father is today I am glad to say I do not know. He sent you to us because he did not want you. No more questions or you will go immediately to bed." She regarded me with narrowed eyes. I did not ask any more.

One day about a week later Miss Kelly asked me to stay a few minutes after class. "Yes, Miss Kelly?" I asked her, going up to the desk after the room had been cleared.

"Don't look so worried, Ariel," she said, smiling. "I just wanted to tell you something, something you should definitely know. I have been making inquiries and I wanted you to know what I had learned." She paused, considering. "What have your grandparents told you about your parents?"

"My—my parents? I know that my mother is dead, Miss Kelly. My grandmother told me so a few days ago."

"A few days ago," she repeated as though to herself. "Do you know anything about your father?"

"No. My grandmother said she didn't know what had become of him. She told me not to ask again." I only knew that he hadn't wanted me, I thought, swallowing hard.

Miss Kelly took my hand in hers. "No, Ariel, your father is not dead. He is an artist, and is becoming very well known, I understand. He lives in England."

"An artist? My father? In England?" It was too much to assimilate.

"Yes, a painter. Of portraits. Some say he is brilliant, I hear. When you were two years old, you were sent from London to live with your grandparents. They have never told you any of this?"

I shook my head. "My grandmother just told me that my mother was dead, and that my father's name was Morrow. You said he is a painter, in London?"

She nodded, straightening. "Yes, a famous one. His name is Lancelot Morrow. How about you? Do you enjoy drawing and painting?"

I gaped at her. "Grandmother told me a long time ago that I must never draw or sketch. She—she burned my sketchbook."

She frowned. "Well, art is a part of our curriculum here. You will certainly paint and draw and sketch for me. All the children do. But you may keep your artwork here at school, in your desk, rather than bringing it home. Tomorrow morning I am going to give you a box of watercolor paints. Would you like that?"

Not trusting myself to answer, I nodded.

"Good. Run along now. Your carriage will be waiting."

Now I knew with a sudden reeling clarity why my grandmother had been so horrified and enraged at the sight of my sketchbook. Not because my childish sketches were not good enough, but because the whole notion of my drawing repelled her.

Chapter Two

I adored Miss Kelly. I devoured all the books she lent me — about fairies and giants and famous people in history, and Greek Gods and King Arthur and children such as Mary Lennox and David Copperfield. And I began to tentatively experiment with pen and ink, and watercolors. Having never painted with colors before, I was thrilled, and the time I spent each day with a narrow brush in my hand was my favorite. School became not a place to which I dreaded going but one for which I longed when I was not there. The other children gradually stopped taunting me as the newness wore off and as I became more like them. I learned the school routine and all the proper songs and stayed quietly in the background, content to read or daydream rather than engage in rowdy games in the schoolyard. With my upbringing, I could not be anything but a loner, and that was not to change.

In the classroom we had books such as *A Drawing Book for Young Ladies and Gentlemen* and *Sketches from Nature,* a book of lithographs, and *The Art of Coloring and Painting Landscapes,* etchings of cottages and gardens that had then been handpainted. These books fascinated me, and I worked hard to copy the plates. There were also black and white etchings of oil paintings by the Old Masters, and by studying them I was introduced to the history of art. My only disappointment was that none of the paintings, all done by famous artists, Miss Kelly told us, who had lived in Europe hundreds of years ago, was in color. It frustrated me not to be able to scrutinize the various palettes the artists had used, not to mention their techniques.

Many times Miss Kelly would look at a piece of work I had done and shake her head, saying, "If only you could have lessons." She herself did not feel capable of providing the special tuition she believed I needed. But we both knew better than to suggest such an idea to my grandparents. If my grandmother had any notion that art, the study and application, was a subject at the Rhinebeck School, she would have withdrawn me instantly, tutor's exorbitant fees notwithstanding. I was very careful not to let her find out.

In those days I was thinking about my parents a great deal. What had my mother been like? Had my room once been hers? It must have been, for some of the furniture was child-sized. What had she looked like? What had she been like? How had she met my father? It was no good asking the servants, for they were new since her time.

And what of my father? What was he like? Had he loved my mother? Had he ever loved me? Would I ever see him again? I used to imagine myself grown up some day, traveling to London and paying him a visit. He would instantly recognize me (because of my resemblance to my mother) and cry, "Ariel! Is it really you? Oh, how could I have let so many years go by!" And he would take me in his warm embrace. The dream always ended with him pleading with me to stay in London and live with him to make up for all the years we had missed together. He would tell me why he had sent me to New York, and ask me to forgive him for his neglect. Both of us would be in tears, and sometimes I wept while I imagined it.

I worked hard at my lessons, did my chores dutifully, and rarely spoke to my grandparents unless one of them addressed me first. Life was easier that way. But inside I was conscious of a burgeoning excitement, a wakening interest which was fast becoming a passion. Life was no longer either boring or fearful. And on warm afternoons I would sit on the back lawn and look out over the broad Hudson to the highlands beyond.

Once Miss Kelly brought me a book she had purchased in New York City, an issue of *The American Art Review*, "a journal devoted to the practice, theory, history, and archaeology of art." In it were etchings of oil paintings by a group of artists who had painted, to my surprise and delight, the Hudson River and its surrounding banks, meadows, hills, and mountains. The landscapes they painted, and the fact that they were American, made them of special interest to me. I loved the enormous use of detail in their paintings, and the way they portrayed nature as beautiful, sublime, and sometimes ominous — the untamed wilderness of America, an enchanted landscape.

My father was to later dismiss these works as highly romantic and rather naive, but I have never lost my love for the members of the Hudson River School — Thomas Cole, Asher B. Durand, Thomas Doughty, Jasper Cropsey, Frederic Edwin Church, John Kensett, among others.

When I was twelve years old something happened which I had never imagined or expected, simply because I never considered that it was remotely possible. My father came to Starlings. I had imagined traveling to London in later years and charming him with my presence, but never once had I imagined him at Starlings, my grandparents' home. And I am certain that it never occurred to them either. They assumed he was finished with me and were more than content that it be so. His appearance was not something which fit into the scheme of things.

It was a Sunday morning and my grandparents had gone to church. Due to a headcold I was in bed; my indomitable grandmother had a horror of illness of any kind. When I was ill I always had to keep to my room so that I would not contaminate other more susceptible people.

The month was October and the day a splendid one. My window was open; the cool fresh air and warm sunshine poured in. About the house the maple trees were the color of ripe persimmons. I lay in bed gazing contentedly at the design they fashioned against the vivid blue sky. I remember hearing a flock of Canadian geese honking their way south, and to this day the same sound brings back in sharp focus that October morning when I first saw my father.

A carriage was coming up the drive, its wheels scraping and crunching on the gravel. It could not be my grandparents returning so soon as they had left a mere half-hour ago, and we never had callers except for delivery men who would never have come on a Sunday.

But the carriage was stopping in front of the house, and I heard someone getting out and walking up the flagged stone steps to the door. Swiftly I jumped out of bed and dashed to the window, overcome with curiosity.

Below stood a man. He looked very well-dressed, fashionably so, so it was doubtful he had come from nearby. I could not see his face under his hat. Whom might he be? Anyone acquainted with my grandparents would have known that they would be at church on a Sunday morning.

I forgot my stuffed-up head and scratchy throat.

Quickly I wriggled out of my nightdress. There came a knocking at the front door. Tossing a dress over my head, I did up the buttons, smoothed my braids, and went out into the hallway.

Janet was just coming up the stairs; ordinarily she would have gone to church as well, but she had been told to stay with me.

"Oh, Miss Ariel, there's a gentleman below who says he wants to speak to you. I don't know what to do, what your grandmother will say. He hasn't told me his name." She was clearly bewildered and uneasy; she didn't know how to handle unexpected visitors.

"Where is he?" I asked tremulously.

"In the parlor. I don't know — your grandmother — I don't think she'll like it. I can tell him you're ill. Oh, do you think you should . . . ?"

Ignoring her, I had swept past and was hurrying down the stairs. Could it be . . . ? No, that was impossible. And yet . . . I went along the corridor to the parlor, my heart hammering in my ears, a lump in my throat.

He was standing in front of an oil painting — a portrait of one of Grandfather's ancestors — a particularly unattractive woman with narrow eyes and a pious expression. It was flat and lifeless; I had never liked it.

I could not say anything; I merely stood there, waiting.

He turned around. "A rather poor example of early American art, wouldn't you say? However . . ." he shrugged as though he hadn't expected anything else.

He was tall and thin, gaunt even. His long face was partially concealed by a beard and mustache; his eyes were large and somber, his nose aquiline. His hair, which had begun to recede from his high brow, was exactly the shade of dark red as my own.

33

"Hello, Ariel," he said.

"Hello, Father. Won't you sit down?"

He smiled slightly and moved away from the painting, taking a seat and setting down his ivory-handled walking stick. He was elegantly dressed in gray trousers and dark coat; there was a jewel pin in his cravat. He looked vastly different from any man I had ever seen. I had not the slightest idea what to say to him and sat there gaping. He was doubtless disappointed in me, plain and tongue-tied, my cold-induced red eyes and nose not improving my looks.

"I don't know how much your grandparents have told you about me," he began. "I have been living in England for many years. But I have just recently moved to New York."

"New York?" He couldn't mean Rhinebeck.

"Yes, New York City."

Of course. What a dolt I was.

"I have a studio on Tenth Street. Do you know New York?"

I shook my head. "I—I've never been there," I admitted, embarrassed. I had never been anywhere, but I hated for him to know it.

"Well, I will be living there from now on. I decided it was time I returned to my own country, and renewed our acquaintance. I have many commissions here, and friends who also rent studios on Tenth Street. I paint portraits, you see."

"Yes, I know," I said. "My teacher at school heard about you and told me. She said you were almost famous."

He smiled and I groaned inwardly. *Almost* famous. What an idiot. I couldn't be making a worse impression. That I was this elegant stranger's daughter he must find as difficult to believe as I did.

"How are your grandparents? They are both, I assume, still living?" Perhaps it was an odd question to

34

ask, revealing that there had never been the slightest bit of correspondence between them in the last ten years, but I did not find it strange.

"Yes, They—they're at church now."

"And you were permitted to stay at home?"

"I have a cold." What a dull conversation when all the while I was dying to know about his life, and what difference his presence in this country was going to mean to my own. "Are you painting a portrait now?"

"Yes. One of a lady with interesting eyes."

"Is she very rich?"

"Very. It is the rich who desire permanence, and who can pay for it."

With a sick disappointment I heard voices, the shutting of the front door, and steps in the hall. My grandparents had returned and I had scarcely spoken to my father at all.

"It's Grandmother and Grandfather," I said, dismayed. "They—they'll wonder whom the carriage belongs to." I bit my lip.

"Well, they will soon learn," he said, unperturbed, and stood up.

The parlor door opened and Grandmother stood on the threshold, her large formidable frame blocking the light from the hall, her broad face grim. I shivered.

"Who is this man, Ariel? What do you want here?" she said sharply.

"I am Lancelot Morrow, Mrs. Van Horn. I am Ariel's father." His voice was cool.

If she had been anyone else I would have felt sorry for her. That his appearance was a severe shock was all too apparent. Her face whitened and then rapidly resumed its ruddy color; her eyes dilated fiercely.

But her voice was her own, cold and stoical. "You did not inform of us your visit."

"No, I thought it best not," said my father. He was totally at ease while on the other hand I was quaking with nerves. My grandfather, standing behind my grandmother, had not spoken. But his expression was belligerent.

Then I sneezed twice in succession. It seemed to break some spell.

"Ariel, you should be in bed," said my grandmother.

"Well, I won't stay longer then," said my father. "But I shall come up from the city from time to time to visit my daughter."

"Have the goodness to inform us of your arrival the next time," said Grandmother.

"I will, madam," said my father, his tone suddenly crisp, "but if you are away from home when I arrive, I will be forced to come unannounced from then on."

Grandmother's color rose; she regarded my father with now-unconcealed hatred.

My father took no notice. "Good-bye, Ariel," he said.

"When will you come again?" I blurted out, fighting an urge to burst into tears. My grandparents had spoiled everything.

"Be quiet, Ariel," said Grandmother. "Ariel. Whatever made you give her such a foolish-sounding name?"

"Your daughter, Mrs. Van Horn, had a fondness for Shakespeare," said my father in slight amusement. "It was her choice." Turning to me, he added, "I'll come again soon, Ariel. Good-bye."

My grandparents said nothing. They merely stepped aside for my father to leave the room. I heard the front door open and shut.

"Go to you room, Ariel, and do not leave your bed again today. Janet should never have allowed that man to enter this house while we were away. Natu-

36

rally a—a bohemian like him would choose a Sunday morning on which to call. After all this time to decide to show an interest in you! However, it is likely nothing more than a passing whim. I don't imagine he'll make the trip up here from New York very often." Her voice held a note of grim satisfaction.

I did as she ordered. Wretchedly I lay down on my bed. What a stupid morning. What a terrible waste. He would never come again.

But he did. Not often, but every few months. Just when I was worried that he had forgotten me, then he would return. We never talked very much. We were both quiet people, and I had not been brought up on the art of conversation. For his part I believe that he wanted to be friends but was as unsure of how to go about it as I was. Neither of us was demonstrative and our conversations were stilted, awkward, but gradually a tentative sort of affection began to grow between us. Even then I was perceptive enough to realize that that was all it would ever be. I was his daughter and now that he was near, he wanted to know me, perhaps out of deference to my mother's memory. But there was no great reconciliation between us, no great bond gripping us which shut everyone else out. For a while I assumed that he was disappointed in me, that it was something lacking in me which caused him to act the way he did. But later I realized that that was not the case. Painfully I realized that he was not capable of deep feelings, except for his work.

My grandparents silently tolerated his visits, which surprised me. He never stayed long, only an hour or so, and that pleased them. They had no wish to see him and would leave us alone in the parlor. Sometimes we walked about the grounds of Starlings.

"Some father," said my grandmother complacently. "He only wants to be bothered with you when the mood strikes him." She meant to hurt me, but she was right in her estimation of him. Yet the anticipation of future visits made my life richer, more exciting.

It was a long while before I summoned up enough courage to show him a few of my sketches and watercolors. I had told Miss Kelly, of course, that he had set up a studio in New York City and that he was painting all the fashionable people there. I pictured the ladies in their magnificent jewels and gowns sitting for him.

I longed to see his studio, to see the city. I loved Dutchess County; I loved its farms and rolling hills and forests and orchards, but I yearned to visit other places as well. I would watch the steamboats sailing down the Hudson from Albany, and I would wish that I stood on one of the levels, gazing ahead down the mighty river, my hair blowing in the breeze.

It was Miss Kelly who urged me to show my work to my father. The idea had occurred to me almost from the beginning, but I was too timid to do it of my own accord.

"I think he'll be very interested," she said to me. "You love to paint and sketch; it's important to you. And you have talent. You must show him sometime, Ariel."

So eventually we selected what we thought were my best works and she put them in a folder for me and tied it with string. My grandparents would assume it was ordinary schoolwork. Since they had never expressed an interest to see any of it before, I did not anticipate a sudden request.

It was another Sunday afternoon the following autumn when the round fat pumpkins were bright orange and the Indian corn hung on the Dutch door. We went into the parlor and, my stomach in knots, I handed him the folder. "I—I like to draw, too," I said.

38

Glancing at me thoughtfully, he untied the string and opened the folder. I held my breath as he looked at the first one, a sketch of Starlings. He looked at it for a long while before putting it aside and taking up the next one which was a watercolor of the school. There was another watercolor of the old Dutch church in the village. The last one was of the Hudson flowing between the high bluffs. Biting my thumb, I waited for him to speak. Why on earth had I shown them to him? They were poor, awful.

Finally he spoke. "How old are you?"

Perhaps a curious question for a father to ask, but, after all, he was no ordinary father. Not offended, I said, "Thirteen."

He slid the papers back into the folder. "Do your grandparents know you can draw and paint like this?"

"Oh, no, Father. I — I'm forbidden to paint or sketch. But these are assignments. I do them at school. Please — please don't tell Grandmother."

"I have no intention of telling your grandmother anything," he said somberly. In his eyes there was an intensity I had never discerned before.

"You have," he said, "fine compositional ability for your age. Your palette is all wrong, but that's more due to the poor quality of paints available to you. Your perspective could be better and your brushwork needs instruction, but you can capture an image — a scene — rather well. I do not know where this will lead you, perhaps nowhere. You are very young. But you should have lessons."

"That's what Miss Kelly says." I was elated; he must feel that I had some talent worth cultivating.

"Well, I will give you some pointers on how these might be improved. You will do some work for me. And we shall see."

After that he began to give me assignments, simple

ones that turned out not to be simple at all such as a pair of hands. I also worked at sketching cubes from different perspectives while he talked of vanishing points and visible planes.

"Your painting will resemble nothing more than a map projection unless you understand the concept of perspective." He would talk of color. "Warm and cool tones create form and space."

Miss Kelly was as delighted by his interest as I. "This is what you've needed all along," she said.

When we were alone in the parlor I would take out the papers I kept hidden from Grandmother and Grandfather and show him what I had accomplished in the time since his last visit.

Once I painted a scene of my own choosing, a child being bullied in the schoolyard by other children. The little boy looked frightened and about to cry, the children about him frankly cruel, gleeful. Father did not like it.

"In art there is no room for sentiment," he said. "The artist must paint merely what a passerby would see with no inclination or temptation to tell a story. You must remain completely detached, no moralizing. Whistler says that art should stand alone without the artist's emotional presence. Art is no longer a moral force, as John Ruskin had it. Simply put, I paint what I see, not what I judge or discern, and so should you."

"I wish—I wish I could see some of your paintings," I said wistfully, not looking at him.

But when I did look at him there was only that now-familiar slight smile, and nothing more.

Sometimes I would ask him about his studio, his subjects. I was interested in the details of his life because it was so very different from the life I knew in rural upstate New York. Although the city was only a few hours away by steamboat or train, it seemed

40

like another world.

He told me that he belonged to a group of artists known as the Tile Club. They met regularly on Wednesday nights at a member's home for dinner and a discussion of the decorative arts or of the changing role of the artist in society. The host provided the meal and the materials, and, after dinner, they would sit and paint white tiles with blue pigment, or plaques, or whatever was taking their interest at that time. Father and a few of his friends had collaborated on a special Christmas issue for *Harper's Monthly*. Winslow Homer was a member of the Tile Club, as was William Merritt Chase, Edwin Austin Abbey, and the architect, Stanford White.

Aside from evenings spent with his friends, I got the impression that he attended few fashionable affairs.

"I am painting Mrs. John Jacob Astor," he said once.

"What is she like?" I asked.

"She is considered a beauty. Her skin is very white and she has dark hair."

"No, I mean, what is she *like?* Her personality."

He looked at me, his brows raised. "I have no idea. Nor do I wish to know."

"Why not? Won't it help you to understand her?"

He sighed. "Ariel, if you are to become an artist, you must accept that we do not *understand*, we *observe*. Portraiture should be wholly impersonal. I deliberately do not engage in social contact with my sitters. I do not wish to know them. If I did, I would not be able to paint what I see. It is the brush on the canvas which should excite the viewer's emotions, not the content of the painting. Technique, method—they are everything."

He brought newly published art journals so that I could study recent European and American works, enabling me to experience first-hand Tonalist, Realist, and Impressionist styles. It was in one of these journals that I finally saw my first Lancelot Morrow.

It was of three lovely ladies, the daughters of a prominent man in England, two seated together on a divan, the other opposite them in a chair. The background was dark, nondescript. All attention was focused on the pearllike transluscence of their faces and slim arms and hands. One of the sitters gazed intently at the viewer. Their poses, at first glance, looked nonchalant, even haughty. But on further study they were tense, slightly nervous, restless. Their gowns were painted with bold fluid brushstrokes so that one could almost feel the stiff fabric, but their faces were as smooth as marble and as white. With quick dabs of paint he had highlighted their touches of jewelry and lace. I had never seen anything quite like it before, I, who had been studying paintings executed hundreds of years earlier. Although my father had clearly learned much from the Spanish and Dutch Masters, his style was uniquely his own. It was a brilliant painting.

My father and I might have continued in this pattern for years, had not my Grandmother one day discovered my art folder. Usually I kept it at school in my desk, bringing it home just before my father was due to visit. But on one occasion, when I was fifteen, he did not arrive on the Sunday he had written he would. I waited all afternoon in the parlor, going to the window and looking out at the bleak wintry landscape, a cloud of my breath forming on the pane of glass.

"No doubt he had something better to do today," said my grandmother with a sardonic smile. "A woman, maybe. He's tired of making all the trips up here to see you, I suppose. When was the last time he was here? Nearly four months ago, wasn't it? I imagine, Ariel, you'll see him less and less from now on. I expect he's bored playing father. It doesn't exactly suit him, you'll have to agree."

I don't believe her, I thought stubbornly. I *won't* believe her. But he did not come.

The following day was Monday and a school day. I rode to Rhinebeck in the carriage, too despondent to remember to bring my folder of watercolors and sketches. But it was under my mattress, safely out of view. Surely it would remain there until I brought it back to school.

In the middle of the afternoon I entered the warm kitchen, eager for my mug of mulled cider and a fresh gingersnap or two. But just as I was sitting down at the round gateleg table that had come from Holland many years ago, Janet came in to tell me that my grandmother wanted to see me in the parlor.

"Perhaps she's had a letter from my father," I thought hopefully.

But Janet looked troubled. "Oh, Ariel, I'm sorry."

"Why? What — what is it?" I asked, paling.

Janet shook her head. "I'm afraid your grandmother is fit to be tied. You'd better hurry."

My heart in my mouth, I hastened to the parlor where each of my grandparents sat in the highbacked chairs. And then I let out a gasp. In my grandmother's hand was my art folder.

"Are these yours?" she asked icily.

I could not reply.

"Did your father give these to you?" she asked.

"N — no — they're mine."

"You drew these yourself?"

I nodded, biting my lip.

"Were you not forbidden to engage in this activity years ago?" she cried, enraged.

"I — Miss Kelly gives us assignments in class. We have art in school, Grandmother. Everyone must par-

43

ticipate."

"Did Miss Kelly assign these things?"

"Well, yes . . ."

"Then why are they not at school? What were they doing under the mattress of your bed? Janet turned it today, and I happened to be present."

"I—I forgot to take them back to school this morning."

"Why were they here at all, Ariel? You know I forbade you to dabble in such foolishness!

Twisting my hands together, I felt my face becoming hot. "Well, I—I had planned to show them to Father. He has been helping me with my studies."

Her eyes narrowed. "With your studies. Do you mean mathematics, geography, literature, history? I was not aware that your father was a scholar."

He was, but I did not feel up to arguing the point.

"Ariel, answer me!"

"He . . . he has been giving me lessons . . . in art."

My grandmother handed my collection of drawing and watercolors to my grandfather. He stood up and moved near the fire, his face as condemning as hers.

"No! Please, he hasn't seen them—I've worked so hard!" There was one in particular of which I was very proud, one I had done of the kitchen at Starlings, the room I loved best. There was the huge fireplace with beehive oven, the farmhouse table with bowls of apples and nuts, the small deep-set windows, the flagged stone floor, the heavy ceiling beams and Dutch door. I was developing a talent for painting the inside of rooms.

"And he never will see them, Ariel," said my grandmother as my grandfather tossed the folder into the flames.

Through a haze of heat and sickness I heard my grandmother continue, "From now on you will not be permitted to see your father. I have already written to tell him so. There will be no more drawing lessons or cozy chats in this room. I should never have tolerated his visits. He has attempted to corrupt you under our very roof, influencing you with his bohemian, depraved ways, just as he did your mother. Heaven only knows what else you have learned, what other things he has exposed you to. But it ends here. That man—your—your *father*—poisoned our only child against her parents, against her way of life. We shall not allow him to poison you as well. From now on your room will be searched every day. There will be no more painting, no more sketching. You will not return to the village school. The expense of a tutor will be tremendous, but it is a burden we must bear. All the influences to which you have been exposed these last three years must be eradicated. It is our duty to you. Now go to your room. You are to remain there until I say."

I said nothing. I went to my room.

Three days later I was still in my room. Janet brought my meals on a tray, but she was forbidden to speak to me. The room was chilled and I lay huddled under the bedclothes, too miserable even to dress. I would be a prisoner at Starlings forever; that was clearly what my grandmother intended for me. It was what she should have done to my mother. She had made one mistake; she was determined not to make another.

That afternoon I heard the sound of a carriage stopping in front of the house. Was it the new tutor already? I thought, heartsick. I won't get up, I said to myself. I won't look. I hate them all.

There were footsteps coming up the stairs. Sitting up in bed, I waited. The door swung open and there stood my father.

"Come along, Ariel," he said as though it were the most natural thing in the world.

45

I gazed at him in astonishment.

My grandparents were behind him, breathing heavily. "How dare you?" shouted my grandmother, her face purple-red. "You cannot do this!"

"This is the child's home," said my grandfather fiercely. "You have no right to take her."

"I am her father," was the mild reply. "And the law is very clear on that. She is coming to live with me."

"To live with you!" cried my grandmother. "When did you ever want her? When did you ever provide for her, except when she was a baby? All you've done for Ariel is to fill her head with your bohemian notions. You want to make her exactly like you!"

"Whereas you, madam, wish to make her exactly like you. Which is why I am taking her away. Come, Ariel. You will not need anything except a coat."

"Who has provided for her all these years, given her everything she has needed? Without thanks or recompense, I might add!"

"Ah, I thought that might come up," said my father softly. Reaching into his breast pocket, he withdrew his billfold and took out a thick packet. "Here is your recompense." He held out the money, a slight expression of disdain on his face.

My grandmother took it. "Oh, yes, you're rich now, I suppose. But you weren't when you married Millicent. You hoped to get her money to support you while you dabbled with brushes and paint. We always knew that," she sneered. "And we saw to it that it didn't happen. Now this is what you've come to, buying your own child. That is what you are doing!"

"And you, madam, are selling her."

My grandmother swelled, her heavy chin jutting out. "Well, get out, the pair of you."

"Ariel may visit you whenever she wishes," said my father, smoothing his beard with his long fingers.

"Good-bye, Grandmother," I said.

"You will never be welcome in this house again, Ariel, if you go with your father now. Remember that, as your mother did. You're making the same choice she made, following in her wicked, foolish ways. Blood will out, even after all our care, our efforts, our—"

"Did you ever consider, madam, that it was because of that care, those efforts, that Millicent did not return?" said my father bluntly. Then he made an exasperated gesture with his hand. "Enough of this. Ariel is my daughter and she is coming to live with me. You will know where to find her."

"Good-bye, Grandmother, Grandfather," I murmured, slipping past them. "If you ever need me or—"

"You'll never get a penny of our money, Ariel!" cried my grandmother, her voice ringing harshly in my ears as I followed my father down the stairs and out to the waiting carriage.

And that was the end of the melodrama. There was no declaration of love and remorse from my father, no warm promise of what was certain to be a better life.

"I've decided you should see more of the world," was all he said.

We rode through Rhinebeck and I determined to write to Miss Kelly and tell her of my changed circumstances. I would miss her. But I could not repress the excitement now welling inside me, the amazed, delirious culmination of years of dreams.

I could not have imagined New York City the way it really was—block after block of buildings, some seven or eight stories high, so many people, so many carriages, shops, churches, the degree of resolute, even frenzied, hustle and bustle—all of it was foreign to me. We lost sight of the Hudson River while still uptown, my last link with the familiar.

In the colossal mansions on Fifth Avenue lived many of Father's subjects, their windows looking out over the towering trees and lush grass of Central Park. There was a great cathedral which was straight out of a history book on the Middle Ages with ornate carving, tracery, and soaring spire. We passed the fashionable restaurant, Delmonico's, where elegantly clad couples drifted in and out. I did not exclaim or badger my father with questions; I only stared out the window of the coach, awestruck.

As we drove further downtown the streets became narrower and, if possible, even busier, the buildings smaller and closer together. This was an older part of the city, some of the buildings dating back to the early Dutch residents. And I noticed the telltale Dutch roofs with steps or curves, and the smaller windows.

We also passed street after street of new brownstone townhouses with steps leading up to the front doors from the sidewalks, and bow windows jutting out from the upper floors.

And then we were driving round Washington Square with its huge granite arch. The carriage stopped before one of the handsome townhouses framing the park.

"Here we are," said my father.

"Is this your house?"

"Yes, and now yours as well."

"Is your studio here also?"

"No, it's some blocks away on Tenth Street."

The front door was opened by an exotic-looking man with black hair and olive complexion who wore a strange red costume.

"This is Omar, Ariel."

Omar bowed. "Very pleased, Miss Ariel," he said showing very white teeth.

48

"Omar is from Turkey. He has been indispensable to me for—how many years is it, Omar?"

"For twelve years, Mr. Lance."

"Yes. He was valet to a dreary English M.P. when I rescued him. Omar, we would like dinner as soon as possible. Have you prepared Miss Ariel's room?"

"Yes, Mr. Lance. All is in readiness." Bowing again, he retreated.

The hall was papered in a design of peacock's feathers, brilliant blues and greens; the ceiling, to my wonder, was painted in patterns of gold and terra cotta with a border of black birds running below the cornice. On a small table was set a large red, black, and gold china plate.

"That is Imari," said my father. "Japanese."

We went up the stairs. "My room is there, yours, down the hall. There is a music room just there, at the front of the house. On the first floor are the salon, the dining room, library, and kitchen at the back."

The house, I learned later, was decorated in the Aesthetic style, with Moorish and Oriental influences as well as Gothic. The walls and ceilings were elaborately decorated in abstract designs, the cornices painted in as many as four or five colors. And the colors themselves were unusual to my eyes—old gold, Pompeiian Red, teal blue, olive green, terra cotta. Used to the monochromatic walls at my grandparents' home, I wandered from room to room, open-mouthed.

My father had a routine he followed rigidly. He rose at seven; he and I breakfasted together at eight. Then he did his correspondence—he had many friends in Europe that he wrote to—in the library before setting out for his studio a little before ten o'clock.

"What about school?" I asked the first morning.

He looked blank. "School?" Smoothing his beard, he acknowledged, "Yes, I suppose it is a necessity. I'll inquire about a good one."

And in several days I was enrolled at a small school for young ladies on the opposite side of the square. "It is convenient," said my father, "and likely no worse than the usual schools for young ladies."

Far more important was my art education, which he himself took in hand.

I learned how to stretch and prime a canvas; using oil paints for the first time, I was instructed in the new *au premier* coup style of direct painting where wet paint was laid on wet paint.

"Your paintings must appear effortless," said my father. "And you must show every nuance of light.

"In oil painting you begin with the middle tone and work up from it toward the dark. This way at the last you deal with your lightest lights and darkest darks. In watercolors, by contrast, you begin with the lightest tones and work through to the darkest."

He showed me the various strokes of the brush from feathery to long zigzags and S and circular strokes. A dry brush was used for fine details, and demanded much precision. According to my father, painting had to be done spontaneously, unhesitantly, and the compositions should be daring and unusual.

I was given brushes of different sizes and shapes—brights, rounds, filberts, flats, chisel-edged—all made of either white hogs' hairs or red sable hairs. Never had I used a wooden palette, never an easel, never a knife for scraping or mixing oil paints—in short, I was overwhelmed at the many things I did not know and was expected to learn.

In watercolor painting, I was told that a limited range of colors was best, that it was often better to mix a color from two already in use than to introduce a completely new one.

"There's an imposed harmony that way," said my father. He suggested I leave parts of the white paper untouched to create highlights, as Turner did.

"Of all the oil pigments, the earth colors are the most permanent — yellow ochre, raw and burnt sienna, raw and burnt umber, Venetian Red, Terra Verte, Van Dyke Brown, and so on. But the most important pigment is white. White should be mixed in with virtually all colors used." He used only oil paints made from cold-pressed linseed oil, and only the purest ultramarine made from crushed lapis lazuli.

I felt ignorant and incompetent. I had to begin at the beginning and learn all over again. But I worked very hard because I wanted to please him, and to please myself.

My father, quiet, self-contained, had many acquaintances but no intimate friends. It was his style to observe life, to stand aside, detached, as a spectator rather than as a participant. His studio was a sociable place, with other artists milling about as he worked, watching him, or talking over glasses of wine while the Society debutantes and matrons, and the Wall Street barons came to be painted. In the way he treated me, he was more like a guardian than a real father. Whether my mother's death had changed him, distanced him from the rest of us, or whether he was always that way, I never knew. But he was well-liked and admired.

For a "bohemian," he lived a very orderly life. Once or twice a week he went out with friends for the evening, and several times a month he gave small dinner parties. But more often he sat in the library in the evenings, reading and smoking his pipe. Sometimes he played his silver flute and I would sit and listen contentedly.

There were nights that I was told he was staying at

his studio, and it did not take me long to realize that he was entertaining a lady, or being entertained by her. But the subject of marriage was never mentioned.

My father did not undertake to create a social life for me. Aside from the pupils at the school, I met no one but his artist friends. And they were not particularly interested in me. Doubtless some of them considered my father to be wasting his time giving me instruction. After all, I was only a girl. But this did not dissuade my father at all; in me he saw a talent he wanted to breed, to cultivate. Where it might lead me neither of us knew or even discussed. But it was our mutual love of painting which drew us together and which was at the very core of my life, now that I did not have to conceal it. At the point of leaving Starlings with my father and going to New York City to live with him, I had embarked on a very different existence from those of other young females, and it was that very difference which was my joy and my bane.

Chapter Three

When I was seventeen I was graduated from the young ladies' academy across the square, but that by no means completed my education. Under my father's tutelage I worked harder than ever. I now had my own easel set up in his studio, and I often painted or sketched the same subjects he did, though not for commissions.

It had taken me years to learn the painstaking process of mixing paints, of selecting the right colors and making piles of varying mixtures to shade and highlight. The background of a painting could never be all one color; nothing in nature was flat; no one color stood out on its own. In nature everything was shadowed or highlighted with nuances of light and hue, and a painting should reflect this. I would begin with an outline, then work on the background and the sitters' clothes, then a little flesh.

"You must paint something of every bit of the painting at the same time," said my father. One of the reasons for this was the pigments that I was constantly mixing on the palette had to be used before they dried.

But although it was a sometimes tedious and gruelling process, it was also enthralling. It was amazing what colors combined to make skin tones when one considered each color on its own. Yellow ochre, white, alizarin Crimson—a deep burgundy—and even ultramarine were mixed to create flesh. Then one had always to add a touch of terra verde, "because the skin has hints of green in the areas under the eyes and about the nose." Then for the facial shadows one might mix alizarin crimson, ultramarine, and white, adding that mixture to the greenish-ochre-white pile for purplish tones. For a face to appear translucent on canvas, the brushstrokes had to be entirely eliminated, and to do that one took a clean dry brush and stroked it over and over the area before the paint had altogether dried.

Over the years I did many paintings which were tossed in the dustbin, but gradually I began to perfect the various techniques I was shown. Earlier I had attempted to copy my father's starkly dramatic style, with its contrasting whites and darks, but later I began to experiment with a lighter, warmer palette in the impressionistic style. My father preferred the deep contrasts between pales and darks, the marble-like luminous skin of his sitters, the white necks against the blue-black gowns. His was a brilliant style, startling and arresting, but after a time I decided that it was not my own and not one that I wished to emulate. Privately I thought that it did not present women in their best light. Often his females were more ghostlike than merely pale, and the intense gazes he gave them were vaguely disturbing. Also the poses he used were strained, exaggerated, almost tortured, so that his portraits conveyed a nervous tension, a restlessness, the impression of an uneasy truce with life.

I decided I would rather work in softer, warmer hues and with subjects of my own choosing. Young mothers with a child or two I was fond of painting, and neighbors would sit for me in their brightest room, or even in the square outside. My father continually urged me to paint just what I saw, and never to allow sentiment to creep into my paintings.

When I was not working in oils I was doing watercolor painting. In this, naturally, an entirely different technique was used. The colors were pigments that had been finely ground into gum arabic. Once dissolved in water and laid to paper, the paint was like a light thin varnish. It was a radiant, expressive way to paint. One laid a flat wash with a large brush, dissolving one brushstroke into another so that the lines did not show. When those dried, further washes could be laid until the final contrasting tones were established.

"You must know how to judge colors and then put them down so that they retain their freshness," said my father. "The lighter areas must have fewer washes, the darkers, more."

If some colors needed to be reduced, one applied a damp sponge or blotting paper to lessen them. A sharp pointed knife was useful for scratching in highlights, and fine brushes or pens for drawing additional details. I learned how to stipple and to scumble, both techniques for conveying texture.

One of my assignments in watercolor painting was to produce an interior of each room in our house. In fact I did many of them over the years. Slowly I improved and continued to practice. Sometimes I put subjects in my interiors, such as my father sitting in his library. I also went to neighbors' homes and painted their interiors, naturally never charging a fee.

It was work I enjoyed, very different from oil painting, requiring a concentration, a precision, and delicacy for which I was suited. One could not be overbold in watercolor painting; the brushstrokes had to be hidden from the viewer, and there were many minute details which were unnecessary in portrait painting—the detailing of Oriental carpets and high relief ceiling patterns, the texture of rush-seated chairs, the rendering of the decorative objects filling each room—all must appear on the paper as they might in a photograph. It was a highly skilled craft to paint a miniature copy of a room on paper, though one that did not require the interpretive power of portraiture.

"In oil," said my father, "the technique should overcome the subject, but in watercolor interiors, the realism is equally significant."

I was twenty-two years old when my career as a professional artist began. My father was at the peak of his career then, and idolized by many, his talents much in demand. But we continued to live a quiet life, though we lived well. The Tile Club had disbanded so his meetings with friends became less regular. He had remained a very private person, though his studio was still a gathering place for old acquaintances and hopeful young artists. One of these young men I had fancied myself in love with, and he had assured me that he was never happier than in my presence. But gradually, painfully, I began to realize that it was my father's presence he actually preferred to my own, and was only professing a regard for me to further his own career. There were often young men surrounding my father and hoping that an association with him would improve their chances of establishing themselves in the art world. But fearing a repetition of my first experience, I was civil to all of them, but distant. I assured myself that I did not require a man in my life. I was to be an artist; I needed nothing else. It was also apparent to me that to some of these young men I posed a threat; after all, I was a female in what was basically a man's world, a man's career. Many of them, though artists themselves, considered it peculiar and improper that I should want to paint professionally and my perseverance and determination made them uneasy, even disapproving. Not that I cared for a moment what they thought; in the years I had lived with my father he had encouraged me to think for myself.

One day I went to my father and told him what it was that I wanted. "I would like to work for commissions like you do, Father." I could feel the warm color seeping into my face. "Do you think I'm good enough?"

"Yes," he said simply, "I do. Your interiors are some of the best I've ever seen."

I was astounded as well as elated; never had he said such a thing to me.

"There are women who make their living painting interiors. There was a particularly good one some years ago in England—Charlotte Bosanquet. She made wonderful use of sun and shadow, of light spilling across one area of a room. You are as talented as she was, perhaps more so. I have spoken to Stanford White and showed him some of your work. He agrees with me."

"Stanford White?" The gregarious red-headed architect who lived rather a wild life was one of my father's old friends from the Tile Club; I had met him occasionally in the last years.

"Yes. He has said you can, if you desire, make a very good reputation for yourself. Painting interiors is once again fashionable, due, no doubt, to the aggressive opulence of the rooms of prominent families. A photograph will preserve the look of a room, but it does not have the appeal of a watercolor interior. A photograph is dead, lifeless. The Society barons want their rooms and houses immortalized as much as they do themselves. Stanford said he will recommend you to a few of his clients. You must do the rest. If that is what you wish."

"I do wish it, Father."

He was thoughtful, stroking his beard. "Your portraits show great promise as well. In France you might be given commissions to paint portraits, but here matters do not progress so rapidly. And you are very young yet. Perhaps some day . . ."

"I'll do the interiors, Father. It's a beginning, and I enjoy doing them." For years I had wanted to achieve the status of a professional artist, not for the money,

57

for we lived comfortably, but for the standing of being recompensed for my work. My ultimate desire was to paint portraits, as my father did, but I was willing to wait and build a reputation. Painting interiors was not something which would win me an exhibit at the National Academy of Design, where my father exhibited his works, but it was a start.

Stanford White was as good as his word. Before long I was asked to bring samples of my work to several mansions on Fifth Avenue. And I began to receive commissions.

It was my first experience to observe the mode of life of the new millionaire class. It was one governed by an elaborate set of rules and regulations created by people such as Mrs. Astor and her second-in-command, Ward McAllister. It was he who had invented the phrase, "the Four Hundred," to signify the cream of New York society, the exact number which would fit into Mrs. Astor's famous ballroom. It was Ward Make-a-Lister's decree that a family had to have made its fortune three generations before, or the gates of Society would remain closed. But Mrs. Astor, much to her chagrin, had been forced to open them a crack to admit the Vanderbilts, grandsons of the Commodore, when her daughter had been overlooked on the guest list of a masquerade ball of Mrs. William K. Vanderbilt's contriving. When Mrs. Astor sent in her card, Alva had stormed the last bastion of Society and declared herself the victor.

My father and I were not on Ward McAllister's list. The millionaires wanted little to do with artists, musicians or writers on a social scale. My father, though illustrious, was not considered an appropriate dinner guest as he would have been in French or English Society whose members deliberately courted creative, talented people.

This bothered my father not a bit. He had even less desire to socialize with the Four Hundred than they did with him. He said they were too busy belittling one another to discuss the arts, and they would not have known what to discuss had they been interested. Richard Morris Hunt had told my father that, to Alva Vanderbilt, anything architecturally old was "medieval,"—she didn't know Gothic from Venetian. To most of the millionaires, the cost of a painting was its only appeal.

So I was regarded as a sort of upper class craftsman. The butlers would admit me, easel in hand, and I would go into the room in which I was presently working and paint until the light began to alter and fade. I rarely saw the members of the families except in passing.

The dowagers would nod coldly, if they acknowledged me at all; the debutantes would smile shyly or pass by haughtily. The most attention I received was from the young men of the households, and it was unwelcome attention.

I was a novelty. I had a famous father, who, though not considered a proper dinner guest, was idolized for his genius, and whose portraits were highly sought after. Not only that, but I was an artist myself—and a young woman. These two facts combined made me an easy target for flirtation, and it did not help that I had greatly improved in looks in the last years.

They were all alike, these young men, spoiled, lazy (for their great-grandfathers or grandfathers had done all the work and made all the money for them), and bored, always looking for diversions. But I never gave them the least encouragement. Nor did I ever set my cap at any of them, which was, no doubt, something their mothers feared. But the matrons could have spared themselves the anxiety. I was no more interested in any of the rich scions of New York Society than I was in the young artists who worshipped my father. To me there was very little difference between them.

The rooms of these mansions had to be seen to be believed. There was none of the aesthetic simplicity of my father's taste or the classical simplicity hailed in the new book on home decorating by Edith Wharton and Odgen Codman. No, it was all gilt upon gilt, marble upon marble; tapestries, paneling, paintings, and wallpaper jostled each other for position and dominance on the walls. The ceilings were painted with scenes of gods and goddesses; mirrors and crystal sparkled in the ballrooms; the eye was continually bludgeoned with a barrage of objects and designs which filled every room. Despite the grandeur of these houses, there was a total lack of warmth and comfort; they were cold, sterile. Theirs was a contrived ostentation in which there was no room for simple domestic pleasures.

Yet in a way these rooms were interesting to paint; they were certainly challenging, as not one space was left untouched on the walls. The furniture was either the gold spindly French sort of the Louis, or the heavy dark Italian stuff, ornately carved and embossed with animals or fruit. The atmospheres in these magnificent homes were always somber, such as one found in museums; in none of these palaces could one find a cozy retreat, a haven. Their wealthy owners must have been in as much awe of them as their poor domestics were.

But it was through the gaudy splendor of the houses that I became a professional artist. I was not inundated with commissions; there were weeks at a time when I had no clients, but that did not depress me. I was beginning to develop a reputation as an artist of merit, and that was all that mattered.

My father and I embarked on a new relationship, one where he was less the instructor and more the fellow artist. Ours was never that of a normal father and daughter, but he was fond of me and I of him, though we did not express it in conventional ways.

60

And I was glad that I now did him credit, and justified his decision to take me away from my grandparents.

For years I had sent Christmas cards and occasional notes to Starlings, but never did I receive a reply. Finally I gave up; they would not approve of the life I had chosen.

My father was a full academician of the National Academy of Design, as well as a member of the Society of American Artists, and his work was exhibited frequently. He had painted a portrait of me which hung at the National Academy. It was titled simply, *Ariel,* and it caused a small sensation. It was a departure from his usual style. I wore white, and there was none of the tension found in his other portraits. This one gave the impression of freedom, of ethereality. Critics recalled Shakespeare's fairy-sprite and made the most of the observation that my father evidently did not view his unusual daughter as one of the troubled neurotic women of the time, caught, imprisoned, longing to escape their bonds but burdened by the trappings of wealth and status. In my portrait I wore a simple flowing gown; my hair fell over my shoulders as I looked away from my viewer. My father refused to sell it, though he had many offers.

We respected one another's privacy, but when we were together my father could be a charming companion. He was well-read, witty, broad-minded, cosmopolitan in his tastes and outlook, and totally devoid of the temper and whims that one often finds in "creative people." This was probably due to his choice to live his life more as a spectator than a participant. His emotions did not run deep; he was not introspective; he accepted life on its own terms and never questioned, never probed.

Looking back now I can admit what was too painful for me to acknowledge then, that I was lonely, that there was something missing in my life. When I was working I forgot myself; I was happiest when engrossed in a project. My father was kind, but it was my work which captured and held his attention, not myself as a child nor as a young woman. This disinterest, this remoteness of his was characteristic, pervasive; he reacted that way to everyone. But in me was a craving to be loved and appreciated for what and who I was, not for merely my artwork, and it was a need which could not be suppressed forever. I was unconscious of it until I began to experience the attention I sorely needed and which had always been lacking in my life, and by then it was too late to be prudent. Starved as I had been for such attention, I could not have shunned it had my life been at stake.

Drew understood because it had been the same for him, always burying his feelings beneath the demands of family loyalty, repressing his own needs for what was expected of him. We found in one another a bond neither of us had encountered before, but it was a bond which nearly strangled us in its grip. The elation swiftly brought with it despair, and even worse, an appalling loneliness, and then, inevitably, tragedy and terror.

I had been painting interiors professionally for about two years when my father died. The month was January and he had gone up to the Catskill Mountains for a week or so to rest. I could not accompany him because I was working on a commission at that time. He had decided rather abruptly to leave the city and had gone alone. While out walking he must have attempted to cross a pond he believed to be frozen, but the ice had broken, and he had fallen through.

I supposed such a death would have been preferable to him than a lingering painful illness when he could not summon the strength or inclination to paint, but the news came as a tremendous shock to me. I had not yet imagined life without him. He was only in his late forties and looked even younger, doubtless due to the calm, orderly life he led. His hair and beard were still untouched by gray; he was never ill.

His friends and cronies clustered round me; reporters from various newspapers waylaid me in the street; his paintings increased in value; the art world of New York, Paris, and London went into mourning. I received letters of condolence from illustrious people I had never met: prominent writers and artists on both sides of the Atlantic, people who had known him years before or merely respected his greatness. For several weeks the letters and telegrams poured in; Omar was inconsolable.

As for myself I took his death harder than one might have expected. I brooded over what might have been between us, but that was maudlin foolishness for nothing would have changed had he lived. I wrote to my grandparents, informing them of his death, but received no response.

The house was very different without him. Every room evoked his personality, his tastes. I began to realize that there was almost nothing of me in our house. I began to feel vaguely uncomfortable there, but lacked the initiative to make a change.

My father had left a handsome legacy to Omar in his will, and lump sums to various art schools to be used as scholarships. The rest was mine. It was not a fortune, but it was large enough to keep me comfortable as long as I supplemented that income from time to time with my own. I think that not leaving me all of his money was my father's way of telling me that he believed wholeheartedly in my career and wished me to go on with it.

The townhouse was now much larger than I needed; I considered selling it and moving to an apartment. I knew that Omar was anxious to set up a business selling men's clothes now that he had the means to do it. Yet he would not leave me until I was embarked on a new life. I was uncertain about what to do. I finished my commission in a sort of numbed daze, and then did nothing. I made no decisions.

My father had been dead for several months when I received the letter from Cordelia Rockwell. In it she stated she had seen some work I had done recently; she wished to meet me and discuss the possibility of commissioning me to do some interiors of her home. I had not had a job in a while and I needed the discipline, the activity. Yet I was reluctant to stir from the listless state I was in. Somehow, though, I found myself standing at the front door of the address on the stationery, and presented my card to the white-gloved footman.

I was shown into a small front salon and sat down to await Mrs. Drew Rockwell, as she had signed herself in the letter. The name was not familiar to me. And after a few minutes she joined me, a tall, beautifully groomed woman of about thirty with chestnut hair and a lilting, affected manner of speaking.

When she walked into the salon that day, I had no notion of how I would come to hate her, or what would be the horrible outcome of a single spiteful act she was to commit.

"How do you do, Miss Morrow?" she said, her voice cool, her gaze passing over my costume, a lavender jacket and skirt with a high-necked white blouse, matching parasol, and hat of lavender colored straw adorned with white roses.

"I believe I stated in my letter that I have seen the interior you did for the Gilmores. Mrs. Gilmore spoke well of you, and of course, everyone knew of your father. I would have liked—but that is beside the point now. I wish you to do a set of interiors of my home. It is a beautiful house, though rather old-fashioned for my taste. However, my husband refuses to change a thing. I am certain you will find the rooms interesting subjects, as for years my husband's family has been involved in trade with the Far East."

"I have no doubt, Mrs. Rockwell," I said. "This looks a very fine house. However, at present I am not certain—"

"You do not understand the matter, Miss Morrow," she cut in with slight impatience. "This is not my house. I am merely a guest here. My home is not in New York, not any longer. What I wish is this: that you come to our home and stay there for as long as it takes you to complete a set of interiors."

Startled, I hardly knew how to answer her. Such an offer had never been made before; I had never traveled in my work.

"Where is your home, Mrs. Rockwell?" I asked cautiously.

"In Newport. But Copper Beeches is not merely a summer home for us. We live there year-round. Or at least my husband does. I usually manage to go abroad in the dreary winter months," she said complacently.

Newport. The summer playground of the fabulously wealthy. In the months of July and August there was an exodus of millionaires from the sweltering city up to the coastal town in Rhode Island. My father had gone up to paint portraits, but I had never been there. I had heard that the Four Hundred had built "cottages" there to rival the great castles and villas in Europe.

"I will be returning at the end of this week," continued Mrs. Rockwell. "The summer season is still some weeks away but I have a great deal to do. I would like you to come in a week or two."

She was assuming that I would not refuse, that I would accept with alacrity. It was characteristic of her that she did not even inquire whether I was working on another commission at the time. But I was used to the imperious demands of the rich, and I would not be intimidated.

"I don't know, Mrs. Rockwell. You see, I have never stayed with a family while I was working for them."

"Oh, there is plenty of room, I assure you," she said, raising one arched eyebrow. "We would hardly get in each other's way. The house is a large one, and there is only my husband, my brother, my sister-in-law. Also my husband's great-aunt comes to us from Boston every summer. Oh, and we have a small daughter, but she won't give you any trouble. Her governess keeps her in the nursery. I rarely see her. So, you see, we are not at all a large household."

I saw nothing of the kind. A six-person household, not counting servants, sounded quite large to me when I had never lived with more than two or three other people. But it was undoubtedly a large mansion. And I did not expect that I would be given a room on the same floor that the members of the family had theirs. So I would very likely have the privacy I was used to. I could probably come and go as I pleased, so long as I worked diligently. When I needed to be totally alone, I could go for long walks. By the sea, I reminded myself.

I began to be tempted. The change of pace and scenery might be the best thing for me at this time. There might even be the possibility of my securing other commissions in Newport, once I finished my work at the Rockwells'. My name was slightly known for its own sake, and very well known because of my father. My work had to stand on its own merits, but I was not too proud to use my father's name to gain a wider audience. I had worked and studied too hard and long to let pride hold me back.

For months I had been grieving for my father, feeling lost and dazed and uncertain about my future. Perhaps traveling to a different location, beginning a new job, was precisely what I needed. I had accomplished very little in New York since my father's death.

Having no real wish to remain in the townhouse, I had still been reluctant to make a move. I had been waiting, biding time. Was this the answer, then? Was this what I had been waiting for, all unknowingly? If I accepted Mrs. Rockwell's offer I would no longer mope about, unproductive, confused, unmotivated. I would be making a firm decision, a step toward my future.

It was time I traveled, I told myself. It was time I broadened, not just my mind and my talents, but my experience. I had not felt altogether comfortable with my father's artist cronies. I daresay, to them, I seemed dull and provincial. I was intense about my work — too intense — and unsure of myself except when I was painting.

There was nothing to keep me in New York this summer.

Omar could open his own business; I had been selfish not to insist he do so before. If I closed up the house and went to Newport, he could do as he liked with no qualms about me.

"The work will take several weeks, Mrs. Rockwell," I told her.

She made an airy gesture with her hand. "Take as long as you need, Miss Morrow. I am certain that no one wishes you to do a hasty job. I have a certain influence. If I am pleased, other commissions may come your way. Surely you would prefer to spend part or all of the summer in a seaside location away from the heat and grime of New York."

"That aspect of it is especially appealing," I told her, smiling.

"So you agree?"

"Well . . ." Why did I hesitate? It sounded ideal, and yet . . . She was regarding me expectantly, a slight pucker in her brow.

"It will take me at least a week to arrange matters," I said lamely. Was it her manner which put me off slightly? But she was only a rich Society hostess; I had dealt with others in the course of my career.

"Naturally I will advance you money for your passage and supplies. I recommend that you travel by steamer. The Fall River line, to be precise."

Everything pointed to my acceptance of her offer. Surely this was the perfect solution to my listless, indefinite state of mind. New work, a totally different location, new faces, experiences . . . My father would have wanted me to take the commission, I realized. He had believed in my career. And I could begin earning an income again, something I needed to do.

"Very well, Mrs. Rockwell. I will agree to come to Newport and paint your interiors."

She nodded, coolly satisfied; she was used to having her way. No person such as I would have dared to thwart her desires. And then I was conscious of a sharp misgiving. It struck me forcibly that I did not like her. And yet what reason was there for this abrupt dislike, this, yes, *animosity?* Her character, her affairs were no business of mine. She was merely a means to attain an end. She was providing me with a new opportunity for my career, a path in which my reputation might grow.

I would be engaged in work I enjoyed in what was considered a beautiful serene spot. My summer sojourn in Newport was likely to be a pleasant one.

But in living with the Rockwells for a time I could not help but be a witness to some aspects of their private lives. This realization made me a trifle uneasy. If I disliked Mrs. Rockwell now, after one brief meeting, how would I feel seeing her day after day? And what of her husband, and of the child she rarely saw? What of the other members of the household?

But many artists over the centuries had stayed with their patrons, I reminded myself. The muralists of the last century had journeyed from house to house, painting scenes of distant places on dining-room walls. I was foolish to allow these misgivings to unnerve me.

I would do my work, explore the old seaport town,

68

and then move on. Mrs. Rockwell, as other Society matrons had done, would likely begin to regard me as a piece of furniture. I would be left entirely to my own devices much of the time. Mr. Rockwell was undoubtedly tied up with business affairs relating to his import firm; the others would have their activities as well. It was doubtful if any of them would give me a second thought or glance.

"I will cable you of my arrival date and time," I said firmly.

"One of the carriages will be sent to collect you at the harbor." She rose. "Good day, Miss Morrow."

The interview was over.

As the days passed, I became convinced that I had made the right decision. That vague feeling of apprehension subsided, or perhaps I somehow managed to push it aside. I was very busy making preparations for the trip and purchasing all that I would require. Mrs. Rockwell having provided me with enough money to travel first class, I made a reservation on a steamboat to Newport. I went shopping for some additions to my summer wardrobe. By the end of the week I was looking forward to leaving New York, and excited at the prospect of spending some weeks in Newport.

Are our lives devised for us so that we are no more than victims or pawns in a vast unholy scheme? Or do we contrive our own destinies, every day making choices, taking steps, unwitting of where they will lead us?

I could not have known how accurate my initial reaction had been and how wrong I was not to take heed of it. When I boarded the steamer which would take me to New England, I entered a maze with high, tangled walls. Unable to go back the way I had come, I penetrated farther into that brambled darkness until there was no escape.

Chapter Four

The steamboat was very luxurious. Richly carved and gilded paneling adorned the walls, and the deck was fashioned of planks of yellow pine and black walnut alternating in a handsome pattern. Through the set of large doors in the after bulkhead I glimpsed elegant staterooms provided for ladies traveling alone, and for families with children. There were also saloons and gentlemen's smoking parlors.

I had no desire to be confined in a stateroom for ladies. I was too restless and excited to sit placidly in a chair surrounded by knitting spinsters. Instead of retiring to one of the inner chambers, I mounted the staircase to the story above.

That deck was open rather than enclosed, and a brass band was gaily playing marches. The steamer was not crowded as I was traveling in the middle of the week; there was plenty of room to wander about and absorb the sights.

It was a magnificent steamer. There were gold Corinthian columns, marble-top tables and velvet-covered chairs. A signal gun heralded our departure from the dock. There was a breathless stirring among the passengers when we felt the first movement beneath us, a smooth glide which cast us into the bay. Walking across the deck, I took hold of the polished balustrade.

As we slipped away from the city, the noise of the

traffic and sounds of the harbor grew muffled and distant. Soon they were drowned out altogether by the martial music of the band. The jumbled outline of the many buildings began to resemble a set of building blocks, and before long the view took on an illusionary quality. As we glided into the Atlantic, the crowded, throbbing city became nothing more than a memory.

I did not feel any sadness at leaving New York. Vacating my father's studio had been difficult because of the time we had spent there together. The lawyers had seen to it that all remaining paintings were wrapped and crated and stored safely, including the portrait my father had done of me. When I finished my work in Newport, I would decide whether I would return to my father's townhouse or sell it and take a flat. Perhaps I might even go abroad, to London. Some of his old friends there had written me warm and sympathetic letters, inviting me to visit them whenever I wished. Just then I felt happier and freer than I had in months; my whole life was before me, rich with opportunities. I felt almost grateful to Mrs. Drew Rockwell for setting me on a new course.

Not for the first time did I pause to reflect on my unusual situation. I saw myself as a woman giving all to her career because it did not seem likely that I would follow the conventional path of marrying and having children. Most men would not have understood or approved of my career, and the unconventional way I had lived in the past nine years without female companionship, spending much of my time at my father's Tenth Street studio, would have made them even more wary. Even at school I had known I was worlds apart from the other pupils, and I was content that it was so. They had been planning to make their debuts or go abroad, whereas I was deeply ensconced in the bohemian world of artists, and wore that like a brand on my chest. No matter that my father and I led rather staid, ordered lives; it was what we chose to do with those lives that set us apart. Any way one looked at it, I was different, and it was that difference which made me threatening. I had sensed it even from my father's lawyers.

And so I was no more prepared for what happened later than if I had suddenly been thrust into an African jungle. I may have lived, I did live, an unorthodox life, but in some ways I was less experienced than any debutante. I had viewed myself as independent, my life following a structured pattern. But that summer my peace of mind and my views on what was right and wrong were shattered. And yet as I stood on the deck of the steamer listening to the cheerful tunes of the brass band, as I watched the waves churn in a broad foamy wake behind us, I had no idea of what would come to pass in that house above the sea, of the evil that simmered, waiting to erupt.

For a time I sat on the upper deck, breathing in the salt air, watching the gentle lapping of the waves. Overhead the the sky was blue with fleecy streams of clouds; it was a perfect day for a sea voyage.

Luncheon was announced by a steward and I joined my fellow passengers in the elegant dining room where the crystal chandeliers swayed slightly with the movement of the steamboat. An orchestra played waltz melodies.

I noticed that I was the only young woman seated alone; the others had evidently remained in the ladies' stateroom to take lunch. I had received a rather odd look from the steward as he handed me my menu, but I had not been governed by the rigid rules of what was considered proper behavior for young women, and I was not going to begin now. It was ironic; in actuality I was much less bold than many strictly reared young ladies, but because I was taking lunch alone I appeared more so. Several of the men cast me curious glances and a few of the women glared disapprovingly.

But I tried to appear nonchalant. I would have felt far more uncomfortable in a room filled with chattering ladies, inquiring into one another's business.

Lunch began with a crab bisque flavored with sherry. There was flounder, delmonico potatoes, and garden peas, and for dessert, peach pie. While I ate I observed the other passengers. The curious ones had become absorbed in their food, a far more enticing diversion than I presented.

There were several couples with children, a few dowagers with dried-up looking companions, and a party of rather boisterous young men who had, earlier, nudged one another and stared across at me in an ill-bred manner.

But none of these people caught and held my attention as did the occupants of the table to my right. I found my gaze returning to them again and again.

Seated there were a man and a child, a lovely little girl. They were both dark with almost black hair and dark eyes. It was evident from the way the steward hovered around them that the man was an important person, and probably someone who traveled this line frequently.

He was in his early thirties, I guessed, and wore a well-cut wheat-colored suit. He was very good-looking, his face strong, determined, and just now worried, his square jaw set, his brow creased. He was bent over talking to the little girl who looked about five or six years old. She was huddled in her chair wearing a white middy frock, her black hair falling in ringlets to her shoulders, one leg underneath her. The man was trying to get her to eat, and she was refusing. Every so often he would say something designed to make her laugh; I could tell because then he would suddenly grin and she would smile wanly back at him. But her food remained on her plate, and most of his looked untouched as well.

At one point he gestured to the steward and made a

73

request; minutes later the steward returned with a bowl of vanilla ice cream. The man urged the little girl to take a spoonful and even fed her some himself, but after a few tastes she shook her head and slouched even more in her chair.

She was very pale, with dark shadows under her eyes. I wondered if she were seasick, or whether there was something more seriously wrong with her.

The man leaned back in his chair, frowning at the child. And an expression came into his eyes which I identified with a slight shock as a despairing sort of fear. Yet what I had observed did not seem to warrant so severe a reaction.

Abruptly he stood up and I saw how tall and powerfully built he was. He picked up the child with no more effort than it would have taken for him to lift a kitten, and, holding her tenderly in his arms, strode from the room. Perhaps she was crippled, I thought sadly.

Other passengers had taken notice of them as well. One of the dowagers was saying something to her companion about them, and several young ladies had watched their progress from the room as I had. And why not? They were a striking pair. I told myself I was fascinated by them as subjects to paint.

Because of my engrossing interest in the man and little girl, I had not noticed that I had again become a subject of interest myself. The three young men who sat together in rather volatile merriment were again staring boldly at me and making comments I was thankful I could not hear. It was time I too left the dining room; I wanted no attention from foolish young men of leisure.

Pulling on my gloves and adjusting my hat, I rose and walked across the room to the paneled doors. Unfortunately I heard the young men following me. Walking hurriedly, I went down the corridor and up the stairs to the deck where I had sat before. But I saw with dismay that it was deserted; even the band had gone below. I turned to retrace my steps, having no wish to be burdened with the regard of three young men on a deserted deck. But at the top of the staircase they stood grinning at me, blocking my way.

"All alone, miss?" said one who wore a wilted-looking flower in his lapel.

"Where are you going?" asked another, revealing prominent teeth.

"My destination and mode of travel are no concern of yours," I said coldly. "Kindly allow me to pass."

I was not frightened, only conscious that they were bored and had drunk enough champagne or beer to make them roguish. They were looking for a diversion on a long boat ride.

"We're just looking for a little company," said the third, echoing my thoughts. "Since you're all alone we thought you might like some company, too."

"I am not alone," I said. "I am traveling with my aunt. She suffers from seasickness and is confined to the ladies' stateroom."

This did not deter them. "Well, you just might as well be alone," said the first.

"I must go to her now," I said. "Excuse me."

When they did not move, I said, "Get out of my way."

One of them grasped my arm. I was alarmed but I dared not show it. I refused to appear timid and feeble in front of them. "If you do not let me pass, I will call for the steward. It is not my desire to make a scene, but I assure you—"

"They're all below. No one will hear you." He smirked, his eyes raking over me.

"All we want is a little kiss," said the one with the large teeth. "Or a few. In a little while you can go back to your aunt."

"How dare you! Let me go at once!" I cried and this time there was both fear and disgust in my voice. I was alone on this level with them. Everyone else was still in the dining room or had retired to a private stateroom to rest. Why had I not gone directly to the ladies' salon?

The young man with the tired flower was pushing me back against the wall. I could smell beer on his breath.

"You're so pretty," he said. "Just give me a little kiss. You can spare a few kisses. We know you don't really want to back to your aunt, if you have an aunt. You were sitting alone in the dining room."

He bent over and I struggled, slapping him with my free hand.

"Now that wasn't nice," his said, his eyes narrowing. "I think we'll have to teach her a lesson."

"Let her go, or I'll teach you a lesson you'll never forget!" thundered a voice. At the top of the stairs stood the man from the dining room, a fierce scowl on his face.

The young man abruptly released me, his face turning beet red. "We weren't going to hurt her. What business is it of yours, anyway?" He jutted out his chin.

"I can easily make it my business," said the dark man. "It's up to you."

The two others looked uneasily at the broad shoulders and muscular build of the older man.

"Let her go, Jeff. Let's get out of here," said one.

"Yeah, come on," said the other. They shuffled down the stairs without glancing back at us.

"Are you all right?" he asked, his frowning gaze on me.

I nodded shakily and then said the first thing which popped into my head. "Where is the little girl?"

"She's asleep in our stateroom."

I colored. As if it were any of my concern. "I — I'm grateful to you, sir, for your . . . assistance."

He regarded me searchingly, but when he spoke I

76

had the impression that he had been thinking of something else entirely. "May I suggest that for the remainder of the voyage you confine yourself to more populated areas of the steamboat? As you seem to be unaccompanied, surely that would be wise."

"I can take care of myself," I said, annoyed at his implicit criticism.

"You were doing an admirable job of it," he said sardonically.

"I won't be blamed for the behavior of those — idiots."

"I'm sure they will not trouble you again. Perhaps it would be prudent, however, if you continued the journey in one of the staterooms reserved for ladies."

"I shall stay where I like," I snapped.

His face tightened, his mouth hardening. "As you wish, of of course. Good day."

Watching him retreat, I could have bitten off my tongue. I realized too late that I had interpreted his concern as disapproval. For all my semblance of poise and assurance I was as inexperienced as he no doubt thought me. I had never before traveled alone; I had not forseen that I might put myself in a position where liberties might be taken. I had been foolish, then rude and ungrateful. His manner had been a trifle overbearing, but he had only been thinking of my welfare.

Rather forlornly I went down the stairs to the main deck following the gilded corridor to the prow. There were others sitting there and I took a seat in one of the plush chairs. The breeze fanned my flushed cheeks and I was calmed by the movement of the steamboat. I fell asleep.

It could not have been much later when I awoke. Stirring, I opened my eyes. I felt groggy and out of sorts. To my astonishment there was nothing to see but a thick whiteness beyond the confines of the boat. Bewildered, I rubbed my eyes. The deck was deserted, but the air was heavy with moisture.

"We've run into a fog bank. It's nothing to be alarmed about."

I had been mistaken; the deck was not deserted. The tall dark man sat in a chair near to me, the sleeping girl in his arms. Her lashes were long and thick and black, crescents against her pale cheeks.

He followed my gaze. "As you can see, I've recalled my responsibility."

"I beg your pardon?"

"You looked rather disapproving earlier when I said I had left her asleep in the stateroom."

"Oh, no, certainly . . ."

"It seems I've been handed two responsibilities this trip. When I walked out here to find the place empty and you asleep, I thought you might be frightened at waking in the fog. Of course, I realize you can look after yourself." An ironic smile curved his lips.

"Thank you," I said, embarrassed. "Again I am in your debt. I—I apologize for seeming so ungracious before." Flushing, I was anxious to change the subject. "Can the crew see to steer the boat?"

"They are used to these waters and these sudden fogs. Chances are we will be out of it soon."

Gazing out at the dense whiteness, I could no longer hear the lapping of the waves against the boat or the screeching of gulls. It was silent and eerie. I had the impression that we would continue to glide through the damp cloying thickness indefinitely, cut off from the rest of the world. If the rest of the world still existed . . .

But curiously these random fancies caused me no alarm, no disquiet. Instead I felt curiously safe, secure. It was an odd sensation, this tranquil acceptance of isolation. And in some strange intuitive way I sensed the man felt it too.

The little girl stirred, mumbled in her sleep, and was again still.

"Your daughter?"

He nodded, his mouth tightening, and again I saw that bleak look come into his eyes.

We subsided into silence, a silence that was both comfortable and comforting. Idle conversation would have been obtrusive.

I had the remarkable feeling that we were sharing the same thoughts, the same mood, when he said, "We might be the only three people alive." There was a strange note in his voice, a sort of brooding wistfulness.

We did not look at one another; we gazed directly ahead, into the fog bank.

It was much later when he said, "I believe we are coming out of it."

He was right. Now it was possible to see beyond the prow; one could also hear the waves slapping. Gradually the whiteness wasted away to a filmy shroud. I could see the waves, gray and choppy, below us. The sudden harsh cry of a gull pierced the vanishing serenity, and when it was answered by further shrieks there was nothing left of that interlude of intimacy, of soothing isolation.

"We must be nearing land," I said, clutching my shawl about me. I felt cold suddenly, and unaccountably depressed.

"Daddy? Are we nearly home?" The little girl had opened her eyes; her tousled head rested against her father's broad chest.

"Yes, darling, it won't be much longer now." But his voice was heavy and his face grim.

Not much longer now before the steamboat would dock and we would go our separate ways, live our separate lives, and the last few hours would become little more than a remote dream, half-forgotten, half-imagined.

He seemed to sense it as well. Straightening his shoulders, he said, "We'll go to the stateroom now and get ready."

"All right, Daddy."

His voice was coolly formal when he spoke to me. "Good afternoon. I hope the remainder of your journey is pleasant."

"Good afternoon," I replied just as formally, just as distantly.

He stood up with the little girl in his arms and strode from the deck.

Then, because I could not bear to remain there any longer, I made my way to one of the ladies' staterooms and sat there the rest of the trip, an open book before me. But I read the words over and over, never once taking them in, my mind picturing his face, the square jaw set, the eyes dark and troubled. Only, for a time as we had sat there in that limbo world, I was certain that they had not been troubled.

By the time we docked at Newport harbor, the sky was clear and blue, the water no longer gray but cobalt. Now even the fog bank seemed something I had imagined while dozing on deck.

The air was soft and shimmering, the late afternoon breeze delightful. My spirits began to lift as I looked out over the coastal town, the shingled or painted Georgian houses lining the streets which rose steeply from the harbor. On the crest of the hill a magnificent white steeple with clocktower and narrow Palladian windows rose like a beacon over the neighboring buildings. The sight was quaint and picturesque in its simplicity, and not at all what I had expected of a playground of the leisure class.

But then I noticed the racing yachts moored alongside weatherbeaten fishing boats, and the line of gleaming carriages waiting on the street to collect the steamer passengers. And I was struck by the incongruity of it all.

With the rest of the travelers I made my way from the wharf up the cobbled alley to the street, hoping that one of the carriages there was for me. My trunks had been carried off the steamboat and I stood beside them, waiting. There was a great deal of confusion, of people milling about. I did not see the tall dark man with his little girl.

Several times as I stepped up to a footman to inquire whether he had been sent for me, he sprang to attention, only to hold the carriage door open for others to climb inside. With interest I noticed the brick Colonial buildings with their Palladian windows and Ionic pilasters which reflected an earlier prosperity. Looking forward to exploring the town at length, I was nevertheless tired and anxious to get settled at Copper Beeches.

Gradually all the carriages pulled away; the wharf grew quieter, the crowds dispersing. I began to feel awkward and annoyed standing there alone, trying to ignore the glances of male passersby. Hadn't Mrs. Rockwell received my cable? I had sent it a full three days ago. Surely she could not have forgotten I was due to arrive this afternoon. She had assured me that I would be met upon my arrival.

Finally I decided that it was foolish to wait any longer. Newport was a small city; I would find my own way to Copper Beeches. Gesturing to a hansom cab, I told the driver my destination, asked him to see to my bags, and climbed inside.

We rode up a steep narrow street leading away from the harbor, past Colonial cottages with gambrel or pitched roofs and many-paned windows. At the top of the hill there was an abrupt change. We turned down a broad avenue, shady with tall majestic trees. Now, rather than passing modest houses like stepping stones, we were driving past stately manors with sweeping lawns and formal gardens. There was a whimsical Gothic wooden mansion, a few built in the "stick style," and a shingle-style villa with a two-story veranda under a tower.

The carriage was slowing and then we turned onto a

long graveled drive. Eagerly I looked for my first sight of the house where I would be staying for weeks to come.

And then I saw it, and could not help a quick intake of breath. It was larger and more imposing than I had imagined, a buff-colored stone mansion built in the Second Empire style with long windows, exposed brackets, and two towers rising from the stately mansard roof. Dahlias, a motif reflecting the Aesthetic movement in art and architecture, decorated the verdigris trim of the roofline.

We drove up the circular drive under a stone archway past towering copper beeches and hydrangea bushes, their blossoms round, fat, and a vibrant violet-blue. The cab drew up in front of the house; the driver deposited my luggage on the front steps, leaving me standing before the two massive medallion-studded oak doors.

After adjusting my hat and smoothing my black watch plaid traveling costume, I took a deep breath and rapped on the door. Within moments it was opened, and I said to the butler, "I am Miss Morrow. Please tell Mrs. Rockwell that I have arrived."

"Mrs. Rockwell is not at home, Miss Morrow. If you will step into the library, I will inform Mr. Rockwell."

At least he appeared to be familiar with my name; my appearance on the doorstep must not have been altogether unexpected.

Entering the house, I passed through a grand hall elaborately paneled in the Eastlake style. There was a fireplace decorated with tiles easily recognizable as the work of Walter Crane, and above my head were three galleries leading up to a magnificent stained-glass window below the roof.

The butler showed me into the library and closed the door. I stood there apprehensively, clasping and unclasping my gloved hands. The woodwork in the room was dark walnut, heavily carved table and chairs and massive bookshelves. Above the mantel hung a painting of a Hudson River scene. I went closer to examine it, a little thrill shooting through me. It was a serene autumn scene, probably by Thomas Doughty, the river placid in the background, with sailboats. Perhaps it was a good omen, I thought hopefully.

Behind me I heard the door opening. I turned, ready to remark on the painting, to share my delight, to meet the head of the household with a new surge of confidence.

Instead I said nothing. I felt the warm color drain from my face and rush back into it, hot now. Lightheaded, I could only gaze in consternation, the solace from the painting evaporating as if it had suddenly been torn from the wall and smashed in two. No, it couldn't be. It wasn't possible. Not *this* man. Not *her* husband.

The man from the steamboat was as stunned as I. Neither of us could speak; we gazed helplessly at one another. And even then I felt with a cold dread that this was no mere coincidence, that something was at play here which we were powerless against.

Then he made a slight movement which broke the spell and we were abruptly just two slightly bewildered people who had happened to meet on a ship earlier in the day.

"May I help you?" he asked. "I am Drew Rockwell."

"I am Ariel Morrow," I said, only a slight betraying breathlessness in my voice.

"Ariel Morrow," he repeated, his gaze suddenly keen. "Of course."

I waited hopefully, but he did not go on, continuing to regard me with that rather disturbing scrutiny.

"I—I've come to do the interiors," I prompted.

He frowned. "Interiors?"

We were going round in circles; I had assumed that my name conveyed my business to him. Didn't he know why I had come? "Yes. Mrs. Rockwell engaged me several weeks ago in New York to execute a series of watercolor interiors of Copper Beeches. You . . . were not aware of this?"

"I had heard you were an artist as well," he said softly.

What was he talking about? "Yes, I am. And Mrs. Rockwell asked me to come to Newport. I cabled her of my arrival time several days ago."

"Mrs. Rockwell said nothing to me about this," he said crisply, his face hardening. "Naturally she would not—" he broke off. "Well, Miss Morrow, Cordelia is not at home just now. She is involved in a very important ritual, on Ocean Drive." His voice was sardonic. "Forgive me. I could have given you a ride in our coach, had I realized Copper Beeches was your destination as well. Are you staying nearby?"

I colored. "I—Mrs. Rockwell gave me to understand that I would be staying here."

His black brows drew together. "Here?"

I was horribly embarrassed—didn't that woman tell her husband anything? Her *husband*. I was still reeling slightly.

"Why on earth she would—" Again he broke off, his eyes narrowing. "Well, Miss Morrow, I apologize for the confusion. I have been in New York myself and have not seen my—Cordelia since returning home. I will see that there is a room prepared for you immediately. Excuse me."

He went out of the library and I heard him speaking to the butler. I wanted to call after him that it was all a mistake, that I had changed my mind, that on second thought I couldn't agree to paint the interiors, that most of all I could not stay under the same roof with him. . . .

When he returned he said, "It appears that Mrs. Rockwell has not forgotten your existence entirely. I'm told that a room has already been made ready for you.

84

One of the maids will take you up, and your bags will be brought to you." He had by now fully recovered his manner and was once again distant, impersonal.

"Thank you, Mr. Rockwell," I murmured and passed through the door he held open for me. A maid stood in the hall and I followed her down a corridor to a landing from which rose a pair of oak staircases, also fashioned in the Eastlake style. The walls were covered in linen painted to look like tapestry. Halfway up the staircases was a breathtaking stained-glass window of a Grecian female figure swaying against a darkly vibrant landscape of greens, purples, and blues. Her face, neck, and arms glowed in an exquisite mauve and opal-hued light that radiated from the upper left corner of the window.

John La Farge. My father and I knew his work well; I had met him on a number of occasions. I had seen a similar scene in oil at the National Academy's recent annual. It was *Dawn Comes on the Edge of Night*. I had admired it greatly then, but in stained glass it was superb.

My room was on the third floor at the rear of the house. From the window was a view of the sweeping lawn, a rose arbor, a fish pond, and farther back, a summerhouse framed with blue spruces and bushes of violet-blue hydrangeas. Beyond the gardens rose enormous trees, the tops glinting copper in the late afternoon sun. And behind them, a band of blue that was the ocean.

"Mr. Rockwell said to tell you that dinner is served at eight o'clock, Miss Morrow. I'm to come back then and show you the way to the dining room."

"What is your name?"

"Nancy, miss."

"All right, Nancy. Thank you."

"Your bath is through there. I put in towels and everything this morning. Is there anything you need just now?"

85

"No, I don't think so. I'm going to have a hot bath and relax until dinner."

"Yes, miss."

When she had gone I went into the bathroom and ran the water in the massive mahogany-framed tub. I washed my face and took off my traveling costume, relieved to at last be alone with my thoughts.

Copper Beeches belonged to the man I had met on the steamboat. He was Drew Rockwell, the husband of the woman who had engaged me and whose commission I had been reluctant to accept. Were my initial misgivings right after all? I had known on the boat that he must be married because he had a little girl. I wished that I had never seen him, that we had not met on the steamer, sharing that peaceful interlude in the fog bank when our thoughts had seemed to come from one mind. . . .

I had to get a grip on myself. I was making far more of that hour or so than there had actually been. So we had spoken on the steamboat, what of it? And it had happened that we shared the same destination. That wasn't as remarkable as I was dramatizing it to be. This was nothing but romantic foolishness, something I had not succumbed to for a long time. There was no fate at work here. There was no reason why I could not stay in this house and do my work, keep to myself, untroubled by the presence of some man I barely knew. All this heart-stopping nonsense and feeling weak in the knees was ridiculous. And potentially quite harmful to me. Yes, he was handsome. He was also my employer—and married. Very married, with a daughter.

It was not at all like me to lose my head in this way. If I were to become infatuated with Drew Rockwell, there would be nothing in it for me but pain and unhappiness. I had come to paint watercolor interiors of this beautiful house and when I was finished, I would leave and never see any of these people again. I had my career to think of, and I was certainly not going to jeopardize it by developing an unbecoming schoolgirl crush on the husband of the woman who had engaged me.

Having taken myself strictly to task, I took a soothing bath and then dressed for dinner in a white taffeta gown with a square neckline and large puffed sleeves to the elbow. Brushing my dark red hair and pinning it in a loose topknot, I clasped a choker of pearls around my neck and was ready when the maid came to fetch me.

The jewel colors in the Dawn window had dulled and glazed; it was dusk. The maid led me down a corridor. "It's just there, Miss Morrow."

I could hear voices. My heart hammering, I went forward, hesitating at the entrance to the room.

"Good evening, Miss Morrow," said Drew. He wore black evening attire and looked rather forbidding. "Allow me to present my sister, Miss Rockwell. Isadora, this is Miss Ariel Morrow."

"Ariel! What a pretty name. And how unusual. Where on earth did your parents get it?" She was a pretty brunette, about eighteen years old, dressed in an apricot gown with yokes of pale blue lace.

I smiled. "From *The Tempest*, I believe."

She wrinkled her nose. "I don't think I've read that one. I like the one about the brother and sister who are twins, and they're separated in a shipwreck, and the sister dresses as a boy and falls in love with a duke who thinks she's a boy, and a lady falls in love with her, also thinking she's a boy . . . oh, never mind about that. You don't look at all the way I pictured you, Miss Morrow, when Drew said a lady artist had come. I couldn't wait to catch a glimpse of you. I've never known a lady artist before. Of course, your father was so famous you'd simply have to be someone special—"

"Dora, I think you are embarrassing Miss Morrow.

Be quiet."

Just then a large old woman entered the room, attired in purple and wearing an alarming coiffure of purple feathers which stuck out in all directions. As she moved forward ponderously I heard the creaking of her whalebone stays.

Her gaze fell on me. "Who are you?" she asked abruptly.

"This is Miss Morrow, Aunt Hermione," said Isadora. "She's a famous artist and has come to paint our rooms."

"To paint them? What in heaven's name for? I should have thought they had enough paint on them already — all those designs my sister's husband, your grandfather, loved on the ceilings, not to mention the wallpaper and panelling."

"No, you don't understand, Aunt," said Isadora, giggling. "She's not *that* sort of painter. How could she be?"

"How? How could she be any sort of painter? What are you talking about, Dora? No one tells me anything."

"Miss Morrow has come to paint watercolor representations of various rooms in the house," said Drew. "She will be staying with us for the present."

"Watercolors? That sounds an affected thing to do, having the rooms painted, I mean."

"Aunt, please," said Isadora, casting an anxious glance at me.

"Cordelia his engaged Miss Morrow to paint some interiors of Copper Beeches, so that the look of them will be preserved for future generations," said Drew dryly.

"Oh, Cordelia," said the old lady. "Well, if I know her she cares nothing for future generations. She must have heard that Alva Vanderbilt Belmont or one of them was having their — whatevers — done and so she just had to follow along." She turned to me. "So you're an artist, are you? What is your name?"

"Ariel Morrow, Mrs. . . ."

"Grant. Where do you come from?"

"New York, Mrs. Grant."

"Miss Morrow and I were fellow passengers on the same steamer today," said Drew. "I had no idea then that we were going to the same place."

Aunt Hermione gave a dry cackle. "Cordelia didn't tell you, eh? Well, what do you expect? Morrow. Any relation to Lancelot Morrow?"

"He was her father, Aunt. Isn't it too exciting?" cried Isadora. "Did he ever paint your portrait, Miss Morrow? But he must have, many times."

"Only once," I said, smiling.

"Where is it now? Do you have it? Or did he sell it?"

"No, it's mine. It wasn't for sale."

"It must be ravishing," she said soulfully.

I glanced across to see Drew regarding me. In words I could barely catch, he said, "It is."

I colored. So he had seen the portrait while it hung at the National Academy. That was why he had recognized my name, and studied me so absorbingly.

"Well, Miss Morrow, there you are."

It was Cordelia Rockwell in a trailing pink gown with seed pearls sewn on the bodice. "I didn't expect that you . . ." She raised her brows.

"You didn't expect that she would arrive today, or that she would be taking her meals with us?" said Drew curtly.

"Don't be foolish, Drew. I knew she would arrive today. I left instructions for a room to be prepared."

"You said nothing to me about it."

"How could I? You've been in New York. What did the doctors say?"

His face hardened. "They spoke a great deal of tedious jargon that, when it came to the point, meant nothing."

She shrugged. "Well, I told you it would be a wasted

89

trip. But no, you knew best. Though why you insisted on going all the way to New York when Dr. Chandler lives next door . . ."

"Prescott Chandler is not a specialist, Cordelia. And he rarely practices these days. Where is Gideon?"

"How should I know?" his wife replied carelessly. "At the Casino, perhaps, or the Canfield House."

"Well, he knows dinner is at eight. We will not wait any longer."

"Thank goodness. I'm famished!" said Isadora.

"I thought you went on a picnic to Portsmouth this afternoon," said Cordelia.

"I did, but I was laced so tightly I could barely eat a thing!"

Cordelia looked pained. "Isadora, really. I hope you don't say things like that when you are out among people. They will get a very odd idea of you."

"At least I don't go about talking like that Mr. Van Alen. He drove out with us today, and everything he said began with, 'Zounds!' or 'Prithee.' And he called one of the footmen a 'varlet' when he dropped a basket. He sounds like something out of Henry VIII's time. Camille and I could barely keep from laughing at him, although no one else seems to pay any attention."

"It is not your place to criticize someone like Mr. Van Alen, Isadora. He is a friend and neighbor of ours, and quite eligible," said Cordelia reprovingly.

"Well, if you think I'd marry someone old enough to be my father, you can think again," said Isadora, unabashed.

"As if he would have you. You're a minx, Isadora," snapped Cordelia.

"Last week at the Casino he held me captive with a long discourse on how he keeps English mustard in an English mustard pot, and French mustard in a French mustard pot," said Drew dryly. "It was enthralling."

"Well, why did you go to the Casino? You detest the

90

place, after all," chided Cordelia.

"Belmont asked me to meet him there. He wanted to buy the new mare. I told him I had no intention of selling her. Besides, I hardly think she would take to life at Belcourt Castle, sleeping in the house on white linen sheets with gold emblems.

"I don't see how Alva puts up with horses on the first floor of her home. Of course, she still has Marble Palace. I daresay one day she'll open it again. If only you would let me redo some of our rooms, Drew. All this wood paneling is so *medieval.* What we need are white columns and delicate French furniture and marble and—"

"Vulgar. That's what it is, Cordelia," said Aunt Hermione.

Cordelia flushed angrily. "Oh, you're as bad as Drew. No one can touch the Rockwell sanctum."

"I confess I was surprised you engaged Miss Morrow to paint our interiors when you are always claiming you want to change them," said Drew.

He turned to me. "The house was built in the 1850s by my grandfather, but my father enlarged it twenty years later. He had visited England on his wedding trip and was very impressed with some of the manor houses he saw there that had been decorated by Charles Eastlake and William Morris. He used their ideas in his renovation of Copper Beeches."

"That's just it, Drew. That was twenty years ago. Now the thing is to have marble floors and white Grecian statues and huge terrains of exotic plants and indoor fountains."

"Unhealthy," declared Aunt Hermione. "I'd be sneezing my head off. And marble is so cold. I'm not ready to take up residence in a mausoleum yet, I assure you."

Cordelia ignored her. "I really do think you might respect a few of my wishes, Drew. I have told you that I cannot bear to drive about with the men not in livery. We are the laughingstock of the town—and I don't mean the locals! The Vanderbilt footmen wear maroon; Mrs. Astor's, blue—"

"We have been over this subject before, Cordelia," said Drew wearily. "I will not have my servants dress in costumes appropriate to a fancy-dress ball. Black and white is much more suitable. The notion of dressing one's staff as they would have been dressed in France one hundred and fifty years ago is absurd. I don't see Mrs. Belmont powdering her hair."

"No, only dying it," giggled Isadora.

" 'To gild refined gold, to paint the lily . . . is wasteful and ridiculous excess,' " quoted Drew.

"What are you talking about?" snapped Cordelia.

"Not I. Shakespeare. *King John,* to be specific."

"Oh, you make me sick. You cling to your stuffy Boston notions and refuse to change. You've got your head buried in the sand, Drew. Well, I've got news for you. Newport has changed. It's not the shabbily genteel place it was in your childhood with all the Bostonians congratulating themselves on their wit and intellect, hobnobbing with poets and artists. You'll find none of that here now!"

Drew gazed down the length of the table at his wife, an ironic smile twisting his lips. "You never spoke a truer word, Cordelia," he said silkily. "My compliments to you."

Her face reddened. In one furious movement she rose, flung down her napkin, and stormed from the room.

Chapter Five

Once Cordelia had stalked from the room, I hardly knew where to look. My own face was scarlet with embarrassment merely for witnessing the scene.

"You shouldn't bait her, Drew," came Aunt Hermione's gruff voice. "It only makes her worse."

"I wonder where Gideon is," said Isadora, obviously trying to turn the subject.

"I am not concerned about him," said Drew heavily. I stole a look at him; he was staring down into his glass of wine, his mouth, hard, his expression grim.

"If you ask me, which you don't," said Aunt Hermione, "the child's condition has something more to it than that bout of scarlet fever. I know the doctors keep telling you that it weakened her constitution, but I've known other children to suffer it and fully recover within a few months. It's been two years, Drew."

"I know precisely how long it's been." There was no curtness in his tone, only a bleak despair.

"Well, that long trip would weary anyone. It's no wonder the child is so pale and exhausted," said the old lady bracingly.

"Blythe is always pale and exhausted," said Drew. He rose, saying, "If you will excuse me, ladies." He had not glanced at me once.

When he had gone Isadora turned to me and said, "I

was so sorry to hear of your father's death. I wish he might have painted *my* portrait. Were you living with him in New York?"

"Yes."

"And did you work together?"

"Well, not exactly. For a long time he was my instructor. Then, two years ago, I began to get commissions to paint professionally."

"Did you always wish to be an artist?"

"I suppose so. Though I didn't believe it could truly happen."

"What does your mother think?"

"She died when I was a small child. I don't remember her at all."

"How tragic," said Isadora musingly. "He could never forget her, and so never fell in love again. But he had you to console him, and so he brought you up to be an artist. What a romantic story."

"Well . . ." I began.

"Stop talking such nonsense, Dora," said Aunt Hermione.

"I only thought it a lovely story, like something out of a novel, not like real life at all. I hope you'll stay here, Miss Morrow, and not change your mind about doing the interiors."

"Why should I do that, Miss Rockwell?"

"Dora means that this is a troubled household, Miss Morrow," said Aunt Hermione gravely. "The fact that you will be living at Copper Beeches for the present . . . well, we wouldn't want our private affairs finding their way into the gossip columns."

"Aunt Hermione!" protested Isadora.

I met the old lady's glare with a fierce one of my own. "I assure you your affairs are no concern of mine, Mrs. Grant. I am here to work, and I am not in the habit of telling tales."

"Now I've made you angry," she said, giving a cackle of laughter. "Good. You look magnificent when you're angry. So did I—once. Dora only manages to look peevish."

"Oh, Aunt, really!"

"Just so we know where we stand," said the extraordinary old woman. "At my age I can say what I like, Dora. It's one of the very few benefits of old age. But I'll say one thing for you, Miss Morrow. You're not one of those pale languishing misses who haven't a thought in their empty heads."

"Have you ever been in love, Miss Morrow?" said Isadora unexpectedly.

Coloring, I stammered, "Well, n-no, not really."

"I've been in love a dozen times," she said feelingly, resting her cheek on her hand. "But it never lasts. I always end up observing them in some foolish behavior, and suddenly they are not dashing, romantic figures at all, but only rather silly boys."

"Plenty of time for you to meet the right man," said Aunt Hermione.

"You were married when you were younger than I, Aunt."

"Yes, but things were different then. We didn't have all this nonsense about making one's debut and going about like sheep in mindless rituals. I met my husband at a ball in New Bedford while your grandmother and I were visiting some cousins. He was a whaling captain, Miss Morrow, just home from a voyage. I took one look at him and knew he was the one for me. And so he proved to be—although he was away at sea so much of the time perhaps that helped the marriage last," she added cynically. "It never had a chance to grow stale."

Was that what had happened to Drew and Cordelia's marriage? Had it grown stale? Were they bored with their lifestyle and one another, or was it something more serious?

"Well, I'm going upstairs now," said Aunt Hermione. She rose slowly from the table, her stays creaking.

I rose as well. "Yes, it's been a long day for me. I'll

say good night to you both."

What exactly was the state of affairs at Copper Beeches? I wondered later while up in my room. That it was a tense, troubled household was apparent even to me. But what lay at the root of the atmosphere?

Somehow the little girl's — Blythe's — poor health was involved. It seemed that her father had taken her to New York to be examined by doctors, specialists. I wondered precisely what was wrong with her. She seemed so listless, so uninterested in her surroundings on the steamer. There were dark smudges under her eyes, accentuating the paleness of her cheeks. And she looked terribly thin. Her father was very worried about her condition, but his wife, the child's mother, had not seemed concerned. Aunt Hermione had mentioned a case of scarlet fever two years before. Evidently the doctors believed that she had never recovered from it.

I saw now why my father had refused to become intimate with the people he painted. He had always asserted that an artist must merely observe and not attempt to delve into the character of the subject. But my father had not been a man of deep emotions; he had been content to go through life as an detached onlooker, never involved, not even particularly interested in other people. I was not like that, I realized. Never would I have been so drawn to Drew and Blythe if I were. And only after a few hours at Copper Beeches, I wanted to know much more about them.

That was the first danger sign.

Feeling rather strained and restless, I was not ready to undress and go to bed. At my window I drew aside the lace curtain and leaned out. The moon was shining and the back lawn was lit with an eerie silvery glow. Further down, the summerhouse was barely discernable in the deep shadows.

From across the lawn came an odd sound, rather like many voices whispering. I realized it was the wind rustling the branches of the enormous trees. In the air there was the faint smell of salt, although I could not hear the sea over the sound of the whispering beeches.

Taking a shawl from the bureau drawer, I wrapped it about me and went out into the corridor. I had no wish to meet any member of the family and so I took a back stairway I had noticed earlier.

Outside, the whispers sounded even louder. I set off across the lawn, drawn by the call of the massive trees in the distance. The grass was damp with dew; soon the soles of my kid slippers were as wet as my trailing hem. But I paid scarce attention. Ahead of me loomed the copper beeches, and another type that I did not recognize. It was the second variety which made the whispering sounds. Branches, dense with leaves, hung down like wild locks on some demented creature's head. In the silvery light they were especially eerie, their trunks wrinkled and huge as elephants' feet. And from their vinelike branches came that unearthly whispering, the murmuring of secrets only they could understand.

I stood there under the trees for some time before turning about and heading back to the house. The breeze had grown stronger and I was chilly in my light shawl. The smell of the sea was acute.

As I neared the summerhouse I decided to get a closer look at it. Pausing by the row of steps which led up to the front porch, I thought what a charming cottage it was, not open like a pavilion, but a real small house with gables and gingerbread.

Suddenly I was gripped from behind. Terrified, I began to struggle, crying out, when a voice I had never heard before said in my ear, "Whom have we here? Not that I'm complaining, not at all, but I would like to know which lady I hold in my arms."

"How dare you?" I cried. "Let me go at once!"

The man released me, chuckling softly. "I didn't think you were one of the servants."

Whirling around, I regarded him furiously. He was young, about my own age. In the moonlight his face was shadowed so that I could not see it clearly, but he was elegantly dressed.

"Who are you?" he repeated.

"I might ask you the same question," I snapped. "This is private property. You have no right to roam about frightening people. What are you doing here?"

"My dear girl, I live here. This is my house, or rather, it belongs to my brother-in-law and my sister. Now who are you?"

So this was Gideon. "I am Miss Morrow," I said stiffly. "I arrived here this afternoon at Mrs. Rockwell's request."

"Are you a friend of Cordelia's?"

"No. She has engaged me to paint some interiors. I am an artist."

He threw back his head and laughed. "A lady artist! And I thought this summer was going to be so dull! Wonders never cease!"

Stung, I said, "I fail to see the humor."

"You do? Well, allow me to enlighten you. I stumble upon a most attractive girl in a beautiful gown, take her in my arms in the moonlight — and then learn that she's a bohemian! And at Newport! Of all the luck!"

"I am an artist," I repeated, tight-lipped. "I paint pictures and charge fees for doing so. That is all. Now if you will excuse me, I am returning to the house."

"Wait a minute. Does Drew know you're here?"

"Mr. Rockwell?" I said coldly. "Yes."

"So he's back from New York?"

"Yes."

"And where did you come from?"

"From New York."

"The two of you, together, today?" There was a gleeful note in his voice. "Are you precisely certain that it was my sister who hired you?"

"I do not like what you are implying, Mr. . . ."

"Lawrence. Gideon Lawrence, at your service."

"Mr. Lawrence. Your brother and I met for the

first time today. Good night."

"I'm sorry now that I missed dinner tonight. A beautiful new face at Copper Beeches is an unexpected pleasure."

It was pointless to respond to him; he wanted only to annoy and embarrass me. Swiftly I moved away from him, but his voice followed me, still softly chuckling, mingling with the whispers of the trees.

In relief I reached the privacy of my room and got ready for bed. Mr. Lawrence might prove to be a bother, but I had met flirtatious young men before who found my choice of career a novel one. I could handle him.

I was awakened some hours later. I had been dreaming of the whispering trees. In my dream I was standing beneath the heavy branches and I was able to clearly understand what they were saying. In the rustling and the swishing were the words, "This is no place for you, this is no place for you." Frightened, I tried to flee but the branches hung down, enclosing me in their dense vine-like embrace while they whispered, "No place for you, no place for you." And then the caresses tightened to a stranglehold, and the whispers became screams until I bolted up in bed, my heart pounding, my face damp, still feeling those branches as they twisted round me, still hearing those ghastly cries.

But my dream was over. I was sitting up in bed and somehow the screams were still going on, faint but audible. I lit the lamp by my bed and listened. It sounded like the voice of a young child. Blythe, it had to be. Getting out of bed, I slipped on my dressing gown and went out into the hallway.

A few of the gaslights were lit, but their light was feeble. My shadow loomed before me, enormous, indistinct. As far as I knew, no other rooms on my corridor were occupied. Therefore, the sounds had to be coming from another wing on the same floor. Moving down to the end of the hall, I opened the door onto another long corridor. The cries had changed; they were softer now,

99

muffled, more like sobs than the shrieks of terror they had been. That a child should be making such sounds . . . What on earth had frightened her so? Today she had seemed frail and wan, but not at all frightened or uneasy.

As noiselessly as possible, I began to slip down the second corridor. And I heard a man's voice, soft and soothing. Drew's voice. Halting, I pressed my back against the wall and held my breath to lis ten. Gradually the child's sobs became less and less until they disappeared altogether.

Reassured by the silence, I turned to retrace my steps to my room before I was discovered in my nightdress in a part of the house where I had no business. But then came Drew's voice again, not gentle and caressing, but tense, exasperated.

"What happened, Miss Simmons? What set her off this time?"

"I have no idea, Mr. Rockwell. She had bad dreams, I expect."

"A child of six does not have bad dreams so frequently and of such a nature as to make her scream her head off unless there is a reason! Besides, she slept undisturbed the three nights we were in New York."

"Well, perhaps it was the excitement of the journey. We both saw how exhausted the poor child was today."

"Yes." His voice had lost its curtness and now sounded weary. "She dislikes doctors and she saw no less than four in New York."

"That must be it then, Mr. Rockwell. The strain of the trip, the tedious examinations . . . You musn't worry, sir. I'm here to look after her. Although in the night when she wakes up frightened, she wants no one but you. A pity your room is—well, so far away."

"You can hardly expect me to sleep in the nursery, Miss Simmons."

"Of course not, sir. I was only thinking that if you are disturbed in the night so must Mrs. Rockwell be, and the others."

"Mrs. Rockwell always sleeps soundly," said Drew stiffly.

"Yes, sir. I suppose she is, well, tired from the dancing and—"

"Was there a light burning in Blythe's room tonight?"

"Why, of course, Mr. Rockwell. I always follow your instructions. I tried to quiet Blythe myself, but it's always the same—she cries out for you."

"I had hoped these night traumas were becoming less frequent. In New York she slept so peacefully."

"What did the doctors say?"

"Oh, the same words over and over. That the bout of scarlet fever weakened her and she should gradually recover from it. But I'm beginning to fear that she—"

"Oh, Mr. Rockwell, you must not think that way. She will recover. It's just that these things take time."

"It's just that the doctors don't know what they're talking about! They cannot determine what's wrong with her so they always hark back to the scarlet fever."

"But it's true that her health has been poorly ever since. When I came she was over the worst of it, but the fever left her blood weak and her appetite diminished. I feel assured, though, that she will continue to improve."

"I hope so, Miss Simmons. Well, it's very late. Good night."

To my horror the words were scarcely spoken before Drew's shadow appeared on the wall several feet from me and he was shutting the nursery door. Swiftly I turned, hoping he might not notice me hovering there in the gloom. But as I was tiptoing away, his voice called to me with a note of surprise.

"Miss Morrow?"

Flushing, I looked over my shoulder. "I—I heard Blythe . . ."

He came forward a few steps. His hair was tousled; he wore a dark blue dressing gown tied at the waist. In the dim glow of the gaslights his face was inscrutable.

"I'm sorry that you were disturbed, Miss Morrow. From time to time Blythe — awakens in the night."

"Her nightmares must be terrible, to make her cry out so."

He shrugged. "I'm a light sleeper. I listen out for her."

"What . . . is she frightened of? Do you know?"

"No, I do not. She never will talk of it, except once in a while to babble something incomprehensible that she is unable to explain. Well, as I said, I am sorry you were disturbed. Good night, Miss Morrow."

"Good night, Mr. Rockwell." I returned to my room but was unable to fall asleep again for some time.

In spite of her fears, Blythe Rockwell was a fortunate little girl to have a father who loved and cherished her the way he did. My grandmother would never have risen from her warm bed in the middle of the night to comfort me. I recalled Mrs. Rockwell's words in reference to her daughter: "I rarely see her." Mrs. Rockwell was very busy.

At least the governess, Miss Simmons, had sounded concerned and sympathetic, as though she cared for the little girl. I supposed I would meet her soon; perhaps we might become friendly.

When I rose some hours later, it was morning and the sun streamed through the lace curtains casting a frosty light over the room. Going to the window, I drew them aside and looked out across the back acres. The copper beeches glinted bronze, their lower branches a darker purple-green. In the distance the summerhouse was a pristine white against the violet-blue hydrangeas and line of blue spruces which shielded the side windows from the lawn. And those trees that had haunted my dreams, those shaggy creatures with their sodden vertical branches that had whispered and stirred last night, they were now still, silent. They were rather like enormous dryads, I thought, spilling their wild thick locks, alluring and mysterious.

After I had bathed and dressed I went downstairs. I

had not known whether I would take breakfast in my room or in the dining room, but as no tray came, I assumed that I was expected to breakfast formally downstairs. Or I hoped that I was. It was characteristic of Cordelia Rockwell that I had received no definite instructions about anything.

This time as I descended the magnificent oak staircase with its latch and key design paneling, I paused on the landing to admire the stained glass window of Dawn. I hoped that I would have the opportunity to paint an interior of this section of the house. I had no idea where Cordelia wished me to begin, or whether she had any preference. I hoped that there would be some message from her this morning; I was anxious to get on with my work. And I hesitated in selecting a room myself in case she had definite notions on the order in which I should proceed. Still, in the mornings it was necessary that I work in a room which faced east, and in the afternoons a room which faced west. That did not mean that I would work on one interior in the morning and a different one in the afternoon. I could only work on one room at a time, and that for only a few hours. By the time the light was altering, I was weary and stiff. But if I were to begin work immediately after breakfast, which I was eager to do, it had to be in a room which faced east.

Isadora was the only one in the dining room. "Good morning, Miss Morrow, I was hoping you would join me."

"Good morning, Miss Rockwell."

"We help ourselves at breakfast. Everything is kept warm on the sideboard. The jam, butter, milk, and sugar are on the table. The coffee and tea were just brought so they are still hot."

"Thank you." Taking a warmed plate, I served myself rolls and sausage, and poured a cup of coffee. The china was a cheerful blue and white Cantonware.

"Do you know they used these dishes as ballast on clipper ships?" she asked. "You see, our family has been in the China trade for generations. So about the house you'll see quite a bit from the Orient. Not only china, but Turkish carpets and Japanese screens and brass tables from India and lots of things."

"Yes, I've noticed. It was Imariware we used last night at dinner, wasn't it? My father was a great admirer of Oriental things as well."

"Cordelia doesn't like them. She'd much rather have French things rather than Oriental. Or Italian. But Drew won't have anything changed, not the way she wants to do it. Besides, as he says, he doesn't have the resources, like the New York millionaires, to plunder English castles and Italian villas for souvenirs."

"Have you seen Mrs. Rockwell this morning?"

"Goodness, no. It's barely nine o'clock and she often sleeps until eleven or later. Why?"

I felt deflated. "Oh, I was hoping to begin work. But last night she didn't have a chance to tell me which room I'm to begin painting, and I hesitate to make the selection myself. If I'm to work this morning it must be in the rear of the house."

"Why don't you begin in the drawing room then? We use it for balls as well, small ones. I'm certain Cordelia would wish that room to be painted, and it does get the morning light. After breakfast I'll show you where it is, if you like."

"Thank you, Miss Rockwell."

"Oh, do call me Isadora. And may I call you Ariel? I can't wait to tell my friend Camille de la Salle about you. A lady artist at Copper Beeches — nothing so interesting ever happens here. Camille is my dearest friend. She'll want to meet you, of course. We have to take luncheon at Ochre Court today. I really don't like going there because I don't care for Mrs. Goelet. She's so cold and arrogant."

"What will you do after that?"

"Well, at three o'clock I promised I would accompany

Cordelia when she makes her calls."

"Whom does she call on?"

"Oh, no one, really. It is the silliest pastime. You don't expect people to be home, or admit that they are! That would be a dreadful *faux pas!* Everyone is out riding down Bellevue Avenue or Ocean Drive delivering their own calling cards. That's precisely from three until four o'clock. And most of the people you call on you just saw at luncheon an hour before! It really is foolish, when you consider it. But a rule of etiquette that Cordelia, for one, would never think of breaking."

I laughed. "I gather you don't mind breaking these rules from time to time?"

"Oh, no, I don't mind. Of course that outrages the dowagers and they talk about me to Cordelia and say that Drew has no control over me. And then Cordelia comes home and scolds me and berates Drew because she says we make her look a fool. So much of the time I endure these tiresome rituals just to keep the peace. Cordelia says I don't behave properly and will have a hard time getting a husband because of it. But I'm certainly not going to marry someone who expects me to carry on this way for the rest of my life. And Drew would never marry me off to a French or Hungarian count, just to improve his status. His and Cordelia's marriage was *arranged,* you see."

"Oh."

"Well, here I am chattering and I daresay you'd like to begin work. I'll show you the drawing room now."

We rose and left the dining room. Isadora went on. "I should tell you that luncheon is served on trays. Cordelia, Gideon, and I are usually out, and Drew eats in town or in the library. Dinner is really the only meal we eat *en masse.* And that's undoubtedly for the best," she added cynically.

There was no need for me to ask her what she meant. Last night's eruptive gathering was štill vivid in my mind.

"So your lunch will be brought to your room as is Aunt Hermione's. I hope she didn't offend you last night, Ariel. She is really a dear old lady and Drew and I are very fond of her."

"She didn't offend me," I reassured her. "Have you seen Blythe this morning?"

She shook her head. "No, but I'll go up and see her before I go out later."

"I heard her crying in the night. I wondered how she was this morning."

Isadora's face clouded over. "Yes, I heard her too. And I heard Drew go upstairs. He's the only one who can calm her when she has these — nightmares, or whatever they are."

"It's terrible for a child to be so frightened."

"And if you had known her before! She was so different before she was ill. So precocious and cheerful. She's completely changed now. Well, here we are — the drawing room."

It was a vast room, the furniture and hangings done in yellow brocade. There was a grand piano at one end. The wall panels were painted with floral designs. Two chandeliers hung from elaborate plasterwork on the ceiling. There were French doors which opened onto a broad terrace.

"Yes, the light is ideal just now," I said. "Thank you, Miss Rock — Isadora. I'm going to get my things and begin." I felt that familiar nervousness mingling with excitement which always came to me before I started work.

Returning to my room, I unpacked the trunk which contained my paper, paints, easel, brushes, and other supplies. When I had gathered together the necessary items, I went back down to the drawing room.

In order to get as much of the room in the painting as possible, I set up my easel in a far corner. Tipping it and securing the board, I laid the flat wash on the heavy-weight cold-pressed paper. Then I took the red sable brushes from the japanned metal tin and began to paint. There was something special about working in watercolors; it was a most expressive and sensitive style of painting, the result both luminous and transparent.

I had been working for some time when I heard footsteps in the hall outside. Assuming it was one of the servants, I did not bother to look behind me.

"Well, you weren't joking. You really are an artist."

With an inward groan I recognized the voice of Gideon Lawrence; his drawling tone with its underlying mockery was unmistakable.

"I should not otherwise be engaged here," I said dryly, turning about.

He was tall and thin, but I had known that last night. His face was boyishly handsome, his hair a light brown, his cheekbones high, his eyes green. But despite these charms there was a vague weakness in his face, a lack of decision and direction.

"That smock is a change from the gown you wore last night. Still, I'm not complaining." He had entered the room, one hand in a trouser pocket and the other swinging the chain of a gold pocket watch.

"Do you mind? I have work to do," I said coolly.

"Go ahead, Miss Morrow. I'm not due at Wakehurst until eleven-thirty, or half past eleven, as Van Alen would say. Everything must be done the English way." He chuckled.

"I cannot work with someone looking over my shoulder." Actually I had done so many times in my father's studio, but this was different.

"As far as I can tell, I'm nowhere near your shoulder, though the idea has a distinct appeal."

"Do you always address ladies in this fashion, or is this peculiar manner reserved for me alone?"

"Do you know that your eyes flash when you are angry? I couldn't tell last night, but now I see quite clearly."

"Mr. Lawrence, I am asking you to leave me in peace so that I can continue my work. I do not have time to banter with you."

"When will you have time?"

"Perhaps never. Now please leave me."

"Why should I? I live in this house. I have as much right to be in the drawing room as in any other room." He strode toward me, still swinging the gold chain.

I sighed. "Mr. Lawrence, I have asked you politely not to disrupt me further. Please be considerate enough to heed my wishes. I have a job to do, and you are keeping me from getting on."

He ignored me, glancing at the easel. "Hmmm. Doesn't look like much yet, does it? Are you certain that you are an artist?"

"I am not going to bother to respond to that. If you must stay here, then kindly go across and sit down — over there."

"What is it like, to be a lady artist?" His eyes raked over me in a way which infuriated me.

"I could just as easily ask of you, 'What is it like to be a gentleman of leisure?' But I think I know. You have nothing better to do than bother people at work. And the word 'gentleman' scarcely applies."

"So the little kitten has claws, has she? I would imagine that the word 'lady' is likely to be inappropriate in your case as well."

"How dare you! I have asked you to respect my wishes and leave me alone. Must I be forced to complain of your conduct to your sister?"

"You have a stray curl that missed the pins," he said, and reached over.

When I felt his fingers on my neck, I took a violent step back. There was a sudden crash and, to my dismay, I saw the easel, paper, and box of paints spill to the floor.

"Oh, look at the mess! And the dirty water spilling everywhere!" I wailed.

"Hang on, I'll ring for a servant," he said carelessly, grinning.

"Just get out!" I cried, and then was horrified to see

Drew Rockwell standing in the doorway.

"What's going on here?" he asked sharply, his dark brows drawn together.

I flushed to the roots of my hair. "I — he — there's been an accident." Picking up the sponge, I began to wipe up the spilled water.

"There's no need for you to trouble yourself with that, Miss Morrow. Gideon, pull the bell rope and then get out."

The change in Gideon from a mocking, flirtatious young man to a sulky, abashed one was immediate. He did as his brother-in-law ordered, not looking at me.

"What was Gideon doing in here?" came Drew's rough voice from behind me.

Slowly I got to my feet. "He stopped in to — to watch me work, I suppose. It was a diversion for him."

"Did you invite him?" His voice was curiously hard.

"Certainly not! I asked him several times to leave. His presence — distracted me from my work."

"How did the easel and things come to spill?"

"He — I was startled and knocked it over myself," I said breathlessly. "Oh, what a mess!"

"Don't worry about that. Molly, please clean this up for Miss Morrow."

The young woman nodded. I had already set up the easel and picked up the paper, paints, and brushes. But my work was ruined — the dirty water I had used to rinse the brushes was spattered across it. "One entire morning wasted! And the light's not what it was," I said mournfully.

"I apologize for whatever my brother-in-law did to cause this, Miss Morrow. He has yet another thing to answer for," he said grimly.

"I believe he will respect my wishes from now on," I said hastily.

"As I know him a great deal better than you do, I put no such faith in your belief. But I imagine he's left the house and will be out the rest of the day, if only to avoid me."

"Well, I am not going to let this day go to waste. Is there a room at the front of the house where I could work this afternoon?"

"The library. I'm the only one who uses that room and I will be out. Please feel free to work in there."

"Thank you, Mr. Rockwell."

He left me and, after thanking the maid, I gathered up my supplies and went to my room. I was still furious with Gideon Lawrence and the way he had provoked me into losing my temper and clumsily knocking over my paints and easel. But I was even more furious with myself; I should have ignored him from the start and not allowed him to see how he had irritated me. His manner had certainly altered at his brother-in-law's appearance, I thought wryly. It was easy to see that he was intimidated by Drew, and held little affection for him.

Because I was a young woman and an artist, Gideon had assumed, as many people did, that I was not respectable. This had angered me at times, but never so much as today. Most men did not understand a woman having a career outside the traditional choices of governess or companion-secretary. My own career labeled me in a way which I did not appreciate. However, it was something with which I would have to live.

Taking off my smock, I washed my face and hands and redid my hair. My face grew warm when I thought about Gideon's fingers on my neck. Thank heaven I *had* knocked over the easel and created a noisy diversion. That was far preferable, I realized, than to have Drew Rockwell come upon Gideon taking such familiarities with me. It might have appeared very different to him from what it actually was.

Hearing voices from my open window, I went across and looked out. Blythe and a young woman were on the back lawn. Miss Simmons (I assumed) was setting up a croquet set. Blythe was not running or skipping or jumping about, but just stood there soberly watching.

I decided to go down to them and introduce myself. In a way Miss Simmons and I were on an equal footing at Copper Beeches, employees but not domestics. If I sought company, she was the person in whom I was most likely to find it. Besides, I wanted to speak to Blythe. I went downstairs and outside.

"How do you do?" I said, smiling.

The governess looked up from pushing the wicket into the ground. She had very fair hair and pink skin. Her eyes were an intense blue and her eyebrows and lashes were almost white.

"How do you do?" she repeated warily.

"I am Miss Morrow. Ariel Morrow. And you must be Miss Simmons."

"Yes." She regarded me curiously. "Are you a guest here, Miss Morrow?"

"No, not at all. Mrs. Rockwell has engaged me to paint some watercolor interiors for her."

"Watercolor interiors . . . You are an artist?" She was frankly astonished.

"That's right." I turned to look down at Blythe. "And you must be Blythe. I saw you yesterday on the steamboat."

Blythe stared at me. I was struck again by her pallor, her thinness.

"Blythe, make your curtsy to Miss Morrow."

"I saw you with your father on board yesterday. I came from New York too. I live there," I went on.

Blythe said nothing. She continued to regard me with her almost-black eyes. Below them the violet stains stood out in her white face.

Miss Simmons frowned. "Blythe should not have had to make that trip. It was too tiring for her. And Mr. Rockwell did not even wish me to accompany them."

"Yes, well, I suppose Mr. Rockwell did what he thought best, taking her to the specialists."

"Did you know Mr. Rockwell before coming here?" she asked, her voice suddenly sharp.

111

"Why, no. We met quite by chance. It was Mrs. Rockwell who engaged me, as I said."

"Oh?"

This was not going as I had expected. I had hoped for some cordial conversation and could not understand Miss Simmons's suspicious manner.

"I see you are about to play croquet. May I join you?" I turned to Blythe, smiling. "Living in a city I haven't had a nice big yard like you have here."

To my surprise and dismay Blythe suddenly flew to Miss Simmons and began crying, "I don't want her to play with us! Don't let her! Make her go away!"

The governess's arms closed tightly about the little girl. "Don't worry, darling. I'm here and no one will hurt you. Daddy and I are here to take care of you. You know that, don't you? Hush now." She looked up at me. "I'm afraid that Blythe is not used to strangers, Miss Morrow." But neither her tone nor her expression were apologetic, despite her words; she looked almost smug.

Flushing, I said, "Oh. Well, I've no wish to upset her." I felt incredibly foolish.

"Good day, Miss Morrow," said Miss Simmons dismissively.

Chapter Six

I had been rebuffed in no uncertain terms. The little girl had clung to her governess and begged her to send me away. And neither had Miss Simmons responded in the way I had anticipated she would. I had thought that as employees we shared a bond, however tenuous, that might at least be the basis for conversation and pleasant companionship. But she had seemed pleased that Blythe had abruptly taken a dislike to me. I recalled the tiny smile curling the corners of her mouth as she bid me good day. And prior to that she had questioned me in an oddly suspicious manner. It was plain that I could expect no companionship there.

Early that afternoon I took my things to the library and began another interior. No one disturbed me, as Drew had promised. It was a room done in the Renaissance Revival style, with heavily carved black walnut furniture and massive bookshelves, a departure from the style of the rest of the house. The floor was marble, and the ceiling had been painted and gold-leafed. Above the fireplace was the painting of the Hudson River scene. I worked for several hours, completely immersing myself in my task.

It was nearly five o'clock when I decided it was time to stop work for the day; the shadows were lengthening as the sun slanted through the long windows, giving the room a different effect than when I had begun.

Gathering up my supplies, I went out into the hall just as Cordelia Rockwell was entering the house. She wore a hyacinth blue gown and carried a matching parasol. She looked polished and elegant; I was suddenly conscious of my drab smock streaked and blotched with paint, and that my hair must be untidily escaping its pins. Not that my appearance was anything other than it should have been, I scolded myself. I was an artist — naturally I had paint on my smock and hands! What on earth had got into me?

"Ah, Miss Morrow, there you are." She made it sound as though she had been searching the house and grounds for me.

"I've been in the library, Mrs. Rockwell."

"The library!" She frowned. "What on earth made you decide to begin in there?"

Coloring, I said, "Well, I had no specific instructions from you, and I needed a room which got the afternoon light. Mr. Rockwell suggested —"

"Mr. Rockwell!" she snapped. "Well, I like that. Giving you instructions when this is scarcely his concern! I wanted you to begin in one of the other rooms — the drawing room, or the small salon." She tapped the tip of her parasol on the floor peevishly.

I did not know how to answer her. I had no wish to explain that I had actually begun in the drawing room that morning only to have my work interrupted and ruined by her own brother. "I'm sorry, Mrs. Rockwell. When I have finished the library, I will begin on the drawing room."

"Oh, very well. I suppose it scarcely matters," she said irritably. "The library is a fine room. The woodwork was designed and completed in Italy, and then crated and shipped here. It's Drew's room."

"I hope I'm to paint the double staircase and landing, Mrs. Rockwell. The stained glass window is magnificent."

"Why not? It's a John La Farge — I suppose you know that. Well, I must get ready for tonight. I've left instructions for you to have a tray in your room tonight, Miss Morrow." She surveyed me ironically. "We are dining out." Then she walked away, her heels clicking on the marble floor.

114

Feeling somehow deflated, I wished that I had not run into her. My spirits had been high as they always were following a productive few hours' work. But now her petty displeasure had brought everything back to me: the strange boat ride, the strained, explosive atmosphere between husband and wife, the child screaming in the night, the episode this morning with Gideon, Blythe's fear of me, Miss Simmon's curiously hostile attitude . . . I was beginning to wish that I had not come to Copper Beeches. I had been here just twenty-four hours, and already I had glimpsed more of the private lives of its inhabitants than I wished.

It was early evening and not time for my dinner to be sent up. Again I was overcome with an uneasy restlessness. From off in the distance the trees whispered to me, their long branches, thick with leaves, waving in the breeze from the sea. I went out.

There were urns on the terrace filled with bright flowers, violet, rosy pink, and white, their delicate blossoms fluttering. Walking past the fish pond, I glimpsed golden flashes beneath the apple green lily pads. Farther down the lawn was the summerhouse, and far beyond it, down an incline and to the left, the greenhouse and stables, a rambling building of red sandstone. But I did not walk in their direction; I moved toward the grove of trees which so fascinated me. In the daylight they resembled gigantic creatures rising from a swamp, dripping wet and covered with clinging algae. The long shaggy branches, dense and vine-like, swayed. And again I heard the whispers, vague indistinct murmurs I could not understand.

There was a stone wall to the right which I had not noticed the night before, and in the stone wall was a curious structure, a huge circle of stone with steps cut into it climbing to a small stone seat at the top. I wondered at the reason for the seat; surely a person was not meant to sit and gaze at the mansion across the road, handsome though it was. But whatever its purpose, I found the round stone gate quite appealing, and could not resist climbing the row of steps

115

up the circle while I held onto the iron balustrade. The house opposite was constructed of rough-hewn amber stone; facing me was a large turret with a conical top which was several stories high. The rest of the roofline was Dutch with whimsically curved gables.

Just as I had decided I had sat there long enough and stood up, a hand on the balustrade, I chanced to glance up at a window in the turret opposite. There was someone there watching me. I could see the white oblong of a face, but no features, no details which identified the person as man, woman or child. And then it was gone. Probably one of the maids, I thought, feeling rather foolish for being spied upon in so childish a pursuit as climbing up a circular gate to a tiny seat. I hurried away from the wall.

It was dark and gloomy under the shielding trees; no grass grew in their shade. Pushing aside the branches, I continued across the lawn which stretched to the cliffs above the sea. As I drew closer, the breeze was heavily laced with salt. I could hear the surf booming as the waves crashed against the land.

When I came out on the graveled path of the cliff, I stood there in awe of the view. High jagged cliffs jutted out into the water; far below the emerald green waves churned white as they drew close to the rocky coast. Rosehips grew in profusion in the dense hedgerow which adorned parts of the bluff. Glancing back toward Copper Beeches, I took in its sturdy granite splendors the way the drooping sun streamed across its mansard roof setting the copper trim ablaze. It looked solid and reassuring, no matter the atmosphere within its walls.

I began to follow the graveled walkway at the top of the cliffs. Below me, on one side, the tide crashed against the boulders. And, on the other side, were magnificent estates. In some places it was difficult to see over the stone walls which framed the grounds, but no walls could shield completely from view those enormous palaces which lined the cliff.

There was a bulky sprawling one of red sandstone, and

one which looked like something out of "Cinderella" — a pale late-Gothic French chateau with turrets and towers and dormers shaped like Turkish helmets. There were older homes — simpler, wooden ones — but it was the stone villas that dominated the shoreline.

After a time I turned and retraced my steps. Some of the rock in the tall cliffs was ocher-colored — a yellowish red — and sparkled like gold. Tiny coves wove their ways in and out of the cliffs. Seaweed swirled amid the glossy stones like heads of brown hair blowing in the wind, and, farther out, moss clung to the rocks, bright and drenched. The surf boomed against the many-creviced cliffs, carving its uneven undeniable course in the rock.

The pale blue of the sky had faded to a lavender which gave the greenish water an opalescent cast. There was a sharp contrast between the palaces fit for kings and queens on one side of the walk, and the rough ragged coastline on the other. The coastline, the cliff, the turbulent surf — they were natural and real in a way that the spectacular mansions were not. The mansions had an illusory quality, newly erected in the styles of others which had stood for centuries on the other side of the Atlantic, and which were set in vast parks far from neighboring estates.

Copper Beeches, at least, looked to be what it was, an American house constructed in one of the prevailing styles of this century. It was large and imposing, but it had no pretentions. As for the others, those French Gothic castles, Italian palazzos, English Tudor manor houses, they were magnificent, but each had a deliberate, self-conscious magnificence whose sole purpose seemed to be to outdo its neighbors and outshine the coastline. But the latter could not be done, regardless of the number of rooms and windows, the towers and tilework, the gryphons and gargoyles, the marble, the columns, the enormous iron gates painted gold.

For a time I stood on the cliff and watched the pounding waves, the sight restoring my wilted spirits.

"Beautiful, isn't it?"

117

I looked over to see an older man standing near me. He had an open pleasant face; the only hair remaining on his head grew at the sides and back. His gray suit was well cut and he carried a gold-tipped walking stick.

"Yes, it is, quite beautiful," I agreed.

"I never grow tired of it. The sea is slowly encroaching and taking the shoreline with it. That's the way of things — the force of the ocean is too strong for the land, the land weakens and is chiseled away by the tides, the strong winning out over the weak." He smiled. "Not that the people in these mansions will have to worry about the land giving way beneath them. Their fortresses will be perfectly safe for several hundred years yet, long enough for the dynasties to prosper."

"Yes, it doesn't seem as if anything could touch these homes," I said.

"They will doubtless be standing long after the originals in Europe have crumbled to dust because their owners no longer have the means to keep them up. Well, I won't disturb you any longer. Good evening."

"Good evening."

He went almost jauntily in the opposite direction after again tipping his hat. Returning back to the house, I felt refreshed and hungry, and relieved that tonight I need not mingle with my employers. And when I slept I was undisturbed by my own dreams and a child's cries.

The following day I decided to explore some of the town. The long morning stretched out before me; I would not resume work in the library until the early afternoon. Dressing in a cambric gown of yellow floral print, I pinned on a straw hat trimmed with yellow ribbons and tiny yellow rosebuds, pulled on a pair of white gloves, and set out.

It was still early; there was no one stirring except the maids. I went down the oak staircase to the side entrance and down the graveled drive. There was little traffic on Bellevue Avenue that morning. A few gentlemen passed me, riding or driving open carriages, but the business of the day, the business of pageantry and exhibition,

118

had not yet begun.

I paused to admire Stanford White's Casino constructed in the Shingle style with green-painted cross gables and mock-Chinese panels. There was a line of exclusive Parisian and New York shops which continued past the Casino in the Travers Block building of half-timbering and brick designed by Richard Morris Hunt.

"Sightseeing, Miss Morrow?"

Drew Rockwell was coming toward me. Flushing, I said, "Well, yes, since I'm painting the library and it gets the afternoon light . . ."

He smiled crookedly. "Relax, Miss Morrow. I'm not scolding you. Would you like to see some of Newport? We can walk together."

"Oh, no. I mean, I don't like to impose . . . you must have many things to do," I said breathlessly.

"None so pressing as all that, I assure you." He stood, hands on hips, looking down at me amusedly.

"Thank you," I said. "I would like that."

And so that morning we roamed the old narrow streets, their austere frame houses elbowing others built in this century. Drew pointed out buildings of special interest such as the Redwood Library, the oldest in the country, designed to resemble a Roman temple; the Georgian-style Touro synagogue, also the first of its kind in America, built by descendents of Jews who had left Holland and Portugal and settled in Newport in the first half of the seventeenth century because of its policy of religious freedom.

"Members of the Massachusetts Bay Colony, including Baptists and Quakers, had broken away from the Puritans and gone to Providence with Roger Williams," said Drew. "But before long they disagreed with him and came further south to Aquidneck Island. Newport became a city of merchants and seafarers."

It had also become a major port in the Triangular Trade.

Molasses from Jamaica was shipped to Newport to be used in the rum distilleries; the rum was sent to Africa to be traded for slaves, and the slaves exchanged in Jamaica for more molasses. The resulting affluence from this dubious economy was reflected in the fine Colonial buildings such as the Brick Market on the waterfront with its Ionic pilasters, and the brick State House which had been designed after seventeenth-century English manor houses with a large wooden cupola perched on the roof. Also there was the beautiful Trinity Church on Spring Street, with its splendid steeple and rows of Palladian windows, built by shipwrights in 1726.

The Revolution, Drew told me, had brought an abrupt end to Newport's prosperity; for two years the British occupied the city using the handsome buildings as barracks, destroying property, wharves, and cutting down most of the trees. Later the French fleet had sailed into Newport harbor, and George Washington had met here with General Rochambeau to plan the battle of Yorktown.

"Most of the summer people don't come down here," said Drew. "They stay on the top of the hill; they know little of the town's history and care even less."

"Have you always lived in Newport?" I asked him.

He nodded, brushing off his sleeve. "My grandfather was from Boston and had Copper Beeches built as a summer house. But when he retired from the China trade he lived there year-round until his death. Then my father had the house remodeled and used it as his year-round residence as well, although he was away for long periods in the Orient. Isadora and I grew up here, when I wasn't away at school."

"And is Mrs. Rockwell from Boston?" I asked him.

His face tightened. "No, Cordelia is from New York. Her father and mine were business associates. She did not take to Newport at first, although she was delighted when Caroline Belmont and Mrs. Astor persuaded their husbands to start spending the summers here. She could only wish that the New Yorkers would take up residence here permanently; at least we've been spared that so far."

"Weren't there summer visitors here before the millionaires began coming up?"

120

"There were, but of a very different sort. Bostonians mostly, and, before the Civil War, Southern planters as well. And artists such as John La Farge and John Kensett, writers — Longfellow, Emerson, Henry James, even Edgar Allan Poe and Robert Louis Stevenson each spent a summer here. And there was a different atmosphere back then. The visitors were intellectuals — professors, ministers. They built or rented simple houses; they took long walks along the Cliff Walk and out to Hanging Rock. They came to relax. There was none of the social competition, the absurd rules and rituals that govern the summers now. Within the last years Newport has become a parade ground in July and August. You will see just what I mean, Miss Morrow, in the weeks to come. Unfortunately her history is forgotten, and now Newport is associated with little else than with dinner guests digging with silver shovels into piles of sand containing rubies and sapphires, and parties for one hundred dogs in fancy dress." There was irony in his tone, and also an underlying bitterness.

"Well," I said self-consciously, "I suppose I should be grateful that some of them want their interiors painted, just as my father painted their portraits."

He studied me from under bent brows. "Forgive me, Miss Morrow, if I seem impertinent, but your father was, I understand, a wealthy man."

"If you are wondering why I seek commissions, there are two reasons," I said frankly. "One, because I am an artist, and to be commissioned to do work is the confirmation of the artist's talent. Secondly, my father left a good portion of his money to several art schools, and it is necessary that I supplement my inheritance with income of my own."

"You are quite remarkable, Miss Morrow," he said gravely. "How long have you been a professional artist?"

"Two years, Mr. Rockwell."

"You are very young."

I shook my head. "Twenty-four. No so very young. And I'm not at all remarkable. It was just that there was never any other alternative for me unless it was to remain with

121

my grandparents for the rest of their lives. But I went to live with my father when he returned from England, and he saw to my art instruction. Eventually it was time for me to utilize what I had learned, that is all."

"I saw the painting your father did of you. It was . . . exquisite. That first day — on the steamboat — I knew I had seen you somewhere before. I tried to buy that portrait, but he refused to sell."

I could not meet his gaze, feeling the warm color seeping into my face. But he abruptly changed the subject, pointing out to me another handsome church, the Congregational, whose interior had been decorated by John La Farge with patterns taken from Oriental carpets.

We walked up the hill past a small park with a circular stone tower rumored to have been built by the Vikings in the eleventh century. Eventually we reached the vicinity of the Newport Casino.

"Stanford White was a friend of my father's," I said. "In fact, it was he who helped me get my first commissions."

"Is that so? I like the architecture of the Casino; the Shingle style White used is very much the old Newport. The property had belonged to James Gordon Bennett, Jr., publisher of the New York *Herald*. He hired Stanford White to build the Casino. Bennett was the one who sent Stanley to Africa in search of Dr. Livingstone, who had no idea he was missing."

I laughed. "But the headlines, 'Where is Dr. Livingstone?' sold a great many newspapers."

Passing the shingled villas and Greek-revival mansions, we came to the graveled drive of Copper Beeches. And on the front lawn loomed another of those whispering trees, its drooping branches thick with leaves.

"What is that tree?" I asked him. "I've never seen one like it."

"That is a weeping beech, Miss Morrow. There are a number of them on the estate, along with the copper beeches, of course."

"They're rather like enormous drenched creatures arising from a swamp, aren't they? I'd like to paint one some-time."

Again he gave me that twisted smile. "You have a very original mind, Miss Morrow."

Flushing slightly, I asked what had been on my mind for much of the morning. "Mr. Rockwell, how is Blythe?"

It was a mistake. His face hardened, and with narrowed eyes he peered off into the distance. I cursed myself for my tactlessness. "Do you mean today," he asked, "or generally?"

Why had I blundered into this? "Well, I — I couldn't help but notice her frailness, and then the way she cried out. . ."

"Blythe suffered a severe shock when she was ill with scarlet fever two summers ago," he said curtly. "From something like that it is difficult to emerge unscathed. And now if you will excuse me, I am going to Boston later today and have to get ready."

Abruptly he left me, and I watched his retreating figure in dismay. I had trespassed on forbidden ground and, in doing so, had spoiled the morning's pleasure.

Inside the galleried hall I nearly collided with Gideon.

"Well, well, the prim and proper Miss Morrow. But I saw you just now with Drew, coming up the drive. Where had the two of you been?"

My gaze met his impertinent one squarely. "I was walking about Newport and happened to meet him."

His eyebrows rose. "Oh? But aren't you supposed to be hard at work on your watercolors? You certainly told me so in no uncertain terms yesterday. Or was that only because I am not the master of the house?"

"Because you saw fit to disrupt my work yesterday morning, Mr. Lawrence, I have since had to begin in a room which gets the afternoon light. I am on my way to gather up my things now. Good day to you."

While I changed my clothes and ate my lunch, I thought about the morning spent with Drew. He had been a pleas-ant and informative companion, and obviously was strongly attached to his hometown. But it was just as obvious to me that he was an unhappy man. I wondered about the severe shock Blythe had suffered, and whether he too had been unable to emerge unscathed.

From Isadora I had learned that his marriage had been arranged for him; he himself had told me that his father and Cordelia's had been business associates in the import business. Had they married in order to please their fathers, neither of whom was still alive? I had observed them together only once, but within minutes their mutual irritation had been made evident.

Cordelia, as a New York heiress, was an aggressive member of the Four Hundred, the group for which Drew professed contempt. They were opposites in that respect, she championing the very clique he disliked. Her favorite time of the year in Newport was the one he loathed, when the sleepy coastal city was transformed into an arena for the New York millionaires.

Because Drew's family had been wealthy for generations, secure in their heritage as Boston Brahmins, they lived well and comfortably, surrounded by beautiful things, but not in the opulence of the nouveau riche. Flaunting whatever wealth they possessed to enhance their social position was a way of life unknown to them — and unnecessary. It was no wonder that Drew despised the conspicuous extravagance and excesses of the summer colonists while looking back with regret to an older, quietly genteel Newport he remembered.

But Cordelia wanted none of the subtle, understated elegance of simpler times. She longed for Copper Beeches to be remodeled from its Aesthetic style to one reflecting the opulence of the present day, with marble columns, gilt and indoor fountains. She wanted their male servants to wear livery.

I wondered to what extent Drew was able to avoid participating in the social events of the summer. Cordelia was in the thick of it; I guessed that he was forced to attend balls and elaborate dinner parties some of the time. Doubtless he had more involvement than he wished.

What happened, then, with the exodus in September? I supposed that Drew would be relieved to have the town left to itself again, but what of Cordelia? The seven or eight weeks the millionaires spent here was relatively a short time. What did Cordelia do the rest of the year? When she had interviewed me in New York, she had mentioned going abroad in the winter, and without her husband.

But all of this was no concern of mine, I reminded myself sternly. Whatever their relationship, it was none of my business. They were married, and that was the one fact I should not disregard.

Yet I appreciated it very much that Drew Rockwell had talked to me as an equal today, and not as an employer. He had not regarded me as a figure of oddity, because I was a female artist, nor had he been disapproving. Interested, yes, but not in the way that Gideon was.

When I resumed work in the library that afternoon, I was half-afraid that Gideon would come in and annoy me since his brother-in-law had left town. But I worked undisturbed. He had been bored that first morning, and I was a novelty. And perhaps even at a distance Drew continued to intimidate him. I was certain there was no love lost between the two.

That evening Cordelia was dining out with friends, but Isadora, Aunt Hermione, and Gideon and I had dinner together.

"Where's Drew?" asked the old lady wearing another alarming coiffure, this one with bunches of cherries pinned to her piled up white hair.

"Oh, he went up to Boston," said Isadora. "He asked whether I might behave myself while he's away." She dimpled.

"And naturally you told him that would be impossible," said Gideon.

"I'm not the one who lost three nights running at Canfield's," Isadora said pointedly.

"Who told you that?" His voice was sharp.

"Oh, I don't remember. But you know what Drew said to

you the last time. You'll run through your inheritance before you're thirty-five."

"It's no business of his. He can keep his nose out of my affairs!"

"And where is Cordelia tonight?"

"At Arleigh." Isadora sighed. "It's Mrs. Lehr and Mrs. Fish and the rest of them. And Harry Lehr, of course. They all find him so amusing."

"I don't find him amusing," declared Aunt Hermione. "Elizabeth Drexel sealed her unhappiness when she married him. If you ask me, he only married her for her money. And her social position. His position as court jester was too tenuous. He wasn't going to end up like Ward McAllister—used and then cast away like an apple core."

"I hear he adores women's clothes and advises some of the ladies on what they should wear," giggled Isadora.

"Popinjay," muttered Gideon.

"How is your work progressing, Miss Morrow?" asked Aunt Hermione.

"Well, thank you, Mrs. Grant."

"Ask her what she was doing this morning," said Gideon, smirking, "not that she'll tell you."

"Mr. Lawrence is referring to my stroll about the town this morning," I said coolly. "I was out exploring and met Mr. Rockwell quite by chance. He offered to show me about."

"You couldn't have had a better guide," said Isadora warmly. "Drew loves Newport."

"Why on earth you should wish to go down there is beyond me," said Gideon. "Lots of shabby old buildings, that's all. And you can s-carcely drive down those narrow streets."

"Everyone doesn't go racing about like you, Gideon, driving at breakneck speed down Bellevue Avenue or Bath Road," said Isadora. "Naturally you wouldn't see any charm in the old sections of the city."

"What did you do today, Dora?" asked her great-aunt, spearing a carrot with her fork.

126

"Camille and I went to Bailey's Beach and then had luncheon at her house. Gwendolyn Chandler was there with her mother."

"Good. That girl needs to get out more," said Aunt Hermione. "Why she makes such a recluse of herself is beyond me."

"She's a grown woman, Aunt," said Gideon. "You can't call her a girl any longer, only a spinster. Still, she *is* an heiress. There is all of Mrs. Chandler's money, after all. Perhaps I'll court her myself. She ought to appreciate some male attention — would probably fall into my arms in gratitude."

"You really are sickening, Gideon," said Isadora witheringly. "As if Gwendolyn wouldn't see right through you."

"I suppose Olive has given up on her getting married," said Aunt Hermione. "How old is she now? Twenty-six?"

"The Chandlers live next door to us at Oaklawn," said Isadora to me. "He is a doctor, though naturally he hasn't a steady practice. They are from New York."

"Is Oaklawn the house you can see from the round stone gate?" I asked.

"The Chinese Moongate? Yes, that's the one. Isn't it charming — the Moongate, I mean? It used to face the sea, you see, with no houses or trees to block the view. It's a wishing gate. There's a legend that if you stand beneath the gate and make a wish, it will come true."

Soon after, Gideon and Isadora left together to attend a musicale at the Casino, and Aunt Hermione retired to her room. I went out onto the terrace to admire the full moon, a great disc of silver above the trees. The mist had risen, gauzelike and smelling of the sea. Tonight the weeping beeches were perfectly still; in the silvery gossamer mist they were illusionary, unearthly.

As I approached them, I heard the sound of a piano, coming, I assumed, from the house opposite. Oaklawn, Isadora had said. I did not recognize the piece but it had a piercing haunting quality; it was exquisitely played. When it was over, I waited to see whether there would be

127

more. But it seemed the person had finished for the night because there was only silence. Slowly I walked away, the strains of the music still in my head.

The heady scent of the roses drifted toward me as I passed the rose arbor and wandered rather aimlessly across the lawn, reluctant to return indoors.

It was then that I noticed a light coming from behind the row of spruce trees which framed the summerhouse. Someone was inside the cottage. As I drew closer, I heard a woman's laugh. One of the casement windows must be ajar. Scarcely knowing why I did so, I went near to the summerhouse and stood there listening.

"Helen will be at Arleigh for hours yet," said the woman. "Don't worry."

"And how did you manage to get away?" came a man's voice.

"Oh, a ravaging headache came over me during the sixth course. I simply had to come home, take my remedy, and go to bed." She laughed again and he joined in.

"I have the remedy for you," he said huskily. "Come here."

As swiftly as I could I walked away, back in the direction of the house. The beauty of the evening had evaporated; the moonlit filmy air was no longer appealing. I had no idea who the man was, but the woman's voice was unmistakeable. It belonged to Cordelia Rockwell.

Chapter Seven

The days evolved into a routine. Completing the interior of the library, I began anew on the drawing room. Rarely did I see the other members of the household except at meals. Some nights they dined out and I had a tray alone in my room. Drew remained in Boston. I was careful not to pass the summerhouse too closely on my evening strolls.

One morning I was joined at breakfast by Isadora, looking her most charming in a white chiffon gown printed with violet-blue hydrangeas.

"What a lovely gown," I complimented her.

"Do you like it? It's the latest from a Paris shop, designed especially for Newport." She frowned. "I do hope I won't see anyone else wearing one."

"Where are you going?"

She had taken a plate and was serving herself from the platters on the sideboard. "To a concert at the Casino. Mullaly's string orchestra will be playing at eleven." Sitting down opposite me, her eyes lit up. "Why don't you join us, Ariel? I'm meeting Camille de la Salle. We'd love to have you."

I hesitated. "Well, I don't know—"

"Oh, do come, Ariel. You really ought to have some fun. The Casino's a lovely place."

"I have finished the interior of the drawing room, and I had planned to begin on the galleried front hall this afternoon . . ." I was letting her persuade me.

"Then you are free this morning. Good. We can leave here at fifteen minutes before the hour. It's such a gorgeous day; we could take the wicker phaeton, but I'd prefer to walk. What do you say?"

"I'd love to see the inside of the Casino," I admitted. "Thank you."

"All right. Camille will meet us there. I'll see you in the front hall, then, at a quarter to eleven."

I changed into an apple green gown embroidered in peach at the bodice, pinned on a hat of peach-colored straw, and took up a parasol. As it was I was ready ahead of Isadora, but she soon joined me, carrying a parasol printed with the same violet-blue hydrangeas as those in her gown. Her broad white hat was trimmed with the flowers as well. We went out the front door and down the graveled drive to Bellevue Avenue.

"I saw Blythe a little while ago. She misses Drew and keeps asking when he'll return. At least she's been sleeping better. I admit I was worried, with Drew out of town."

"I suppose her governess looks after her well."

"Yes, I daresay." But her voice held a note of uncertainty. "She's an odd person, Miss Simmons. She often makes me feel as though I'm not welcome in the nursery. She always reminds me, 'We don't want to upset Blythe, Miss Rockwell,' when she and I are only playing. I know Blythe is delicate, but she's too quiet. She needs to run around and make a rumpus once in a while. I certainly did that often enough! And so did Blythe used to."

"I suppose I was more like Blythe now," I said. "Very quiet, I mean. My grandparents wouldn't have permitted any other sort of behavior."

"Your grandparents?"

"Yes. I was sent to live with them just after my mother died. I was only two, so I had no memory of either of my parents. It wasn't until years later, when I was fifteen, that I went to live with my father in New York."

"Where did your grandparents live?"

"In upstate New York, on the Hudson. They have an old Dutch house, very handsome, with a lovely view of the river."

130

"Do you go back often for visits?"

I shook my head. "I haven't seen them in nine years. I don't even know if they are both still living. When I decided to leave them and live with my father, they said — well, they made it clear that I would never be welcome at Starlings again. They had disowned my mother when she married my father, and they also washed their hands of me."

"But why?"

"They never approved of my father. You see, he and my mother eloped while she was making the Grand Tour with a schoolfriend's family. New Yorkers, I suppose. She met my father in Paris. My grandparents never forgave her for what they viewed as her rejection, her betrayal of them. So later when my father took me away, it was another betrayal — this time by me. To them, artists are not . . . respectable people."

"Families can be so beastly, can't they? Not mine really, because Drew is a dear, but our father pressured him to marry Cordelia when he was very young, only twenty-two. He won't ever do the same to me. I wish I could only say that about my friend Camille. Her mother is very busy trying to land the ideal husband for her. Ideal meaning some foreign duke or count. There is one her mother has her eye on now. He's years older than Camille and has a silly mustache that he waxes and curls."

Passing the row of exclusive shops, we made our way through the Casino's wide entrance. Once on the other side I saw a windmill-style clock tower with a bell-shaped roof. Palladian windows, dormers, and portholes adorned the shingle and brick structure. The courthouse was framed with double verandas, meeting in a rotunda of Chinese latticework. Above the entrance were three cantilevered lanterns with elaborate iron supports.

Inside the courtyard was a small green. There were a number of people milling about. The orchestra had already begun to play, but their audience could not be said to be listening quietly. I realized that the music was merely a pleasant backdrop for the more important business of the day. Women in broad flowery hats talked animatedly while seated in boxes, and the men strolled about, pausing here and there to speak to them.

"Oh, there's Camille," said Isadora, touching my arm. I followed her across to where her friend sat alone in a box.

"Late as usual, Dora," said Camille. "Thank heavens you're here. I just caught sight of Count what's-his-name. Not that he's definitely decided on me. I hear he's a constant visitor at The Breakers, so perhaps he'll choose Gertrude over me." Camille had blond hair and delicate, elfin features.

"Miss de la Salle, Miss Morrow," said Isadora formally as we sat down.

"How do you do?" I said.

"Oh, hello. You are the artist. I've heard so much about you from Dora. We've been talking about how fortunate you are, living your own life the way you do and doing whatever you like. Not that Dora has anything of which to complain. She doesn't have a mother like mine."

"No, but I have Cordelia," said Isadora and both of them giggled.

A tall girl glided over to us. "Ah, Camille, Isadora. I see you bought the chiffon hydrangea gown. I considered it, but decided it was a trifle too ingenue. But it suits you." Her haughty gaze moved to me.

"I daresay you are right, Maude. You won't see twenty again, will you? Or even twenty-one," said Isadora sweetly. "Oh, this is Miss Morrow. She is our guest at Copper Beeches. Miss Morrow, Miss Drayton."

She nodded coolly at me. "Miss Morrow . . . ? I don't believe I know—"

"Oh, you knew her father. Lancelot Morrow, the famous painter. He painted your portrait, didn't he? Or so you're fond of telling everyone."

Miss Drayton flushed. "He did, indeed. It's quite a good likeness, I believe. Your father, Miss Morrow, was quite . . . capable." She passed on with a contemptuous curl of her lips.

"How I hate that cat!" cried Isadora. "If she *had* bought this gown I'd have been obliged to toss mine into the fire! The idea of describing your father as — as *capable,* as if he had laid the bathroom tiles!"

Soon after another young lady paused at our box. "Just look at my new earrings from Tiffany's. I suppose you heard about Pop asking that dreadful woman from Narragansett to be our weekend guest at Wakehurst."

"Well, no, actually . . ."

"Oh, yes, he had planned an elaborate luncheon party, but the ladies all cried off when they got wind of this other guest. Pop was desperate. He begged me to act as his hostess so that all the ladies would be induced to come." She paused expectantly.

"Well, what did you say, May? You're obviously dying to tell us," said Camille.

"I told him I would, but on one condition. That he'd have to pay me five thousand dollars. But that's not all I said. 'For five thousand dollars I'll come to your party, but if you want me to talk to your guest and be polite to her, you'll have to make it ten.' "

The three of us regarded her in astonishment.

"So he wrote out the check then and there and handed it to me. Of course the luncheon party was a great success. *And* I got the earrings I'd seen at Tiffany's for ten thousand dollars. I guess Pop will let me choose the guests the next time," she finished complacently.

"Lovely earrings, May," said Camille dryly.

"That was May Van Alen," said Isadora after she had left us. "She and her father live near us at Wakehurst. Years ago Father sold some of our land to the Van Alens. Wakehurst is a wonderful house, really. It looked like Mr. Rochester's house in *Jane Eyre.*"

"Imagine, blackmailing your own father!" cried Camille.

"Ten thousand dollars, just to be hostess at a luncheon," agreed Isadora. "It's rather revolting. Now that I think of it I do remember Cordelia mentioning something about it."

"Look, there is that German baron Mrs. Mills is thrilled to have at Ocean Lawn," said Camille. "She thinks she has one up on Mrs. Belmont this summer. Mrs. Belmont has only an ambassador staying with her at Belcourt. Mother says a baron is far more distinguished than an ambassador."

"With that double chin and those side whiskers? I don't think he's at all distinguished."

"Not him, his title," said Camille. "You know the way people fall all over themselves for the privilege of entertaining foreign nobility. And usually they're the most difficult of guests, and so insufferably proud."

"Good morning, Miss Rockwell, Miss de la Salle," said a pleasant, slightly familiar voice.

It was the man I had spoken with on the Cliff Walk recently. Today he was in the company of a short, plump woman, her ruddy complexion subdued barely but not effectively by a quantity of loose powder on her cheeks.

"Oh, good morning, Dr. Chandler, Mrs. Chandler," said Isadora, smiling. "How are you both?"

"Very well, thank you." He turned to me. "It's my friend from the Cliff Walk, isn't it? I'm delighted to see you again."

"Dr. and Mrs. Chandler, may I present Miss Morrow who is staying with us at Copper Beeches. The Chandlers are our closest neighbors at Oaklawn."

"How do you do, Miss Morrow?" said the doctor. "Are you from Boston, perhaps? I know Miss Rockwell has many friends in Boston."

"No, from New York. Actually I am working at Copper Beeches, painting interiors. I'm an artist," I said.

"Is that so?" asked Dr. Chandler with quick interest.

"Her father was Lancelot Morrow," said Isadora.

"You don't say! A genius, a brilliant man! Did you hear that, my dear?"

Mrs. Chandler did not return my smile. As she gazed at me, something flickered in her eyes before she said to her husband, "We had best be leaving, Prescott. You know we're expected at Belcourt for luncheon."

"Olive is right — we don't want to be late. I look forward to meeting you again, Miss Morrow, and furthering our aquaintance. Good day, ladies." Bowing slightly, he took his wife's arm and they walked away.

"I wonder where Gwendolyn Chandler is," said Isadora.

"At Oaklawn, of course. Mother says she rarely leaves her room. Even in the winters in New York she doesn't mix with people."

"I expect she's sick of all the tedious balls and dinners and things. I heard at one time she wanted to be a concert pianist but her mother forbade her. She plays so beautifully, you know. Once in a while when I'm on the back lawn I hear her."

"Oh, I must have heard her, too," I said. "One night a week ago. She is very talented." Naturally I did not mention what else I had overheard that evening.

Shortly after I returned to the house, leaving them at the Casino. That afternoon I worked in the galleried entrance hall for several hours, and was finishing up when Cordelia sailed in from her afternoon calls and drive around the ocean.

"If Mrs. Herbert Wooley comes by again this afternoon, you are to give her the same message, Merriman," she said to the butler.

"Yes, Mrs. Rockwell," he said impassively.

She swept past me and down the corridor. Some minutes later I was folding up my easel when there came a knock at the studded oak doors. Merriman opened them and I heard him murmur something. To my consternation there was a cry of anguish, and a woman pushed past him and into the hall. She was a striking brunette, elegantly dressed, her features marred by a look of terrible distress.

"Please tell Mrs. Rockwell that I need only a few minutes of her time," she pleaded to Merriman.

"I am sorry, Mrs. Wooley, but regrettably Mrs. Rockwell is unable to see anyone this afternoon," said the butler gravely.

"I don't believe you! It's me she doesn't want to see — only me!" The woman pressed a crumpled handkerchief to her tearful face.

"Perhaps you could come back another day," I said to the lady consolingly. What on earth was her pressing need to see Cordelia, and why was Cordelia apparently avoiding her?

She looked up then, her dark eyes brilliant, her pale face blotched. "I have come every day this week," she cried in desperation, "and always the answer is the same. 'Mrs. Rockwell is unable to see you.' 'Mrs. Wooley is not on Mrs. Rockwell's calling list this afternoon.' Always it is the same. Why, oh why, won't she receive me? Am I so unacceptable? I wish her to do me one favor, just one. And it would be so easy for her. My husband and I were good enough to dine with in Paris some months ago, but it seems we are not good enough for Newport society! I wanted her to procure an invitation for my husband and me to attend Mrs. Belmont's ball. That is all. Then I would not trouble her again. She knows this — and she refuses to speak with me! My whole life rests on this — she holds my entire future in her hands — yet she refuses to help me!" Mrs. Wooley burst into renewed sobs while I regarded her in horrified pity.

The front door opened again and in came Gideon, stopping short when he saw the scene in the hall. Merriman stood by woodenly, but I fancied he was not as impervious to Mrs. Wooley's anguish as he appeared. Certainly I felt helpless and dismayed.

As Gideon drew close to her, she looked up and her brilliant eyes became filled with a desperate hope. "Oh, Mr. Lawrence. I'm so glad you've come! I know you'll help me. Please entreat your sister to receive me. Certainly you can persuade her. I need her entrée in order to be invited to Mrs. Belmont's ball next week. It's more important to me than anything in the world! I must be at that ball. Please say you will speak on my behalf. If Mrs. Rockwell knew how dreadfully important it is . . . why, she couldn't be so cruel!"

Gideon pulled at his collar as though it were too tight.

"Mrs. Wooley, I'm afraid there's nothing I can do. I have no say in these affairs, I assure you. If my sister will not receive you, nothing I could say to her would change her mind."

She regarded him feverishly. "But you'll go up to her, ask her—"

His voice was irritable. "I've told you I don't get involved in these matters. My sister would not appreciate it if I did. If she will not see you, then I cannot move her. Now isn't it time for you to return home?"

Mrs. Wooley turned and walked a few steps, giving one terrible choking sob after another. It was appalling to watch this poor woman's disintegration, her desolation. And for something so frivolous as an invitation to a ball. She was crying as though she had lost her child. I could not understand it, but my sympathy for her was real.

"I must go to that ball!" she shrieked. "I must!"

She crossed the threshold, swayed, and then collapsed on the doorstep. The three of us had not noticed that a carriage had driven up. Its door was flung open and Drew jumped out, striding up to Mrs. Wooley. I had rushed over to her side as well.

"It's Mrs. Wooley, isn't it?" he asked gently. "What is it? Are you ill? Shall I send for your husband?"

She sat up, shaking her head. "No, you mustn't do that. He—he'll be so angry. He told me not to come."

"Take some deep breaths, Mrs. Wooley. That will help stop the trembling."

She did as he suggested, her hand to her throat. Her face was ravaged, but her manner was calmer. "I must go home," she whispered. "I must go home."

"Let me help you to your carriage," said Drew, lifting her to her feet. Gideon, Merriman, and I watched as Drew led her down the steps to her carriage. She climbed in, Drew spoke to the driver, and the carriage rolled away.

"What on earth was that about?" asked Drew as he entered the house.

"Oh, some silly ball or other," said Gideon carelessly. "I

gather she wasn't invited. Foolish woman."

"Why did she come here?" he asked, frowning.

"She came to ask Cordelia to persuade Mrs. Belmont to send her an invitation. Apparently Mrs. Wooley isn't finding the Newport season all that she hoped it would be," drawled Gideon.

Drew said stiffly to me, "Good afternoon, Miss Morrow," before leaving the front hall. Folding my easel and gathering my things, I then went upstairs. But as I neared the second-story landing on my way to my room, I could not help but overhear what happened next.

"Cordelia! Where are you?"

"No need to bring the house down, Drew. So you've returned, have you? Has that dreadful woman gone?"

"If you are referring to Mrs. Wooley," said her husband icily, "then, yes, she is gone. What in God's name did you do to distress her so?"

"I distress her! What about me? Do you think I enjoy having such scenes in my home? I always said she had no breeding. Thank heavens no one else decided to call on us while she was running amuck in our entranceway!"

"Why did you refuse to see her, Cordelia? I gather she merely wanted to ask you a favor," said Drew quietly.

"What would have been the point? I knew what she wanted. She wanted me to procure her an invitation to Alva's ball."

"And for once couldn't you have shown a little human kindness and put in a word for her? After all, she's no stranger to you."

"If I sponsored everyone who opportuned me, Society would be in a sorry mess! Do you have any idea how many gatecrashers there are every year? We should not be able to refer to the members as The Four Hundred if we allowed just anyone in."

"As I recall, Mrs. Ogden Mills considers Society to have only two hundred members. In fact she claims that there are only twenty families in New York that she recognizes. I wonder if yours is among them." His voice was sardonic.

"Just why are you bothering about that insignificant Wooley woman and her husband, may I ask?"

"Not so insignificant, Cordelia. I understand his company in the Midwest made ten million dollars in one year. They seem like decent enough people. I'm sure they know which fork to use." His voice was dry.

"He is in trade, Drew. And that is just not acceptable. Mrs. Astor used to say that the people who sold her her carpets, no matter how well-off, would never be invited to walk on them!"

"Cordelia, that woman downstairs had nearly lost her reason. It meant so much to her, though why on earth she should want to waste her time at one of these ridiculous, self-indulgent affairs is beyond me. The last dinner party we attended, with fish swimming about in the center of the table, was unappetizing to say the least."

"Every one else admired the effect excessively," came Cordelia's cold voice. "The Wooleys should never have rented a villa for the entire season. You know what Harry Lehr says: that Newport should be avoided like the plague until you are certain you'll be accepted there. The Wooleys could have gone to Bar Harbor, or to Saratoga, which are not so exclusive. Here they are getting what their audacity deserves. They are being ignored. And there are many others like them. I heard O. H. P. Belmont say that there are nearly four thousand millionaires in this country. Only a few will be admitted into Society."

"Tell me," Drew asked silkily, "on what do you base their admittance? The men could care less. After all, few of them have any scruples. Many of them made their fortunes on swindling the Union government, selling ships to the Navy that weren't seaworthy, and defective rifles to the Western army which had been condemned by Army inspectors in the East. But that didn't worry certain profiteers, whose names, as you know, are among the exalted of today. It meant nothing to J. Pierpont Morgan that the soldiers had their thumbs blown off. It meant nothing to old Commodore Vanderbilt that his fleet of ships carrying

139

hundreds of men almost didn't make it to New Orleans. He committed his own wife and son to lunatic asylums for periods of time when he didn't like what they were saying or doing!

"So what criteria do you and the other all-powerful matrons set down as crucial for one to pass through the Hallowed Gates?"

"You know as well as I do that the family fortunes must have been made three generations previously," said Cordelia angrily. "In certain circumstances, members of the second generation may be recognized, but that is rare. The family must be accustomed to having a fortune and live with it for a number of years, providing them with comforts, luxuries, proper education, and behavior."

"A proper education? Do you pretend that that is the case with Mrs. Fish? She can barely read and write! And as far as behavior goes, why do you think she and Harry Lehr stayed on the terrace at Wakehurst during the last musicale there? Van Alen told them they made too much noise! Face it, Cordelia, the people you go around with are no more cultured and educated than those they trample on, many times less so. Their rudeness, the way they prey on one another, would not be tolerated by the middle or lower classes. Most of them haven't a spark of decency, compassion, wit, or intellect! They wouldn't have a leg to stand on without the money."

"How can you say that?" his wife sputtered. "How can you say they are not cultured? Why, have you no idea of the priceless treasures, the ancient things they have preserved!"

"Ransacking monasteries and castles in Europe for mantels and paneling and statues is not what I'd call evidence of culture," he said dryly. "Anyone with a heavy purse can do that. Mrs. Belmont scarcely knows one style of architecture from another, and she has no knowledge of history, despite all the antiques she's collected."

"Not everyone cares to be as high-brow as you, Drew, buried in your books. Why, if you didn't have such fine stables, you'd be dull as dishwater. Your contempt for my friends is well-known. If it weren't for *me, you* might not be recognized, despite your heritage. How would you like that?"

"As I have as little to do with these people as possible, I could think of far worse things. I'm living with far worse, am I not, *Madame Wife?*" His voice was knife-edged.

"Oh, I know you dislike me heartily, Drew. We haven't been very fortunate in our marriage, have we? Two sickly children and the one left practically demented. But just now I enjoy being Mrs. Drew Rockwell, as long as it's in name only. And if I ever do decide to divorce you, I can promise you I'll take Blythe. I'm certain to get the house as well. It may be dreadfully Gothic now, but I daresay I could change all that with the right decorator. Ogden Codman, for example." Her voice was taunting.

Drew did not answer her. I heard a door slam shut and then, Cordelia's low laughter before her door, too, was closed. All this time I had been gripping the staircase bannister, unable to move. But now that the coast was clear, I hurried on up to the third floor.

Cordelia had referred to two children. That had come as a shock to me, that there had been another child besides Blythe. Not only was one child gone, but the one remaining was not well. Was that the reason for the bleakness, the pain I had glimpsed in Drew's eyes? Whatever loss he and Cordelia had suffered, it had certainly not brought them closer together. Even though Cordelia had lost one child, she neglected the one still living.

I had known that she had a lover; now I knew that she preferred to hold fast to a loveless marriage rather than be labeled a divorced woman. Knowing full well that Drew would not risk losing Blythe to her, her position was safe and secure. From the bit of conversation I had overheard in the summerhouse, I gathered that her lover was also married. Neither, apparently, was willing to make a change in his or her marital status. Besides, divorces were difficult to obtain.

141

It was about eleven o'clock that night when I was ready to retire that I heard the screams again. Blythe, I thought with dismay. What ailed the poor child? Tempted to put my hands over my ears to shut out the sounds, I waited for them to cease. But after some minutes of listening to the little girl's terror, I could endure it no longer. I remembered that the family had dined from home this evening and were probably still out. I had considered it singular that Drew and Cordelia could battle fiercely and then put on a united front as they went out to dinner mere hours later. But doubtless they had years of practice of doing just that.

Buttoning my dressing gown, I went down the corridor to the nursery wing. The cries grew louder and more anguished as I approached. They were chilling to hear. What on earth was frightening her?

Outside the door to the nursery, I not only heard the little girl's shrieks, but shouting as well. I recognized the voice as Miss Simmons's. Without bothering to knock, I flung open the door.

To my surprise the room was almost in darkness, with only the light from the streetlight shining in the window and forming shadows on the walls. Blythe stood rigidly against one wall, her arms at her sides, her eyes shut. She was shrieking as hard as she could.

Miss Simmons faced her. Neither of them had noticed me. "Stop it, Blythe! Stop this at once! Your father has not come back! He is not here, do you understand? So there is no point to any of this — no point at all!" There was no sympathy in her sharp tone, only anger and frustration.

"Miss Simmons!" I cried accusingly.

She whirled around. "What are you doing here, Miss Morrow? This is not your part of the house!"

Ignoring her, I went over to the gas globe and turned up the light. It had not gone out altogether, but the light it cast had been very weak. Now there was a warm soft glow about the room which dispersed the shadows and lit up the corners.

Kneeling down beside the screaming child, I took her arms in a firm grip and said, "It's all right. Blythe. There is nothing here to hurt you. See, I've turned on the light. Open your eyes."

She refused, struggling, but I did not release her. I continued to speak soothingly to her until gradually her cries diminished in intensity. She still remained alarmingly rigid.

"Get a wet cloth," I said over my shoulder. "She's terribly hot." Her normally pale face was red and damp.

"Mr. Rockwell won't like this. Blythe doesn't take to strangers. You'll only make her worse," said Miss Simmons.

"I'll take the responsibility. Just please get that wet cloth."

When she did, I held it against the child's forehead while she flinched. Then I pressed it to her cheeks and eyes.

"Open your eyes, Blythe," I said.

She shook her head violently.

"Why not?"

She shook her head again.

"Tell me why you don't want to open your eyes, darling."

"Even if she tells you, it won't make any sense," said Miss Simmons witheringly.

Ignoring her, I repeated softly, "Tell me, Blythe. Why won't you open your eyes ? What are you afraid of?"

"I don't want to see them!"

"What? You don't want to see what? Tell me, darling."

"The — the leaves," she said between her teeth, "on the wall, dancing."

"The leaves?" What did she mean?

"The shadows — on the wall . . ."

"Blythe, there are no shadows at all. Open your eyes and you will see for yourself. The shadows have all gone. The room is bright and you are safe."

For a few moments I thought she did not believe me, but then her eyelids relaxed and she blinked rapidly, squinting. Assured that I had spoken the truth, she opened them all the way.

"It was dark," she whispered. "I don't like it dark."

"Isn't the light supposed to be kept burning in here?" I asked.

"It was on slightly, you saw that for yourself," said Miss Simmons sullenly. "Sometimes when the gas is turned up in one part of the house, it is lowered in another."

Yet something told me that that was not what had happened. I wondered whether the light in Blythe's room had been turned down deliberately, so that the little girl woke to a gloomy, heavily shadowed room. But what reason would Miss Simmons have for doing such a thing? I could not believe she would torture the child, encouraging her to be fearful. There must be some other explanation. Perhaps one of the servants *had* turned up the gas on a lower floor of the house.

"Blythe, everything is all right. The room is warm and bright and you are safe. Now you must get back in bed."

Lifting her, I carried her to the bed, her frame slight and frail in my arms. "You are perfectly safe, darling," I said, smoothing back her dusky curls. "Haven't you heard about the good fairies who look after children?"

Regarding me somberly, she shook her head against the pillow.

I pulled the coverlet over her. "You know what fairies are. Lovely tiny creatures with wings like lace. They watch over children and keep them safe from harm."

"Like the one in my window?"

Glancing over to where she gestured, I saw that one of her windows was indeed a stained-glass scene of a fairy and an elf. The elf wore a sugar-loaf hat and sat on a lily pad, playing a reed, while beside it danced a curly haired fairy.

"Yes, darling, just like that pretty fairy," I said. "The next time you think of something or see something that makes you feel afraid, I want you to think of that lovely fairy and her friend the elf who are watching over you."

She yawned and closed her eyes.

"Fairies! What nonsense!" said Miss Simmons acidly. "You're going to give her sillier notions than she has already."

Humming a little melody, I continued to smooth her hair and soft cheeks until I was certain she slept.

Then came the sound of footsteps in the hall. Rising, I turned toward the open door.

"Oh, Mr. Rockwell," began Miss Simmons, flushing.

He glanced from her to me. "Merriman said Blythe had been screaming," he said. He still wore black evening attire; he had obviously just returned.

"Miss Morrow and I managed to calm her down and get her back to sleep," said Miss Simmons breathlessly.

"How on earth were you able to do that?" he asked, but he was not looking at Miss Simmons.

"She was crying out for you, sir. I — I hoped that you had returned," said the governess.

"I cannot always be with her, Miss Simmons. That is why I employ you. I thought you said that she slept soundly on the nights I was away in Boston."

"Yes, that's true. I don't understand why tonight . . . Perhaps you should stay a while, sir, in case she wakes again. It may not be so easy to soothe her the next time."

"I'm going to bed, Miss Simmons. If she wakes again, I'll hear her." He gazed across at me. "Thank you, Miss Morrow. I'm sorry you were disturbed again."

I smiled slightly, shaking my head. Glancing at Miss Simmons, I was startled to see the malice in her eyes as she regarded me.

But then she was smiling sweetly at Drew. "Good night, Mr. Rockwell. And don't worry about Blythe. She will be fine now that you have returned to Copper Beeches."

"Well, good night," I murmured and went from the room.

"Wait, Miss Morrow." Drew was behind me, closing the nursery door. "I appreciate very much whatever it was you did for Blythe tonight." I started to demur, but he interrupted me. "I know it was you who calmed her and sent her back to sleep. I am in your debt." His warm gaze brought the color to my cheeks.

"Oh, no, sir, it was nothing. It just distresses me so to hear her screaming the — the way she does."

"I know," he said wearily. "I can't make sense out of her fears. They don't only arise at night, I'm afraid. Once she became terrified when a flock of birds suddenly flew out of a tree and across the sky — the sudden movement or something. Perhaps she thought they were going to attack her. It took me nearly a half an hour to quiet her down after that, and she refused to go outside for several days." He shook his head. "How did you manage to calm her?"

"Oh, I told her about the good fairies, and how they would protect her if she believed in them. I don't think Miss Simmons approved. But I can't see any harm in make-believe. She is only a little girl, and she needs something pleasant and comforting to think about when she feels frightened."

"I am very grateful, Miss Morrow." He took my hand and held it in a strong grip. "Not that I'm surprised. That day on the steamboat I felt that you — that I —" He broke off abruptly, his face hardening, and dropped my hand. "Good night, Miss Morrow," he said, his voice suddenly curt.

"Good night, Mr. Rockwell," I said softly, and went to my room.

It was a long while before I slept. In the past hour several things had been made clear to me. First, Miss Simmons was far from being the ideal governess for Blythe. Shouting at her while she was pressed, terrified, to the wall, was one of the worse things she could have done. I was convinced that she harbored no affection for the little girl, and I suspected that she might even use Blythe and her fears for her own purposes. I had no proof, of course, except for the turned down gaslight. Had Miss Simmons actually lowered the flame on purpose, believing that Drew had already returned from the dinner party and would hasten to the nursery? It was in the nursery where Miss Simmons was likely to see Drew, and his beloved child screaming with fright was the likeliest thing to lure him there. Was that the reason for Blythe's undisturbed nights while Drew was in Boston? Had Miss Simmons kept the light burning brightly on those nights as there was no chance of him hearing her cries and coming to her aid? And now that he had returned, had she actually *dimmed* the light knowing that Blythe would wake and be frightened, and that Drew would come?

Except he had not come. He had still been away from the house. It was I who had heard, and who had come.

Miss Simmons was in love with Drew Rockwell. Now I understood her initial suspicion of me, her hostility. She had feared that I, as another young woman in the house, might be a threat to her. She must know as well as I did the state of affairs between Drew and Cordelia; she had been living at Copper Beeches much longer than I. Did she actually hope that he might return her affections? Did she even dream that he might some day marry her?

There was one thing of which I was certain. Miss Simmons enjoyed Drew's nocturnal visits to the nursery. Whether she instigated them or not, she lived for those visits. And that was the reason she looked after a little girl for whom she had no affection, no love. She used Blythe for her own ends, as a way to her father's heart.

Some days later, I was working in Cordelia Rockwell's bedroom on the second floor. It had been recently done over in the prevailing French style with Louis XV furniture painted gold, apricot damask walls highlighted with Corinthian pilasters, and a ceiling fresco of cherubs playing in the clouds. I guessed it was the one room Drew had permitted Cordelia to change.

As I worked, I heard Cordelia welcoming a group of ladies into her adjoining sitting room, a room I had not yet seen. The door was slightly ajar, so their voices could be clearly heard.

"I do like this room since you've had it done over," said one lady. "And those Sèvres pieces are so charming."

"It was perfectly hideous before, wasn't it? It had belonged to Drew's mother, and was so *Victorian,* if you know

147

what I mean," said Cordelia. They assured her they did in suitable tones of disgust.

"I hear you had a visit from that Wooley woman last week," said one. "She had come to me before. I told her there was nothing I could do for her."

"Certainly not," said Cordelia, tittering. "The brazenness of some people! Why, if I were to take up everyone that asked me — ! Drew actually felt *sorry* for the creature!"

"Men — a pretty face and they're all the same. Just like J. J. Van Alen inviting that woman from Narragansett to be his guest. After she had gone, he explained that the sea air did not agree with her. She was not able to keep her hair in curls, if you please. She should have come to us, I told him, we'd have curled it for her!" The woman gave a hoarse, macaw-like laugh.

"I declare I am furious with Alice Drexel for going off to Europe and leasing Fairholme to those Leeds, those dreadful Tinplate people. The entire house will have to be disinfected afterwards!"

"It was the same with that creature at the Horse Show last summer. Imagine having the audacity to sublet one of the boxes. And to send out invitations as cool as you please to a party at the Casino pavilion. I stared at her in outrage and so did everyone else. And not a soul came to her party," announced the woman with satisfaction. "The last I heard she had given it out that she and her husband had to leave Newport due to a death in the family. In actuality they merely sailed to Narragansett and registered at one of those vulgar hotels."

"Are you going to Harry Clews's 'Servant's Ball'? I hear Harry Lehr is going to act as butler. It sounds the greatest fun!"

"Dear Harry. He always knows how to enliven the season. It would be so dull without his notions. Do you remember when he pretended to be the Russian Czar, Mamie?"

"I can't decided whose luncheon to attend next Wednesday — Alva's or Alice's," moaned a voice. "I'm in *such* a quandary. Such a terrible predicament. You know Alva only announced she was having a luncheon after she learned that Alice was!"

"She's still furious at the way the other Vanderbilts have treated her since the divorce."

"Yes, but what shall I *do?*" moaned the lady who had never been in such a terrible predicament.

"Maisie, all of you, you must see my new bracelet and necklace. Sapphires and diamonds," said Cordelia.

"Tiffany's?"

"Yes, on my last trip."

Sounds of approval and admiration all around.

"Olive Chandler had a new stomacher on the other night. All diamonds, some as large as my fingernail. She said it was a present from Dr. Chandler."

The harsh laugh came again. "You know what that means, pet. She bought it herself. We all know Olive carries the purse in the family."

"But Dr. Chandler is so distinguished. And his family is an old one, even if he hasn't Olive's money."

"Distinguished, eh? I'd only take that as far as I could throw it. Too bad he can't do anything for Gwendolyn. 'Physician, heal thyself' — or thy family, in this case."

"Gwendolyn is not ill, Mamie."

"No, pet, just odd. And that's even worse."

"One feels sorry for the Chandlers. Gwendolyn is scarcely a credit to them. There is no strong line to survive there."

What stupid women, I thought, repelled. Nothing to do but gossip and appraise one another's jewelry. Naturally they would consider it amusing to dress as their servants for a night's entertainment just so long as they would not have to lift a finger the following day. I was relieved when the gathering broke up a short while later.

That evening Cordelia and Gideon were dining out. Drew joined us but he was remote and preoccupied. After we had finished eating, he left the dining room rather abruptly, his face grim. He had scarcely spoken at all.

"I wish Drew wouldn't brood so," said Isadora worriedly. "He looks so wretched sometimes. I've tried to talk to him, but he won't talk. You know how he is."

Aunt Hermione sniffed. "I do. But he must make his peace with it someday."

"I don't think he'll ever get over Nathan's death," said Isadora. "If Blythe were well, he might not feel it as much. But I think he's afraid of losing them both."

"Cordelia certainly got over it quickly enough. Inhuman, that's what she is," said Aunt Hermione gruffly. She shook her head. "I'll never understand it."

"You'd think she didn't have a daughter at all," said Isadora.

"Nathan?" I asked softly.

Isadora turned to me. "Oh, Ariel, I'm sorry. Of course you don't know. Blythe had a younger brother. They both had scarlet fever, but he . . . he died of it. I'm afraid Drew has never gotten over Nathan's death. He was such a dear little boy, so lively and mischievous."

"The doctors said he might never learn to walk," said Aunt Hermione. "It was his leg, twisted, you see. But Drew worked with him every day until he was able to run almost as fast as Blythe. It was a joy to watch the three of them together."

"How terrible," I said.

"I've told you how different Blythe used to be, Ariel," said Isadora. "But the illness and losing her brother affected her deeply, left her sickly and fearful. They shared the nursery, and it was Blythe who found him in the morning. It was horrible — and for a child . . . He had died sometime the night before."

Chapter Eight

Some days later I was painting the first-story landing with its magnificent Eastlake double staircase paneled in white oak, and the stained glass window of *Dawn Comes On the Edge of Night* by John La Farge. It was my favorite room, if one could refer to it as that, in the house. To create the predominently purple hues of the breathtaking window, I was mixing alizarin crimson, ultramarine, and white in various proportions.

"Miss Morrow."

It was not the first time that my heart began to race when I heard that voice. Setting down my brush, I turned. "Yes, Mr. Rockwell?"

He was dressed for riding, his boots dusty and his dark thick hair windblown. But evidently the gallop had not improved his mood; he looked forbidding, and there were tight lines about his mouth.

"Miss Morrow, we are having guests for dinner this evening. Our neighbors, the Chandlers, will be joining us."

"I understand, Mr. Rockwell. Mrs. Rockwell wishes me to have dinner in my room. Of course."

He raised his brows. "I have no idea what Mrs. Rockwell wishes. I would like you to join us. We will be gathering in the drawing room at eight o'clock."

Before I could respond he had turned and walked away. That evening I dressed with special care in a teal blue taffeta gown with a slim skirt that widened in a flounce above the hem. It was simply cut, but elegant and becoming to me. Putting up my hair, I fastened it with two seed pearl clasps, slipped on my pearl choker, and sprinkled lily of the valley scent on my lace-trimmed handkerchief.

At a few minutes past eight, I went downstairs to the drawing room. The family and guests were just taking their seats; Merriman was pouring champagne.

As I entered, Cordelia looked up in mild surprise. Her arched brows drew together. "I thought I had instructed one of the maids to bring you a tray, Miss Morrow. We have guests tonight."

My face flooding with color, I stood rooted to the spot. But Drew said easily, "I asked Miss Morrow to join us. She's something of a celebrity, you know. I was sure that Prescott and Olive would be interested to meet her."

Dr. Chandler rose, smiling. "Indeed. Olive and I have already had that pleasure, haven't we, my dear? Miss Rockwell introduced us to Miss Morrow at the Casino last week. How do you do, Miss Morrow?" His smile was warm and friendly.

"Good evening, Doctor. Good evening, Mrs. Chandler," I said. She nodded coldly to me. She was wearing a dark blue gown which set off the diamond and sapphire stomacher she wore. I recalled the recent conversation in Cordelia's sitting room.

"May I present my daughter, Miss Chandler, Miss Morrow? I think the two of you have not met before," said the doctor.

So this was Gwendolyn. Her brown hair was scraped back from her forehead and pinned in an uncompromising knot at the back. Her eyes were large and well-shaped. They would have been her best feature had they been a darker shade. As it was they were a very pale green, and disconcerting. She extended her hand. I took it, feeling no grip at all. Her attire differed greatly from her mother's; her gown was rather severe and of a drab color. She wore no jewels. It was difficult to see her in the role of a great heiress.

"How do you do, Miss Chandler? I believe I have had

the pleasure of hearing you play the piano. In fact, I could not move until you had finished, I was so taken with the way you played."

There was a palpable silence. Gwendolyn regarded me with that slightly disturbing gaze, saying nothing in response. Then her father said warmly, "Yes, we are very proud of our daughter. She has been given great talent. Allow me to say, Miss Morrow, that the art world suffered a great loss when your father passed away."

"Thank you."

"Olive and I were once in London and saw some of his work at the Royal Academy. The world needs many more talented men like him, not only artists, but great men of any ability."

"Did we, Prescott? I don't remember," said Olive Chandler. Whether she actually remembered seeing my father's work or not, she was not going to give me the satisfaction of admitting it. It was apparent that she resented me, an employee at Copper Beeches, being made one of the dinner party.

"I wish he had painted my portrait," said Isadora. "Perhaps you could do it, Ariel."

"Don't be foolish, Isadora," said Cordelia. "Miss Morrow paints watercolor interiors, a vastly different thing from a portrait in oils."

As if you would know the difference, I thought irritably. "As a matter of fact, Mrs. Rockwell, I have painted portraits. I studied with my father for many years."

"Oh? And whom did you paint?" she asked airily.

"People my father and I knew in New York. No one with whom you would be familiar." My voice was stiff.

"But you did not receive commissions, did you?" she asked haughtily. Tonight she wore a lace gown of dull gold. "Practicing on street vendors is scarcely the same thing, is it?"

Flushing, I did not answer her. I should not have allowed her to needle me into this conversation.

Gwendolyn Chandler gave an abrupt laugh. We all

turned to her in surprise. "Imagine, the freedom to paint street vendors. You do not know how fortunate you are, Miss Morrow."

I had no idea how to respond to her. The others were evidently used to her strange remarks; Drew said something to Dr. Chandler, and Cordelia began talking animatedly to his wife.

Gideon leaned over and said in a mocking undertone, "Are you truly free, Miss Morrow?"

"I don't understand what you mean, Mr. Lawrence," I said coldly.

"Gwendolyn obviously envies you. Though it's always difficult to know just what she means. But she's right, you know. You put Gwendolyn and our own dear Isadora in the shade. You are able to do what you like with your life, without censure from anyone."

"I listen to my own conscience," I said. "Perhaps you should try it."

Gideon chuckled. "Why do you dislike me so, Miss Morrow? I assure you I am your devoted admirer."

"I can live without your admiration."

"But can I live without giving it, without acting upon it?"

I was spared answering him by the appearance of Merriman who announced that dinner was ready. At the table I was seated beside Dr. Chandler. He was interested in my life with my father, asking me questions and encouraging me to talk. Once or twice I intercepted a look from Olive Chandler who clearly did not appreciate his efforts to draw me out. Her heavily powdered face was pinched and stiffly disapproving.

Gideon had been recounting what was, to him, an amusing story concerning himself and one or two friends. I missed most of it, but did hear Isadora make a scathing comment about the police.

"Oh, they have no authority over us," blustered Gideon. "This town knows which side its bread is buttered on. It would rot if it weren't for the summer residents."

"It would serve you right to be thrown in jail one night,"

said Isadora, "you and a few of your charming friends. Haven't you got anything better to do than steal weathervanes off barns, or go into churches late at night and ring the bells? If Drew finds out, he'll cart you to the police himself!"

"I suppose you're just dying to tell him," said Gideon, casting a glance at his brother-in-law at the far end of the table. "Don't be such a spoilsport, Dora! If you weren't so pretty, none of my friends would pay you any mind."

"As if I would want anything to do with your horrid friends!" cried Isadora hotly. "Why, if they were the last people on earth, I wouldn't like them!"

"I think I'd like to be the last person on earth," said Gwendolyn musingly. "All those great glittering palaces lining the cliff and not a soul in them. I could throw away every pair of white gloves I own." There was a strange glint in her pale luminous eyes.

"You know, funds are needed for a few of the buildings downtown," said Dr. Chandler. "You and I must do what we can, Drew."

"I do not see why the burden should fall on us, Prescott," said his wife. "We are here only two months out of the year."

"I know, my dear, but people such as ourselves must support these endeavors. Those buildings are of great historical and architectural significance. They must be preserved. We can never have too much beauty or culture or learning in the world. It is the other things — the ignorance, the poverty, the imperfections of our society which must be fixed or rooted out."

"Prescott is always so concerned with the duties that fall upon the shoulders of people such as ourselves," said Olive complacently to Cordelia.

"We should not regard them as duties, but privileges, Olive," said her husband. "We were born to them and we have a responsibility. Ignoring the unpleasant is unworthy of us, unconscionable. The more effort we put into building and improving the society we live in, the better it will be."

"That's quite a pretty speech, Prescott," said Aunt Hermione. "But despite that I have lost all pretentions to beauty, I'm not ready to be rooted out just yet."

Everyone laughed, and Dr. Chandler made the old lady a gallant answer.

I turned to Gwendolyn. "You really do play very beautifully, Miss Chandler. I heard you once when I stood at the Chinese Moongate." I assumed now that it was her face I had seen at the turret window.

"Did you know, Ariel, that my grandfather built Oaklawn?" Isadora asked.

"Oh, really?"

"The two houses are related, Miss Morrow," said Gwendolyn, her eyes fixed on me. "Connected." I saw Gideon roll his eyes at Isadora who pretended to ignore him.

"If you have all finished, we can go into the drawing room," said Cordelia. "Perhaps Gwendolyn can be prevailed upon to play for us."

"What do you say, my dear?" asked her father, smiling.

"I don't feel like playing tonight," she stated flatly.

Gwendolyn was certainly a creature of moods and whims, I thought. Dr. Chandler seemed slightly embarrassed by her blunt refusal, but Cordelia covered up the awkward moment by launching into a story about a pianist who had walked off the stage in the middle of a concert in Paris. After some further talk, the Chandlers took their leave.

"I hope I shall see you again soon, Miss Morrow," said Dr. Chandler.

"I hope so as well, Doctor. Good night." At least he did not treat me as though I were little more than a servant. He seemed a man of high ideals and principles, motivated to do what he could for those less fortunate. Perhaps that was because he had married into great wealth rather than having had it from birth. His daughter was certainly not made happy by her fortune. She was very ill-suited to the gay, glittering world of the millionaires. A recluse much of the time, she dressed more like a schoolmistress than an heiress. Olive Chandler, arrogant, and as conscious of her status as Cordelia, must despair of her.

The following morning I was having breakfast with Isadora when Cordelia stormed into the room. She was not yet dressed, but wore a lilac chiffon wrap. Flinging something on the table, she snapped, "Where's Gideon?"

"He went out riding a few minutes ago," said Isadora, "and then he's having lunch at the Clambake Club. Why? What's wrong?"

"What's wrong? He's disgraced us again, that's what!"

"How do you mean, Cordelia?"

"Just look at this!" She picked up what she had tossed on the table and handed it to Isadora.

"Oh, *Town Topics*," said Isadora. "What else is new?"

Town Topics was a New York scandal sheet reporting on misconduct and indiscretions made by members of The Four Hundred. On the cover were two ladies in silhouette, whispering to one another.

"Read the 'Saunterings' column," said Cordelia.

Sighing, Isadora found the page and began to read. " 'A certain young lady in the English Set suffers from some kind of throat trouble — she cannot go for more than a half an hour without a drink, preferably champagne. A divorceé dwelling over the stables dyes her hair. Her hands are wrinkled as a laundress's.' "

"Not those," cried Cordelia impatiently. "Go on."

" 'A gentleman from Philadelphia much admired by the females is not to be seen in Newport this summer. He is now residing in an exclusive hospital in Europe, suffering from a result of that admiration.' Oh, this is sickening. Really, Cordelia! 'A Prince of Wall Street whose house bears the name of a certain tree found in Newport entertains some delectable young women from the theatre on his yacht while his wife sits alone on shore in their great house. A widowed lady with three children and a brick house on Narragansett Avenue, that exclusive Newport address, drove out to Hanging Rock, a picturesque geological formation along the coast recently. Was it the contemplation of the view, we ask, or something else entirely which kept her away for hours, in the sole company of her handsome coachman?' "

"Not that drivel! Haven't you found it yet? Here, give it to me." Snatching it from Isadora's hands, Cordelia skimmed the contents. "Here it is: 'A young man visiting in one of Newport's older cottages built by a Boston Brahmin'—now don't tell me that isn't Copper Beeches—'has taken up a pastime enjoyed years ago by a newspaper editor, that is, driving his open carriage down Bellevue Avenue at breakneck speed in the wee hours of the morning wearing nothing but his skin. If this gentleman is not careful he may go the way of his mentor, who was forced to retire to Paris because of his scandalous behavior.' There. What do you think of that?"

"So Gideon has been riding about naked in the middle of the night as James Gordon Bennett used to," said Isadora. "I'm not surprised. He's always looking for some new amusement. It could be much worse."

"Worse!"

"Yes, they could have talked about his incessant gambling, or the maid you had to pay off a few months ago in New York—"

"The mere fact that he was alluded to at all is intolerable," said Cordelia, two bright spots of color in her cheeks. "I don't care the slightest what he does, but he must learn to be discreet enough so that the gossip columnists don't get wind of it. Where is Drew?"

"Are you looking for me, Cordelia?" Drew was standing in the doorway.

"Take a look at this!" She pointed a finger at the print.

"I would have thought the past few nights a little chilly for that sort of activity," said Drew dryly. Isadora giggled.

Cordelia's eyes narrowed. "This is nothing to make light of, Drew. I want you to know what you are going to do about it."

His raised his brows. "I? Nothing at all."

"Nothing! Does it mean nothing to you that a member of

158

this family has been libeled in such a way? That our privacy has been invaded!" she cried indignantly.

"The boy has done far worse, Cordelia. If I go to Rowe or even Mann himself, they'll be alerted to some of Gideon's less harmless escapades. If we ignore this, it will blow over."

"That's easy for you to say, Drew," said Cordelia. "You sit in your ivory tower here and care nothing for public opinion. But I choose to go among these people!"

"Then you'll have many shoulders to cry on. I notice that several of your friends are referred to as well. Gideon's offense is really insignificant compared to the allusions to alcoholism, promiscuity, unmentionable diseases, and various other delights. Or is it not that reference to Gideon which really disturbs you? Did that strike too close to home for comfort? Are you afraid, Cordelia, that you may be next?" His tone was silky, his expression coolly appraising.

Cordelia gave him a venomous look, turned on her heel, and left the room. Drew left as well, leaving Isadora and me in an uncomfortable silence. Evidently Drew knew about Cordelia's assignations in the summerhouse.

"Oh well, Gideon will be off at the end of August to somebody's hunting lodge in North Carolina," said Isadora.

"Did I hear someone mention my name?" Gideon strolled into the room, his hands in his pockets. "I'm flattered to be the subject of a discussion between two such lovely ladies."

"Oh, stop it, Gideon," said Isadora. "Don't waste your charm on us. And before your head gets too swollen, understand that we weren't lauding your good points, if you have any. Cordelia is very angry with you."

"I'm positively trembling with fright. What is she angry about?"

"Don't you know you are mentioned in 'Saunterings'?"

"Oh, that." He took out his pocket watch and began to swing it to and fro. "Drew ought to be more careful whom he employs. No one saw me but a couple of the grooms I woke up to harness the horses."

"With or without your clothes on?" asked Isadora sweetly. "Besides, it is far more likely one of your cronies let it out. But if you are uncertain, next time harness your own horses. I'm sure the grooms would appreciate an undisturbed night's sleep."

A short while later I was once more at work on the first-floor landing. Camille de la Salle paused to speak to me on her way up to see Isadora. She seemed filled with a suppressed excitement; her eyes were shining and her cheeks had a rosy glow. She very politely admired my work, but I could tell her thoughts were far away. She had something of a confidential nature to report to Isadora; vaguely I wondered what it might be.

There was another visitor that day, but not for Isadora. A woman, heavily veiled, passed me and swept up the stairs.

Two of the maids were in the corridor; I had not paid attention to their chatter as they worked, but something one of them said broke through my concentration.

"That was Mrs. Leander — the one written about in that *Town Topics* this morning. I heard Mr. Merriman speak to her," said one.

"Oh, What did they say about her?"

"A widowed lady with three children, they said. I stole a look at Mrs. Meredith's copy in the kitchen."

"That could mean anyone."

"No, it's her, I tell you. Mrs. Meredith says she lives in a brick house on Narragansett, just like the column said. Matilda from Oaklawn stopped in for a chat and I heard them talking about it. Mrs. Leander is the only widow that lives on Narragansett."

"Well, what did they say about her?"

"That she and her coachman drove out into the country."

"What's so awful about that?"

"Don't be an idiot. A lady like her drives out to Hanging Rock alone, stays there all day, with no one but her coachman? I've seen him at the Forty Steps on some Thursday nights. He's a handsome one, with shoulders like an ox."

160

"Oh, I think I know the one you mean. Lots of the girls had their eyes on him. Red hair, right? But he didn't ask none of us to dance."

"That's the one. Thomas, his name is. Tom Bateman. I'll tell you why he don't want to dance with us maids. Cause we aren't good enough for him. He's looking a lot higher. Mrs. Leander, to be exact."

"Oh, go on! A lady like that — not with a coachman!"

"Ask Mrs. Meredith if you don't believe me."

So the veiled lady was another victim of *Town Topics*'s malice. And her offense, were it true, was far more severe than Gideon's in the eyes of Society. I felt sorry for the widowed Mrs. Leander.

A few days later Isadora came looking for me and asked, "Ariel, I wonder whether you'd like to ride the Ten Mile Drive along the ocean with me this afternoon. It's very pretty. Say you'll come."

"All right, I'd like to very much."

That day I finished the interior of the landing. It was just after three o'clock when I folded my easel and carried up the paper to my room to dry. I felt drained, my neck and shoulders stiff. I was supposed to meet Isadora at four o'clock in the front hall. A ride in an open carriage would be very pleasant; it was sweet of Isadora to have invited me. She was another who treated me as an equal, never as an inferior, hired to do a job.

After taking off my smock and washing my face and hands, I changed into a white gown trimmed with red ribbons. Isadora met me below, her own gown a striped pink and white affair, and we climbed into the waiting black wicker phaeton with red wheels. The afternoon was lovely, the sky a vivid blue, the breeze cooling and smelling faintly of the sea.

Just as we were ready to drive away, Cordelia came out of the house with Blythe in tow. I realized that it was the first time I had seen them together. They both wore white and would have made a pretty picture had not Blythe looked so reluctant.

161

"You're taking Blythe with you on Ocean Drive?" asked Isadora in surprise.

"And why shouldn't I?" asked Cordelia.

"You never have before, that's all."

"It will do the child a world of good to see all the fine carriages and the ladies and gentlemen, won't it, Blythe? She can't remain a recluse — I refuse to have another Gwendolyn Chandler in my house!"

Blythe looked unhappy; it was obvious she didn't want to accompany her mother. Another carriage had pulled up; Cordelia led Blythe up to it and instructed the footmen to lift her inside.

"I do hope that Blythe will be all right," said Isadora worriedly. "However, maybe Cordelia is right. A ride in the fresh air and some time with her mother . . ."

"We'll go first," called Cordelia. Their carriage moved past ours and down the graveled drive to Bellevue Avenue.

"At least we can keep an eye on her ourselves," said Isadora. "I'm glad you decided to accompany me, Ariel."

"Where is Miss de la Salle today?"

Her face clouded over. "Oh, she had another engagement this afternoon. She — she was to meet someone at the Redwood Library."

"A young man?"

Isadora nodded. "I met him yesterday. He's quite nice. I liked him. But if Camille's mother were to find out—!"

"Why? What's wrong with him? He's not married or . . . ?" I flushed.

She shook her head. "No, nothing like that. But, Ariel, he's not at all the sort of person her mother would consider suitable for her to speak to, much less meet in secret! He's . . . he's . . ."

"Poor?" I asked.

"Yes, by Camille's mother's standards. He's an ordinary young man; his father has a shop, I believe, on Thames Street. They are respectable, but far, far removed from Camille's situation."

"Are the two of them that serious about each other already?"

"I don't know, but Camille is only permitted to speak to and dance with men that are the sort she might marry. William is most definitely not of that sort. Oh, he's gentlemanly, well read — he's a schoolmaster — and Camille's rather a bluestocking herself. But if Mrs. de la Salle ever found out, Camille would be in terrible trouble. The kind of trouble that Consuelo Vanderbilt was in. And you know what happened to her, forced to marry the English duke. Mrs. de la Salle wants Camille to marry a European nobleman just as Consuelo did, and you know that count is dancing attendance on her. Her mother is not pressing her yet, but if she heard about William, I dread to think what would happen. Newport is a small city — one can't avoid being seen forever. You saw *Town Topics*. That's the sort of thing they love to pounce on with horrible glee. I'm worried for Camille."

"What does Camille say herself?"

"Oh, she's paying me scant attention. Not that I blame her. She's happy, you see. And it's obvious that William adores her. But her mother would never agree to their marriage in a million years."

We were riding down Bellevue Avenue away from the town in a long train of carriages, passing palatial summer residences. Isadora dropped the subject of Camille and pointed out a few of them: Beechwood, belonging to Mrs. Astor who, it was rumored, had lost her reason; Marble Palace, with its towering Corinthian columns, built for the former Alva Vanderbilt as a birthday gift from her husband just a few years before their divorce; and Belcourt Castle, a Louis XIII hunting lodge where Alva now lived with her new husband, O. H. P. Belmont.

"You're not supposed to look at anyone on the Drive, you know," said Isadora. "You're supposed to sit straight as a poker and gaze directly ahead. But I don't bother — it's just too tedious. And I always get an itch or something when I do."

"I wonder how Blythe is doing," I said. Glancing ahead, I

could just see the top of the little girl's head. Cordelia was paying her no attention, sitting ramrod straight, just as Isadora had said was de rigueur.

The long line of carriages skirted the rocky coastline. Hedgerows grew on one side and there were salt ponds on the other. Scrub pine trees rose stunted and twisted on the shore's edge, and below them were tiny coves scooped out of jagged rock formations which stretched like jetties into the sea. The sun was warm, the water a clear cold blue with no trace of green.

The line of elaborate carriages, phaetons, demi-deaumonts, landaus, and victorias stretched far in front and behind. The attending footmen wore livery; the vehicles were glossy without a speck of dust or streak of grime. The horses' short manes were braided, the tails clubbed. But there was a curious lifeless quality to the procession. It was wholly devoid of enjoyment, of the sort of delightful ease which one might expect. The faces of the participants were as stiff as their postures, and as unrelaxed.

And then the atmosphere changed altogether, in the way that Isadora had feared it would.

Ahead of us, Cordelia's coachman had raised his whip and it somehow became entangled in an overhanging branch. He jerked it once or twice and freed it, but the branch itself was violently shaken, the leaves springing up and down just above Blythe's head. I scarcely took this in at the time, and it would certainly have passed out of memory as quickly as it had occurred, were it not for one thing.

Blythe began to scream.

"Oh, my God," said Isadora. "Not here!"

Blythe's arms were over her head, but they did not muffle her terrified shrieks. Their coachman halted and so did ours, and the ones just ahead stopped to stare back, the mouths of their occupants open.

Cordelia was gazing at her daughter in horror, not making one move to calm her or quiet the screams which tore from her throat. Then I saw Cordelia's arm raised and her hand strike the child.

Instantly Isadora was out of the wicker phaeton and reaching for Blythe. Without a word to Cordelia, she lifted the now-sobbing little girl from the carriage and carried her to ours.

"Take us home," she said crisply to the coachman. "Just turn around the best way you can and take us away from here."

"Yes, Miss Rockwell."

Cordelia's carriage was already moving forward; she sat staring straight ahead as though the last few minutes had not happened at all.

On the way back we met the curious, appalled glares of the other carriage occupants; they were, for once, breaking their rules of not glancing at passersby, and of not speaking. Some of them spoke excitedly to each other, their afternoon enlivened sharply.

Blythe was trembling and weeping in Isadora's arms. In great relief we reached the driveway and headed toward Copper Beeches. As we pulled up, the front door opened and Drew came running out.

Blythe sobbed, "Daddy!" and he took the distraught child in his arms.

"What happened?" he asked savagely. "I couldn't believe it when Merriman told me that Cordelia had taken Blythe on that stupid procession!"

"I don't really know, Drew," said Isadora.

"She became startled when a branch flew almost in her face," I said.

"It's all right, darling. Daddy is here now. Dora, how did she get these red marks? Did the branch scrape her face?"

"No. Cordelia slapped her," said Isadora deliberately.

Suddenly Blythe spoke, her head still against her father's shoulder. "It was the *leaves* . . ." And the horror that was conveyed in that whisper struck a chill in my heart.

Chapter Nine

Leaves again! What so obsessed her about leaves? In her bedroom she had been terrified by shadows of leaves on her wall. And this afternoon when the driver's whip had caught on a branch and shaken it, she had again been prey to a horror we could not comprehend.

Isadora and I followed Drew as he carried Blythe up to the nursery. Miss Simmons met us in the doorway.

"What has happened? Blythe, darling, what is it?" Her voice throbbed with concern.

"She should never have been taken out in that ridiculous parade," said Drew curtly. He went over to Blythe's bed and sat down with her in his lap.

"I agree with you, Mr. Rockwell," said Miss Simmons warmly. "I did suggest to Mrs. Rockwell that it was not advisable in the circumstances, but unfortunately my words held no weight with her. These fits come upon her with no warning at all."

"My child does not have fits, Miss Simmons!"

She flushed scarlet to the roots of her hair, her pale lashes and brows standing out in contrast. "I should not have used that word, Mr. Rockwell. I am very sorry."

He nodded wearily, his face still grim.

She went on, "Perhaps if you could stay with Blythe for a little while . . . She is always better when you are near. I think, however, that she needs to be quiet, with few people about." She looked deliberately at me.

"I'll be back in a while," said Drew, setting Blythe off

his lap. "First I want to talk to my sister and Miss Morrow. Sweetheart, you stay with Miss Simmons. She will look after you and keep you safe. You're home now, and there is nothing to be afraid of."

Blythe did not respond to him, and after a few moments he straightened, frowning, and the three of us left the nursery.

In the library Drew said, "I want to know exactly what occurred this afternoon."

"We scarcely know, Drew," said Isadora. "Ariel and I were talking; Blythe and Cordelia were in the carriage just ahead of ours. Blythe hadn't wanted to go with her mother, but Cordelia had insisted."

"Don't tell me she was suddenly overcome by maternal stirrings, long dormant!"

"Well, other children are sometimes brought along. I suppose Cordelia just felt inclined to take her this afternoon."

"No doubt thinking that the two of them made a pretty picture of virtuous motherhood," he said cynically.

"Then, out of the blue, or so it seemed to me, she was screaming, and their carriage had stopped. Ours, of course, did also."

"What was this about a branch?"

"The coachman's whip had become twisted in an overhanging branch. It was twitching up and down—and Blythe was screaming," I said.

"And while she was screaming Cordelia slapped her," he said through his teeth, raking his fingers through his hair.

"I suppose she thought it might stop the hysteria," I said uncomfortably. Not that I wished to defend Cordelia's action.

"And naturally it had just that effect," he replied sarcastically.

"I think I hear a carriage," said Isadora. "It must be Cordelia returning."

After a swift glance out the window, Drew strode from the room out into the front hall. We heard him dismiss the butler.

"Oh no, they're really going to have it out now," said Isadora nervously. "I think I'll go up to my room."

"Yes, so will I."

But the raised voices had already reached us. We stood there, frozen. Molly, one of the maids, had come out of the drawing room and hesitated on the threshold, also uncertain.

"You are never to lay a hand on Blythe again, is that clear, Cordelia? You do and I'll kill you!"

"Let me go, Drew! I only slapped the child. And it was high time, if you ask me. She needs precisely more of that when she becomes hysterical, so she will snap out of it!"

"And did she snap out of it?" His tone was cuttingly sardonic.

She ignored him. "You have no idea what it was like — the sheer mortification I went through! Screaming like that, like some wild animal, in front of all those people, shaming me like that! I'll never forgive her!"

"Shaming you! As if that were possible! You may think the behavior you indulge in is kept secret, but I know exactly what you do, and with whom!"

"I don't know what you're talking about. I'm going up to my room. My nerves are completely shattered. It took all I had to continue that ride."

"Perhaps the world would have found your role of a dutiful mother more convincing had you chosen to accompany your child home. You thought she would add to your consequence, didn't you? Or that a reminder of her existence might dupe the moralists?"

"She's completely deranged, I tell you! She wouldn't add to anyone's consequence. She ought to be locked up!"

Cordelia stormed past the library door and caught sight of us. She paused, smiling. Her eyes glittered and there were two spots of color in her cheeks. To Molly she said, "Don't you have anything to do, you foolish girl?" When the maid had scurried away, she said to Isadora and me, "Well, Blythe's two rescuers. I'd like to know, Miss Morrow, why you were present this afternoon."

"I invited her, Cordelia," said Isadora quietly.

"It does you little good, Dora, to be apparently on intimate terms with a female artist. You ought to safeguard your reputation a bit better in future."

My face hot, I followed Isadora out of the library and into the galleried hall. "Don't pay her any attention, Ariel," said Isadora. "She's just angry that we reported to Drew what happened on Ocean Drive."

"I apologize, Miss Morrow, for my wife's remarks," said Drew stiffly. "The truth is that Isadora could not do better than to be seen with you." We watched him furiously fling open the front door and go out.

I went up to my room but did not remain there long. Feeling in the need of a brisk walk, I went down the back stairs and across the lawn to the cliffs. The water was a cobalt blue, rippled and calm as a lake. On a boulder sat a number of dark sleek cormorants, their necks long and slim. They must have had their fill of fish for they sat perfectly still, silhouettes against the lapis water. Manes of seaweed clung to the other rocks, the heavy tangled strands swirling in the current. Across the water a strip of farmland stretched out like a long finger. Far below the Cliff Walk the waves rolled in gently over the jagged shoreline.

"Miss Morrow, good afternoon."

Looking up, I saw Dr. Chandler making his way toward me. "How are you, Miss Morrow? I was hoping I would see you before long. How is your work progressing? I hope that Mrs. Rockwell will invite Olive and me to view your interiors."

I murmured some conventional reply and he regarded me closely. "Forgive me, Miss Morrow, I've no wish to be impertinent, but you look troubled. Is there anything that I can do?"

"Oh, it's not really my business," I said hesitatingly. "But this afternoon something—upsetting—occurred. About Blythe Rockwell."

"Will you tell me about it? I can see how distressed you are."

I was grateful for his concern. "Well, Miss Rockwell and I were on the Ten Mile Drive just behind Mrs. Rockwell and Blythe. Blythe became frightened and began to scream. She does this from time to time, as I daresay you know. Just out of the blue, she becomes terrified, and no one understands why. In any case there was rather a scene and Miss Rockwell and I were obliged to take Blythe back to Copper Beeches."

"And how is she now?" he asked gently.

"She was calm when we left her in the nursery with her governess."

"Poor little girl," he said, shaking his head. "Her illness two years ago left her much weakened in body, and, I'm afraid to say, in mind as well. Drew has taken her to the best doctors in Boston and New York, all specialists in their fields. They hope she will outgrow these fears of hers. But I'm afraid that what ails her goes deeper than the scarlet fever."

"What do you mean?"

"Are you aware, Miss Morrow, that she had a little brother? A sunny little fellow. He was born with a twisted leg. He and his sister were very close—she was very protective of him. They had scarlet fever at the same time."

"Yes, I did know, Dr. Chandler. Nathan, the little boy, died."

He nodded gravely. "It was a terrible tragedy. But he was never strong, always susceptible to colds and influenza."

"I understand that Blythe was different before her illness."

170

"Yes, she was highly spirited, healthy, strong." He shook his head. "You would scarcely recognize her today if you were unaware of all that had happened. But Nathan—I'm afraid that he did not have as much chance as she as surviving into adulthood. I have known both of them almost from birth. If it had not been the scarlet fever, I'm very much afraid it would have been something else. Blythe became ill first, rather surprisingly, and then Nathan as well. She was strong enough to withstand it, but it seemed to have sapped most of her strength. She has never been the same since."

"Do you think it was losing her little brother that has made her so fearful?"

"I now believe—and I'm certain the family does as well—that the cause must be attributed to more than a bout of scarlet fever. I wonder if she has ever accepted her brother's death. Some people are, shall we say, enfeebled by tragedy; they never fully recover their former health and energy. It's almost as if they waste away, in body or in mind, or both. We do not understand the human mind, although Dr. Freud in Vienna thinks he is making tremendous strides in that direction. I consider most of his theories outlandish and sensationalist. But it's quite possible that past events can trigger patterns of behavior. Lady Macbeth compulsively washing her hands after Duncan's death, for instance.

"But in Blythe's case, I don't pretend to understand or to be able to explain. I'm afraid it's just as possible that she may have inherited some . . . well, weakness of the mind which was not noticeable until now. It may get worse. In my own family—" he broke off, frowning. I realized that he was thinking of his daughter, Gwendolyn, who was certainly odd. "Sometimes, for some unknown reason, the mind begins gradually to deteriorate. Someone can be perfectly normal for years and then. . ."

171

"You think Blythe's condition may worsen?" I knew that Drew feared this too, and it haunted him.

"I hope not. Perhaps with the best care and attention from a loving father . . ." As he had tried to give Gwendolyn, I thought, again reading his thoughts. Yet how much had she responded? She seemed distant from both parents, remote from everyone. She would startle people with her unnerving remarks and then retreat into herself again.

We walked for a while in brooding silence and then he turned the subject again to my work. I answered his questions readily, eager to latch on to something else.

"Your father was one of the greatest artists this country has ever known, but then he would have been outstanding in any country. Few people are blessed with such gifts. I was once a talented surgeon, but when I married, my wife was not enthusiastic about my continuing to practice regularly. So I gave it up. But once I had the gift. I believe we must do everything in our power to encourage those of us who are blessed with particular talents. We must provide opportunities wherein those talents can be nurtured. In my youth I was sent to medical school by a very wealthy man. As far as the arts go, many of our friends here are not overly interested in them. But I've tried to make them see that their money can be put to good use by supporting the arts. Unfortunately, as you know, there is a current trend now to purchase only things European, that American literature and paintings, American music, are inferior, provincial, crude. I think that it is a serious mistake to think that way. We must extol what is fine in our society, just as we must be able to discern what is unworthy of our regard."

We walked for a while longer before turning about and retracing our steps, saying good-bye on the cliff near Copper Beeches. Dr. Chandler, in marrying his wife, had given up something he loved, the practice of medicine. It sounded as though he regretted it from

172

time to time. But it would not do for one of the members of The Four Hundred to work regularly in a New York hospital. He must have felt rather suffocated, as Drew did, by the demands of Society, and the limitations it placed on his life. And so he did what he could as a philanthropist to make up, perhaps, what he was not able to do any longer as a talented surgeon. I wondered whether he was often depressed by the shallowness of the lives and interests of the people around him, especially his own wife.

It was the next afternoon when I was working in Cordelia's sitting room that I heard sobs coming from her bedroom next door. Astonished, my brush poised in midair, I wondered whether she herself was crying. But then her voice came to me through the connecting door. "Why on earth did it have to be *him*, Maisie?" Her tone was heavy with scorn.

The sobs became indistinguishable murmurs.

"All right, it's done now. But you must decide what to do. You've made your bed, as they say."

"I know what to do," came the muffled response.

"Go to Europe, I suppose," said Cordelia.

"No, not that."

"Well, what then?"

There was an answer but I could not make it out, and then the two of them left the room.

Maisie could only have been one person — Maisie Leander, who had been alluded to in the recent issue of *Town Topics*, the wealthy widow who spent much of her time alone in the company of her coachman, Thomas Bateman.

When I had finished work for the day, I cleaned my brushes and left the picture to dry. Changing out of my work clothes and smock, I put on my apple green gown and went to the nursery. I had not seen Blythe since the carriage ride yesterday, and I wanted to see how she did.

But I did not reach the nursery. As I passed a door

along the corridor, I noticed it was ajar. Faintly I heard the sound of singing. I pushed open the door, curious.

Blythe was sitting in a small rocking chair. It was she who was singing. Her back was to me.

Hush a bye, hush a bye,
Go to sleep, little baby,
When you awake you will have cake,
And all the pretty little horses.
Black and bay, dapple and gray,
Coach and six and little horses.
Hush a bye, don't you cry,
Go to sleep, little baby.
When you awake you will have cake,
And all the pretty little horses.

As she sang, I glanced about the room. It was a child's room, or at least the furniture that was in it had belonged to a child. The furnishings were not arranged, but had obviously been taken from another room and put there. There was a child's bed, bare of sheets and pillow, a dresser painted with toy soldiers, a toy chest, a small white table and chair, also decorated with toy soldiers, and a cupboard. Pushed into a corner was a rocking horse, its paint still bright, its dark eye staring across the room. The shelves on the cupboard were filled with toys — stuffed animals, a jack-in-the-box, and a line of tin soldiers. One had fallen over and lay toppled on its side, forever halting the progress of those behind it. The air in the room was close, the dust thick.

These must have been all be Nathan's things, and they had been removed from the nursery and stored in here after his death. I wondered how often Blythe was permitted to come in here. She was still singing in a reedy little voice, rocking back and forth in the rocking chair.

"Blythe?" I said softly, not wishing to alarm her.

She jerked in the rocking chair and swiftly looked around at me.

"Why don't you come with me, Blythe, and we'll look for Miss Simmons?"

She shook her head, her dusky curls shielding her face.

"That was a lovely lullaby you were singing."

Still no response.

"Come along, darling, we'll go back to the nursery." I felt uneasy in this room with all its unused furnishings just stashed away; it could not be healthy for the child to sit here and brood.

Reaching for her hand, I pulled her gently from the chair. And then she began to shout.

"Stop it! Leave me alone! Go away! "She twisted out of my grasp and fled from the room while I followed, chagrined.

Miss Simmons came out into the hallway just as Blythe reached the nursery door. "What is it, Blythe? Where have you been?"

"I found her in the room down the hall—I'm certain you know the one I mean," I said. "When I tried to get her to come out, she got angry."

"What are you doing here, Miss Morrow?" Miss Simmons cried, her arms folding about Blythe. "You have no business on this corridor at all, snooping and prying."

"I merely came to see how Blythe was," I said stiffly.

"Well, she *was* fine. In fact, she's been sweet and quiet all day. But now you've come and upset her— again."

"I found her in that room, Miss Simmons. Do you allow her to go there often? It can't be good for her."

"Blythe is *my* concern, Miss Morrow. Just because you interfered the other night—just because you were invited to ride with Miss Rockwell—you assume you have free run of the house. Well, you have no right to come to this wing. Why don't you go back to your

175

painting, to what you were hired to do? You may be asked to dine with the family, but you are not welcome in my nursery! I won't have Blythe upset by you, do I make myself clear?"

"It was only when I tried to make her leave the room that she became upset. You make it sound as though I am persecuting the child!"

"Please go now, Miss Morrow. I would not like to complain to Mr. Rockwell about you."

You would like nothing better, I thought, and you will undoubtedly do so at the first opportunity. But I said nothing. Miss Simmons was grimly triumphant that I had inadvertently caused another of Blythe's tantrums. And nothing would have pleased her more than for Drew to come along and see for himself the havoc I had created.

I realized that she was extremely resentful of my standing in the household, that I took most of my meals with the family, that I had accompanied Isadora on several outings, that Drew had clearly been grateful to me the night I had soothed Blythe and sent her to sleep, something Miss Simmons had never been able to do.

She had no real affection for the child, but made herself seem indispensable to Blythe by playing on her fears, even encouraging her tantrums as she was doing now, and then making a big show of calming the little girl. Rather than providing a tranquil, comforting atmosphere for the child, I suspected that she kept her on edge and fearful. Whether this was intentional or not, I could not tell. Miss Simmons loved Drew with a sick, pent-up sort of love, and she used Blythe to be near him. One way, I guessed, was by turning down the light very low in the little girl's room from time to time, knowing she would wake and be frightened, and he was sure to come if he heard his daughter's cries. And then he would see Miss Simmons in her ruffled nightdress, her pale hair falling about her shoulders . . .

Without another word, I turned and left the nursery

wing, stopping only to close the door of the room where Nathan's furnishings were stored. But despite my suspicions concerning Miss Simmons, I could not go to Drew and say, "I don't believe Miss Simmons is the right governess for Blythe. It's just a feeling I have . . ." Blythe even seemed fond of her; I might do more harm than good. Neither could I say to him, "Why don't you give these things away, get rid of them?" Who was I to interfere in these peoples' lives? Before long I would leave Copper Beeches and doubtless see none of them again. And I was filled with desolation at the thought.

That evening Aunt Hermione, Isadora, and I dined alone. Weary and tense, I said little. As soon as I was able I left the dining room, and took a shawl from my room. The stained glass window of Dawn was dull and murky.

The twilight was deepening; a smoky lavender light drifted over the lawn and the grass was damp with dew. Faint glimmers of stars pricked the sky like tiny pins. The white roses in the arbor looked silver-violet in the dusk; their heady sweetness floated on the air.

Rather aimlessly I wandered across the lawn until I found myself nearing the summerhouse, the line of blue spruces like sentinels along its wall. And I heard muffled voices, laughter, as I drew close. So again Cordelia was entertaining a male guest in the summerhouse — and this time she had not waited for Drew to leave town.

Abruptly I moved away and hurried across the lawn in the opposite direction. Night had almost fallen, the stars brightening in the plum-blue sky. Behind me the house was a bulky dark mass, its tower and turret fading into the surrounding gloom.

The group of weeping beeches loomed ahead, black shaggy monsters rising from the earth. Tonight there were no whispers. The Chinese Moongate glowed eerily, its pale stone shape just visible. Standing by it, I glanced over at Oaklawn, the Chandlers' home. The first and second floors were well lit, but the steeplelike turret rooms were dark.

Just then I heard a horse's hooves coming down the side street which divided the two estates. I could not see who the rider was until he had climbed down off his horse and pushed open the wrought-iron gate.

"What are you doing out here, Miss Morrow?" asked Drew Rockwell roughly.

"I — I merely wanted some fresh air. Do you have any objection to my walking about the grounds?" I asked, dismayed.

"Of course not." His voice was still curt. "I'll walk with you back to the house."

"Isadora tells me that if you make a wish under the Moongate, it will come true." I laughed nervously, happening to glance up at one of the dark windows of Oaklawn. There was a pale form that had not been there before, but it was gone as soon as I had noticed it. Gwendolyn Chandler, I thought, and I was conscious of a nameless misgiving, almost a dread. It was the thought of being watched by those pale green eyes. . . .

"Wishing for things is not the way to attain them," he said, a strange hard note in his voice. "Surely your experience of life has taught you that."

I did not understand what he meant; I had only spoken a foolish thought aloud. At least we had not met near the summerhouse, I thought, relieved. From here no voices could be heard, no laughter. Still I found myself glancing across the lawn. I could just barely make out the glow of the light in the cottage from between the spruce trees.

"What is it, Miss Morrow? Has my wife shocked you with her use for the summerhouse?" he said sardonically.

I caught my breath. "You knew that she was — ?"

"Of course I knew."

"But . . ."

"You don't understand, do you, Miss Morrow? You

178

don't understand why I don't sue my wife for divorce when she is obligingly providing me with grounds."

We had stopped walking and were standing close, looking at one another. His face was inscrutable in the darkness. Behind us the horse snorted once.

"Blythe?" I asked softly.

"Precisely, Miss Morrow. With your usual perception you have grasped the situation exactly. If I were to name my wife in court as an adulteress, and show proof of her behavior, it would be . . . unpleasant, to say the least. Not that I care for her or for myself. But I don't want Blythe touched by scandal." He paused, and when he spoke again the harsh irony was gone from his voice. "She has already endured—a great deal."

"I see."

Abruptly he began striding away and I hurried to catch up with him. "How is your work progressing?" he asked. "You must be nearly finished by now." His voice was cool, impersonal.

"Yes," I said, biting my lip. Thank goodness for the velvety darkness separating us. For he could not see my stricken face. As I could not see his.

We had reached the terrace. "Well, I will be certain to give you an excellent recommendation, Miss Morrow. Good night."

Watching him, or rather hearing him, ride off toward the stables, I realized that there was only one reason for the brutal desolation I was feeling.

I had fallen in love with Drew Rockwell.

It was about noon on the following day. I had been working feverishly all morning, possessed with only one thought: to finish my work and leave Newport as soon as I was able. Returning to my room, I took off my smock and washed my hands. Glancing about the room, I noticed an envelope lying on the carpet by the door. I had not noticed it earlier as I had been carrying my painting supplies, and they had blocked my view of the floor as I entered the room.

There was no name written or printed on the envelope. I picked it up and drew out the letter inside. The print was in large capital letters.

A WOMAN HIRED TO PAINT SHOULD DO HER WORK AND NOT GO OUT AT NIGHT TO MEET HER MASTER.

That was all. Staring down at it, I wanted to laugh. It was so absurd. Who in the world had written it and slipped it under my door this morning while I worked? Someone, I supposed, who had noticed me returning to the house with Drew. One of the staff, perhaps. The butler? No, surely this sort of thing was beneath Merriman's dignity. One of the maids or menservants? I did not think so; it was written, I thought, by an educated person. Almost anyone might have seen us; we had not attempted to conceal our movements. Our meeting last night had been perfectly innocent.

What about Gideon? It was likely the sort of thing he would do and take amusement in. He doubtless found such actions diverting. And he resented me, I was certain, for not returning his interest, and for rebuffing him in no uncertain terms. If he happened to see Drew and me outside at night, he would enjoy concocting an ulterior motive, an assignation. Even if he did not believe it of us, he would take pleasure from the accusation.

I could not believe that either Aunt Hermione or Isadora would write a poison-pen letter. And Cordelia would not use this method to express her malice. She would choose something melodramatic, humiliating, were she to suspect her husband and I were meeting in secret. If she cared at all, that is. Besides, she had been fully occupied last night in the summerhouse.

Who else could it have been besides Gideon? Suddenly I thought of Miss Simmons. She might be *capable* of writing an ugly note, but had she actually done it?

Her room, and Blythe's, were on the front side of the house. From her window she could not see the back lawn or the terrace. I supposed that she might have been somewhere else and seen us. But I still considered Gideon the likeliest suspect.

No matter who had written it and pushed it under my door, I would ignore it. It was sly and cowardly; I would not let on to anyone that it had disturbed or dismayed me.

That night Drew was absent at dinner, but Cordelia was there and in no pleasant temper. She found fault with every dish and tongue-lashed the serving maid so severely for spilling a few drops of cream sauce on the tablecloth that the girl left the room in tears.

"Stupid girl," she said scornfully. "These footstools haven't the least idea how to be good servants."

"Don't use that word, Cordelia," said Aunt Hermione.

"Why not? Don't you find it amusing? It's what Harry Lehr calls the Newporters. 'Our footstools.' After Louis XIV, you know." She tittered.

"America was deliberately not established on royalty and nobility, Cordelia. I wish you and your friends would realize that. You ought to be ashamed of speaking to that poor girl the way you did."

"Why, Aunt Hermione! I had no idea you were so puritanical. Miss Morrow, I should like to know how many interiors you have left to paint."

"Just two, Mrs. Rockwell. Miss Rockwell's bedroom and the Turkish sitting room."

"What about my bedroom, Miss Morrow?" asked Gideon outrageously. "Aren't you going to paint that? Or Drew's either?"

I flushed rosily and Cordelia snapped, "Oh, hush, Gideon. Sometimes you are too foolish for words."

But Gideon was not at all abashed. He was regarding me with amusement, and I felt more certain than ever that it was he who had written the poison-pen letter. He must have spotted me walking with Drew and thought it would be humorous to accuse me of meeting him by design. Whether he believed we had met by accident or intent was not the point; his enjoyment was in the execution and delivery of the letter, and in his speculation of my reaction.

And so, when, an hour or so later, I heard someone whistling a popular tune, and looked out the window to see Gideon standing on the terrace, I was overcome with annoyance and went down to him.

"Why, Miss Morrow," he said as I closed the French door behind me. "What a pleasant surprise." Grinning, he took his cigar from his mouth. "And just when I was thinking about you."

"I want to know, Mr. Lawrence, whether you wrote a foolish note to me this morning and left it in my room."

"A note? You mean an anonymous letter? Don't tell me you actually received one! What did it say?" His voice was lively with amused interest. I could not read his expression in the darkness.

"That's none of your concern," I said coldly. "It was personal — and rather rude. And wrong in its implication. If you wrote it, then you know very well what it said. I ask you again, did you write it?"

"It seems to have distressed you, Miss Morrow. What could it be about, I wonder?" The tip of his cigar glowed red. "What subject would do that? Your talent, perhaps, your profession? But no, you said it was personal. Personal and rude. And something obviously close to your heart." He paused. "Could it have been about . . . Drew?"

"So you did write it," I said angrily.

"I did not say that, Miss Morrow. But you've told me what I wished to know." He chuckled.

Whirling around, I moved toward the French doors, but he caught my arm and pulled me back to the edge of the terrace.

"Let me go," I said between clenched teeth.

"You came out here to talk to me, to accuse me of something. So say what you have to say." He dropped the cigar.

"Let me go. I can't talk seriously to you. You are only good for saying spiteful things and writing spiteful notes."

"Whoever wrote this note to you struck a very raw nerve. Do you still have it? I'd like to read it."

"You know very well what it said. I'm not fooled by you. Now let me go or I'll call Isadora or your sister."

"They've gone out. Party at Mrs. Kernochen's."

"One of the servants then."

"They're belowstairs. Can't hear you. Not that any of them would cross me if they did. Do you think I really don't know what was in that letter? Not that I'm admitting anything, mind you. But it was about you and Drew, that much is clear."

He drew me closer to him. I was trembling with rage. "I'll scream my head off!" I cried.

Suddenly his hand was about my throat, squeezing it. "You make a sound and I'll throttle you senseless. If you're a good girl, no one has to know. But if you make trouble for me, I'll tell everyone it was you who asked me to meet you out here. Whom do you think people will believe—a female artist, or a gentleman?"

"You're no gentleman!" I gasped. His hand came off my throat and covered my mouth as he dragged me across the dark lawn.

"If Drew, then why not me? Surely he hasn't a monopoly on your favors," Gideon said in my ear.

In response I kicked him as hard as I could. Swearing, his grip loosened for an instant and I pulled away and began to run across the lawn. But he was behind me quickly and reached out, grabbing me, so that I lost my balance and fell forward on the grass. Before I could get up again, he was on top of me, his hand fumbling at my bodice, his teeth on my neck. I cried out in pain, struggling, and his hand went round my throat again.

"Gideon!"

I shuddered in relief at the sound of that voice. Gideon was pulled off of me; shakily I sat up, covering my face with my hands.

"It wasn't what you think, Drew," said Gideon. "She — she asked me to meet her here tonight. I couldn't be so ungallant as to refuse. And we both know what she must be." He tried to laugh with some of his old bravado.

I heard a smack followed by a groan and a thud. I looked up to see Gideon sprawling on the grass.

"You repeat that and I won't answer for the consequences," said Drew savagely. "Now get out of here."

Slowly Gideon got to his feet, rubbing his jaw. "So that's the way the wind blows. I'm not good enough for the lovely Miss Morrow, eh? It has to be the master."

Drew made another move toward Gideon, but I said, "Don't. Let him go."

Gideon turned and walked away, back to the house. Unsteadily I rose to my feet. We heard the sound of the French doors closing.

"Did he hurt you, Miss Morrow?" asked Drew, his voice curiously remote.

"I — I'm all right," I replied shakily.

"I don't think he'll trouble you again."

"No. Thank you, Mr. Rockwell, for coming by when you did and . . ."

Still he did not look at me. It was an oddly formal conversation, following so closely on an emotional scene. I wanted desperately to get back to my room, to flee this cold, detached stranger. There was tension in every muscle of his hard broad frame; his profile was stony against the night sky.

"Good night," I murmured brokenly.

Abruptly he turned, and his gaze was neither cold nor detached. He drew in a sharp quick breath, his eyes burning into mine. And then suddenly the rigidity left

184

him. He reached out and I was in his arms, crushed against him, his head bent, his mouth bruising mine, his fingers entangled in my tumbled hair. My lips parted under the exquisite pressure; the taste and feel of him flooded my senses. I could scarcely breathe, and his breathing was ragged as well. I clung to him, his heart thundering against mine, my body responding to the desperate passion in him, and prompting it to inflame even further.

But though there was a fierce delight, a wild joy, in our embrace, I found it a torment as well. And somehow there were tears in my eyes. For there could be no happy ending; what we shared could only be stolen. When I finally drew away, he did not detain me, and when I hurried to the house, he did not call me back.

Chapter Ten

The following morning I was awakened by a rapping on my door. I had spent a restless exhausting night in a misery of longing and despair, and I had not fallen asleep until nearly dawn.

"Who is it?" I asked groggily, sitting up in bed.

"Nancy, Miss Morrow."

"Come in, Nancy," I called out, wondering what it was she wanted; the maids at Copper Beeches did not wait on me as a rule.

She opened the door and gazed across at me with wide expectant eyes. She looked feverish. "I — I thought you'd like to know, miss. That is, none of the family is up yet except Mr. Rockwell . . ."

"What, Nancy?"

She came closer to the bed, her voice eager. "It's outside, Miss Morrow. On the Cliff Walk."

"What is, Nancy?" I asked impatiently. "What are you talking about?"

"If you go to the window, you might be able to see," she said excitedly moving over herself and drawing the lace curtain aside. "There's a big crowd there already."

Swiftly I got out of bed and went over to the window, looking over her shoulder. "What is it? Why is the crowd there, Nancy? Has something happened?" I felt a cold prickle of fear.

"It's a body, miss. A lady, I think. She went over the cliff. They're bringing her up now. One of the grooms came to the kitchen and told us."

"And you wanted to tell someone," I said faintly. "Who is it?"

"I don't know yet, Miss Morrow. The groom, Peter, could not get close enough to see."

"Is — is she dead?"

"After a fall like that? She must be all broken. I'd say the world's seen the last of her."

I straightened abruptly. "Well, you've told me. You can leave me to dress now."

"Yes, Miss Morrow. I just thought you'd want to know." Did her eyes hold a knowing gleam, or was it my fancy? Why had she rushed up here to tell me? Was it merely because I was another employee like herself and she would not have dared wake up any of the family? She had been bursting with the news. I was too afraid to ask her whether she had a notion who the dead woman was.

Could it be . . . ? But no, that wasn't possible. It couldn't be Cordelia's body which lay broken and battered on those jagged rocks far below the Cliff Walk. Shuddering, I wrapped my arms about myself. Last night Drew had gripped me to him hungrily, and this morning a woman was dead from a fall from the cliff near Copper Beeches . . .

I had to know. Peering out the window, I could just see the group of spectators gathered above the faint strip of gray which was the water. But the scene was too far in the distance for me to make out any details, any activity.

Once dressed, I hastened down the stairs and out the side door. Who could the poor woman be, I thought, my heart hammering? Who had been killed by a fall from that cliff? Nancy was right — to survive that fall would take a miracle.

Who was it, who was it, whispered the weeping beeches as I approached them. It was then that I heard the piano music. At first I paid it no mind, so bent was I

187

on learning the identity of the woman. But as I passed the Moongate I heard it loudly and clearly. With a jolt of stunned horror I recognized the piece being played, *Danse Macabre,* the Dance of Death by Saint-Saëns. Why in heaven's name had Gwendolyn Chandler chosen to play *that?* The eerie music was wild, expressive, rollicking. Clapping my hands over my ears, I raced away to the top of the cliff.

The crowd was strangely silent. It was an odd mixture of servants in formal livery, townspeople, and a few members of the summer colony, not looking their best in the gray light of the early morning. I hurried along the outskirts of the crowd gathered on the graveled path until I found a place where I could see what was happening below.

When I reached an area where the cliff jutted out, I paused on the bluff and looked down at a nightmarish scene. The drop was particularly high, the cliffside sheer rock all the way down with nothing to have broken her fall, no sloping earth with bushes to cushion it. Below were outcroppings of large boulders whose very size and sharp edges made me feel faint. The water was a poisonous pale green at the shoreline, an evil unnatural color.

There were policemen below, waving and shouting. They had climbed down a long rope ladder which was fastened to a stone balustrade.

"Who is it?" asked a woman. "Do they know yet?"

The man beside her shrugged. "One o' *them,* I guess."

"Well, she'll have a better trip up than she did down," said the woman and gave a muffled snigger.

I moved away from them, feeling ill. Whose body was it? It had been wrapped in a red blanket. The red color was jarring against the gray granite rocks.

"Who is it? Does anyone know yet?" asked a late-comer.

"A lady from one of the houses, I heard."

"No! A lady?"

My blood ran slow and thick, my eyes were riveted on

that long stiff form in the red blanket. People about me watched the scene with shock and a gloating interest. I did not want to be among them. But I could not return to the house until I knew.

"Look, they're bringing her up now."

The men below had fastened a rope around the body in the blanket, and two policemen at the top of the cliff were raising it slowly. At one point the red bundle knocked against the sheer side of the cliff with a sickening thud; a ripple of horror moved over the crowd, and several women covered their faces with their hands.

"Who is it?" someone asked again, the same question which reverberated frantically in my own mind. I held my breath as the red bundle reached the top of the cliff and the two policemen gripped it, lowering it to the ground. Eagerly the crowd edged closer.

"All right, all right, get back, all of you," growled the policeman before he bent down on one knee and began to untie the rope from about the long stiff form.

But when the policeman began to draw aside the blanket, I could not watch. Turning away, I looked out across the sluggish bayberry water. Sullen, dingy clouds were suspended above it. My nails dug into the palms of my hands.

Then suddenly a murmur went through the crowd, and another and another, as the identity of the woman was passed along.

"It's that Mrs. Leander."

"Mrs. Leander, of Rosehips."

"She lives down Narragansett."

"Where?"

"In that brick mansion with the high wall around it."

"She's a widow."

"Do you think she jumped?"

"Jumped? No! She must have been out walking and fell over."

"Who'd be out walking this path in the dark?" The voice was scornful.

189

Mrs. Leander. Maisie Leander, Cordelia's friend. Only today she was not wearing her veil; her face was revealed for all to see the blank gaze, the bruised and cut cheek.

I swayed, feeling my knees give way.

"Miss Morrow, are you all right?" A steadying arm was placed about my shoulders. I looked gratefully up into Dr. Chandler's concerned face.

"You shouldn't be out here, Miss Morrow. This is no sight for you. I just came to see if I could be of any help, but unfortunately there is nothing I can do. Come, I'll take you to the house. You'll be better after a cup of tea. Or perhaps some brandy. Come along, my dear."

I could not answer him. He continued to speak soothingly as he led me away from the Cliff Walk. I scarcely knew what I was doing, but when I realized that we were nearing an ocher-colored stone house with a Dutch curved roof rather than Copper Beeches, I paused. Vaguely I recalled the chilling music I had heard. But now the piano was silent.

"It's all right, Miss Morrow. This is Oaklawn, my house. I'm going to take you inside and give you some tea. And you are going to drink it, and the shock will lessen. Then, when I am convinced you are thoroughly recovered, I will take you back to Copper Beeches. Trust me, Miss Morrow. I was once a very fine doctor."

"You are — very kind," I murmured.

"Nonsense. Now, careful. There are three steps here. That's right."

We went inside the house and down a long hall flanked with Italian dower chests, heavily carved. Then we entered a drawing room with French furniture upholstered in red brocade. The shade reminded me of the swaying bundle moving up the side of the cliff, and I shuddered.

"What is it, Prescott?" Olive Chandler rose from her seat, her eyes narrowed in the full roundness of her face.

"Miss Morrow has suffered a bad shock just now, my dear," said Dr. Chandler, easing me into a chair. "I'm go-

190

ing to ring for a pot of strong tea."

"What shock? Where were you?" Her voice was sharp, suspicious.

"I'm afraid there's been a tragic accident, Olive." He yanked the bellpull, and when the maid came, ordered tea. The maid glanced at me curiously.

"Mrs. Leander took a fall from the cliff sometime last night or early this morning. She is dead, Olive," he said quietly.

Olive's pudgy hand flew to her throat. She had paled under the powder and I noticed the magnificent jeweled rings she wore.

"How — how could it have happened?" I asked weakly.

Dr. Chandler shook his head, his usual jaunty manner gone. "The police will have to determine that, I suppose."

"That woman — she was likely going to meet someone last night. Why else be on the Cliff Walk in the dark? You know what everyone was saying of her." The shock had worn off; now Olive Chandler had no pity for the dead Maisie Leander.

"My dear, please. She must have been very troubled. Ah, here is the tea. Now you sip this, Miss Morrow. You will begin to feel better."

"People were talking about her and that coachman of hers," continued Olive harshly. "I, for one, never liked her and thought it was all you could expect."

"She had been left alone to raise those children," Dr. Chandler replied, "perhaps she was lonely. Those poor children . . . but as I remember they have relatives who will take them in."

I stood up, anxious to leave, to get away from Olive Chandler's malice. "Well, I should be going now. I'm much better. I've taken enough of your time."

"Wait, Miss Morrow. Have another cup of tea. You still are very pale."

"No, really, I'm better now. Not nearly so unsteady. Besides, I have work to do. I must get back."

"Very well. I'll take you home in the carriage."

"Oh, there's no need, Dr. Chandler. It's just a few steps to the grounds of Copper Beeches."

"I insist. You have had a shock, Miss Morrow, and I'm going to assure myself that you get there safely. Drew would do the same for someone in my household."

I smiled feebly, having neither the strength nor the inclination to protest further. "Good day, Mrs. Chandler."

She nodded coldly to me. "Please come straight back, Prescott. You know we are to take luncheon at Vernon Court."

"Yes, I remember." He sighed.

In the carriage he said, "Please try not to dwell on what you saw earlier, Miss Morrow. These tragedies happen sometimes in life, as you know from your own experience."

He was referring to my father's death; numbly I nodded. When the carriage stopped in front of Copper Beeches, he helped me down from the carriage.

"I'm very grateful to you, Dr. Chandler, for your kindness and solicitude. I'm sorry to have been such a nuisance."

"Not at all, Miss Morrow. You should not have gone down to the Cliff Walk — the news would have reached everyone soon enough."

"Yes, I know," I said dully.

I could not tell him that I could not have waited patiently in my room until Nancy learned the identity of the dead woman and told me; I could not admit that I had had to discover for myself, as soon as possible, who she was.

If she were Cordelia Rockwell . . .

For the sharp sensation I had felt when I learned she had been Maisie Leander was relief, and that relief had made me giddy, dazed. In those minutes following the identification of the poor crumpled creature in the red blanket, I had not been myself. But not precisely for the reason that Dr. Chandler assumed.

Had I actually believed that it was Cordelia who,

192

wrapped in the red blanket, had thudded against the sheer ochre cliff? And had I actually feared that someone had sent her purposely to her death?

Not just someone. Drew. I relived his powerful embrace, our desperate yearning for one another. Suddenly I was ashamed of my wild fears and speculations. How could I have ever considered that Drew had murdered Cordelia—for me? I must have been mad. And what had we shared last night? A kiss . . . nothing more. For all I knew it was not his first outside the bonds of matrimony. How egotistical I had been, to suppose that he might kill his wife just because he had reached out to me and I had gone to him willingly. I was a fool. It was likely that last night had meant little to him, no more than it would mean to Gideon. Most men considered me an easy target for amorous advances, simply because of my work. A female artist had little or no reputation. If Gideon could desire me, why not Drew? It was just that his methods were different.

To distract myself from the pain I was feeling, I tried to think things out. The dead woman was Maisie Leander, Cordelia's friend. The one who had visited Cordelia, heavily veiled, on the day *Town Topics* had come out. There had been some foolishness about her in "Saunterings" implying that she was too fond of her coachman. Olive Chandler had smugly referred to the same gossip. Maisie Leander had obviously been very distressed over the reference to her in that malicious column. But surely she wouldn't have committed suicide over it.

Suicide. Now why had that idea struck my mind? She must have merely stumbled and fallen as she walked too closely to the edge of the cliff. If she had been walking in the dark it would have been an easy thing to happen, the graveled path veering away from her without her realizing it. But why on earth had she engaged in such a hazard, walking the Cliff Walk at night?

Isadora and Gideon were in the dining room having breakfast. I didn't feel in the least like food, but I wanted

193

a cup of coffee. Perhaps it would help dispel the vagueness, the dazed state I was still in.

"Ariel, hello. I thought I heard someone come in the front door. Was it you?" asked Isadora.

I nodded, careful to ignore Gideon. "Dr. Chandler drove me here in his carriage."

"Dr. Chandler! Where on earth were you?"

With fingers that still trembled slightly, I poured coffee and cream into one of the blue and white Chinese cups. "You haven't heard? Nancy woke me up to tell me." My voice was dry.

"You mean about Maisie Leander throwing herself over the cliff?" asked Gideon carelessly.

"Gideon — of all the inhuman — ! Yes, we heard about it. You — you didn't go out there!"

I nodded. "It was . . . horrible. People standing around like eager ghouls. And I was one of them." I shivered.

"I just don't understand it. How could she have fallen? What on earth was she doing out there?"

"Dora, it was no accident, I'm convinced of that. No sane person walks by the cliffs at night when there is no moon. It's lunacy," said Gideon.

"What's this I hear about that poor woman?" Aunt Hermione ambled into the room, her stays creaking. This time her white hair was unadorned, merely pinned in a simple topknot. "I never thought that poor woman had much sense — few of Cordelia's friends do, for that matter — but this . . ." She shook her head.

"May I get you something, Aunt?" asked Isadora.

"No, I've had my breakfast, child. I had the news about Mrs. Leander over tea and toast a little while ago. Nancy couldn't wait until I'd eaten to tell me."

"She woke me with the news," I said. So it had merely been an overwhelmingly eagerness to share the groom's story with anyone which had sent her directly to me. I had feared she had singled me out for entirely another reason.

194

"Well, I daresay the girl has few excitements," said Aunt Hermione tolerantly. "Still, this is one we could all have done without."

"You know that there was gossip about her," said Isadora uneasily. "Do you think there could be any connection?"

"I don't see how a bit of drivel in a scandal sheet could have any bearing on this tragic accident."

"But that's just it, Aunt," said Gideon eagerly. "It may not have been an accident."

"What do you mean?"

"I mean, dearest Aunt, the woman could have killed herself," he said coolly, his eyebrows raised.

Aunt Hermione stared at him. Then she said abruptly, "No. I don't believe it. Over that paltry gossip? The idea's absurd. She may have wanted to leave town until it blew over, but kill herself? Ridiculous."

"There is another possibility." It was apparent that Gideon was enjoying himself; his disgrace last night was far from his mind. He paused expectantly.

"Oh, do tell us, Gideon," said Isadora. "You know you're just dying to."

He glanced at each of us in turn. "She might have been pushed."

"If that isn't just like you, to think of the most horrid thing!" declared Isadora disgustedly.

He shrugged. "Things like that happen all the time, Dora. If you don't believe that, you're a fool."

"But not in Newport! Not practically at our back door!"

"Well, who pushed her then?" asked Aunt Hermione, frowning.

"Damned if I know. Her coachman, perhaps?" He chuckled. "Perhaps he didn't like his good name being bandied about with hers."

"Oh, you're determined to make a joke of everything," said Isadora. "Why should he of all people want to kill her, if the gossip about them was true?"

195

"How should I know? I wasn't in the silly woman's confidence."

"Perhaps someone was," said Aunt Hermione meaningfully.

Isadora's head jerked up. "Do you think Cordelia knows anything?"

I stared down into my coffee cup. I had just recalled something. The muffled sobs coming from Cordelia's bedroom. Cordelia's scornful voice telling her that now that she had made her bed; she must lie in it. Had Maisie Leander decided on suicide as an end to her troubles, whatever they were? It had to be more than just that there was ugly gossip about her. Cordelia had suggested she go to Europe — was that to escape whatever predicament she was in? Was it to get away from her lover, the coachman? Thomas Bateman, his name was. I remembered the maids mentioning him.

Then there came the sound of heels clicking in the hall, and in came Cordelia herself in a morning gown of periwinkle blue. Her face was pale, but her eyes were overbright.

"Well, what are you all staring at?" she snapped. "Can't I come down to breakfast once in a while?"

"We were wondering whether you'd heard about Mrs. Leander," said Isadora quietly.

"Get me some coffee, Gideon. Yes, I've heard."

"Do you think she fell or . . . ?"

Cordelia regarded her sister-in-law cynically. "No, child, I don't think she fell."

"Then—"

"She was a fool and a weakling. So she took the easy way out." Cordelia's tone was damning.

"Remind me never to become your friend, Cordelia," said Aunt Hermione.

Cordelia's color rose. "You sound just like Drew. He came and broke the news to me. I suppose he expected me to break down and sob and wring my hands. Well, I have no use for people who won't help themselves.

196

Maisie was like that. She let herself get into trouble, and then she let it destroy her."

"What are you talking about, Cordelia?" Drew stood in the doorway, his black brows drawn together. Hastily I looked away.

"Oh, it will all come out anyway. She was going to have a child—a servant's child! I told her to go off somewhere and discreetly have it with no one the wiser. But she had other ideas. I didn't know that this was one of those ideas."

"So she killed herself rather than face having the child," said Aunt Hermione. "Poor woman."

Cordelia stood up. "Well, don't let me inhibit your period of mourning. But I have a full day ahead." She swept past Drew.

"Inhuman. She has no more feelings than a cat. It's exactly the way she was over little—" Aunt Hermione broke off, glancing at Drew's forbidding face.

"Not even death must be allowed to interfere with the business of leisure," said Drew, and he was gone on those words.

But the business of leisure was certainly vitalized by the news of Maisie Leander's death and the possible reasons behind it. Cordelia did not have to admit what she knew about Maisie's condition because the police questioned her personal maid who had observed certain signs for herself. And on the strength of her testimony, and that of Dr. Chandler, who had examined the dead woman, a verdict of suicide while of distraught mind was brought at the inquest. Thomas Bateman, the coachman, was interrogated, but he denied knowledge of her pregnancy. Mrs. Leander's character was dragged through the mud in the newspapers, and her unfortunate intimate association with one of her servants gloated over. Every domestic had his or her story to relate; people came forth who claimed they had seen Mrs. Leander in the company of her coachman on all sorts of occasions. However, as the judge pointed out dryly, every lady in Newport was seen in the company of her coachman every day, and so these enthusiastic witnesses were given short shrift.

Naturally I did not attend the inquest, but Gideon did, and it was all in the newspapers the following day. I felt sickened at the way the woman's private affairs were made a public sensation. "Well, she brought it on herself, taking that way out," said Cordelia scornfully.

Cordelia continued her busy social life. One day I happened to glance out the window and I saw a man handing her down from a carriage. He was good-looking in a florid, fleshy sort of way; I watched as he lifted her hand to his lips. Was this the man she had been meeting in the summerhouse? And then she said something, and I heard him laugh, and I realized that it was.

On another occasion I was passing the drawing room when I noticed them sitting together inside, talking. Still, I thought cynically, there was little chance of Cordelia herself being involved in a scandal when the man dropped by during the day. Cordelia was not one to risk gossip as her friend Maisie had.

As I was going up the oak paneled staircase, I met Drew coming down. I had not seen him alone since the night he had come upon Gideon and me; I had gone out of my way to avoid him. Coloring, I would have passed him without a word had he not taken my arm.

"Come out with me, Ariel," he said softly.

"Out . . . ?"

"Yes, now. We'll go for a drive." I noticed he was dressed for riding in a brown coat, buff-colored trousers, and brown boots.

I wondered whether he were asking me because his wife was entertaining a male guest in the drawing room. Dismayed and uncertain, I did not know what to say.

"This has nothing whatsoever to do with Cordelia," he said roughly. "I want to be with you." Then, ruefully, "You can trust me, you know."

Flushing, I looked up at him. "All right. I'd like to go

198

for a drive. I'll just get my hat."

I would have liked to have changed my work clothes for a more becoming gown, but I sensed he was impatient to leave the house. Soon we were riding down Bellevue Avenue in a small open carriage. I was conscious of the curious glances leveled at us by women in grand glossy vehicles, but Drew gave no sign that he was aware of their interest. He drove himself, and I sat beside him in the box. When we turned down Bath Road, I was relieved to get away from the more fashionable part of town. Drew expertly threaded us through the throngs of vehicles headed to Easton's Beach, and after that the road became practically deserted. On one side was the water, on the other, seas of bulrushes, tall and purple-tipped. The breeze was fresh and strong, the ocean's waves peaking and foaming.

Gradually I began to relax, feeling the distress and tension of the past week drain from me. For several miles we drove along the curving shoreline. Then Drew stopped the carriage. "Let's walk a while," he said. He had not spoken to me since leaving the house.

We found a path through a field of dense purple-crowned thistles, delicately fashioned Queen Anne's Lace and blooming rosehips fluttering in the breeze. In the distance we glimpsed the bright blue water. Swallows flew overhead, whole flocks of them moving swiftly across the sky. White moths floated in and out of thickets, and crickets hummed and chirped in secret places. Just ahead a cotton-tailed rabbit hopped out of the hedgerow, across the path, disappearing into the green on the other side. As we penetrated this remote spot, it became impossible to see over the sides of the bank. We were secluded in the high thickets of the field.

But then we rounded a bend and ahead was the blue water tipped with white. The black sleek cormorants sunned themselves on the rocks before taking their long dips beneath the surface in search of fish.

We emerged from the grassy headland and made our

way down to the shore. The beach was littered with huge quartz-like boulders, opalescent in the sunlight. There was very little sand between the rocks. It was a wild, desolate beach, very far removed from the mansions of The Four Hundred. Auburn strips of seaweed crunched under our feet as we walked.

It was a strange mood which possessed us that day. Words were not necessary, at least not then. Drew took my hand and we climbed over the gray and salmon-hued rocks, stepping on piles of brittle blue-black shells. At the water's edge the rocks were covered with swaying seaweed like thick wet manes of hair.

There was a feeling of serenity which flowed through us both. There were no plans to make, no decisions to be forced. We were living in the moment, and not concerned with what had come before or what lay ahead. It was enough for me, and for him as well, I sensed, to be together on the lonely beach. Just as we had shared that time in the fog bank on the steamboat.

We climbed over the boulders until we came to a narrow cove where the water lapped gently against the bright moss-strewn rocks, where the granite crags rose on three sides, where topaz clumps of seaweed shifted in the water between the stones. Directly ahead was the vast ocean with no fingers of land to impede it. Above us the bluffs were dense with hedgerows. In this cove, as in the fog bank, we were the only two people in the world.

I sat down on a rock and slipped my fingers into the cool water, vaguely humming a tune that had been running through my head.

Glancing up at Drew, I was startled to see a stricken look on his face. "What is it?" I asked in dismay. I had broken the spell.

Abruptly he straightened and peered out to sea. "That tune — I haven't heard it in a while, that's all. What made you sing it?"

"It's one I heard Blythe singing a while ago, a lullaby."

"You heard Blythe singing it?" His gaze was sharp.

200

I nodded. "I think you should know, Drew, that I found her in the room down the hall from the nursery. The room where her brother's things are kept."

His eyes narrowed. "I didn't know she ever went in there. That melody—it was a lullaby I used to sing to them. And I taught it to Blythe so she could sing to Nathan at night when they were alone."

"Tell me about Nathan, Drew."

The brutally naked pain in his eyes was almost too much for me. With difficulty I suppressed an overwhelming urge to go to him and cradle his head to my breast. But I remained where I was with the rocks separating us.

"He was . . . a great joy to me. Both of them gave my life a meaning it had never had. My daily life with Cordelia . . . well, let's just say that they far outweighed what was lacking in our marriage and provided me with the only justification for it that I could accept. When Cordelia was pregnant for the second time I kept asking myself how I had allowed it to happen. But when Nathan was born he was reason enough.

"The doctors had said he wouldn't be able to walk. But my old nurse looked after them before she died and she said not to pay attention to what they had said, that he could walk and we could teach him. And so we did, the winter before he became ill. From the first Blythe was so protective of him. He loved her very much. She was "Bie" and I was "Dew," never "Daddy." After he died, Blythe began calling me "Daddy." I should have got rid of his furniture. Cordelia wanted to—that's why I didn't, I suppose. Until I have the time to see to it, I'll tell Miss Simmons that Blythe is not to go in there unless I am with her."

When I did go to him, I felt him trembling and I held him tightly. At least he had talked a little bit about Nathan, and I had listened. I could not know what it was like to lose a child, but I loved him and it hurt me deeply to see him so unhappy.

201

He drew me closer and began to kiss me urgently, desperately, as though to blot out the pain. His mouth devoured mine before blazing a trail across my cheeks to the softness of my neck. I began to respond to his fierce embrace, the heat coursing through my body, my senses singing, clamoring.

My hat fell to one side as his fingers pulled the pins from my hair. Our bodies strained together, relishing the feel of one another. A pulse throbbed wildly in my throat as his hard mouth moved lower, burning through the thinness of my gown.

"Ariel," he said hoarsely, "how I've wanted you, longed for you—every day, every minute. You're a fire in my blood. To have you in my house, to see you across the room—it's been the worse sort of torture."

"I didn't know it was that way for you, too," I said breathlessly. "I only know I've been miserable, longing to see you and afraid to as well."

"I'd been wishing that you'd never come, that I'd never seen you, spoken to you."

"I too."

He held me tightly against him, stroking my hair. "But that's foolish. It's like saying I wish I never had had Nathan for a son. No matter what happens, Ariel, I love you. And that will never change."

"Oh, Drew," I sighed, and then his lips took possession of mine again. I felt the hot passion rising in him and I gloried in his craving of me, meeting it with a craving of my own. Reaching for his hand, I drew it to my breast.

But then he was dragging his mouth from mine. "No, Ariel," he said huskily. "Any more and I'll be lost."

"Let's be lost together," I whispered. "It's better to be lost than to be alone."

He shook his head. "I'm not going to ruin your life. Mine is already a shambles. I haven't lain awake night after night struggling with myself only to give in now. Do you think I haven't longed to claim you as my own? But I haven't sunk that low yet." He released me, his face hardening, staring out to sea.

"But I wouldn't ask anything. I wouldn't make demands," I said wretchedly.

He turned to me, his voice rough. "But you should, Ariel, that's just it. You deserve so much more than a sordid affair with a married man. You know the way things are. I — I've lost Nathan. I must put Blythe above everything else. I can't offer you anything. And so I'm not about to commit the supremely selfish act. You'd hate me for it, resent me —"

"I wouldn't!"

"Yes, you would. Perhaps not now, but later, in years to come. You have your career ahead of you; you have so much to offer life. I've made a mess of everything by agreeing to my father's request that I marry Cordelia. I won't ruin your life as well. I could never live with myself. You deserve so much more than to be my mistress. And they would find out, you can't keep these things secret for long. I'm known in Boston and New York; so are you. What it might do to your career . . . If I took you now, Arel, on this rocky beach, I could never let you go. When you leave it's going to be intolerable in any case. If we made love we wouldn't be able to part for good. And we must."

I began to cry miserably. He sat down on a boulder and drew me onto his lap, kissing my hair and my wet cheeks. I had never felt so unhappy, so cheated and frustrated in my life. Yet I was not angry with Drew; I understood that he was sacrificing his own happiness for Blythe's. If only Cordelia would agree to divorce him and not hold on to Blythe, but she had made it clear that she wanted no changes made.

"I will never love anyone else," he promised me. "Every day I will think of you, every night in the darkness I will hold your image to me."

Eventually we got up and began to walk along the shoreline. I was calm and dry-eyed. We climbed over massive gray boulders, carved with many ledges. To one side the ocean tossed and crested; to the other loomed the headlands, swallows swarming, stalks of thistle swaying in the breeze.

And then we rounded a point of land and were suddenly facing Newport, and that comforting feeling of aloneness, of seclusion, vanished for good. Far across a stretch of water was the Cliff Walk. The palatial cottages which lined the bluff were discernible even at this distance. From here they resembled dolls' houses, tiny, insignificant. But they were the symbols of a society we could not fight, a society whose rules and mores made a mockery of our love for one another and our desire to be together. And in one of those houses Cordelia Rockwell entertained her lover, her reputation unsullied, her position unchallenged.

Hand in hand we left the rocky beach, following the path through the thickets to the carriage. Then we drove along past the seas of purple bullrushes bent low in the wind, and back up the long hill to Newport.

At the gatehouse I got down from the carriage. Drew and I exchanged one long look before he drove down the graveled drive to the stables. I turned and walked toward the house, only to meet the man with whom I had seen Cordelia. I wondered uneasily whether he had seen me get down from Drew's carriage.

He lifted his hat to me, a smile I did not quite like on his fleshy face. I nodded coolly to him. He was a large, beefy man, dapperly dressed, a flower in his lapel.

"Miss Morrow, isn't it? I wondered when I should have the pleasure. Daughter of the great Lancelot Morrow. He painted my wife, y'know. Not that she did him justice." He laughed. "I am Bartholomew Reed."

"How do you do? Now if you'll excuse me, I have some work to do."

"Work, eh? Was it work that took you off with Drew Rockwell? I wondered where he was all day. Not that I blame him, not at all. There's something fascinating about the idea of a lady artist." His gaze was lingering.

"I was under the impression that you had other fish to fry," I said deliberately.

He grinned. "I'm beginning to envy Drew, really I am. If you are ever interested, think of me. I have a lot more money than Drew, and I can be a lot more fun."

"Get out of my way," I said between clenched teeth.

Laughing, he stepped aside, making a bow so exaggerated as to be insulting. I swept past him and through the galleried hall, sudden tears pricking my eyes. This was what I would have to put up with if I became known as Drew's mistress, I realized. And it was these sorts of altercations, these slurs from which he wished to spare me. I would not have a shred of reputation; I would be hard put to be hired by a respectable client.

Drew was right. As his mistress I would have nothing but a few stolen hours with him once in a while. I would have no career except as a kept woman. That was not what I wanted for myself. I had not worked so hard all those years with my father to throw away my career now. In New York I would no longer be known as "the lady artist who paints interiors," but as "Drew Rockwell's mistress." And those circumstances just might destroy the only thing I would have left: my love for Drew.

This was not Paris or London where these things were viewed with more tolerance, where my private life might not taint my public one. Drew knew the harshness of the world better than I, despite my unorthodox career. He knew precisely what would happen if we defied convention and chose to be together.

There was also the possibility that Cordelia, in retaliation, would sue for divorce, citing me, and win custody of Blythe. Drew could countersue, as Cordelia had many times provided him with cause, but then the very scandal would arise from which he wanted to spare Blythe. He had lost one child, and Blythe's health, both physical and emotional, was fragile. I did not blame him for wanting to protect her from a situation which might easily become sordid and notorious.

That evening after I had worked on what was my last interior of the house, I went out for a walk. As always I found my steps taking me past the rose arbor, the fish pond, and down the length of the lawn to where the weeping beeches loomed enormous, their shaggy branches dense with leaves that fluttered and swished.

And somehow I found myself standing beneath the Chinese Moongate, wishing silently for a resolution, a way out of the seeming hopelessness of my life and love. Behind me the weeping beeches murmured and whispered as though they understood, and offered solace.

After a while I wandered down to the cliff's edge. Gazing far down at the jagged boulders piled along the shore, I could not help but think of Maisie Leander. Poor wretched Maisie who had sought a death so horrible because she had broken one of society's rules.

"That's where she went over."

Catching my breath, I saw Gwendolyn Chandler coming toward me on the Cliff Walk. Shuddering, I answered, "I know. It was terrible."

"She was going to have a baby. But she didn't want it. She wanted to kill it." Her voice was harsh.

I did not know what to say. It was dusk and her face seemed eerily lit, a white blur in the plum twilight. Her pale green eyes were luminous, filled with an almost unnatural glow.

"I wanted a baby once," she said.

"Perhaps you'll have one someday," I said uneasily.

"I'll never have a child." Her tone left no room for doubt. It was strangely flat.

"Well, if you marry and —"

Her gaze mocked me. "I'll never marry. Haven't you heard? I'm different, peculiar."

"You're an artist, like me," I said. "You play the piano, I paint. I'm also considered different, odd."

Suddenly her eyes narrowed; her expression became ugly, hostile. "Don't mock me, Miss Morrow. You have no idea what you're talking about. *You and I are nothing alike.*" She turned to go and then glanced back over her shoulder. "You see, I've seen you. At the Moongate . . . with him."

And on those words she moved swiftly away, her form disappearing like a wraith into the deepening night.

Chapter Eleven

Now I knew for certain whose face I had seen at the turret window of Oaklawn, the pale blur which had appeared and disappeared so suddenly. Gwendolyn Chandler had watched me from her tower, had observed Drew and me together at the Chinese Moongate that night he had ridden up on his horse.

I did not understand her rapidly changing moods, her cryptic comments. Had she some interest in Drew herself? What had she meant by her scornful accusation, "You and I are nothing alike? I could not have mistaken the malignant tone in her voice.

The next morning I worked for several hours. At noon I stopped, cleaned my brushes and straightened up before my lunch was brought to me on a tray.

The afternoon stretched ahead of me. I decided to take what might very well be my last walk about the town. Again I was charmed by the quaintly shaped Colonial homes with their tiny window panes, their graceful but austere symmetry, the decorative woodwork or fanlights over the doors. I discovered an old graveyard dating back to the seventeenth century, the stones carved with skulls, angels, and bleak weather-beaten verses.

As I made my way along one of the streets above town I could glimpse the blue of the harbor at every crossroads, forested with masts of the many sailing

vessels moored there. On the cobblestone streets sloping down to the water the houses leaned together as
though for support with little or no grass or cultivated
gardens between them. Roaming the narrow twisting
streets for several hours, I was enchanted by the snug
homes, shops, and stone or wooden churches. The atmosphere was vastly different from the chateaux and
villas a mere mile or so away.

Passing a tea shop with lace curtains at the window,
I went in and ordered tea and blackberry pie. A
young couple was seated at the back in a corner; I recognized the young lady as Camille de la Salle,
Isadora's friend, whom I had met at the Newport Casino. Her companion must be the one Isadora had
told me about with such trepidation, the young man
who would be considered most unsuitable by Camille's
mother. Not once did they glance in my direction, so
absorbed were they in one another. Watching them
gave me some misgivings; I did not sit long over my
tea.

When I reached Copper Beeches and was climbing
the staircase to my room, I heard two of maids talking
excitedly on the second-story landing.

One of them was Nancy. "Molly, what do you think
I've just heard? You know Matilda, Mrs. Chandler's
personal maid over at Oaklawn, the one that comes to
visit Mrs. Meredith?"

"Yes, I know her," I heard Molly say.

"Well, you remember Thomas Bateman, Mrs.
Leander's coachman, the lady who killed herself because everyone said she was going to have his baby?"

"The one who jumped off the cliff?"

"That's the one. Well, now he's dead, too!"

"No!" came the faint shocked whisper.

"Matilda told Mrs. Meredith that he shot himself to
death last night. One of the grooms found him this
morning. He was an awful mess, so she says."

"Why did he do it?"

"Couldn't live without her, I guess. Or blamed himself for her death. The house was to be sold and all the servants let go. He had lost his position and I suppose wasn't going to find it so easy to get another after all that had gone on." Their voices faded as they went down the back stairway.

Mrs. Leander and her unborn child were dead, and now her lover, the child's father. What was the point of it all? Why had both of them chosen suicide as a way to solve their problems?

The daytrippers that came to Newport to gawk at the mansions and hope for a glimpse of their inhabitants doubtless assumed that the rich hadn't a care in the world. But it seemed that there were as many tragedies being played out in the palatial cottages as in the humblest of dwellings. There was no poverty or starvation of the body, but perhaps of the spirit.

I myself was deeply enmeshed in the troubles at Copper Beeches; I had observed the circumstances at Oaklawn: the strangeness of Gwendolyn Chandler, and her father's philanthropic zeal which did not quite take the place of the surgeon's career he had left behind years ago when marrying Olive and entering her world of The Four Hundred.

There was lovely young Consuelo Vanderbilt who had been made a prisoner at Marble Palace until she had succumbed to her mother's wish that she marry the Duke of Marlborough. Now living in an authentic palace across the ocean, she was doubtless no happier than when she had lived in a sham one.

And now one other death had followed the scandal and tragedy of poor Maisie Leander.

The next day I was working when one of the maids came to tell me that Mrs. Rockwell wished to see me.

"Very well. Please tell her I shall be with her in a few minutes." I took off my smock and tidied myself before going to Cordelia's sitting room.

She was drinking a morning cup of chocolate and

reading some letters. "Ah, there you are, Miss Morrow. You are finished with most of the interiors, are you not?"

"I am."

"Well, go and fetch them, if you please. I wish to see them."

"Now, Mrs. Rockwell?"

"Yes, of course, now," she said, raising her brows.

"Very well."

Gathering up the interiors in my room, I returned to the second story. She studied each one in turn while I stood there, hoping she would be pleased. As for myself, I considered them some of the finest work I had ever executed. "These are quite satisfactory, Miss Morrow," she said. "Are you working on the last now?"

"Yes."

"And do you have another commission following the one here?"

"Well, no, I thought I would return to New York and . . ."

She raised her hand. "Good. I have something else I wish you to do."

"And what is that, Mrs. Rockwell?" I asked warily.

"I wish you to paint my portrait."

I was astonished; never had I expected such a request.

"You said once that you had painted many portraits, that you worked with your father."

"That is true, Mrs. Rockwell, but I believe you know that I have never been professionally engaged to paint a portrait."

"What does that matter? I shall be the first. Alva is always saying that she is the first in everything. Well, I will be the first to have my portrait done by a lady artist, Lancelot Morrow's daughter, no less."

I could only regard her in dismay. Why had my chance come now, with this woman, in this house? I had longed to get commissions to do portraits, but if I

211

accepted her offer it meant prolonging my stay at Copper Beeches. Both Drew and I knew that I needed to leave soon, for both our sakes.

Taking a deep breath, I said, "I'm afraid I cannot accept your generous offer, Mrs. Rockwell. I—I shall have to decline." Realizing that I was deliberately rejecting an opportunity which might never again come my way, my heart felt like a stone.

"Come now, Miss Morrow. Don't be coy. I am doing you a great favor, as you must be well aware. For one portrait I will pay you twice what I agreed to pay for an entire set of interiors. And I am not without influence. If I am pleased with the likeness, as pleased as I am with the interiors, I will not hesitate to recommend you to my wide circle of acquaintances."

"Mrs. Rockwell—"

"Think, Miss Morrow. Your interiors are very good. But consider how your reputation as an artist will grow when you paint a Society hostess. You could have an entirely new career ahead of you. Imagine, your work displayed at one of those annual exhibitions! Has that ever happened before, Miss Morrow?"

Gazing at her, I realized I had never hated her more than I did at that moment. She knew exactly what to say to make the offer irresistable to me. Painting portraits rather than an endless procession of lifeless rooms. If I were truly serious about my career, as serious as I had always believed, I could not refuse her.

But what about Drew, and our feelings for one another? How would he feel about my painting his wife's portrait? And might we be headed directly into danger if I continued to stay at Copper Beeches?

Cordelia's lips curled. "I think you are a little afraid, Miss Morrow. If you are that uncertain of your talent, then there is no more to be said."

I met her cool gaze with one of my own. She had challenged me and there was no turning back. I would not throw away this chance just because my heart was bruised and sore. I had to think of the future, *my* future. Drew would have no place in it, but I would always have my work. If I were careful not to reject my greatest opportunity so far.

"All right, Mrs. Rockwell. I will paint your portrait."

She surveyed me ironically. "That is more like it, Miss Morrow. When will you begin?"

"The day after tomorrow, I suppose. I have to put some finishing touches on the last interior. And I will need supplies, things for oil painting."

"Well, whatever you need we can order from Boston. There is no hurry, after all. It must be the finest work you have ever done, Miss Morrow." She set down her cup of chocolate. "Well, I must change for luncheon. When you have all that you require to begin, we will arrange a schedule for the sittings."

Now that I had made the decision, I felt the excitement bubbling within me. I realized that I had been manipulated into accepting, but what I also realized was that I had wanted to accept from the first. No female artist in her right mind would have refused such an offer, the offer of a glittering future seldom presented to those of my sex, and at the age of twenty-four.

There was one part of me which cared nothing for the commission, the treacherous part that thought only of Drew. But in my exhileration I did not examine that part. I refused to believe then that I was adding fuel to the fire, that by extending my stay in this house I was plunging into circumstances which would swiftly become a nightmare, a nightmare I could not have imagined in my worst dreams.

I disliked Cordelia Rockwell more than ever, but I was determined to produce a splendid portrait of her. It was ironic that the tangible thing Drew would have to remember me by would be the portrait of his despised wife. The ancient Greeks believed that the gods placed mortals in just these situations for their own amusement. I wondered whether someone somewhere were laughing now. . . .

That evening I joined the family at dinner. We were eating stuffed veal roast with tiny carrots and new potatoes when Isadora said, "I suppose you'll be leaving soon, Ariel. Are you going to be in Boston at all this fall? Perhaps we could make arrangements to see one another; I always spend some time with Aunt Hermione in the autumn."

"Well . . ." I said, feeling my face growing warm.

"Miss Morrow is not leaving yet, Isadora," said Cordelia grandly. "She is going to stay and paint my portrait."

There was a palpable silence. Fearfully I glanced down the table at Drew. He was regarding me intently, black brows drawn together.

"Oh, Ariel, how wonderful!" cried Isadora. "And perhaps after Cordelia's you might do mine?"

"No place else to go, Miss Morrow?" asked Aunt Hermione, her sharp eyes on me.

"I'm surprised at you, Cordelia, trusting your likeness to a novice," said Gideon spitefully. "If Miss Morrow makes a mess of it, don't complain to me." He was trying to appear nonchalant, but the hostility in his eyes gave him away.

"What do you mean, Gideon? I'm not the first person Miss Morrow has painted. The first member of Society, though, who has offered her a commission. What do you say, Drew?"

His voice was curt. "Do as you please, Cordelia, you always do." Then he added in a slightly softer tone, "I'm certain Miss Morrow will do an admirable job."

"I've decided that if I am pleased with my portrait I shall give a reception to show it to all my friends. Miss Morrow may attend as well."

"That's very generous of you, Cordelia," said Drew ironically.

Briefly our gazes met again and I knew that he understood and accepted my decision. Even so, I perceived in his eyes a sort of desperation, and knew it was reflected in my own.

It was the following day that I received the second poison pen letter. It had been slid under my door just as the first. My stomach tightening, I resisted the urge to destroy it unread, and opened it.

STOP MEETING YOUR EMPLOYER, YOU
FILTHY SLUT.
BAD BLOOD WILL OUT.

I stared down, aghast, at the bold printed lettering on the white paper. This one was far worse than the other. The first had been merely sly and unsavory; this one had a vindictive quality, a note of venom, even hatred, which had been lacking in the first. There was apparently no doubt in the writer's mind that Drew and I were conducting an illicit affair. And what on earth was meant by "bad blood will out?" Was the sender referring to my father, assuming that because he was an artist, he was therefore immoral, and so was I?

Somewhere I had an enemy. But it was an enemy who was concealed, observing me as I could not observe him or her. I felt chilled and shaken. Who disliked me that much to pen these nasty notes, to refer to me as a "filthy slut"? To whom did I pose a threat?

I recalled Gideon's look of vicious dislike at dinner. Had he written this note because I had rebuffed his advances, and encouraged Drew's? The first note struck me now as a sort of playful admonishment more than an actual warning. Could Gideon have seen Drew kissing me that night after he himself returned to the house? Had he watched us drive out of town that day and jumped to his own conclusions?

I was certain one of the servants had not written it because of the quality of the paper. Of course, one of them might have helped himself to a piece of stationery, but I doubted it. And I recoiled at the notion of questioning them. I had no desire to publicize the disgusting note. None of them would admit to it, and I would only be providing them with food for speculation. If they were not already watching Drew and me, they would begin to.

The sender must have banked on just such a reluctance. That was part of the cowardly art of poison-pen letters. Make them so malicious and lurid that the receiver would wish only to destroy them.

There was also Miss Simmons. I had suspected her from the first, although I had believed that it must be Gideon. Now, the more I considered her to be the writer, the more sense it made. Miss Simmons was in love with Drew and she perceived me as a rival. It was not difficult to believe that she would call me a "filthy slut" if she thought I had succeeded where she had failed. And with her obsession for Drew, she might make a practice of observing his movements whenever possible.

She was the likeliest person to have sent the two letters. I was not convinced of her guilt, but I was determined to question her. This sickness had to stop; I would not remain a passive recipient of these horrid notes any longer. I would not be called foul names and threatened.

Just now it was early afternoon; Blythe was probably taking a nap. I would go to Miss Simmons's room and ask her point-blank if she had written the two poison-pen letters. If she denied it, which she likely would, I could voice my intention of showing it to Drew, and carefully watch her expression as I did so. Surely if she had written them, something would be revealed in her face. As an artist, I flattered myself that I was a good reader of faces. If Miss Simmons was penning these dreadful things, she might be thrown off balance by my confronting her.

But as it happened, I never asked her. Softly I crept down the corridor of the nursery wing, careful not to awake Blythe if she were sleeping. Pausing outside Miss Simmons's door, I was just about to knock when I heard her voice answered by a man's. His was too low for me to identify.

Appalled, I backed away. Could it be Drew? Whom else? Was he a cynic who toyed with the emotions of different women? The sounds left no doubt as to the activity in the bedroom. I had to get away from there.

Turning, I saw with another shock that Drew was coming down the hall toward me. "Ariel? Is something wrong? You look as though you've seen a ghost," he said as I hurried to meet him.

I had to keep him at the far end of the hall. "Oh, no, I —" Taking a deep breath, I began again, "Drew, I've been meaning to explain about my agreeing to do your wife's portrait. You see, it —"

"There's nothing for you to explain, Ariel. I would be very selfish if I prevented you from doing something that could so boost your career."

"I'd like to show you the interiors I've done. I — Would you come now and see them?" Desperately I tried not to reveal my anxiety. If he should discover Miss Simmons with a man in her room while his daughter was close by, napping . . . Miss Simmons might be a spiteful unhappy woman who wrote poison-pen letters, but I did not wish to see her so horribly exposed. Such a thing was unthinkable.

"I'd very much like to, Ariel. I must talk to Miss Simmons now, when Blythe is asleep. Perhaps afterwards."

"No, now!" I said vehemently. He looked slightly taken aback. Laughing nervously, feeling my face as red as a beet, I added, "I mean, I'm going out later —

with Isadora."

"Well, later this evening then. Just now I need to talk to Miss Simmons. I haven't had a chance to tell her that Blythe is not to go in that room there."

Hurrying after him, I gripped his arm. "Drew, please . . ."

He frowned. "What is it, Ariel?"

"I must tell you. Today I received a note, a nasty, disgusting sort of note. Anonymous, of course." I was babbling; I hadn't meant to tell him, but I had to keep him from approaching Miss Simmons's room.

"What did it say?" he asked grimly.

"Oh, awful things. I—I have it right here." Taking it from my pocket, I handed it to him. If only he would leave the nursery wing with me. If only he would abandon his resolve to speak to Miss Simmons now.

Glancing down at it, his face hardened. Then, scowling, he said, "This is revolting. Who could have sent it?"

"It's not the first one I've received," I said. "I got another several weeks ago, but it wasn't as bad. Please, Drew, we need to talk."

"We'll talk," he said. "But first I'll see Miss Simmons." His voice was flinty. "Frankly, I think she may have sent it."

My ruse to show him the letter in order to distract him had done the opposite. He was striding down the hall, intent on confronting Miss Simmons.

"No, Drew, stop! Don't—don't—"

But he was rapping on the door. "Miss Simmons, are you in there?" he called out sternly.

"Drew, no, there's someone—" My eyes implored him.

"She's with someone now?" His gaze narrowed incredulously.

The door was opening. In dismay I saw Miss Simmons standing there in her wrap, her pale hair falling over her shoulders. She had expected to see Drew because she had heard his voice. But when she saw me her expression became malevolent.

"You brought him here," she hissed.

"No!" I cried, aghast. "It wasn't—I tried—"

"It doesn't matter. I'm leaving anyway. I've had enough of this place."

Over her shoulder I saw Gideon come up behind her. "Well, well, if this isn't cosy," he said, amused.

"Get out of here, Gideon," said Drew softly.

"Oh, get off your high horse. I've done nothing more than you've been doing with our artist-in-residence here."

"I said, get out."

Gideon flushed. "Stop treating me like a child, damn it! You wouldn't give Miss Simmons the attentions she craved, so I obliged. Now everyone's happy."

"You are to leave Copper Beeches today, Gideon."

His jaw dropped. "Now wait a minute, Drew. I don't think you understand. I know I got a little out of hand with Ariel that night, but this wasn't at all like that. Tell him, Jennifer. I wasn't forcing anything on you."

But Miss Simmons merely smiled, glancing from Gideon to Drew. Her mocking bravado hid her humiliation. I felt humiliated as well, and revolted by the entire scene.

"You are never to set foot in Copper Beeches again, Gideon," said Drew, still in that quiet steely voice. "You've disgraced yourself in my home for the last time. Now get out."

Gideon stared at him a few moments longer before rage transformed his features. "All right, I'm going! I have plenty of friends who'll put me up. But you'll be sorry, you bloody hypocrite! Because I'll tell everyone about you and the lady artist here—"

It was then that Drew lunged forward, grasping Gideon by the collar, his eyes blazing his fury. "You say one word about Miss Morrow and I swear I'll beat

219

you within an inch of your life. I've stood your filthy insinuations long enough. You aren't fit to wipe Miss Morrow's boots. She and I have nothing to hide, not that you would ever believe that. I've put up with your viciousness because you're Cordelia's brother, the way I've put up with a great many things. But no more. You're a weak, selfish, spoiled boy. Oh, I'm aware that you're twenty-five years old, and there are only six years between us. But you're a boy all the same. Now get out of my sight. And one word about either Miss Simmons or Miss Morrow and I'll hunt you down like a dog!" He threw Gideon from him who collapsed on the floor. Closing my eyes, I heard Gideon get to his feet and go down the hall.

"I do not blame you, Miss Simmons," said Drew heavily. "But I think it would be better for all concerned if you found another position. I will write you a recommendation."

"How charitable of you, Mr. Rockwell!" cried Miss Simmons, her eyes sparkling. She was almost arrogant. "I'm leaving, and I'll take that recommendation." Then, abruptly, her face crumpled. "I told you I loved you. But it made no difference to you, did it? I only embarrassed you. That was when I decided to go. You're in love with Miss Morrow—any fool can see that, despite your protestations of innocence! I'm only a governess, not at all glamorous like a lady artist. She can't love you—she's probably had lots of men. She's nothing but a slut!" Sobbing, she covered her face with her hands.

I knew then that Miss Simmons had indeed written the two poison-pen letters, hoping to warn me off Drew. But I no longer cared. This whole affair had been sickening in the extreme; I would never have wished on her a disgrace so devastating, so complete.

"Daddy?" said a small voice. Blythe stood in the nursery door; we had not noticed her opening it. Her dark eyes were troubled, her face pale. "Why is Miss

220

Simmons crying?"

"She's had some bad news, Blythe. She'll have to go away. Come with me now, darling." Picking her up, he strode down the hall. Without a backward glance at Miss Simmons, I followed him.

Miss Simmons left a few hours later. I had expected another vicious argument between Drew and Cordelia over Gideon's banishment, but none occurred that I witnessed or overheard. Perhaps Cordelia was fed up with Gideon's behavior as well; I knew that she had had to dismiss one or two of the maids at their family home in New York where he spent much of the winter. It was one thing for Cordelia to carry on a love affair with a man of her own class, but quite another for Gideon to go about seducing servants. That simply was not done.

Determining in which room to paint Cordelia took some time. I considered several rooms with an eye to colors, light and backdrops. My own style of portrait painting was not the striking dramatic contrasts of whites and darks that had been my father's trademark. I liked to use warm colors and soft, blurred contrasts between hair and clothing and flesh. Not for me the sepulchral women in black velvet. And because I painted interiors and was interested in their details, I paid attention to the background behind the sitter, adding it to the painting. My father, on the other hand, had preferred nondescript backgrounds that would taken nothing away from the drama of his portrayal.

Finally I decided on the drawing room as the best setting. The wall panels of floral bouquets were painted in yellow, faded rose, and apple green. They would make a charming backdrop for Cordelia's chesnut hair and peaches-and-cream complexion. She could sit in one of the yellow damask chairs before a section of the wall. The light in the mornings would be ideal.

While I was in the drawing room, Molly was also there, lowering the chandelier so that she could wipe the huge crystal teardrops free of dust. I was surprised to see Blythe suddenly appear in the doorway, her dark curls tousled and a smudge of jam on her cheek. The maids were taking turns looking after her until a new governess was hired, and the results were not altogether successful.

"Hello, Blythe," I said. "Where is Nancy? Isn't she playing with you today?"

She stared at me solemnly for a few moments before answering, "She's in the kitchen with Mrs. Meredith."

"Well, shouldn't you go back there? She must be looking for you."

Blythe shrugged and I realized the foolishness of my statement. It was doubtful that Nancy, gossiping, had not even noticed that the child had left the kitchen. And she was so quiet most of the time that one tended to forget her presence.

"Well, come along," I said. "I'll take you to her."

Just then Molly, who was standing on a stepladder, lost her balance and gave a small cry. She managed to steady herself without falling, but not before she had nearly toppled into the lowered chandelier, knocking it back and forth.

Certain that she was all right, I turned back to Blythe. But the child had gone rigid, a frozen look of horror on her face, her skin as white as paper, her dark eyes wild, terrified.

"Blythe, what is it?" I asked in quick alarm, steeling myself for the screams to begin.

But they did not. Instead the little girl gasped out, "Make it stop! Make it stop!" The last word was almost a shriek.

Molly leaned forward and took the chandelier by its central bar.

"There, look, it's stopped now, Blythe."

Abruptly the tenseness left the child, her body

crumpling into involuntary shudders.

Molly glanced at me, shaking her head. I could read her thought: What's the matter with the daft thing now?

Kneeling down, I took Blythe by the shoulders and held her against me. To my surprise she did not struggle. "It's all right, darling. It was only the chandelier swaying. Molly fell against it—you saw her. Is that what frightened you? Were you afraid she would fall and hurt herself? She's fine."

When her trembling had slowed, I led her across the room and out the French doors to the terrace.

"It's a lovely day, isn't it? Come, let's take a little walk." She allowed me to take her across the lawn to the fish pond.

"Remember what I told you about the good fairies looking out for you?"

She made no response.

"Well, do you see the lily pads on the surface of the water? Sometimes fairies use them as rafts, to float gently about the pond."

"Have you ever seen one?"

"No, I'm sorry to say I never have. But fairies aren't allowed to be seen by us, you know. They throw dust in our eyes to prevent us seeing them when they are out at night. When you wake up in the morning and find sand in your eyes, that is the fairy dust."

"It is?" Her dark eyes were wide. "What else do you know about fairies?"

"Well, their favorite holiday of the year is Midsummer Eve, when they light a bonfire in a glen in the forest and dance around it. They have a wonderful banquet, too, but people like us must be careful never to eat fairy food because we might become enchanted."

"What would happen?"

"You might be changed, different. Or your world might be. Do you know the story of Rip Van Winkle, and what happened to him when he came upon the little men in the Catskill Mountains of New York?"

She shook her head. So I told her about Rip slinking off from his chores and his nagging wife, and how he and his loyal dog had climbed up into the mountains one autumn day. They came upon Henry Hudson's crew playing ninepins, and he joined them in drinking their potent brew.

"He fell asleep. And when he awoke it wasn't the next morning at all, but one many years later. His hair was gray and he had grown a long beard. Everything he knew, even his house, had changed, because the drink of the little men had bewitched him so that he even slept through the Revolution. All his friends were gone, and so was his wife, but his daughter, who was now a grown-up lady and a mother herself, recognized him and welcomed him back."

"But where did the little men come from? Where do fairies live?"

I paused, trying to remember all I had read as a child in Miss Kelley's class. "Titania, the Queen of the Fairies, and naturally the most beautiful, lives in a bower of flowers. Some fairies live inside hollow hills, and some in caves and in woods, in mountains and in trees. If you see a tree with a hollow in its trunk, it just may be that brownies live inside, or in the ground beneath it. Inside the tree are tiny winding stairs which go up the trunk and lead to tunnels below in the roots.

"Some fairies are said to live on islands—magic islands covered in mist that people can only see once in seven years. Seven is always a magic number. But when the sailors get too close, the island melts away."

"What does this island look like?"

"Oh, it's always spring, always peaceful and beautiful. There are high mountain peaks covered in snow, but the fairies never get cold. The fairy palaces are made of crystal and gold, and there are flowers everywhere because fairies love flowers. Fairies can live forever on these magic isles. That is why King Arthur was taken to the Isle of Avalon where he could be brought back to life someday."

"Was King Arthur a fairy?"

"No, but he was a great king, and well-loved by all the creatures with magical powers. He had a wise old magician named Merlin."

"We have a fairy doll on top of our Christmas tree every year," said Blythe.

"I'm sure she's very beautiful."

"Yes, she is. Tell me more about fairies."

"Well, let's see if we can find a circle of dark green grass — darker than the rest of the lawn."

We walked about for a while, searching.

"Here it is! I've found one!" she called excitedly. "What is it?"

"It's a fairy ring. It's supposed to mark the spot where fairies dance, and there may be an underground fairy palace beneath it. You must never sit inside a fairy ring on Midsummer Eve or you might be whisked off to fairyland."

"I wish I could be whisked off to fairyland," said Blythe a little forlornly, her black curls shielding her face as she looked longingly at the dark green circle.

"I don't think you'd find it very comfortable there," I told her. "Remember, fairies — and elves and brownies and piskies — are very tiny, so they can live in small places you and I would never fit in. And we wouldn't like what they eat at all: roasted ants, flies' eggs, a worm's heart."

"Eew." She screwed up her face and then giggled, an awkward, uncertain sound.

I had recalled something else. "Is there a horseshoe above the stable door, by any chance?"

She nodded.

"Well, some people claim it's for good luck. But there's really another reason. You see, fairies love horses. They love to borrow them and ride throughout the night so that they are too tired to pull carriages or take humans on their backs the next day. Fairies are mischievous creatures, and like to annoy people. But if there is a horseshoe above the stable door, fairies will keep away because they don't like anything made of iron. Fairies were on the earth long before people began to make things out of iron, and they were chased underground and into the deep woods when the iron-making people came."

"Is this really true?"

I laughed. "Well, I don't know. But it's fun to think about, isn't it?"

She smiled, nodding.

"Well, perhaps you had better go and find Nancy now. She may be worried."

Without a word she took off, her pink dress floating behind her, her dusky curls bouncing. She looked like a little fairy herself. When she reached the terrace, she turned and waved shyly at me.

"Blythe, there you are." Isadora was standing by the French doors. "Nancy has been looking for you. It's time for lunch. But first give me a kiss." Blythe reached up and kissed her cheek before going inside, and Isadora walked out onto the terrace to meet me.

"She looked almost cheerful, the way she was running. What were you talking about?"

"Fairies," I said, feeling a little foolish.

"Well, something tells me you've made a friend, and that is no small accomplishment. But I must tell you, I've had a wonderful idea! You must simply say yes!"

I regarded her excited face a trifle warily. "What is it?"

"There's going to be a ball next week at Hedgerow. It's one of the most important events of the season, and I want you to come."

"Oh, no, I couldn't."

"Don't say anything yet, Ariel. Just listen. It's a masquerade ball. All the guests will wear masks and costumes. No one will know who anyone else is, at least not until the unveiling at midnight. And I've already procured an invitation for you. I simply told Mrs. Evans that we have a houseguest staying with us. She's very easygoing, not at all like most of the Society hostesses around here. She immediately wrote an invitation out for you and gave it to me."

"But, Isadora, I am not a houseguest," I said, distressed.

"Oh, pooh, what does that matter? Who's to know or care? You must come, Ariel. It will be so much fun. And you can leave before midnight with no one the wiser, just like Cinderella."

"But Mrs. Rockwell — I'm certain that she would not approve of you or me deceiving Mrs. Evans."

"Oh, Cordelia won't know. She's far too caught up in her own affairs. No one will know. Don't be prudish, Ariel. You're an artist. You're supposed to do daring, exciting things. You're supposed to be unconventional. There will be so many people milling about that you can be one of the crowd. Please come! I'm going to be Cleopatra, and I have the most *divine* costume!"

"Well . . ."

"It will be our secret," she said, her eyes glowing. "I'll see to all the arrangements, order a second carriage for you after we leave. You do have an invitation, after all. You're not a gate-crasher. It will just be for two or three hours. And no one will know your true identity. You must say yes."

To my amazement I heard myself saying, "All right, Isadora. I'd very much like to go."

She was delighted. "Oh, wonderful! Now there's the matter of your costume. Who shall you be?"

"I'll figure something out." If I were actually going to attend this affair, I wanted to give a great deal of thought to what I would wear.

"Well, there's a good seamstress who lives in town.

I'll give you her name and address. She could sew your costume."

"All right."

"Remember, it's in ten days time."

"Will—will the family attend?"

"Drew and Cordelia, you mean? Yes, they both go. Aunt Hermione won't, though."

I did not care whether Aunt Hermione attended or not. I only wanted to be certain that Drew would be there.

Chapter Twelve

It took me some time to select a persona for the masquerade ball. In my room I sat with a sketchpad before me, rapidly drawing various characters and costumes. Juliet? Marie Antoinette? No, there was surely to be at least one representative of those famous ladies. And whoever heard of a Juliet with dark red hair? But I had no inclination to be Queen Elizabeth, just to oblige my hair color. A lady of ancient Greece? A character out of a nursery rhyme, or fairy tale? Guinevere?

Nothing seemed right. After drawing nearly a dozen sketches, I tore them each in half. This was going to be more difficult than I had anticipated. But I was grateful to Isadora for giving me the name of the seamstress. When I had decided what my costume would be, I would go and see her. But I had better decide quickly; the night of the ball was approaching.

A little later I went to Cordelia's room and knocked on the door. I wanted to set up a firm schedule, if possible, for her sittings. But there was no answer. I was moving away when a door opened behind me and I heard Drew's voice: "Ariel."

My heart skipping a beat, I said, "Yes?"

"If the invitation still holds, I'd like to take you up on it," he said, coming towards me.

"Invitation?"

"To see your interiors. I apologize for the other day.

I take it you were aware that Gideon was with Miss Simmons?"

Coloring, I nodded and then said quickly, "The interiors are in my room. Should I bring them down?"

"No, I'll come up with you."

I went ahead of him up the stairs and into my room. While he studied the watercolors I stood nervously at the window, gazing out over the lawn. Yet I took in none of the view, conscious only that we were alone in my bedroom and he was scrutinizing my work.

Finally he spoke. "These are exquisite, Ariel. You are very gifted."

"Thank you." I was rosy with pleasure.

"And to think I was against the idea at the beginning. I saw it as merely another foolish whim of Cordelia's. I — was against your being in the house — my house — because earlier, on the steamboat, I had felt such an undeniable attraction to you. No, it was more than that — a bond with you. Something I was not prepared for and didn't understand. And something I've tried very hard to resist these last weeks."

He raked his fingers through his hair. "Ariel, I can't tell you how difficult it is for me, night after night, thinking of you up here. I don't know whether I can —" he broke off roughly, turning away. But after a moment he looked back, his face softening, his smile crooked. "Blythe talks about you all the time now. She calls you the fairy lady. And she's right in a way. Even your name . . . You're like one of those mystical ladies in a Burne-Jones painting. Later, if I ever find myself wondering if you were real, I'll have these."

He picked up the interiors. Straightening, his cheeks slightly tinged with color, he went on, "In the meantime, I will arrange for them to be suitably framed. And this is for you. Cordelia doubtless forgot."

It was a check. And he was right; Cordelia had

made no attempt to pay me for the work which I had accomplished.

"Thank you," I said, biting my lip. To my dismay I felt tears pricking my eyes. I wanted terribly to throw myself into his arms but I sensed that now I must be the one to hold back, that he would not be able to retain his iron control if I made a move towards him. And if we gave in to the powerful temptation, it would not be for the last time, and sooner or later we would be forced to pay the consequences.

So I watched him open the door and go out, the interiors under his arm, while I ached with misery and longing.

I remembered what he had said. He had compared me to one of Burne-Jones's female figures, those lovely, graceful Pre-Raphaelite women with flowing red hair, skin like porcelein, and faraway, otherworldly expressions.

And then I knew. That was what I would be for the ball, a Pre-Raphaelite model. There had never been any other real choice. Taking up my sketchpad, I began to draw.

The following morning I began work on Cordelia's portrait. She had agreed to sit for me at eleven; I had managed to gather all the supplies I needed and was anxious to begin work.

Cordelia sat in a yellow damask chair in front of a decorative wall panel. Her gown was a rose-colored watered silk which matched the shade in the floral bouquet of the panel. Glinting in the sunlight, it had an elaborate lace collar. Her hair was swept gracefully up from her slim white neck. She looked very beautiful.

I tried to do what my father had always advised, to paint the sitter as merely an object with no thoughts about his or her character. For the first time I truly understood and appreciated his style of being an observer, of resisting the urge to convey an opinion about his subject.

That was what I must do with Cordelia. Stoically I would put aside my contempt for her, my jealousy, and paint just what a casual observer would see if he or she stepped into the room: a lovely woman in a sunlit drawing room on a summer's day. It would be my technique, my brushwork, which would be the lure of the painting, and not the personality of my sitter.

First of all, I sketched the painting that I wanted to do. Her head was turned a little to one side, her body positioned the way I requested, the fingers of one hand curled, palm side up, the other hand almost lost in the folds of her gown.

Then I used a wash of paint to quickly outline the portrait. The colors of the palette I had selected were laid out before me. To keep the colors in their various combinations, the same combinations, I had to paint something of every area of the painting—the floral panel, the chair, her hair, her gown, a little flesh. I did not want Cordelia's gown to contrast starkly with the backdrop, but to blend in. I wanted the effect to be soft, warm, blurred, impressionistic. My brush strokes were now wet; later they would be dryer, smoother, with a buttery quality. I worked swiftly, with a minimum of strokes, as my father had taught me. Yet this portrait would be totally my own.

"I must have someone in tomorrow to talk to me while I sit," she said. "This is dreadfully tedious."

I made no comment. I was not about to enter into a conversation with her because into my work might creep a subtle slant of feeling, a hint of intimate knowledge of this woman whom I detested. If she wished to have a friend with her during the sitting, I had no objection. That way she would be further distanced from me.

"I really cannot sit here one minute longer," she declared later. She fidgeted in her chair, her brow creased, her foot tapping on the floor.

"Very well, Mrs. Rockwell. That's all we need do today."

"I should certainly say it is, Miss Morrow. I've sat here for over an hour. I really must get ready for luncheon." Without another word she swept from the room.

After I had eaten my own lunch, I put on my hat, gathered up the sketches I had done of my costume, and left the house. The seamstress lived in one of the narrow streets on the Point, one of the original sections of Newport which had seen more prosperous days. Her cottage was painted dark green and looked very old, late seventeeth century, perhaps, or very early eighteenth. It stood next to a tidy garden.

The woman who answered the door was tall and reedy.

"Mrs. Perkins?"

She nodded. "You would like something sewn, I suppose."

"Yes. Miss Rockwell gave me your name."

She glanced up the cobblestone street. "You come in a carriage?"

"No, I walked. I — I'm employed at Copper Beeches. My name is Ariel Morrow."

She studied me, frowning slightly. Then she said, "Well, come inside, Miss Morrow. You must be tired. I'll make some tea."

"That's very kind of you."

"Work at the house, do you? Looking after the child?"

"No. I'm painting Mrs. Rockwell's portrait."

She gave me another intent glance before leaving me in the parlor as she went to make the tea. The room was small but charming. The wide-board floors were polished to a high gleam; the mantel and wainscoting were painted a bright blue. It reminded me a little of Starlings. The ceiling was low, and the floors pitched, due, I guessed, to the cottage settling over the years. I was surprised to see some very fine examples of Colonial furniture in the room — a tea table, a lowboy with shell motif, a bookcase with glass doors. It was saying a great deal for Mrs. Perkins that she had not cast them aside for the new, factory-made things of today.

When she brought in the tea tray, I said, "You have some beautiful pieces."

She nodded briskly. "Made here in Newport over one hundred and fifty years ago. My daughter says I ought to sell them, buy new things. I won't."

"You are wise."

She handed me a cup of tea, another surprise. The cup was a delicate eggshell Oriental one. "All these things have been in my family for many years. Now, let's see those drawings."

"They're for a costume ball, you see," I said, feeling more than a little foolish. Unrolling the sheets, I smoothed them out. "It's a Renaissance-style gown — full sleeves, billowing skirt, high-waisted. And I'd like the color to be emerald green. I'll need a mask as well."

She nodded. "When do you want it?"

"In a week?"

She nodded. "You better come back in three or four days for a fitting.

"Thank you, Mrs. Perkins. I'll pay you now so you can get the fabric and things you'll need."

"I used to sew for Mrs. Rockwell, not the one up there now, but Miss Rockwell's mother. The present Mrs. Rockwell wouldn't be caught dead coming down here to me." She almost smiled. "It's just as well. I can't abide those New Yorkers. It's a shame Mr. Rockwell ever married her. A shame about that little boy, too."

She took my measurements and we set up a time for a fitting in several days. I felt that my costume was in very good hands. There was also something I sensed which puzzled me. She seemed curious about me without asking any questions, no, more than curious. She seemed almost apprehensive. And I did not think it was because she did not have the confidence to create the costume. It was something else entirely, a personal feeling about me. Yet she was not an open, garrulous sort; I did not feel comfortable asking her whether anything was wrong.

The following day Cordelia sat for me again, and Bartholomew Reed was her chosen companion. Lounging on the sofa, he filled the room with cigar smoke and the sound of his deep laughter. He wore a diamond ring on his finger which glittered in the sunlight and shot a circle of light on the wall across the room.

Most of the time he talked about men who, according to him, had made foolish investments on Wall Street, or who were "too soft" for business and as a result had lost a great deal of money and property. Mr. Reed had no sympathy for these unfortunate acquaintances. "They didn't have what it takes to stay on top, giving ridiculous sums of money away to charities rather than putting them in the right places where they could grow. And what's the purpose of those charities anyway? To provide aid to the poor and sick so that they can live long enough to produce more poor and sick. They ought to be weeded out. 'A drunkard in the gutter is just where he ought to be,' as that fellow says."

I was relieved when the sitting was over.

When I returned to Mrs. Perkins's cottage for my fitting, I knew that my confidence in her had not been misplaced. She had fashioned the gown precisely as I had drawn it; the material was rich and jewellike, the style full and flowing. When I tried it on, I felt I was one of those allegorical ladies against an Italian landscape. With my hair down and pulled away from my face, the effect would be just as I wished.

Glancing over at Mrs. Perkins, I started to express my admiration for her skill. But I was startled to see a strange look on her face as she studied me in the gown. It was a look of misgiving, almost fear.

"What's wrong, Mrs. Perkins?" I asked.

Abruptly she shook her head and the expression was gone. "Nothing, Miss Morrow." Her voice was brusque.

"But there is. I—I noticed it before. Is something wrong?"

"No." But then she pressed her lips together and her intent gaze did not waver. "I'll tell you. It'll be worse if I don't. My head will ache and who knows, I might be doing you some good. My daughter doesn't like me to talk like this, she takes after her father that way. Miss Morrow, you ought to leave Newport."

"Leave—Newport?"

She nodded grimly. "Ever since I first saw you, I had a sense of something. Something you ought to be afraid of."

I stared at her in consternation. "What do you mean?"

"Nothing may come of it, but then again . . . sometimes things happen. Bad things. You go to that ball if you like, but finish your work and leave. You shouldn't stay here."

"Why do you say that? Do you think something bad will happen to me?" In spite of myself I felt cold prickles creep along my spine.

She shrugged. "You're in love, aren't you? In love, and unhappy."

I could not deny it. To have done so would have been foolish and a waste of time. Somehow she *knew*. Baffled and distressed, I could not answer her.

Briskly she began to unfasten the gown. Her manner had abruptly altered. "I'll have this ready in two more days. Come back for it then. I'll have the mask

236

sewn, too. Same color, I think, not black."

"All right." She seemed annoyed now, with herself and with me. There was no offer of tea; she seemed eager to be rid of me, as though my presence somehow unnerved her.

In a daze I walked back to Copper Beeches, unable to free my mind of her words. Some of the joy, the anticipation, had gone from the prospect of attending the costume ball. I wondered whether, indeed, I should not go. But I already had my costume, a wonderful one, and Isadora would be disappointed if I abruptly changed my mind. And after all, I *was* leaving soon after the ball, just as soon as Cordelia's portrait was completed. There was no question of my remaining in this house to paint Isadora or anyone else. Both Drew and I realized that to prolong my stay any further would be foolhardy, even intolerable.

I could not have imagined then just how intolerable my life would become.

When I returned to Mrs. Perkins's cottage to collect my costume, she was gruff and impersonal. It was as though she resented the feelings I had aroused in her. But she had warned me and could now wash her hands of me with a clear conscience. I thanked her for her splendid work and left.

That evening there was talk of the masquerade ball at the dinner table.

"Drew, if Gideon is present, do not get into an argument with him," said Cordelia. "The entire town is buzzing about him leaving Copper Beeches, and his version of the event is vastly different from yours."

"It would be," said Drew dryly. "You can relax, Cordelia. I want nothing more to do with your brother."

Cordelia flushed angrily, but before she could retort, Isadora said hastily, "I'm so pleased with my costume this year. It's all gold and black and there's a marvelous wig. I sincerely hope that no one will have the slightest notion of who I really am."

"I don't know whether it's suitable for you to be Cleopatra," said Cordelia, distracted from her annoyance with her husband. "Surely some other choice would have been more appropriate for a girl your age."

"I refuse to follow the lead of the other debutantes and be something so insipid as Little Bo Peep!" she declared. Grinning, she added, sending a defiant glance in Cordelia's direction, "I even have gold snake bracelets to wear round my wrists!"

Aunt Hermione was shaking her head. "Tomfoolery. In my day we didn't go in for such things as masquerade balls. Would have thought it vulgar, play-acting."

"Times change, Aunt," said Cordelia profoundly. "Drew doesn't like it either, but this is one ball I insist he attend. It's the most important of the season. Deciding what to be, what to wear — why, people plan for months ahead! I decided on Madame Du Barry last February when I was in Paris. Who are you going to be, Drew?"

"I have no idea," said Drew shortly.

"You have no idea! Are you mad? It's tomorrow night!"

"I have better things to do than plan ridiculous costumes, Cordelia. And since your brother has displayed no inclination or ability to take some of the business dealings off my hands, which is just what your father and my father hoped he would do, I am very busy. I'll come up with something before the ball."

"Well, see that you do," she said, slightly mollified. "I hear Harry Lehr is going to be the Sun King."

"That comes as no surprise. There's nothing your friends like better, Cordelia, than playing royalty. I'll escort you and Isadora, but don't expect me to stay long."

Just long enough to dance with me once, I thought.

"Camille is going to be Maid Marian," said Isadora.

"I understand the Count is becoming more pronounced in his attentions. Her mother seems in no doubt that he will propose."

"But she loathes him!" cried Isadora.

"She'd be a fool to refuse him. They say he has two castles and three hunting lodges."

"Is Miss de la Salle interested in hunting?" asked Drew smoothly.

"Camille says he doesn't bathe often enough," said Isadora in disgust.

"Isadora, really! How can you? And at the dinner table!" cried Cordelia. "At any rate, it scarcely matters what Camille says or thinks. Her mother is determined to see them engaged at the end of the season."

"Parents always know best, don't they, Cordelia?" asked Drew silkily.

Cordelia ignored him, and I thought with pity and concern of Camille and her young man, the schoolmaster from Newport; they had looked so happy and so absorbed in one another at the tea shop that afternoon.

The following day Cordelia did not sit for me; she had one hundred and one things to do to get ready for the ball that evening, and the next day she would be too tired, having stayed up half the night.

Isadora came to my room, eager to see my costume. "Oh, Ariel, it suits you perfectly! How clever of you to think of being one of those models. Isn't Mrs. Perkins a wonder? The only reason I didn't ask her to make my costume was that it was really too exotic. I couldn't have expected her to provide the gold bracelets, leather sandals, and all. I had to send away for it. Camille and I both did."

"I saw her in the tea shop recently with . . . her friend."

"You mean William Everett, I suppose," she said, looking troubled. "She is continuing to meet him in secret, going places none of her mother's friends would go. She is bringing him tonight."

"William?"

She nodded. "I told you she was going to be Maid Marian. That's what she wants everyone to think. Actually, she's going as Juliet and William will be Romeo. Not very subtle, I told her. They think no one will recognize them. But I think it's a terrible risk. William wants to marry Camille, but she doesn't want to elope and that's the only way she'll be able to marry him. She keeps hoping that somehow something will happen and her mother will give them her blessing. I tell her she is mad to think that way. In her mother's mind she and the count are already engaged."

"Mrs. de la Salle really desires this man as a son-in-law?"

"She likes what he represents and that's all she cares about," said Isadora cynically. "She's not interested in what sort of person he is, or whether he will make Camille happy. Could you marry someone called Count Drago? And he even looks a bit sinister. I know Camille will be miserable if she marries him. It's all so pointless! He only wants her inheritance, probably to restore his horrid crumbling castles and hunting lodges, and to spend on his mistresses! William doesn't care a thing for her money. He knows that if she marries him she'll be disinherited. But he cannot persuade Camille to go openly against her mother."

"It's a shame," I said inadequately. "I understand how you must feel."

"Arranged marriages rarely work out," she said with a rather wordly air. "But still people have them. I can hear Mrs. de la Salle saying, 'Only this way will the pure lines of ancestry be maintained.' She's always saying things like that. But I wanted to tell you about the arrangements for tonight. At nine o'clock a carriage will take Drew, Cordelia, and me to Hedgerow,

I've ordered another one to collect you at a quarter past nine. Soon after that I'll be looking out for you. Now you're not going to lose your nerve, are you? You're going to look quite fabulous in that costume!"

I didn't go down to dinner that evening. I was too excited to eat. And for some reason I did not want to see Drew or any of the others so close to the time of the ball, the time of magic. For I was foolishly imagining the next few hours as a time when I would be, not myself, but someone else entirely outside of time. And if I were someone else, so would Drew be. My only worry was that he might decide not to attend, or that he might leave before I arrived.

Finally it was time to put on the heavy emerald gown with its full sleeves and wide folds of skirt. No jewelry was necessary, but I did thread a gold ribbon through my hair which I had curled and left down. When I was ready I looked in the mirror and scarcely recognized myself. For one night I would be a mysterious beauty, a mythical creation of one of my favorite artists who had been a friend of my father. When I tried on the mask of the same green as the gown, the transformation wash complete.

Just before I went down to wait for my carriage, I went along to the nursery wing to see Blythe. The maids were still taking turns looking after her until a new governess arrived. Tonight it was Molly's turn, the rest of the servants having been given the night off except for the coachmen who were to drive us to the ball.

Molly was dozing in the rocking chair; Blythe was sitting up in bed, a picture book on her lap.

"Hello, Blythe," I said.

She looked up, smiling shyly. "Are you going to the ball, too?"

"Yes. Do you like my costume?"

She nodded. "If I were going, I would be a fairy with a silver dress and silver wings."

"Oh, Miss Morrow," said Molly. "I didn't know you at first. Are you going to that costume ball, too? You look very grand."

"Thank you. I had better go. I just wanted to say hello and good night to Blythe."

"Hello and good night. At the same time!" Blythe giggled.

"You're a cheerful one tonight," said Molly. "And here it is past your bedtime and I'm the one falling asleep."

"Well, good night, both of you," I said.

On the second-story landing I met Aunt Hermione coming out the Turkish sitting room. The gaslights were turned down low, leaving much of the area in shadows, and she gasped when she saw me.

"It's Miss Morrow, Mrs. Grant," I said hastily, a little embarrassed.

She pressed her bosom. "Oh, Miss Morrow. So you're going to that ridiculous affair as well?" Her voice was sharp.

"Well, yes. Isadora persuaded me and I thought there would be no harm in it. I'll only stay a little while."

"No harm in it?" she asked severely. "You're playing with fire, Miss Morrow."

"I—I don't know what you mean, Mrs. Grant," I said, flushing. "I do have an invitation, as a guest of Isadora's. I know it's deceitful, but I will leave before the unmasking and Isadora said Mrs. Evans would never know."

"I'm not concerned about Mrs. Evans, and well you know it. I suppose you think you can act as you please with no one to notice, being in costume. Don't look so astonished. I have eyes, you know. And if Cordelia weren't so self-absorbed she'd have caught on by now."

"Caught on to what?" I asked faintly.

Her face softened. "Come now, Miss Morrow. I'm not censuring you. I realize these things happen. But

242

for your own good you and Drew must be very careful."

I bit my lip. "It's not like that, Mrs. Grant. Drew doesn't even know I'll be attending tonight."

"He'll know soon enough," she said gruffly. "I don't suppose you're going to the ball looking like that to meet anyone else. You know what will happen if Cordelia begins to suspect there is something between the two of you, don't you? She can do as she pleases, and she does, but that doesn't mean she would look the other way while Drew found what was missing in his life. If she suspects that he is in love with you, she'll fight back with every vindictive bone in her body."

"It's just for one night," I said, my eyes filling with tears. "I'll be gone soon — we both know it's for the best."

"I'm sorry for you, Miss Morrow, and desperately sorry for Drew. If only he had never agreed to his father's wish that he marry Cordelia. But what's done is done. Well, go on. But be careful, Miss Morrow, be very careful."

Mutely I nodded, and then went down the double staircase to the carriage waiting outside.

In the entrance hall at Hedgerow the pink marble columns were entwined with English ivy and white roses. The ballroom was paneled entirely in gold, with rococo carvings of faces, sunbursts, fleur-de-lis, cherubs, shells and wreaths. There were life-size bronze sculptures of Venus and Mars at the marble mantel. The room was enormous, but crowded with exotic people: kings of England and France, Julius Caesar, a Viking or two, Greeks, pirates, Joan of Arc, Sir Lancelots or Gallahads, Mother Goose, Madame Butterfly in red silk kimono, an Empress of China with a lunar white face and slashed black eyebrows.

"There you are, Ariel. I was beginning to think you had changed your mind." Isadora made a stunning Cleopatra. She wore a narrow gold mask, and her eyes were heavily painted in blue, black, and gold. On her head was a gold Egyptian headdress.

"Isadora, how wonderful you look!"

"Shhh. No names. That's one of the rules at this ball. Until the unmasking, that is. All this paint is making my face itch. I'll probably be all red tomorrow. I don't know how Cleopatra stood it. But I'm willing to bet that no one recognizes me." She smiled enigmatically, achieving the proper effect. It was likely she had been practicing all day. Just then Julius Caesar approached us, asking Cleopatra to dance. Waving at me, she went off with him.

The orchestra was playing a waltz, but I could not see the musicians through the throng of people. I caught sight of a tall lady in powdered wig and low-cut satin gown with wide *panniers*. She was dancing with Sir Francis Drake; I had no trouble recognizing Cordelia and Bartholomew Reed.

"Burne-Jones or Rossetti?" said a voice beside me, and I turned to see a man dressed like a judge in an English court, in white wig and black robe.

"Burne-Jones," I said, smiling at Dr. Chandler.

"Are you enjoying yourself? I feel a fool at these types of affairs, but my wife insists on going. She enjoys it. Even Gwendolyn is here tonight. My daughter is Lizzie Borden. A rather questionable choice, I'm afraid."

Ulysses came up then and asked me to dance; afterwards I danced with Henry VIII and Cardinal Richelieu. My partners used various ruses to try to get me to identify myself, but I evaded their questions.

"Can't be your real hair," mused Henry, "or I'd know you for sure. Oh well, I'll know at midnight, won't I?"

I still had not seen Drew, or even someone I suspected might be he. I had looked twice at a tall, dark-haired Roman gladiator, but realized swiftly that the man wasn't he.

Romeo and Juliet whirled past, and I remembered Camille's and William's costume choices. If the young lady were Camille, she was unrecognizable in a dark wig covered partially by a beaded velvet cap. Cleopatra danced by with a Highlander. Isadora was greatly enjoying herself this evening, playing the alluring Queen of the Nile.

And then I looked down to see—yes, it was—an *axe* with what looked like blood crusted on it. Gwendolyn Chandler stood beside me, holding the axe.

"They never found the dress, you know," she said abruptly. "The one she wore. The one that must have been covered with blood."

I did not know what to say. I felt repelled by her pale green eyes, luminous through the slits of her mask.

"She burned one she said had paint stains on it. Brown stains. Do you think she did it, Miss Morrow?"

"I—I don't know," I said, my mouth dry. "I didn't follow the case."

"I followed it very carefully. I read every article I could. She especially hated her stepmother, but she loved her father very much. You know that Fall River is very close to Newport, don't you? Imagine, killing your father and mother, hacking them with an axe—and getting away with it. All because you teach Sunday school."

"You won't be able to dance, holding that thing," I said, wincing.

"I didn't come to dance," she replied scornfully. "Why did *you* come, Miss Morrow?"

When Robin Hood approached and asked me to dance, I went with him in relief. Gwendolyn Chandler was too strange; I had felt almost frightened of her.

Where was Drew? Had he decided not to come after all? I should have asked Isadora what his costume was, but I had been reluctant to show an interest in him.

"Well, I never expected to see you here," said another Roman. "Are you a gate-crasher?"

"Certainly not," I answered Gideon. "Isadora procured me an invitation."

"Did she? Resourceful little thing, Isadora. I wonder whether our hostess, Mary, Queen of Scots, knows who the lovely Renaissance maiden is. Oh, I won't tell her. Not if you dance with me, that is."

"Haven't you caused me enough problems—and also yourself? I'd sooner dance with the devil!" I cried angrily.

He laughed. "Don't you know I *am* the devil? Or a form of him. I'm Caligula."

"The only thing I know about Caligula is that he made his horse a senator. I thought you were another Caesar or Marc Antony."

"Oh no, too dull by far. Have you seen Lizzie Borden? Now if I were Dr. or Mrs. Chandler I'd be more than a little worried." He chuckled. "Dance with me, Miss Morrow, or I'll expose you here, now, as someone even the easygoing Mrs. Evans wouldn't have on her guest list."

"You wouldn't dare!" I hissed.

"Oh, no? I assure you I will. I have a bone to pick with you, Miss Ariel Morrow. You're the reason Drew threw me out of the house." Through the slits in his mask his eyes held a threatening glint.

"I'm the reason! I suppose you've forgotten what you were doing that afternoon. You ought to be ashamed of yourself, taking advantage of Miss Simmons the way you did!"

"I took advantage of her? That's rich! It was more the other way round. I don't like being a stand-in for someone, especially my brother-in-law!"

"I'm leaving," I said furiously. "I'm going back to Copper Beeches." The night was ruined. Drew was obviously not here and not coming, and I refused to stay and argue with Gideon Lawrence. That was not the reason I had ordered this costume.

But suddenly there was a hand at my elbow and a tall masked man was standing beside me. He wore a tricorn hat. His black cape, which fell to the top of his glossy riding boots, was opened to reveal a pearl gray waistcoat, white ruffled shirt, and dark knee breeches. Beside him Caligula looked rather ridiculous in his gold-leaf head wreath and white muslin tunic.

"I believe this next dance is mine. Or should I say merely, 'Stand and deliver'?" said Drew ironically. And then he had taken me in his arms and swept me away.

"You're a *highwayman*," I said, relief so heady it made me giggle.

"And you are enchanting. I'm certain Burne-Jones would agree."

"It was you who gave me the idea, you know," I said shyly. "I—I was afraid you hadn't come."

"I nearly didn't. I went back after bringing Cordelia and Dora. I didn't think I could stand another one of these absurd affairs. I went to Blythe's room to say good-night, and she told me she'd seen the fairy lady on her way to the ball. So I came back."

"You don't mind, do you? It was Isadora's idea. She seemed to think I would be lost in the crowd, that no one would notice me."

"That, my lovely one, is scarcely possible," he said in my ear.

We danced several waltzes in succession and then he said, "Let's get out of here. I've had enough of this, and I want to be alone with you."

I, too, was ready to leave, the amusement of the evening wearing thin. I had had my fill of kings, queens, powdered wigs and masks.

Once in the darkness of the carriage, he pulled off his mask. "Enough of this foolishness," he said huskily and pulled me to him.

But the ride to Copper Beeches was too short. Just as we were climbing out of the carriage, there came a loud cry from above. Shocked, I looked up, scanning the row of windows.

"Mr. Rockwell, help! come quick."

"My God, it's Molly—the nursery!" He dashed into the house, taking the stairs three at a time. I followed him as rapidly as I could. When I reached the nursery wing, I was conscious of a strong, deadly smell—gas.

Molly was weeping in the corridor, her apron covering her face. Drew came out, cradling his daughter in his arms. Her face was white, but no whiter than his.

"Oh, my God," I cried in horror.

"She's still alive. Open all the windows, Molly. The entire floor must be aired out."

"Yes, sir. Thank the Lord you came home when you did. It's a miracle, it is. If I hadn't waked up and smelled the gas . . ."

The stained-glass window in Blythe's room was raised a little, and I realized that Molly must have called down to us from there.

"Was that window open?" I asked.

"Yes, miss. I had opened it because the night was so warm. Then I sat back in the rocking chair and fell asleep."

"Molly, get the coachman to go for Dr. Chandler. He is at Hedgerow, but leave a message at Oaklawn that I want him to examine Blythe tonight," said Drew. He turned back to Blythe, bending over her. "Wake up, darling, wake up." Gently he tapped her cheek.

"How did it happen, Drew?" I asked him when Molly had gone. "I smelled the gas as soon as I reached the corridor."

"The gas was turned on, but the lights were not lit. I turned off the jets myself. Molly had already dragged Blythe off the bed and almost out the door."

"She woke up just in time to save Blythe and herself," I said. "Thank God the window was slightly open!"

"Molly has a great deal of explaining to do," said Drew grimly. "Wake up, Blythe. Wake up for Daddy." There was a note of desperation in his voice.

Eventually she stirred, frowned, and opened her eyes. I realized I had been holding my breath, as frightened as Drew, and sighed in great relief.

"Daddy? Why are we out in the hall? I'm sleepy."

"Are you sweetheart?"

She had closed her eyes again. "The smell is gone now," I told him. "You can put her back in bed."

He carried her into her room and set her down gently on the bed, but did not leave her side. Silently he stroked her dark curls and pale cheeks. We did not talk; I realized that he was almost dazed with the effects of terror and relief.

Dr. Chandler came a while later, his white wig and black robe discarded. "The maid tells me Blythe inhaled gas fumes!" Drew got up so he could examine the sleeping little girl. He listened to her heart.

"She's very fortunate, Drew. She'll be fine. Tomorrow she'll likely have a headache and her throat may be sore, but that's the extent of it."

"Thank God," breathed Drew. His face was still ashen.

"How on earth did such a thing happen?"

"That's what I'm going to find out. Molly? Come in here, please."

Her eyes were red-rimmed and she was twisting the corner of her apron around one finger.

"Molly, when I entered this room, the gas was escaping but the lights were not on. Can you explain why?" Drew asked her sternly.

"I don't know, sir! I can't imagine how it happened. I'm that certain I turned off the gas when I put out the light. I *couldn't* forget a thing like that!"

"You're new here, aren't you, Molly?" asked Dr. Chandler.

"Yes, sir. I came this past May."

"New to America?"

She nodded miserably.

"Where did you come from? Ireland, isn't it?"

"Yes, sir."

"Belfast? Dublin?"

"No, sir, not the city, the country."

"The country," repeated Dr. Chandler. "And how did you light your cottage?"

She looked surprised. "Why, with candles. And with one oil lamp."

"No gas?" he asked gently.

"No, sir." She bit her lip. "I know we didn't have gas, but I've lived here for three months and I know just how to use it. I swear to you, by the Holy Mother, I'd never have made such a dreadful mistake!" She was in tears again.

"Well, you have both been very fortunate. Blythe will be fine, and you, Molly, should try to get a good night's sleep."

"Thank you for coming, Prescott," said Drew, stretching out his hand. "Can you find your own way out? Most of the staff have the night off."

"Of course. Good night, Miss Morrow."

"Good night, Dr. Chandler."

When he had left Drew again turned to Molly. "Don't you know that at least one of these lights is to be left on at night? If you had followed my instructions, this would not have happened."

Her face went scarlet. "I'm that sorry, sir. I—I forgot. Miss Blythe was already asleep and I was so sleepy meself. I didn't remember about the light being left on all night. But I know I turned off the gas!"

Drew sighed heavily. "I should discharge you, I suppose. But I won't. Now go off to bed. You must be

250

feeling poorly yourself. I'll stay with Blythe. Don't be so careless again."

"Yes, sir," she mumbled brokenly and slipped gratefully away.

"I better go to my room, Drew," I said. "If Cordelia should return . . ."

He came over to me. "I'm sorry the night had to end like this, Ariel."

"Don't say that. Thank heavens we left the ball when we did. And remember, no matter what Molly did with the gas-light, she was getting Blythe out of the room."

He followed me out into the hall and held me tightly against him, his face buried in my neck. "For a few moments, I was so afraid—it was almost like that time with Nathan. I don't think I could have stood it, again."

My neck was damp. "I know, I know. I love you, Drew." There was nothing else for me to say.

Chapter Thirteen

When I was having breakfast the next day, Isadora came into the dining room, very distraught.

"I've just heard what happened to Blythe! She and Molly might have — if you and Drew hadn't come home early and found them."

"It was a miracle that we did," I agreed. "You see," I explained awkwardly, "I did have to leave the ball before midnight, and your brother was kind enough to escort me back to the house." My face warm, I wondered if she suspected, as Aunt Hermione did, that there was more between us than merely the relationship of an employer and employee.

"Did you enjoy yourself last night, Ariel?"

"I did, very much."

She smiled. "I think several of your dancing partners were looking about for you at the unmasking. I must tell you, I shocked many people when I revealed who I was! It was great fun. Of course, now when I think that while I was enjoying myself, Blythe nearly died . . ."

"There's no way you could have known," I said. "And it's all over now — they are perfectly safe."

"How could Molly have been so careless? It makes my blood run cold to think what might have happened."

"Well, Molly did wake up in time and dragged Blythe out of bed. And the window, thank heaven, was raised a bit."

"I think we'll all feel better when the new governess comes," she said.

"Has your brother found one?"

She nodded. "A woman in Boston. The family she has worked for there are going to Europe and will not be taking

252

her. Hopefully she will be an improvement on Miss Simmons. I never felt she was right for Blythe, though she did seem attached to her. Blythe, I mean. Miss Simmons never seemed truly fond of her."

After we had finished breakfast, we went upstairs together. On the second-story landing I was turning to climb the remaining flight to my room when a door was flung open and Cordelia, attired in her lilac chiffon dressing gown, glared at me accusingly, two bright spots of color in her cheeks.

"Well, Miss Morrow, I hope you are pleased with yourself!"

"What — what do you mean, Mrs. Rockwell?" I asked, taken aback.

"It seems you and my husband are getting yourselves talked about!"

I flushed scarlet to the roots of my hair, heat rushing into my face like a wave. "T-talked about?" I asked feebly.

Isadora giggled. "Don't be foolish, Cordelia. Who is talking about them?"

"Oh, nearly everyone by now, I should imagine!" Cordelia thrust the latest edition of *Town Topics* in front of our faces.

I bit my lip.

"Oh, that piece of trash! Honestly, Cordelia! You know they invent most of their items, or twist the real facts!" cried Isadora with scorn.

"You obviously have forgotten about Maisie, Isadora. Just listen: 'There is a charming new addition to the household of one of the older Newport mansions, the daughter of a famous painter who is also, quite remarkably, an artist herself. Is she the red-haired beauty we have noticed in the company of the master of the house, walking and riding about town?' Cordelia stopped and glared at me. 'And is she behind the feud which exists between him and his brother-in-law who, we understand, is no longer welcome in that house?'

"Oh, that had nothing to do with me!" I protested.

"It's all nonsense, Cordelia! Surely you don't believe that filth — they are only insinuating! We all know why Drew forced Gideon to leave, and it had nothing whatsoever to do with Ariel!" said Isadora.

"Once I was exploring the town, Mrs. Rockwell, and I met up with Mr. Rockwell quite by accident —"

"Oh, I know there's nothing truly in it," said Cordelia, tapping her foot on the wooden floor, "but it makes us all look so ridiculous!"

"Why do you bother to read that rubbish?" asked Isadora. "Every issue carries in it something which, one way or the other, manages to upset you."

"It's essential to keep abreast of what is being said, Isadora. Perhaps you should read it yourself. There's an entry here you are bound to be interested in," Cordelia told her complacently.

"Why, am I in it?" asked Isadora, delighted.

Cordelia threw her a withering glance and began to read. " 'Love is blooming everywhere this season, and between the unlikeliest couples. The latest romance, we are told, is that of a young heiress with a French name, and one of Mr. Lehr's 'footstools,' a worthy young man, no doubt, but scarcely one to be accepted by the heiress's mother who is looking favorably on the suit of a European blue blood. Which man, we wonder, will be the fortunate one?' "

Cordelia regarded Isadora with mocking triumph. "And that heiress, if I'm not much mistaken, is your dear friend Camille. Just who is this footstool, Isadora?"

Isadora's face had gone quite pale. "Let me see that," she said faintly. Cordelia handed the copy to her and she scanned the paragraph. Then she turned to me, her face stricken. "Oh, no, if Camille's mother sees that, then something quite dreadful is sure to happen! I must go to Camille right now."

"So *Town Topics* is all nonsense, is it, Isadora? Well, perhaps not every time," said Cordelia, satisfied that her dart had found its mark.

Isadora did not answer. She hurried into her room and

closed the door.

I was moving up the staircase when Cordelia called to me. "Well, Miss Morrow, I should be more careful of my behavior from now on, if I were you. Having your name linked with your employer, however mistakeably, will not endear you to those who might consider employing you in future. I have friends who would definitely think twice about engaging a female artist about whom the rumors were flying."

What about *your* behavior, I wanted to ask. Why isn't there gossip about you? I also felt unaccountably annoyed that she had so quickly assumed that there was "nothing in it." Did she think Drew was made of stone, that, locked in a sterile marriage, he might not ever fall in love? But not with a female artist. That would be too vulgar by far.

But she was right about one thing. Were there ugly gossip about Drew and me, my career, my professional reputation, would suffer. And I could very well be burdened with the advances of future male employers who assumed that if I had dallied with a former one, why not with another?

Drew and I had to be very careful from now on, until I left Copper Beeches and we were parted for good. I realized it had been very foolish to attend the ball last night, and hoped that no one, reading the scandal sheet this morning, had put two and two together. If only Gideon had not recognized me. As for Dr. Chandler, I was certain he would say nothing.

Anxious to get my mind off myself and my troubles, I went to Blythe's room. She was listlessly fitting a puzzle together while Nancy sat in the rocking chair, mending.

"Blythe, would you like to go for a walk with me?" I asked. "If you feel strong enough, that is. How do you feel?"

"All right. My throat hurts just a bit, but not as bad as it did last night. Daddy stayed with me all night," she said importantly, "until Nancy came in this morning with my breakfast. Do you know what, Ariel? Molly told me all about the little people in Ireland last night. Her grand-

255

mother used to leave them a bowl of milk and some food outside the cottage door! Do you think we might do that?"

"Well, we could ask Mrs. Meredith, I suppose. Would you like to?"

"It's all she talks about, Miss Morrow," said Nancy, "fairies and such." She shook her head.

"Don't you believe in fairies, Nancy?" asked Blythe solemnly. "Ariel does, and so does Molly."

"I've never seen one, have I?" But then she relented, seeing Blythe's crestfallen expression. "But I had a great-uncle, a sailor, who believed in mermaids, and nothing anyone said could make him stop."

Blythe and I went downstairs to the kitchen. Mrs. Meredith was sitting at the table with another woman whom I knew to be Matilda, Olive Chandler's personal maid, who came over from Oaklawn from time to time to chat with Mrs. Meredith. Mrs. Meredith had always treated me with civility, but Matilda eyed me suspiciously, her face tight. I wondered whether the two of them had seen the last issue of *Town Topics,* and felt my face growing warm again.

"Well, Miss Blythe, and how are you?" asked Mrs. Meredith, getting up from her chair. "I thought you'd be in bed all day after what that foolish Molly did. I told her she was a lucky girl to still have her post here — it was more than she deserved."

"Are there any cookies, Mrs. Meredith?" asked Blythe, single-minded.

"Why, of course. Would you like some with a glass of milk?" asked the cook indulgently.

"Yes, please, and could we have some for the Little People?"

"For the what?" Mrs. Meredith turned about, her hand poised above the cookie jar.

"You know, the Little People, the fairies," said Blythe earnestly. "Molly says they come to your back door and, if you leave food for them, they bring good luck to your house."

"That good-for-nothing Irish baggage," mumbled Mrs.

Meredith. "Little People! All that will come will be nasty squirrels and ants and things. Oh, very well, Miss Blythe. Go on, take two cookies and put the plate outside. I suppose we need good fortune as much as anybody else, isn't that so, Matilda? But I won't have pests coming near my kitchen!"

"Oh, they won't bother anything," said Blythe and she took the plate to the door, setting it out on the step.

"Why don't you take your cookies outside and eat them as we walk?" I suggested. I did not feel comfortable with Matilda's hostile gaze on me.

Blythe agreed and we took a walk about the grounds, searching for signs of fairies.

"They might like the weeping beeches," I said. "The long, heavy branches would keep them from being seen, and there is plenty of room for them to dance underneath. Listen, can you hear the whispering sounds the leaves make?"

"Maybe it's the fairies and elves who are making the sounds," she said. "Maybe that's how they laugh and talk!" She pushed aside the branches and we stood beneath the huge tree. "They don't dance during the day," I reminded her. "And their footprints are too light and tiny for us to see."

"Do you think they'll like the cookies?" she asked. "I broke them into tiny crumbs."

"I'm certain they'll be very grateful," I told her, making a mental note to go and remove the cookie crumbs from the plate later that day.

"Daddy says a new governess is coming to take care of me. I wish it was you."

Touched, I said, "Darling, I'm not a governess. But it makes me happy to hear you say that."

"You'll stay here, won't you, Ariel? You'll stay and help me look for fairies?"

I bit my lip. "I'll have to go back to my own home soon, Blythe. But perhaps your new governess will help you look for fairies." Whatever the new woman was like, I hoped she had an imagination, the sort of imagination which could fit into a child's world.

After I had taken Blythe back up to the nursery, I returned to my room. Isadora came in search of me shortly after. She was terribly agitated.

"Oh, Ariel, I'm so glad you're here! I have to talk to you."

"What is it, Isadora? What's wrong?"

"It's Camille. I went to her house. Her mother wouldn't receive me. The butler told me that Camille was ill and could not see anyone. I *know* she's not really ill! It's all due to that horrible *Town Topics!* Her mother has found out about William!"

"Oh, Isadora, I'm so sorry—for both of them! Maybe her mother will come round. She's probably very angry now, and that's why she wouldn't admit you into the house, but later—"

"No, Ariel, you don't understand! Mrs. de la Salle will *never* permit Camille to marry William, never in a million years. He may as well be the Man in the Moon! Their only chance in being together was in eloping. I know Camille's not ill. She's being kept in that house like a prisoner, until her mother can do something!"

"Isadora—"

"Listen to me. I know what I'm talking about, although to you it probably sounds like something out of a melodrama. Mrs. Vanderbilt, I mean, Belmont, did the same thing to Consuelo. She kept her a prisoner in Marble Palace until she relented. Until she promised to marry that awful Duke of Marlborough. And today, at Camille's, when I was leaving, that Count Drago drove up. He bowed very low to me, an odious smile on his face. He knows I don't like him, and that I knew about William all the time. He knows Camille loathes him and he doesn't care. I'm so afraid she'll be forced to marry him. She'll be wretchedly unhappy!"

"Isadora, it's a terrible thing, but I don't know what can be done," I said helplessly.

"If only William could get word to Camille, if only there were a way they could elope. Why did they wait? I was afraid that something like this would happen! But now Camille is locked up, and I'm not allowed in the house. Perhaps—perhaps we might go and see William. Only I don't know what good that would do."

"It might do him some good, to see you, to talk to you."

"All right. But please come with me, Ariel. Perhaps the three of us can come up with something."

I nodded. "I'll come. Do you know where he lives?"

"Yes, I think so. We'll go this evening."

But we did not go that evening. Because by then Cordelia had learned that Mrs. de la Salle and Camille had left on the steamboat to New York, accompanied by the Count. Their engagement had been hastily, though not formally, announced. They would be married in New York and leave for the Continent shortly afterward.

"Mrs. de la Salle is forgoing a large society wedding," said Cordelia. "What a shame, not to be able to bask in the envy of her acquaintances! She's accompanying them to Europe, I understand. I wonder if she fears Camille will try to throw herself overboard. She's very angry with you, Isadora, and everyone knows it. You were well aware of Camille's unfortunate attachment to that unsuitable young man."

Isadora said nothing, staring down at her plate.

"And Drew, while I'm on the subject . . . you know that you and Miss Morrow have been the subject of speculation among the gossips."

He looked up, frowning, and shot a swift keen glance at me.

"People will begin to talk about the two of you," warned Cordelia. "I'm certain you don't wish that to happen."

He regarded his wife sardonically. "We can do what we like just so long as people do not talk, isn't that it, Cordelia?"

There was an awkward silence. Cordelia reddened, glaring at him with venomous dislike. But at least she put no faith into what the gossips were saying. It had not occurred to her that the implications might be true.

I had to leave Copper Beeches as quickly as possible. I had to finish Cordelia's portrait.

The following morning I was eager to get back to work. Before Cordelia came into the drawing room, I set up my easel and began to mix the colors I would need. Venetian red and umber for her hair, mixed with a little linseed oil to give it a sheen. To create a glowing, translucent look to her face, eliminating all brush strokes, I would use a clean dry brush, stroking it over and over before the paint had altogether dried.

While I was working intently, Bartholomew Reed came in; I did not notice him until the smoke from his cigar wafted toward me. I told Cordelia she might relax for a while as I was going to do some work on the backdrop of the floral panel.

Cordelia was saying, "And Bart, our dear Isadora knew all along that Camille de la Salle was meeting that schoolteacher! That's probably what we have to look forward to in this family — that Isadora will disgrace us by marrying someone quite unacceptable! Then Drew will sing a different tune. He actually said that Eleanor de la Salle should have permitted Camille to marry this boy! And you know how permissable he is with Isadora. Apparently Camille even brought this boy to the masquerade ball. Isadora said they went as Romeo and Juliet — how very affecting! Camille wore a dark wig. The Count, I understand, spent the entire evening looking for a blond Maid Marian!" She laughed.

"Well, that's the purpose of a masquerade ball, isn't it, my dear? To do things in the guise of another? Things one can't or shouldn't do oneself? I noticed your husband doing just that," said Bartholomew Reed.

"Drew? What are you talking about, Bart? He wasn't even there. I knew he would hurry home as soon as possible."

"I hesitate to correct you, Cordelia, but he was most certainly present that night. And rather preoccupied with a mysterious red-haired beauty, I observed."

My hand froze on the canvas.

"What do you mean, Bart? You must be confusing Drew with someone else. There were other highwaymen, I daresay."

"Perhaps. But none, I'm forced to admit, with your dear husband's bearing. It was certainly he. As to the red-haired beauty clothed in green, I'll leave it to you to guess her identity."

"Just what are you implying?" asked Cordelia sharply.

"Why, nothing at all, my dear. Only that at midnight he and his partner were nowhere to be found. So you see, he is not so impervious to female charms as you have believed."

Cordelia laughed a bit harshly. "The only red-headed lady I can think of is Alva Belmont. And you can be sure that Drew was not suddenly captivated by *her*. The lady you speak of might have been wearing a wig." She paused. "Or she might have been Miss Morrow."

My head shot up; I gazed at her in dismay.

"I had come to the same conclusion myself," said Bartholomew Reed dryly.

My face was hot. Before she could say anything, I blurted out, "I did attend the ball, Mrs. Rockwell. Isadora insisted, and I allowed her to persuade me. I suppose I shouldn't have. But I was only there a short while. Mr. Rockwell escorted me back here—and that was when we found Blythe unconscious."

Cordelia regarded me with amusement. "Do not look so distressed, Miss Morrow. I'm not at all surprised to hear about Isadora's part in this. And I suppose attending a most important social event such as that was a novelty for you. Well, I've had enough for this morning." She yawned. "I must change for luncheon."

When she had left the room Bartholomew Reed got up and came over to me, glancing at the easel. "Hmm. It's good. You must be relieved, Miss Morrow, that your secret is safe, at least for the time being."

"What secret is that, sir?" I asked coldly.

He smoothed back his hair from his forehead, the diamond ring sparkling. "Cordelia can be remarkably obtuse at times. But you don't have to play coy and innocent with me."

"I resent what you are implying, Mr. Reed, and I won't beat about the bush with you. Mrs. Rockwell has nothing to fear from me."

"Then Drew must be a fool. What could be simpler? A lovely lady artist living in his house, and it's common knowledge he and Cordelia detest one another."

Taking up my things, I left the room, my heart pounding. First Gideon had guessed the nature of Drew's feelings for me; then Aunt Hermione. And now Bartholomew Reed. He seemed to enjoy toying with people. But Cordelia had evidently not taken him seriously, and for that I was grateful.

Later that afternoon Isadora asked me to accompany her to William Everett's house.

"But Camille is gone now, Isadora. What good will it do?"

"You said yourself he might need to talk to someone. Perhaps he would appreciate a visit from me."

"But hardly from me. I've never even met him."

"You don't have to come inside the house. You can stay out in the carriage. Just come with me, please."

"All right. I could use some fresh air."

But it was a dreary day. In the mottled sky the clouds hung low; it was sultry and windless. We rode down Bellevue Avenue in the wicker phaeton, saying little.

We drew up outside a modest house with a front porch which Isadora said belonged to William's parents. Climbing down from the phaeton, she gave me a faint smile before going up the walkway.

I leaned back in the phaeton, immersed in my own thoughts. The portrait of Cordelia was good, very good. I wished that my father might be here to see it. Yet I realized that I did not need his confirmation of its worth. I now had an opportunity to have a successful career as a portrait painter, something even he had believed might be beyond my reach. Now I was close to obtaining my dream, yet somehow the allure was not as strong. I felt strangely low and almost apathetic.

Isadora was coming out of the house; I was surprised to see her so soon. Her face was pinched with horror; despite the oppressive humidity of the day I felt a sudden chill.

"Oh, Ariel," she began, climbing into the phaeton and taking the reins. "Something terrible has happened!" Her voice was barely above a whisper.

"What is it? Did you see William?" I asked urgently.

She shook her head. "I—I couldn't. They wouldn't let me. I mean, there was an accident last night!"

"What sort of accident?" I asked, my heart slowing to a dull thud.

"To—to William. He had gone out for a walk, I suppose. At any rate, a carriage struck him down as he was crossing the street."

"Oh, my God. He's not . . . ?"

"He's still alive. But his legs were horribly crushed, and his back. Oh, Ariel, the woman who answered the door told me he'll never walk again!"

"Oh, Isadora!"

"I suppose he was so upset about losing Camille that he didn't notice the carriage. And it was dark."

"The driver didn't stop?"

"No. He was probably drunk. William was unconscious when they found him. I can't believe it—it's too awful to contemplate! And Camille . . ."

We rode back in silence. Perhaps it was the oppressive, unbreathable air. Perhaps it was unhappiness of my own hopeless situation. But as we drove down Bellevue Avenue with its elegant shops, its magnificent houses and gardens, I began to be frightened. I began to feel that there was something horribly amiss in this jewelled city by the sea. Maisie Leander's suicide followed by that of her coachman, the spiriting away of Camille de la Salle and her brutally forced marriage to a man she detested and doubtless feared, and now this dreadful accident to William Everett who had loved a young woman above his station.

In addition to the luxury, charm, and beauty of our surroundings, there was something else. Something that was spinning out of control, something evil . . .

I told myself I was being ridiculously fanciful. What on earth had William Everett's accident to do with Maisie Leander's suicide? But it wasn't just that; it was Blythe's brush with death several nights ago; it was the malicious gossip in *Town Topics* which was insidiously ruining lives. There was also the eerie warning from Mrs. Perkins, her insistence that I leave Newport before it was too late.

All these things combined now to make me uneasy, even vaguely alarmed. But I was beyond understanding my impressions. As we turned into the entrance to Copper Beeches, the weeping beeches towered like hideous shaggy monsters, sinister and ominous. Today there was no charm in the whispering of their leaves.

The following day Cordelia announced that she was going to give a dinner party when the portrait was complete.

"I want everyone to see it. Naturally you will be invited, Miss Morrow, as I said before. We'll hang the portrait on the drawing-room wall and keep it covered for effect. Then, when everyone has gathered there after dinner, I will have it unveiled for all to see."

This was too melodramatic for my taste. "Thank you, Mrs. Rockwell. But I am anxious to return to New York once the portrait is finished. I — I have some business matters to attend to concerning my father's estate."

"Well, you must delay your departure until after the dinner party. Surely one extra day will make no difference. And I'm certain you wish to procure other commissions. That evening will be the ideal time for our guests to view your work. They will be returning to New York themselves in a few weeks' time. If they have the opportunity to meet you, then you may very well line up a number of commissions. That is, if you are desirous of doing so."

Again she knew just what to say. I wished nothing better than to receive commissions to paint portraits. Working on

Cordelia's had been an exhilarating experience for me, despite my dislike for her. I could not go back to painting rooms for the rest of my life. Now that I had accepted one commission to paint a portrait, I wanted there to be more. No, I could not spurn Cordelia's patronage so easily.

"Very well, Mrs. Rockwell. You are very gracious. I will stay until after the reception."

The new governess arrived a day or so later. Her name, Nancy told me, was Miss Janet McCready, and she spoke with a thick Scottish burr. She was middle-aged, and a very different sort of person from Miss Simmons.

Blythe and I were playing underneath the weeping beeches when we heard Drew call, "Blythe, where are you? There is someone I'd like you to meet."

They could not see us through the heavy branches of the weeping hemlock, nor could we see them. Blythe, reluctant to meet someone new, answered, "There is no one here but the Fairy of the Hemlock."

I was about to take her hand and lead her out from under the tree when to our surprise a strange voice replied, "But if I walk widdershins about this tree nine times, the fairy must come out."

Blythe stared at me, wide-eyed. We heard someone walking around the circumference of the hemlock again and again. Blythe was giggling.

Then came, "I have now completed the spell to make the fairy come out of hiding. She must now do as I wish."

Blythe walked out from under the huge bushlike tree, and I bent my head to do the same. Standing outside was a slight small woman with pale red hair. She wore a dark blue gown with white collar and cuffs. Drew was gone.

"Well, what a bonny fairy. Never in the Highland glens have I seen such a one. And now you must grant me a wish."

"What wish?" asked Blythe, delighted.

"Well, I must think now. What shall I wish for? A big house and a lot of money? Shall I wish for all the freckles to leave my face? Or shall I wish to see the little girl named Blythe that I've come so far to look after? Bonny Fairy of the

Hemlock, be good enough to summon Miss Blythe while I turn about and shut my eyes."

As she turned around Blythe looked at me and giggled again. Then she said in a solemn voice, "Your wish is granted."

The small lady turned around and her cheerful face lit up. "Well! Never did I expect to meet up with magic here. I thought I had left all that behind me in Scotland when I was a girl. For it's a verra old country, much older than this one, with much magic left in it from the Old Ones who were there long before the coming of Christ."

"What sort of magic?" asked Blythe.

"Oh, I could tell you about the kelpies who live in streams or wells, and the selkies who come ashore and shed their seal skins, taking human form, and the wee folk who live under the hills, and the giants who live in the mountains —"

"Oh!" exclaimed Blythe. "Ariel and I don't know those stories. Please tell us!"

"I'll tell you," said Miss McCready, "but first things first. I am Miss Janet McCready."

"I am Blythe Rockwell."

"How do you do, Miss McCready? I am Miss Morrow." I gave her my hand.

"Where is Daddy?" asked Blythe.

"Oh, he dinna know how to walk widdershins about the hemlock, so he had to return to the house," said Janet McCready severely.

Blythe laughed and so did I.

"Now, I'm thirsty for a cup of tea. I always carry my own with me. Queen Mary. Why don't you and Miss Morrow show me the way to the nursery and we'll all have some. I have my own special biscuits as well. Not as good as scones or shortbread, but they'll do."

So the three of us went up to the nursery. Miss McCready looked about her with satisfaction. "This will do verra well. And what luck it is to have a window with two of the wee folk on it. They'll look after you. And there won't be anything to be afraid of, not with Janet McCready here."

So Drew had given Miss McCready an idea of Blythe's sudden and inexplicable anxieties. And as I sat in the nursery drinking tea and listening to her tell stories to Blythe, I felt that she was just the person to deal with them.

That night at dinner Cordelia was full of plans for the dinner party, and the "unveiling" of the portrait, as she called it. The whole notion made me uncomfortable, but I told myself that it was her own vanity which was impelling her to make such a presentation.

"I thought not too large a party. Fifty guests, I daresay. That will be more intimate."

"Fifty is all the dining room will hold," said Drew dryly.

"Anyone not present will hear all about it the next day. I'm inviting only the most important people, Miss Morrow. Eight courses, I thought. As for the flowers, I've decided on gardenias. Bowls of them everywhere. And I'm going to take Mamie Fish's advice and serve nothing but champagne. Wine makes everyone too dull."

"I'd like to see the champagne that can keep your friends from being dull," said Drew bluntly.

Cordelia ignored him. "I wonder whether I should send to New York for a French chef? Mrs. Meredith is fully capable, I suppose. I only want the best for this dinner party. The portrait will be a wonderful surprise. I know you were against Miss Morrow being here at first, but surely you've changed your mind?"

"Miss Morrow is very talented," answered Drew coolly.

Cordelia changed the subject to that evening's musicale at Wakehurst which she and Isadora were planning to attend. As quickly as possible after dessert, I excused myself. But as I was going up the stairs, Drew caught up with me.

"Come out to the Moongate at ten o'clock," he said in a low voice.

It was now not yet nine. I went upstairs to my room, my heart racing. Why did he wish to meet me? Wasn't it taking too much of a risk? I had only another week here at most; I did not want any more complications. Yet desperately I longed to be alone with him again.

Shortly before ten o'clock, I went downstairs and outside. I moved slowly across the lawn, suddenly shy and filled with misgiving. We should not be meeting in secret this way; it was too dangerous. If Cordelia were to find out. . . . Ahead of me rose the weeping beeches, faintly rustling in the night air.

Drew was waiting for me at the Chinese Moongate. I paused before I reached him, hesitating, but in two strides he had crushed me to him, his mouth claiming mine.

"Oh, Ariel," he said hoarsely, his breathing ragged, "I can't be strong any longer. It's too much — more than I can bear. I refuse to let you go. I'm going to talk to Cordelia. There must be a way. She can have the house, anything. Except Blythe. She must let me go!"

"No, Drew, don't — don't talk to her." Pushing him away, I said, "I — I'm frightened. Something's wrong somehow. We mustn't talk this way." I shivered.

"There's nothing to be afraid of, sweetheart," he said, his arms going round me again, his hand stroking my hair. "But I'll wait. I'll wait to talk to her until after you've gone. But I won't live this way any more, Ariel. I won't let you go. When I've worked things out with Cordelia, I'll come to New York."

"What was that?" I whispered, tensing.

"What?" He nuzzled my neck.

"I thought I heard something." I peered through the dense branches of the weeping beech into the darkness of the lawn.

"It's nothing, love. Just the wind in the branches."

"But there is no wind now, Drew. The branches are perfectly still."

"There's nothing out there. We're all alone. Now kiss me . . ."

Chapter Fourteen

Drew and I decided that I would leave Newport the day after the dinner party. Once I was in New York, he would decide on the right time to speak to Cordelia about a divorce. He did not wish her to suspect the nature of his feelings for me because, if she knew he were in love with someone and hoping to remarry, it was likely she would not agree to divorce him, or would do so in a way which would lead to the notoriety we wished to avoid at all costs. Cordelia's position as Mrs. Drew Rockwell was very important to her, as her marriage was not, and we knew she would not relinquish it unless matters were handled very carefully.

If everything worked out to Drew's satisfaction, we would take Blythe and go abroad. Isadora and Miss McCready could accompany us if they wished. Aunt Hermione would doubtless return to her home in Boston. And, as soon as Drew's divorce was final, we would be married. Whether we would return to New England or continue to live abroad and maintain his business affairs from there, only time would tell.

But for now it was essential that Drew and I were never alone together. We could not give anyone, not even the servants, the slightest sign that we were involved.

The dinner party was in a few days' time. I finished the portrait, leaving it on the easel to dry thoroughly. Cordelia had ordered a handsome gilded frame for it, and it would be hung on the drawing-room wall covered with a black cloth. After dinner, when the guests had retired to the drawing room, Cordelia would give the word and the portrait would be displayed before all.

"Not exactly subtle, are you, Cordelia?" asked Aunt Hermione. "But then modesty was never one of your strong points."

Cordelia waved her hand in a dismissing gesture. "Oh, Aunt, don't be so stuffy. I assure you it will be most effective."

I was proud of the portrait. Several times a day I would go in and look at it, just to reassure myself that I had actually painted a portrait for a commission — and done it well. It was undeniably the best work I had ever done.

Drew went to Boston on business. He had affairs to attend to, and I suppose he had decided that it was easier on the two of us were he not in the house and likely to give his feelings away.

"Just so you return for the dinner party," Cordelia told him airily. "Remember, you are the host." On the night before the dinner party, I was awakened by the sound of crying. Blythe, I realized, and Drew was away in Boston.

Quickly I threw on a dressing gown and hurried down the corridor to the nursery wing. But the sounds had ceased before I reached the little girl's room, and when I entered it was to find her clasped in Miss McCready's arms.

"Is everything all right?" I asked breathlessly.

"Quite all right, Miss Morrow. Blythe had a wee fright, but she's a brave lassie, aren't you, pet?"

Blythe nodded.

"It was my own fault," said Miss McCready ruefully. "I'd forgotten how she likes the light left on. And when she awoke she saw something on the wall that frightened her. The shadows of the leaves made by the street lamp, that's all. When the wind blows, the leaves dance and sway, don't they? And so do their shadows, there on the wall. 'Tis nothing at all to be afraid of."

"Well, I just wanted to make certain that Blythe was all right," I said. "I'll go back to bed now."

"Good night, Ariel," said Blythe.

"Good night, Miss Morrow. And don't worry. Now, Blythe, shall we turn off the light for a minute and see the shadows of the pretty leaves? Just for a moment, now. See, just like fairies' wings, they are. They canna hurt you."

Closing the nursery door, I went back to my room. Tonight Blythe had not called for her father, and Miss McCready had managed quite easily to calm her. Blythe's chances of getting better and becoming more like a normal child were improving. And for that reason alone it was essential that Cordelia not be antagonized in any way. Were she to insist on custody of Blythe and be granted it, I trembled to think what would happen to the child. Drew and I did not wish to build our life together on that foundation.

Dancing leaves, a swaying chandelier, birds suddenly flying upwards—I still did not know what to make of Blythe's fears. But it was saying a great deal for Miss McCready that she had soothed the little girl so quickly.

The following morning Isadora and I went to the Newport Casino to listen to a concert. She was still brooding over Camille's sudden departure and the news of William Everett's accident, and I was rather apprehensive about that night, so I had suggested we do something to pass the time.

We listened to the music, and then as we were leaving the Casino, we passed Olive Chandler's box.

"How do you do, Mrs. Chandler?" asked Isadora politely. "We'll be seeing you tonight, of course. Cordelia has a wonderful surprise for everyone."

"Indeed?" said Olive Chandler, glancing coldly at me. "So you are still here, Miss Morrow? I thought you were to leave once your work was finished."

"I will be leaving shortly, Mrs. Chandler," I said coolly.

"Awful woman," said Isadora as we walked away. "She's like an iceberg, stiff and freezing. I always feel she disapproves of me, though I don't know why."

"She is certainly very different from Dr. Chandler," I admitted.

"Isn't he a dear? I don't know how he could have married her. She was from an old Knickerbocker family, and so was he, although he hadn't any money. Perhaps their parents arranged it as Drew and Cordelia's marriage was arranged. And poor Camille's," she added forlornly.

When we reached the house Isadora went inside to change her gown and I followed the sound of voices to the fish pond where Blythe and Miss McCready were bent over, peering into the water.

"What are you doing?" I asked.

"We're looking for a kelpie," said Blythe.

"A what?"

"A water creature," explained Miss McCready. "They live in deep wells and bogs. But not in fish ponds where one can see through to the bottom."

"What do they look like?"

"A black fierce horse," said Blythe. "People in Scotland say charms to keep them away. I'm glad we haven't any here." She ran off, chasing a butterfly.

"She is so much better than she was when I came here two months ago," I observed. "She never laughed or ran about then."

Miss McCready frowned. "But she shouldna be frightened the way she is. I canna understand it."

"Yes, I know. It's horrible. She'll be quiet and calm, and then suddenly, out of the blue, she'll become terrified." I told her about the ride on Ocean Drive and when Molly had knocked the chandelier back and forth.

"Hmm. And the shadows moving on the wall . . ." Miss McCready pressed her lips together, her bright blue eyes staring ahead. "I wonder, Miss Morrow, if these things are connected."

"Connected?"

"If they remind the child of something, something which frightened her in the past. When I was young there was a man in the village who couldn't bear to be in a room without windows. His mother would lock him in a trunk when he misbehaved as a lad, you see."

"I'm certain that Blythe has never been mistreated," I said rather stiffly.

"No, Miss Morrow, I didn't mean that. But something may have frightened her years ago, something she has now forgotten. That man dinna remember being locked in a trunk. His older sister told me about it. These things that frighten Blythe — they may remind her of something that happened before. Whatever it is, 'tis too terrible for her to remember. But the *feeling* of the fear she felt then stays with her."

"I don't know if I understand," I said. "But I'm sure that what you are thinking has not occurred to anyone." I frowned. "You know that two years ago her little brother died."

Miss McCready replied, "I did know. And she herself was ill, poor bairn."

"She changed after that. The doctors assured Mr. Rockwell that she would fully recover, but somehow she never has. She would not speak to me when I first came here. Now she is running about with some color in her cheeks. But she's still much too thin."

"I'm going to build her up, Miss Morrow, don't you fret," said Miss McCready. I regarded the small, slight woman with her freckles and her wide smile and her hair blowing untidily about her head, and I believed that she would.

That afternoon I went to the drawing room. The portrait had been fit into the frame and now hung on the wall between the two sets of French doors. Tonight it would be covered with a black cloth which would then be drawn aside to reveal the painting underneath. Closing my eyes, I imagined the room filled with people, jewels glittering, heads craned to catch the first glimpse of their beautiful hostess . . . As Cordelia had said, it would be most effective. My father would have loathed such a theatrical spectacle and refused to take part in it, but then he had not needed the exposure the dinner party was sure to bring to me. His name was well-known when he arrived in New York.

It was when I went up to my room that I saw it.

An envelope on the carpet near the door, just as the other two had been weeks before. *But that's impossible!* shrieked a voice in my head, *Miss Simmons is gone!* With shaking fingers I picked up the envelope and pulled out the folded paper. And as I read the contents my blood ran thick and slow.

I WARNED YOU TO GO. BUT IT'S TOO LATE NOW. I WILL EXPOSE YOU AS HIS MISTRESS. I WILL RUIN YOU, YOU VILE DAUGHTER OF A SLUT.

Putting my hand to my hot cheek, I stumbled across to the window to take in the fresh air. I dropped the letter as though it scalded me. Breathing deeply, my stomach heaving, my body trembling, I tried to get a grip on myself. In a very few hours I would be meeting influential people. I had to be calm, gracious, poised.

Who could have written this vicious thing? Miss Simmons had left weeks ago, hadn't she? Was it possible that she might have returned today to pick up something she had left behind? Had she then become enraged to learn that I was still at Copper Beeches and so felt compelled to write one last note?

I went downstairs to the kitchen. The maids and cook were very busy preparing for the dinner party, but I had to ask them.

"Mrs. Meredith, has Miss Simmons been here today, by any chance?"

She looked up at me, her rolling pin in midair. "Miss Simmons? I haven't seen her, Miss Morrow, busy as I've been in here all day."

"I—I thought she might have returned to fetch a belonging she left behind," I said lamely, realizing that Mrs. Meredith did not appreciate the interruption.

"Oh, did she leave something? I wouldn't know about that. Did any of you see Miss Simmons today?"

The maids shook their heads, staring at me. I must be a sight, I thought, if I looked as distraught as I felt.

"Well, I'm sorry to have troubled you," I said and hurried away.

If not Miss Simmons, then who had written such a vile note and slipped it under my door? Not note, notes. Three of them, all penned by the same person. The block lettering, the ink, the paper—all the same. I had believed that Miss Simmons was responsible, especially since I had not received one since her departure. But it must be someone else entirely. Who hated me that much to call me filthy names and accuse me of being Drew's mistress? And what was the reference, again, to my *mother?*

Picking up the letter and envelope, I shoved them into my drawer underneath a pile of clothing. I resisted the urge to destroy it as I had destroyed the two previous ones after Miss Simmons had left. Perhaps I should show it to Drew. I was leaving for New York the following day, so it was likely that I would never find out who had penned it. But I wanted to know. There was something horribly chilling about being the target of so much hate, hate from an enemy who refused to come out in the open. It was impossible to fight an enemy of that sort.

Someone in Copper Beeches must have written it, along with the others. Gideon had left the house, but he had not left Newport, I reminded myself. Had he slipped into the house this afternoon, knowing that Drew was out of town? He had recognized me at the masquerade ball and threatened to expose me then and there. And the author of the poison-pen letter was determined to expose me as Drew's mistress. Not that he would have the opportunity, as I was leaving on the morrow.

Yet, if Gideon suspected that I was Drew's mistress, why had he not told Cordelia? Perhaps he was angry with her as well for not standing up for him when Drew had thrown him out of the house.

On the other hand, if he had spoken to Cordelia, then perhaps it was she who had written the letters. But somehow I was certain that it was not Cordelia's style; she would take a more direct, damaging approach in expressing her outrage. So whom did that leave? And what of the continued references to my mother, the talk of "bad blood"?

Could Aunt Hermione have known my mother years ago? Had she known my father? Did I pose a threat to her? Was she fearful that somehow I would take Drew away, leaving her to fend for herself in her last years?

I pictured the old woman, alone in her bedroom, writing these letters in an attempt to frighten me away. But she had such a blunt way of speaking; would she be the sort of person to cravenly write the things she hadn't the courage to tell me to my face? But there was a power in writing poison-pen letters, I realized. Protected from scrutiny, knowing I was helpless and unable to fight what I could not see, the author could do whatever he or she wished.

Sick at heart, I began to lay out my clothing for the dinner party. Now I had no desire to go through with it at all. I wanted only to leave Copper Beeches.

It was nearly dark when I dressed in a new ivory taffeta gown with seed pearls and appliqués of lace sewn onto the bodice. Pinning up my hair, I secured it with pearl clasps and fastened my choker around my neck. I wanted to look my best tonight when I was presented to Society as a painter of portraits. I had to put all thoughts of the letters out of my mind. I would not allow my enemy to ruin this night for me. It was the triumphant realization of all my dreams, and I was determined to make it a success.

When I went downstairs to the crowded first-floor landing, I entered the throng of guests milling about and observed my surroundings. The women sparkled with literally hundreds of magnificent jewels; the men in their elegant black and white were mere foils for their partners, providing a place for the eyes to rest before one's glance moved on to the next glittering lady. These were America's fittest, the most prominent people in the country.

"I've got a new team that will beat Reggie's," announced one man.

"The stock closed at two hundred and sixty," declared another.

"Worth is late with my gown. I simply refuse to pay the price we agreed on!"

"We're going to Hot Springs. It will be *such* a relief to rest. I'm simply *exhausted,* my dear."

"Such a sickening thing happened today. One of our gardeners *died.* Can you believe it? Right in the rose garden. Why he hadn't the decency to pass away in his own home, I don't know. We were forced to deal with the arrangements *ourselves!*"

"I know I've seen her gown before. I'm sure it's the one she wore to Beaulieu one evening earlier in the season. Her memory must be going, poor dear."

"Common varlet, he'll not work in my stables again. Zounds, there's a delectable wench." This from a tall man with a monocle.

"Why on earth did you wear *that* gown? You look a fright," said a large blond man to the striking brunette with him. Her cheeks were tinged with color, but she smilingly greeted those about her.

"Harry!" Someone called, and the blond man waved.

"I must have twenty swans for my Bal Blanc," said one woman.

"I would not acknowledge Alva in Trinity Church last Sunday. Say what you will, I do not believe in divorce. I always thought she was a little too fond of O.H.P. Belmont when she was married to Willie. Those long cruises they all took together . . ."

"Did you read *Town Topics?* Not that I normally do, of course, but our cook had a copy. It mentioned Drew Rockwell with a woman. I wonder who she is—perhaps she's here tonight!"

I froze.

"My dear, I hardly think so," tittered her companion. "Mr. Rockwell would have better judgment than that. She's an artist, I understand. Someone said they were together at the masquerade ball at Hedgerow."

"No! Does Cordelia *suspect*, do you think?"

Backing against the wall, I felt my face on fire. So there was already gossip about Drew and me, thanks to that slanderous *Town Topics*. Tonight when Cordelia's portrait was revealed, some people would realize that I was the artist whose name was being bandied about with his. Much worse, if the talk should reach Cordelia's ears, all our plans might be ruined.

But I was leaving tomorrow. Surely that would put an end to the gossip. There was no fire without fuel. Besides, the summer season was nearly over and these people would be going to other mansions in other locations. And they would rapidly become absorbed in new tittle-tattle. After all, Cordelia had read *Town Topics* and had not taken it seriously. If she had she would never be giving this dinner party and the "unveiling" afterward. She would have insisted that I leave then and there.

The ancient Chinese gong sounded then, three times, and gradually the crowd began moving out of the landing and entrance hall into the dining room. Two long tables had been set up to accommodate the large number of guests. The scent of gardenias was heavy in the air; usually it was one I loved, but tonight I found it cloying and oversweet.

Feeling a hand at my elbow, I looked up to see Dr. Chandler. I was relieved to find a friendly face in the midst of the crowd.

"Good evening, Miss Morrow. I understand this is to be a night of triumph for you," he said, his eyes twinkling.

"Oh, you know about the portrait?" I asked him, smiling.

"Hermione told me. I am greatly looking forward to seeing it. Will you partner me at dinner? My wife is one of several making much of a Russian grand duke this evening."

"Thank you, Dr. Chandler, I should like to very much." He must have realized how nervous I was and I was grateful to him.

Across the room I saw Drew talking with a group of men. Near to us Cordelia sat with Bartholomew Reed on her right and the man with the monocle on her left. She wore a gown the color of dry sherry with three long strings of pearls, and gardenias in her hair. I saw Isadora seated at the other table; she waved across to me.

"Did you know that Blythe has a new governess, Dr. Chandler? She's quite remarkable. I believe Blythe is showing great improvement already."

"I'm greatly relieved to hear it, Miss Morrow. I confess I was very worried that night when the Irish girl failed to turn off the gas." He shook his head. "Very careless. To think of a fine family such as the Rockwells suffering the loss of one child and the illness of another. The little boy was too frail for this world, and I was beginning to think Blythe was as well."

"She is fortunate to have Miss McCready looking after her."

"May I say, Miss Morrow, that you look — a bit worried. Is anything wrong?"

"Wrong? N-no, indeed."

"I was afraid you might be brooding over that nonsense in *Town Topics.*"

I regarded him in dismay.

"Forgive me for bringing it up, Miss Morrow. Olive read it and told me. They are always writing the worst foolishness about someone. Some years ago it was Gwendolyn, implying that she was infatuated with her piano instructor. We ignored it and the talk soon died down. It is mere spite and jealousy written by those and for those who wish to make fools of the wealthy and powerful members of Society, many of whom have done great things. You must not allow it to trouble you, Miss Morrow. Gossip passes quickly if it is ignored." He shook his head. "If only Mrs. Leander had not let her judgment be affected, she might be with us here tonight. If only she had come to me for advice — I am a doctor, after all. Anything she told me would have been held in confidence. That something like that should have happened to such a fine person — it's a terrible tragedy. I'm certain that you, Miss Morrow, would not allow the rantings of a scandal sheet to affect your good sense."

Fortunately for me the talk became general after that as we began our meal. Dr. Chandler meant to be kind and supportive, but I felt uncomfortable thinking that even he knew that there was talk about Drew and me. Uninformed, aimless talk, but talk all the same. I was content to listen and observe, every once in a while stealing a glance at Drew who sat at the head of the other table.

"What did you think of Jack Evans's new yacht, Prescott?" asked one man. "I'm tempted to order one like it for myself."

"You know I'm not much of a sailor, Henry," answered Dr. Chandler. "I haven't ridden on it. I leave that sort of thing to the rest of you. I did hear from Olive that it is magnificent, though."

"Where is your daughter tonight?" asked a woman.

"You know she is not fond of large gatherings," said Dr. Chandler. "I'm afraid she is a creature of moods. Olive and I wished that she felt more comfortable around people, but we would never force her. I was hoping, Miss Morrow, that you and she might have become friends. Gwendolyn needs someone to draw her out." His tone was wistful; it was obvious he cared deeply for his daughter.

I happened to glance over at Cordelia and noticed that she had been listening to some of our conversation. She was regarding Dr. Chandler with disbelief. Naturally she would consider it most unsuitable for Gwendolyn Chandler to become friends, as Dr. Chandler put it, with a female artist. But he had never treated me with any trace of snobbery. It didn't matter what Cordelia thought — Gwendolyn Chandler had never acted as though she wanted to get to know me better.

We ate course after course; fish, veal, duck, all prepared excellently by Mrs. Meredith. Several people remarked on the result achieved by a local woman and not a French chef. "I'd snatch her away in an instant if I thought she'd come. And she wouldn't have to be paid nearly as much as a chef!" This from a woman whose throat was a mass of rubies.

Before the dessert course was over, I excused myself from the table and went up to my room to have a few moments alone. The reference to *Town Topics* had upset me, and I hoped that no others would suspect that Drew and I were involved when Cordelia introduced me as the artist of the portrait. I wanted to be offered new commissions once the New Yorkers had returned to their city sometime in the fall. I did not want gossip to blight what could very well be a new career for me.

I had to have confidence in my talent; I had to let the portrait convince people of my worth, and not fear a few idle speculations. Feeling better, I went back downstairs.

I was passing the library on my way to the dining room when I heard Cordelia's voice raised in fury. Oh, no, I thought, is she arguing with Drew? Has she heard some of talk about us? My heart hammering, my mouth suddenly dry, I paused outside the door.

"Don't bother to deny it!" she was saying. "You lied to me — you were together that night. You're not going to get away with it, I can promise you that!"

It must be Drew she was talking to, I thought, heart-sick. She had found out that he loved me. I went into the dining room where most of the other guests still were, sitting over their champagne. But I did not return to my seat because Isadora motioned for me to join her. I did not see Drew.

"Isadora tells me you were the mysterious lady I danced with at the masquerade ball," said a young man. "I looked for you at midnight. You remember Henry VIII, don't you?"

"Oh, of — of course."

"Dora tells me you are leaving for New York soon. Perhaps I'll see you there."

I was spared having to answer him because just then Cordelia entered the room, requesting that we all go into the drawing room where she had something to show us. Isadora winked at me as we rose from the table.

This was it, the moment I had longed for and dreaded at the same time. Taking a deep breath, I moved with the crowd down the corridor and into the drawing room.

Cordelia was standing beneath the portrait, waiting expectantly. When she saw me, she motioned for me to join her. On her face was a slight smile, the anger gone. The room was rapidly filling up. Drew stood in a far cor-ner of the room; his eyes met mine briefly and he gave a reassuring nod. Whatever he and Cordelia had been ar-guing about, he was unperturbed.

Abruptly my apprehension fell away. I had worked very hard to achieve this moment, to be accepted as a talented portrait painter. Nothing was going to mar it. Whatever the future, I should have my career, my work.

The room was very close now with all the guests crowding into it. Expensive perfumes of various kinds were thick in the air. The guests were speaking in softer voices, conscious that something was about to happen, but uncertain as to the nature of it. The room was heavy with anticipation.

"Ladies and gentlemen," began Cordelia, "I ask that

you give me your full attention for the next few minutes."

Glancing over my shoulder, I saw the piece of black cloth covering the portrait. On either side of it stood a manservant. Cordelia was determined to make this event as dramatic as possible.

"I have something to share with you tonight," she went on, a stunning regal figure in her pale gown and ropes of pearls. "Standing beside me is the daughter of Lancelot Morrow, Miss Ariel Morrow." The gazes shifted to me; I flushed slightly. "Miss Morrow's works of interiors are known to some of you. She has been staying at Copper Beeches this summer, and has just completed something very special. It is a portrait which I wish to share with all of you."

There was a ripple in the crowd; an old lady lifted her lorgnette for closer scrutiny.

"When you have seen her work," Cordelia went on, "I am confident you will consider her as fine a portrait painter as her late father. And now I present to all of you — the portrait of myself by Miss Ariel Morrow."

All eyes were now on the black rectangle; I was holding my breath. Cordelia made a gesture to the two menservants. In one simultaneous movement they pulled off the piece of covering.

Once as a child I had fallen from a low branch of a tree onto my stomach. It was the same — the ground rushing up to meet me, the powerful jar which knocked all the wind from my body, then the dazed sensation, the feeling that what had happened, what was happening, couldn't be real . . .

The crowd was silent for a few moments and then began the murmurs, the whispers, the stifled exclamations. And still I gazed at the painting, mesmerized. All the blood drained from my face so that I felt lightheaded, and possessed of a bizarre inclination to laugh.

For it was no longer the portrait I had so painstakingly created out of the best that was within me. Cordelia's face, her chesnut hair which had taken so many piles of color combinations to achieve, the lace at her throat, the floral wall panel behind her — all was a horrible muddled blur. Her features — eyes, nose, mouth — were smeared, distorted, awash together in a grotesque parody. The brown of her hair had run into the delicate rose and yellow of the panel, her taffeta gown blending hideously into the once-yellow damask chair.

My stupefied gaze shifted from the painting to Cordelia's face. Her brows raised, she was smiling.

"It seems that Miss Morrow quite lacks her famous father's talent," she stated with undeniable satisfaction.

The crowd of onlookers were uncertain of how to respond. Some were perplexed and uneasy; there were a few snickers. No one moved.

Suddenly my knees gave way and I would have collapsed there on the floor had not two strong arms gripped and supported me. Stricken, I looked into Drew's face, into his eyes which blazed with fury. I had been too dazed to notice his approach.

As from far away I heard him say, "That is not Miss Morrow's painting, Cordelia. What did you do to it?"

"I? What did I do to it?" She laughed. "Why would I destroy my own portrait? Something must have gone wrong with Miss Morrow's paints — the drying of them. I suppose I deserve that for engaging an amateur. I am sorry that I cannot recommend this artist to any of you. I did have such high hopes of her," she announced to the crowd.

"I saw that portrait this afternoon," snarled Drew, "and it was magnificent. You ruined it yourself, Cordelia. I want everyone here, all your dear friends, to know the truth!"

Cordelia's expression changed from a gloating one to one of rage. "Do you truly wish them to know the truth, Drew? Because I am quite willing to oblige. I *did* destroy the portrait, and I know everyone present will understand why. I refused to keep and display with pride a portrait painted by my own husband's mistress!"

There were gasps and cries; I closed my eyes as if that would cause the entire scene to vanish.

"She's nothing of the kind, Cordelia! Although I've been hard put not to make her so!" cried Drew.

"Deny it if you will! But I'm no fool. The two of you, in my own house, did you think that I would never suspect? That's what I get for engaging a woman of her sort. But I'll see to it now that she never has a chance to destroy a marriage again. Your precious, talented Miss Morrow will never get another commission to paint anything!"

"Destroy a marriage!" Drew shouted bitterly. "That's rich! When did we ever have a marriage, Cordelia?"

Her cheeks stained crimson, she struck him across the cheek. Then she pushed her way through the mass of horrified guests.

They had not moved or spoken up until then, but with her departure came more audible gasps, titters, and excited whispers. And, as one, they began to disperse from the room as quickly as they could. Never had they imagined such a resounding finale to the evening. What a night! They would be able to discuss it for weeks to come without the story growing stale.

The dazed state evaporated, leaving me cold and shivering.

"I have to leave . . . I have to leave . . . I have to leave . . ." I scarcely knew it was my own voice saying those words, babbling them over and over again like a gushing fountain. I struggled for Drew to release me.

But he would not. "We'll both leave — tomorrow," he said savagely.

"Leave!" cried Isadora. "Where will you go?"

He did not answer her. "But first I will see my . . . wife." The last word was ground out; a muscle jerked in his hard square jaw.

Isadora put a hand on his arm. "No, Drew! Not tonight! There's been enough harm done already. Don't go near her. You're — you're too angry. Wait until tomorrow morning," she pleaded.

"Dora is right, Drew," said Aunt Hermione heavily. "Wait until you've both calmed down."

"I've stood her viciousness long enough," he said curtly. "Stay with Ariel, Dora." He strode from the room.

"Cordelia!" we heard him shout. "Cordelia!"

Without a word to Isadora or Aunt Hermione I hurried after him down the corridor. A few of the servants were in the dining room as I passed. At the foot of the double staircase I halted: Drew had bolted up, taking the stairs three at a time. Above me the stained glass window was dark and murky, her pose strained and in vain. Dawn would never come.

Drew was on the second-story landing, shouting at Cordelia. "You've gone too far this time! I'm leaving tomorrow. I'm suing you for divorce."

"Suing me! If there is a divorce to be got, I'll be the one to get it!" she cried. "You and Miss Morrow—you must have thought I was blind! I saw you together in the trees by the Moongate. You thought I was at Wakehurst and the coast was clear. That's what I wanted you to think. I was going to go up to Miss Morrow's room, but there was no need for that. I saw the two of you together before I had even reached the house!"

"Isn't that the pot calling the kettle black? A judge might be interested to hear to what use you've put the summerhouse! You and Bartholomew Reed, this summer. Shall I name the others from past summers? I can play as dirty as you can, Cordelia. If you dare to bring Ariel's name into the legal proceedings—"

"If I dare! You must be mad if you think I won't, Drew! All this time—in my own house! Not your mistress—do you expect me to believe that? And neither will a judge. I'll take this house and Blythe and anything else I want."

"I'll see you dead before you take Blythe one step away from me! You'd make her life a living hell, as you've made mine these last nine years!"

A door slammed; I stood clutching the bannister, my

knuckles white, my body trembling. Drew came down and put his arm around me. "It's all right, Ariel. Come, I'll take you upstairs. We're leaving here tomorrow. We'll take Blythe and go — somewhere, anywhere. If Cordelia names you in the divorce proceedings I'll come back with every affair she's ever had."

"Oh, Drew!"

"I suppose you heard her. She's going to demand custody of Blythe as well, and she'll win, unless I can show her to be an unfit mother. It's going to be hell. Hell for all of us. But there is no other way. I can't allow her to destroy Blythe's life."

"You can't risk losing Blythe to her, Drew. I'll go away to Europe. To England or France. My father had friends in London; some wrote to me after his death. They will help me. I could go there and work. Or I could go to France." I laughed bitterly. "In France they don't mind these scandals. They even enhance one's career."

He grasped my shoulders. "Don't talk that way, Ariel, do you hear me? We haven't gone through all this to be separated now. We'll go abroad together."

Once in my room he said in a gentler tone, "I'm sorry about the portrait, Ariel. It was very beautiful, even if it was of Cordelia."

"It was, wasn't it?" I said, a catch in my voice.

"Don't cry, my love," he said, holding me tenderly against him. "Don't cry." He kissed my eyes and cheeks, and I was passive in his embrace, the tears spilling unchecked down my face.

He wiped my face with his handkerchief. "No matter what happens, we won't be parted, Ariel. I told you . . . you are a fire in my blood."

Suddenly I was no longer in need of comfort. I lifted my mouth to his, opening it against his hard mouth. The misery and despair fell away, blotted out by the raging desire which coursed between us, a desperate hunger which this time we could not deny.

"Ariel . . ." he said huskily, slipping my gown off my

shoulders, "I've wanted you so. I've been nearly crazy with wanting you." His voice was slurred, his breath hot on my bare skin.

"I, too," I whispered, and then we spoke no more, consumed by the fierce urgency of our bodies, my own yielding to the power of his until that heart-stopping time when we were propelled to a white-hot state of agonized bliss. And in my ears were his triumphant cries answered with those of my own.

Chapter Fifteen

Hours later I awakened to see Drew pulling on his shirt and trousers in the semidarkness before dawn. I sat up, hugging the sheet around me.

"Drew?" I said softly, feeling the rosy color seep into my face.

"Go back to sleep, love. I'm only going to my room. I can't be here when the servants get up." He bent down and kissed me, a swift hard kiss. "We'll talk in a few hours."

I lay back against the pillows. "What time is it?"

"Almost five-thirty."

"Are we still leaving together today?"

"Of course, Ariel. But first there are things I must discuss with Cordelia." He sounded weary, and I guessed he was dreading a further ordeal.

"I heard you and Cordelia last night in the library, before everyone gathered in the drawing room," I said. "I should have realized then that she was going to do something awful. She accused you, I heard her."

He frowned. "Ariel, I don't know what you're talking about. I was never with Cordelia in the library last night."

"But you weren't in the dining room after dessert."

"I stepped out to speak to Merriman for a few minutes; I never saw Cordelia."

"Then whom could she have been talking to? She

said, 'You were together that night. You're not going to get away with it.' She sounded very angry."

He shrugged. "Well, that's her concern. I could care less whom she has offended, or the other way round."

With a sharp pang I recalled my ruined portrait. "Turpentine."

"What?"

"Turpentine. That's what she used, with a brush or a cloth. On the portrait."

He had been shrugging on his evening jacket, but at that he came over to the bed and took me in his arms. "You'll paint many other portraits, Ariel. And you won't need the commissions of Cordelia's friends to do it, I can promise you. But now I must get downstairs. I don't want to give Cordelia any blatant evidence to use in court." His smile was twisted. "I can't really continue to deny that you and I are lovers. Not that you can be unfaithful to someone you haven't been intimate with in years." He paused. "When Nathan died, she stood there in the nursery and said . . . it was just as well."

"Oh, Drew, we'll be happy," I told him. "We'll begin all over again."

When I awoke for the second time that morning, the sun was streaming through the lace curtains. Lazily I watched the dust floating on the rays, warm with the memory of Drew's taut hard body against mine and the way his arms had cradled me as we slept.

And then the screams began.

It's all right, Miss McCready is with Blythe, I reminded myself.

But then it struck me that these screams were different—they were not the screams of a child, but a woman. Bolting up in bed, I listened with sick horror. The warmth and comfort I had been feeling was gone, blown out like a candle. The sunlight was harsh and sterile, the room chilled.

With an effort I got out of bed and slipped on my

290

dressing gown. Something was terribly wrong. Oh, God, please, don't let anything have happened to Drew, I begged. Forcing myself to open the door, I stepped out into the hall.

"Sir! Mr. Rockwell!" a man was shouting. It sounded like Merriman's voice, his usual phlegmatic tones now frantic. Oh, God, something had happened—Drew. Drew . . . No! I couldn't bear it.

The woman's screams had turned to moans and sobs. My throat was tight; I could not swallow. Standing at the top of the stairs, I could not move.

Then I heard doors opening, and Drew's voice saying, "What is it?"

Faint with relief, I stumbled down the stairs, gripping the bannister.

"It's Mrs. Rockwell, sir," said the butler.

"Yes? What about Mrs. Rockwell?" Drew asked roughly.

"She—she's dead, sir."

"No!" I heard Isadora gasp.

I saw my knuckles go white but I could not feel anything, not the hard polished wood nor the strained pressure of my fingers.

"Where is she?" came Drew's voice, curiously flat.

"In the summerhouse, sir. Liza here found her when she went in to tidy up."

At that the maid broke into fresh weeping. "Oh, it was horrible—horrible!"

Aunt Hermione's door opened and she came out, a huge billowing figure in purple. "What's happened? What is all this noise?"

"It's Cordelia, Aunt," said Isadora. "She—Liza found her in the summerhouse. There must have been an accident." She cast a swift glance across at Drew's grim face and then looked up to where I stood on the stairs.

"Mrs. Rockwell—she's dead, Mrs. Grant!" cried the maid.

"I'm going out there," said Drew, and went down the stairs.

"An accident, you said, Dora?" said Aunt Hermione faintly.

"I — I don't know. Merriman, tell us. What do you know about — about the way Mrs. Rockwell died?"

"I am afraid, Miss Isadora, that — " he broke off, his lips tightening.

"Well, man, speak up," said Aunt Hermione. "Did she fall or — or what?"

"It didn't appear to me as though there had been an accident, ma'am," said Merriman, his voice strained.

"What do you mean, Merriman?" asked Isadora softly.

"Oh, miss, she's been strangled!" cried the maid. "The poor lady — she's been murdered!" She covered her face with her hands.

As from far away I heard Aunt Hermione say, "Take Liza below and tell Mrs. Meredith to give her some brandy."

"I don't believe it!" said Isadora, putting a hand to her throat. "Not — not *murdered!*"

"Isadora, bring Ariel into my room. I think she may be going to faint."

"No, no." I shook my head, pulling away from Isadora. "I'm going down there."

"Ariel — no! You've had a shock — you mustn't. How can you want to see . . . just come with me."

Ignoring the two of them, I hurried down the stairs, scarcely feeling my feet touch ground. Racing to the drawing room, I went through the open French doors. Several of the maids stood on the terrace, whispering. Brushing past them, I moved across the damp grass. Ahead of me the white summerhouse glowed like a pearl against the violet-blue hydrangea bushes and row of blue spruces.

And then, as suddenly as it had overcome me, the urgent energy was gone. The sun hurt my eyes. Very slowly I walked toward the summerhouse, the blood inside me slowing to a sluggish crawl. Some men stood at the bottom of the stairs, silent. They turned to look at me as I approached, their gazes speculative, intent. By now all the servants must know about the ruined portrait, Cordelia's accusation before Newport Society, about Drew's rage . . .

Somehow I was standing on the summerhouse porch. The door was open; I moved as if through water over the threshold into the cold gloom inside.

Drew was on his knees, bending over a sprawled form. I would not scream. I put my crooked thumb in between my teeth and bit hard. The slim bare arms were white in the darkness of the room, white arms, white face, even the eyes . . . Oh, God, the eyes!

"She's been dead for hours," said Drew.

And then I dropped like a stone to the floor.

When I came to myself I was in my bed and Isadora hovered above me, pressing a cool cloth to my brow. I must have called out in my sleep, and Isadora had heard me. It was only a nightmare, a grisly nightmare.

"How are you feeling, Ariel?" she asked. "I wished you hadn't gone out there."

And then I knew that none of it had been a dream, not the sobbing, terrified maid, not the summerhouse glinting in the sunlight, not the pale heap on the floor with eyes rolled back . . .

I began to shudder uncontrollably.

"Give her some brandy," ordered Aunt Hermione.

A glass was lifted to my lips; I welcomed the strong searing liquid until I began to cough, and some of it spilled down my chin onto the bedclothes. But then I drank more, preferring the taste of the brandy to the violent trembling.

"Where—where is Drew?" I asked when I was able.

"He's sent for the police. He's waiting for them downstairs. I told him I'd look after you."

"The . . . police?"

"They'll have to conduct an investigation, you know," she said gently.

"An investigation?" Why did I keep on repeating what she said?

But suddenly the words came tumbling out, and I had no more control of them than I had had of the tremors. "Drew didn't kill her! He couldn't have—he wouldn't have. Even when she said Nathan was better off dead, he didn't. It's—it's not his fault. It's not *my* fault!"

"Hush, Ariel, we know Drew didn't do it," said Aunt Hermione. Her purple dressing gown covered her bulk like a sultan's robes.

"You must rest, Ariel," said Isadora. "Lie back down."

I gripped her arm. "I must see Drew. I must speak to him."

"He wants you to remain up here. There's nothing you can do now, and it's better if you stay up here for the time being."

"But the police . . . they might think . . . last night, all those people—!"

"Drink a little more, Ariel. You must be calm. You must try to get a grip on yourself."

"Why?" I asked wildly. "Why should I be calm? How can I?"

"Because the police will want to question you," said Aunt Hermione bluntly. "And you must be very careful about the way you answer them."

With renewed horror I gazed at them both. And the fear I knew must be in my eyes was reflected in theirs.

"We're going to leave you now, Ariel," said Isadora. "We have to get dressed, and so do you in a little while. Would you like me to send up one of the maids to help you?"

"No!" I couldn't bear the eager, searching glances, the barely repressed excitement. "No, I can manage on my own."

At least getting dressed gave some purpose to my movements, some direction to my thoughts. Camisole, pantalettes, corset, petticoats, gown, shoes . . . I recalled the last time I had dressed — for the dinner party the night before. My "night of triumph," Dr. Chandler had called it.

It had been the last time I had seen Cordelia alive, when she had brazenly announced to all the guests that her husband and I were lovers as she stood beneath the ruined portrait. Then she had left the room, and the guests, either from disgust or embarrassment, had fled the house as though from an outbreak of Bubonic Plague.

I had heard the fierce argument between her and Drew, her jeering threat to take Blythe away from him forever, and his savage reply that he would see her dead before he allowed that to happen.

Before dawn Drew had left me to return to his room. Had he decided that he couldn't wait to talk to Cordelia, that he had to have things out with her then and there?

What if he had gone to her room and found it empty? Had he gone to the summerhouse in search of her? Had there been another battle between them? Had Drew lost control of himself for a few moments, his hands going round that slim, white neck?

No! I shuddered. It was impossible. He could never have murdered Cordelia. If he were truly capable of such an act of violence he would have demonstrated it earlier. I had observed their arguments before; never had he even raised a hand to Cordelia. If he had not even struck her when she had declared Nathan better off dead, because of his twisted leg, then nothing could send him over the brink. Nothing, perhaps, except the loss of his daughter, the relinquishing of her into the sole care of a woman who would make her future even bleaker than the last two years had been.

Blythe, full of fears and delicate as she was, could become severely unbalanced without the constant love and attention from her father to sustain her. Cordelia had not the slightest interest in her, and absolutely no patience. We had all seen what had happened the day on Ocean Drive, when mother and daughter were together only a short while.

Cordelia would destroy Blythe. And no one knew that better than Drew.

But what of his intentions to prove her to be an unfit mother? There was only one hitch to that plan. He might not win.

What was the matter with me? How could I even entertain the thought for an instant that Drew had killed Cordelia? He had hated her and resented her bitterly, but he could not have killed her.

But someone had. Someone had gone to the summerhouse in the dead of night and strangled her. Why?

There was a knock on the door.

"Yes?" I gasped out.

"Excuse me, Miss Morrow, but it's the police. They want to see you."

So it was beginning.

And now I knew why Aunt Hermione and Isadora had urged me to rest, to compose myself, to gather and smooth my unruly thoughts. I had to choose my words and determine my actions very carefully from now on.

In the library I stood before the two policemen, neither of whom was in uniform. They were detectives from Providence; the Newport police, it seemed, were only too relieved to hand over the case to them. A wealthy woman found strangled—things of that sort just didn't happen in Newport, not in the place where the rich frolicked against a backdrop of elegant, though faded, gentility.

In this room over two months ago I had undergone

a very different sort of interview. I remembered I had been charmed by the oil painting of the Hudson River scene, and then I had turned to see the man from the steamboat. . . .

One man asked all the questions; he had a bony, angled face and sharp shrewd eyes. The other man was short and swarthy, and took notes in a small book with a lead pencil.

"Please sit down, Miss Morrow," said the detective, a Lieutenant Pierce.

When I had done so, they sat too, and the man went on, "I want you to tell me exactly what happened last night."

"You mean, at the dinner party? I—I assume you've heard about that."

"Did you see Mrs. Rockwell at an earlier time yesterday?"

"No."

"Then I think we can begin at the dinner party."

I took a deep breath. "I had painted a portrait of Mrs. Rockwell which was to be presented last night to the company. Mrs. Rockwell had planned a formal dinner party and then everyone was to see the portrait. I had hoped it would further my career, but now I see that although she may have originally planned to display the work untouched, she must have decided a while ago to destroy it, and humiliate me."

"What was Mrs. Rockwell's behavior like at dinner?"

"She was a hostess in her element. Talking . . . laughing."

"What happened after the dinner was over?"

"You must have heard," I said, a trifle impatiently.

"We want to hear it from you, Miss Morrow," and there was a hint of steel in the lieutenant's tone.

"Mrs. Rockwell made an introduction of me—about my fine work, how I was going to be as famous as my father. It was all very flattering," I said bitterly. "Then, when the portrait was shown to the guests, it was— well, I'm sure you've seen it."

"We have. And before then you had no suspicions about the condition of the portrait?"

"No."

"When you first saw the portrait, Miss Morrow, whom did you think had destroyed it? Whom did you blame?"

"No one. I—I—"

"Did you think the paints had run together by accident?"

"Of course not! Such a thing was impossible. But I was shocked, dazed. I couldn't think at all."

"And then what happened?"

"Mr. Rockwell pushed through the crowd and accused Mrs. Rockwell of tampering with the portrait herself."

"It is here you begin to interest me extraordinarily, Miss Morrow. Why should Mr. Rockwell, in front of all his guests, accuse his wife of doing such a thing? He could have handled his suspicions very differently."

"She had spoiled the portrait."

"Yes, but it was her own portrait, was it not? She had engaged you to paint it; you were to be paid. Why shouldn't she do what she liked with it? Why did Mr. Rockwell take such offense—and in public? He could have waited until they were alone, surely."

"He was angry!"

"Why, Miss Morrow?"

"Because it was my first commission to do a portrait. I had worked very hard. He believed in my work. He knew instantly that Mrs. Rockwell had deliberately destroyed the painting to . . . to . . ."

The clock was ticking in the walnut bookcase. Its monotonous ticking frayed my nerves.

"To what, Miss Morrow?" came his insistent voice.

"To make me appear incompetent, ridiculous. To ruin my chances of acquiring further commissions.

To—to humiliate me." My face was hot in remembered mortification.

"And Mr. Rockwell realized this? Was this the reason he became so enraged and forced a scene with his wife?"

"Yes," I whispered.

"Why, Miss Morrow? Why so extreme a reaction from him?"

"He was disgusted by her behavior. She was not exactly a—nice person."

"Why should she go to such lengths to destroy you, Miss Morrow?"

"I beg your pardon?"

"Why should Mrs. Rockwell wish to disgrace you so thoroughly and in public? She, I understand, hired you in the first place."

"I—I don't know," I said wildly.

The lieutenant got up and went over to the window. "You realize, Miss Morrow, that we are going to be questioning many of the guests who attended Mrs. Rockwell's dinner party last night." He turned back to me. "Perhaps they will be able to tell me why she disliked you enough to ruin the portrait you had done of her."

My face tightening, I met his gaze squarely. "I've no doubt they will be eager to do so. Mrs. Rockwell suspected that her husband and I—that he and I were lovers."

"And are you?"

"It—it wasn't true, what she believed. Mr. Rockwell and I had never . . . what she accused us of was untrue," I finished lamely.

"Just what did Mrs. Rockwell say?"

I hesitated.

"Remember, Miss Morrow. We are going to check your story against all the witnesses last night. Fifty is more than an adequate number."

"She announced before everyone that—that I was

her husband's mistress."

"And then?"

"Mr. Rockwell said it wasn't true. She didn't believe him. She accused me of destroying their marriage. She said she would see to it that I never worked again."

"Go on."

"Then she slapped him and left the room."

"I am going to ask you a question, Miss Morrow. And I want nothing but a direct answer. Are you in love with Drew Rockwell?"

"I—" The ticking of the clock was growing louder, more jarring.

"Are you in love with Drew Rockwell, Miss Morrow?"

"Y-yes," I whispered.

"And is he in love with you?"

The sound of the clock was strident in my ears. Didn't they notice it? How could I answer the questions when all the time the clock was driving me mad? I wanted to hurl something at it, smash it, anything to stop the ticking, anything to stop the questions. . . .

"I repeat, Miss Morrow. Is Mr. Rockwell in love with you?"

"Yes, yes, he is!"

"And Mrs. Rockwell found out?"

"You don't understand, Lieutenant! She cared nothing for Drew, or for either of their two children. They hadn't been—she hadn't been faithful to him in years. Her latest lover is—was—Bartholomew Reed of New York."

Now that the words had come I could not speak them fast enough. "Drew probably did not tell you all that, but it's perfectly true. I saw them together on numerous occasions. They used to meet at the summerhouse. Why, he might have gone there last night and killed her himself! I heard her in the library after dessert last night, shouting at someone. She said, 'So you

300

were together that night.' Don't you see, it must have been he in there with her. She must have found out he had another mistress, or perhaps she was talking about his wife, I don't know."

"You did not hear or see this man?"

"No, it could even have been a woman. I have no idea who was in there with her. I thought it was Drew, but he said no, he hadn't gone into the library."

"He told you this? Did you believe him?"

"What do you mean? Of course I believed him."

"All right, Miss Morrow. We will question Mr. Reed later. Now I want to know what happened after Mrs. Rockwell left the drawing room. What time was it?"

"I'm not sure. The dinner party began at nine. Sometime between eleven and twelve, I suppose. When Mrs. Rockwell left the drawing room, the guests began to depart as well."

"Did any of them speak to you?"

"No. Miss Rockwell and Mrs. Grant came up to me, though."

"Neither of them went after Mrs. Rockwell?"

I looked up, startled. "No."

"Why not? She may have been in need of comfort as well as you were."

"Cordelia Rockwell was never in need of comfort," I said crisply. "She had planned, staged this entire evening with one goal in mind. To disgrace me."

"Yes, but you were a threat to her, Miss Morrow. I only wondered why Miss Rockwell and Mrs. Grant remained with you in the drawing room."

"They were concerned about me. They have always been kind—"

"But Mrs. Rockwell was a member of their family, while you are merely an employee."

"Yes, but—"

"Were they not fond of Mrs. Rockwell either?"

"I have no right to make assumptions on either Miss Rockwell's or Mrs. Grant's feelings," I said stiffly.

Still standing, he grasped the back of the chair. "Come now, Miss Morrow. You have lived in this house for close on three months, I understand. You have been privy to some of the private affairs of this family. Surely you would not be merely making assumptions. You must know very well how the two ladies feel about Mrs. Rockwell. But I will pass over that for now."

If I felt any relief then, it did not last. He continued, "But you, Miss Morrow, how did you feel about Mrs. Rockwell?"

"How did I feel?" I repeated stupidly.

"Yes. In the beginning, did you like her, admire her?"

"She was beautiful," I admitted.

"But as a person. Did you admire her character?"

"No, Lieutenant Pierce, I did *not* admire her character."

"And why is that?"

"I scarcely knew her; we were hardly on intimate terms," I said impatiently.

"Miss Morrow, I am asking you directly. Did you like Mrs. Rockwell?"

"No, I did not. She was interested in nothing and no one but her own pleasure, her own amusement. She never spoke a kind word to anyone that I overheard. She never spent any time with her daughter except one afternoon when she took her on a carriage ride, and then slapped her when she became afraid and began to cry."

"And to her husband? She never spoke a kind word to him?"

"Least of all him," I said bitterly. And I could have bitten off my tongue.

"They did not get on, Miss Morrow? They were not happy together? What exactly was the nature of their relationship? Aside from the fact that Mrs. Rockwell, you claim, was not faithful to her husband."

"They did not get on, as you said," I said shortly.

"And why was that?"

"Really, Lieutenant, it's not for me to judge."

"Did you ever hear any arguments between them?"

"Well, yes . . ."

"And what was the source of their discontent with one another?"

I took a deep breath. "I cannot answer that. There were many things. She was always needling him."

"How frequent were these arguments?"

"Well . . ."

"Every day?"

"Oh, not every day," I said, relieved. "Sometimes Mr. Rockwell went away on business." *You idiot,* I told myself.

"I accept that they were unable to argue when Mr. Rockwell was away from home, Miss Morrow," said the lieutenant dryly. "But when he was at home, was it common to hear verbal battles between them? I am going to question the servants as well, of course. In my experience they are remarkably aware of the most intimate details of their employers' lives."

I glared at him. "They argued frequently."

"And he ever strike her, to your knowledge?"

"No!"

"Let us get back to last night. You have told me that Mrs. Rockwell left the room and the guests left the house. You, Miss Rockwell, and Mrs. Grant remained in the drawing room. What did Mr. Rockwell do?"

"He went after Mrs. Rockwell, up to the second-story landing."

"How do you know this?"

"Because I followed him."

"And did you hear what passed between them?"

"Some of it."

"What did they say?"

"He wanted a divorce. She said she wanted one too.

303

She said she would take their little girl away from him. And he threatened to have her proven an unfit mother in court."

"What happened after that?"

"Mrs. Rockwell went into her room and Drew came down the stairs and—and saw me."

"And then what?"

Coloring, I murmured, "He accompanied me to my room. I—I was shaken."

"And how long did Mr. Rockwell remain with you, Miss Morrow?"

It was the clock again. Ticking. Tocking. Back and forth, as clamorous as his endless questions.

"Miss Morrow?"

Suddenly the clock chimed, a series of harsh, loud gongs sounding again and again. I clasped my hands over my ears, blurting out, "He stayed until five-thirty!"

There was a pause; the clock had ceased its striking. I did not look at either man.

"So the two of you were together from about midnight until five-thirty in the morning?"

"Yes." Abruptly I thought of a question of my own. "When did Mrs. Rockwell die?"

"We have not precisely determined that yet, Miss Morrow, but it is likely she died sometime before five-thirty. Possibly between two and four o'clock."

So Drew could not have gone to the summerhouse at dawn. He had not been aware of Cordelia's death until Merriman had informed him of it. "Well, Drew was with me then. He couldn't possibly have had anything to do with it. You did suspect him right away, didn't you?" I said accusingly. "But now you see he couldn't have done it."

The detective's sharp eyes did not waver from my face. "I very much regret that I see nothing of the kind, Miss Morrow."

"What—what do you mean?"

304

"I mean precisely this: that I cannot rely on your word alone that Mr. Rockwell was with you. You have admitted that you are in love with him, that he was planning to leave his wife for you. You have a great deal at stake here, Miss Morrow."

"I don't understand."

"What was going to happen once Mr. and Mrs. Rockwell were divorced?"

"I—I don't think he had thought that far ahead. Everything happened so quickly—"

"Was he planning to marry you?" The question shot out and hung in the air between us.

There was a cold hard knot at the pit of my stomach. "We had discussed it."

"Mr. Rockwell is in love with you and is planning to marry you. With that knowledge I have to consider the possibility that you may not be telling me the truth, Miss Morrow."

Aghast, I stared at him. "How can you say that? Haven't I just told you terribly private things? How dare you accuse me of not telling the truth!"

"You may be sacrificing your reputation to protect him, Miss Morrow. I cannot rule out that possibility. Also, you may have fallen asleep and not realized he had left your room. He may have gone to the summerhouse, killed his wife, and returned with you none the wiser."

"That's absurd!"

"There are other possibilities as well," he said, smooth and relentless as lava. "You may even be an accessory. You may have accompanied Mr. Rockwell to the summerhouse between two and four o'clock this morning and stood by while he strangled his wife. You certainly wouldn't admit that to me, would you? But you had as much reason to hate her as he did, after what she had done to your portrait, and what she had said about you in front of fifty people."

I could not answer him; I could only gaze at him,

dumbfounded.

"I have no more questions at present, Miss Morrow. But you are not to leave Newport under any circumstances. Sergeant, escort Miss Morrow to the door."

Out in the hallway Drew was waiting. "Ariel, what is it? What did he say to you? Sergeant, what is going on? You can observe for yourself the state Miss Morrow is in!"

"What is it, Mr. Rockwell?" asked the lieutenant, coming out of the library.

"I want to know why the two of you have been called here in the first place. Where are the local men, the men I know?"

"They felt this case was a bit over their heads, Mr. Rockwell. They wired to Providence for assistance. They also felt that, under the circumstances, they might have difficulty being objective."

"What do you mean?" asked Drew harshly.

"I mean, Mr. Rockwell, that you are well-thought-of in Newport. But a very serious crime has been committed, one that requires an entirely unprejudiced investigation."

"What have you been saying to Miss Morrow?"

Lieutenant Pierce's eyebrows rose. "Just the usual line of questioning, I assure you. And it won't be the only time we talk to her." He turned to his assistant. "I want to see Mrs. Grant. And then Miss Rockwell."

Scowling, Drew took my arm and led me down the corridor. "Let's get out of here. I need some air." His face was set in tight grim lines. We went out the French doors and set off across the lawn. I was careful not to look in the direction of the summerhouse. Ahead of us loomed the massive weeping beeches, unearthly, monstrous. Their whispering was calculated, malicious.

"They—they think you killed her, Drew!" I gasped out. "Or that I helped you!"

"Of course they do," he said sardonically. "It's so

306

easy. After last night . . ."

"Someone took advantage of that, Drew," I said urgently. "Someone killed Cordelia and knew the police would suspect you, and probably look no further."

"But who on earth would do it? I thought I was the only one who hated Cordelia and was hated by her in return. She had countless friends—or what passed as friends by her standards."

"Lieutenant Pierce said he is going to question all the guests. They all know you. They'll tell him you couldn't have done it."

He gripped my hands. "They'll say nothing of the kind, Ariel. Someone also took that into account; someone planned this very well. We all played into the murderer's hands last night. Cordelia declared you my mistress in front of all the guests—why shouldn't they believe her? I can guarantee that all—or most of them—left Copper Beeches convinced we were lovers."

"Not all, not Dr. Chandler."

"One in fifty?" He shook his head, releasing me. "Not a good number, Ariel. First she disgraced you in no uncertain terms. And then they witnessed my reaction. I could have strangled her on the spot last night! And they all knew it."

"But you didn't, Drew! Do you actually think that any of those people suspect that you went to the summerhouse and killed her hours later?"

"Of course they suspect it! Wouldn't you—if you had been witness to such a scene? I am the likeliest suspect. The husband always is, in the case of the wife's death. And after Cordelia's—exhibition—last night, there is not a soul in Newport who would testify that we were happily married."

A muscle worked in his jaw. "And another thing, Ariel. The lieutenant said that I am well-liked by the people of Newport. He meant the local people. I have never concealed my disdain and contempt for the summer colonists who make this town a three-ring circus for two months of the year. I have no real friends among those people, and because of that the scales are heavily weighed against me. But as far as you having any hand in it, why on earth should they suspect that?"

"Well, the police know how we feel about one another, Drew," I said, twisting my hands together.

"Oh, Ariel! Damnation! You didn't tell them about last night—about our—about my being in your room?"

"Yes, I did. Didn't—didn't you?"

"No! I didn't want you to become involved in this." His face was hard.

"But Drew, I *am* involved! You were with me when the murder was committed. I am your alibi!"

"But now that they know how we feel about one another, Ariel, they know you have reason to lie. Of course you'll claim I was with you, no matter what. Don't you see? I told them there was no truth to Cordelia's accusation. But now that they know we spent last night together, they'll never believe it was for the first time. Their knowing about us only makes things look worse. Especially since I withheld it earlier. Oh, hell!" He raked his fingers through his hair.

"They'll find the murderer, Drew," I said softly. "The real one. I told them I heard her arguing with someone in the library last night. Whomever she was with may have come to the summerhouse and killed her. In the meantime, there are other considerations. Blythe, for one."

He sighed. "Blythe, yes. Poor darling, she's another motive for them to have. I better go up to the nursery now and see her. God knows what she's heard today. God know what will happen to her. . . ."

"Don't, Drew. Don't say that. And she does have Miss McCready."

"Are you coming back to the house?" he asked.

"No, I think I'll take a walk." I tried to smile reassuringly at him.

His black brows drew together. "Are you all right, Ariel? When you came out of the library you looked shattered."

"I'm all right. Go and find Blythe."

Watching him go across the lawn back to the house, I then moved out from under the secluding beeches. To my dismay there were two women standing on the graveled path of the Cliff Walk.

"Is that she, Mother?" said the younger of the two eagerly. "You said she had red hair."

"Yes," said the matron, glaring at me with repugnance. "Walking about in public—and poor Cordelia not yet cold."

Whirling around, I fled. I did not slow down until I was halfway across the lawn.

"Well, well," said a voice behind me when I stopped to catch my breath. "If it isn't Miss Morrow."

It was Gideon. "What do you want?" I asked bitterly.

He spoke viciously. "Need I remind you that my sister was killed—*murdered*—on these grounds some hours ago? What do you think I want? I've come to pay my last respects. And to help the police with the investigation. I hear there are detectives from Providence already on the case. Worse luck for Drew. None of his friends to hold his hand."

"How can *you* help the police?"

"Oh, I think they'll be very interested in what I have to tell them. I suspected you and Drew all along, you know. Miss Morrow, always so prim and virtuous, with your, 'Please leave me to work in peace, Mr. Lawrence.' Well, I'll wager you didn't mind Drew interrupting your work! I saw the two of you together at the masquerade ball, or have you forgotten? And everyone in town read about the 'mysterious redhaired beauty' in *Town Topics*." He tapped his breast pocket. "I brought along a copy to show the detective, just in case he hasn't caught on to the two of you."

"You're too late," I said almost smugly. "Haven't you heard about the dinner party last night? Cordelia accused us in front of everyone."

"Yes, I know," he said, his eyes glinting. "I wish I'd been there. One can't say that Cordelia didn't go out with a bang."

"How can you talk so glibly about your own sister's death!"

"Oh, there wasn't much love lost between us. We weren't exactly a loving family. But I didn't dislike her nearly as much as Drew did."

Gripping his arm, I cried, "Gideon, you know that Drew did not kill Cordelia! You can't truly believe he did!"

He shook me off, his eyes narrowing. "What does it matter what I believe? My sister is dead, strangled. Most of Newport saw them at each other's throat. And they know about you."

"But he didn't kill her. He was angry, yes, enraged. He wanted a divorce. But he didn't kill her. Someone else did, someone—"

"What do I care whether he did it or not? He's the one who'll hang for it!"

I flinched. "But Drew was with me all last night. I don't care—make it as sordid as you like. But he was with me when she was killed."

"I've lived with the two of them, remember? Until Drew threw me out. I've seen Drew look as though he could wring Cordelia's neck more than once. And that is what I shall tell the detective. He may then draw his own conclusions."

"You're so transparent, Gideon. He'll be able to see right away how much you hate Drew."

He shrugged, brushing a speck from his sleeve. "So what? He'll listen to me. My regard—or lack of it— for my dear brother-in-law is immaterial. What matter are the facts. I will provide the detective with

310

them, just practicing, you know, for the real thing."

"The real thing? What real thing?"

"The trial, Miss Morrow. The trial of Drew Rockwell for the murder of his wife and my sister, Cordelia Rockwell."

Chapter Sixteen

The two detectives remained in the house until early evening. When they were finally gone, Drew, Isadora, Aunt Hermione, and I sat down to a silent uneasy meal in the dining room. We knew it was merely a brief respite; the probing questions would begin again, for all of us. And they did.

On the day of Cordelia's funeral, the police left us alone. I did not attend, for obvious reasons, but apparently most of the summer residents did. It was held at the family church, the Congregational one on Spring and Pelham Streets. I could imagine how hot and airless and crowded it was on that August day, and how the flamboyant murals designed by John La Farge might seem a trifle jarring. Isadora told me later that one woman fainted and had to be carried out.

"They came more to gape at Drew and the rest of us than for the sake of Cordelia's memory," she said with disgust. "And afterwards, Dr. Chandler and one or two others were the only ones who spoke to Drew. They've condemned him, you see, and it's so unfair!"

Drew had ordered a lavish luncheon for the mourners but the only guests who gathered with the family in the drawing room were Prescott, Olive, and Gwendolyn Chandler. Isadora urged me to come

312

down and join them, and I reluctantly agreed.

The ruined portrait had been taken down from the drawing-room wall and a mirror rather hastily put up in its place. I caught sight of my reflection as I entered the room — cheeks flushed, eyes overbright, my expression tense, anxious. I did not look well.

Isadora and I sat down on the yellow damask sofa. I felt, rather than saw, Olive Chandler's disapproving glare, outrage in every ounce of her tightly corseted figure. Naturally she considered it to be in very poor taste that I was joining the mourners. It doubtless was; I should not have allowed Isadora to persuade me.

Gratefully I took a glass of sherry from the tray Merriman held. Perhaps it would help to steady my nerves.

Gwendolyn Chandler was staring ahead at nothing in particular, her pale green gaze more than a little disturbing.

"There was nothing you could have done, Prescott," Drew was saying. "You did right to take Olive home that night."

"But I could have given Cordelia a sedative. Instead I ran with my tail between my legs like everyone else. But at the time I believed it was best if we all left as soon as possible!"

"You were right." said Drew curtly.

There was an awkward pause; I took a gulp of sherry.

"I want you to know, Drew, that if anything should come of all this, that if by some absurd throw of the dice you are — well . . ." There was a look of pained embarrassment on Dr. Chandler's normally bright face. "Just know, my boy, that you can count on me to — to testify as to your character." He spoke the last words in a rush.

"Oh, Dr. Chandler, don't!" pleaded Isadora. "Don't

313

even say such a thing! Surely that won't be necessary!"

"The feelings are running high against me. I know that," said Drew, staring down into his glass of wine.

"Olive and I simply cannot for the life of us imagine who would have done such a dreadful thing," continued the doctor.

"Prescott feels that the only person capable of such a foul act must be a vagrant, a thief wandering the grounds that night." Mrs. Chandler did not look as though she agreed with her husband.

"He must have known it would be impossible to break into Copper Beeches, so instead he chose the summerhouse as an easier target. Cordelia must have startled him. He may not have meant to do more than frighten or stun her, but when he realized what had actually happened, he fled without taking anything after all. Is the summerhouse kept locked?" asked Dr. Chandler eagerly.

Drew frowned. "No, it's not. There is nothing inside of any real value. I never considered it necessary."

I wondered whether Dr. Chandler and Olive had any idea why Cordelia should go to the summerhouse at night. I supposed that they merely assumed that, after the scene with Drew and me, she had fled the house.

"To think that a crime such as that—something one would associate with mean city streets and the desperation of the poor and weak—to think that it could happen here, of all places," said Dr. Chandler, shaking his head. "And to one of our finest families. The realization is shattering to me."

"You forget Lizzie Borden, Father," said Gwendolyn.

We all turned to her, startled.

"Fall River is not Newport, Gwendolyn," said her mother sharply. "And I have forbidden you to mention that woman's name in my presence."

"Why, Mother?" asked Gwendolyn sweetly. "She was proven innocent. It's just as you and Father were saying. Mrs. Rockwell must have been killed by a wandering vagrant, just as Lizzie's parents were."

"You don't think it's possible that someone meant purposely to murder Cordelia, someone who knew her?" asked Isadora rather breathlessly.

"You don't mean someone we all know!" said Olive Chandler, aghast.

"Well, if Drew can be suspected, why not anyone?" Isadora said defensively.

Gwendolyn Chandler stood up. "I think I shall play a little," she said calmly, and went over to the piano.

"A good idea, my dear," said Dr. Chandler, relieved. "A little music would be just the thing." If there was music, we would not be forced to converse in this unnerving way.

But when she began to play, it was with difficulty that I suppressed a gasp of horror. For the piece she had selected was that diabolical *Danse Macabre,* the Dance of Death. The same piece she had played on the morning Maisie Leander's body had been found. Why was she playing it? It was shocking, horrible under the circumstances. Did she find it amusing somehow? She must be as mad as everyone said.

Dr. Chandler rose to his feet, but Drew, shaking his head, motioned for him to sit down. We sat there listening to the gleeful ghosts rising from their graves and dancing manically about the graveyard. And I could not help but see Cordelia's moon white face, the marks on her throat, her eyes . . . My nails dug into my palms.

Gwendolyn was playing the eerie melody faster and faster, her fingers flying over the keys. It was ghastly, monstrous. I could feel the look of sick frozen horror on my face; Drew's expression was rigid; Isadora was biting her lip; Aunt Hermione's eyes were closed, her

315

face sagging. Yet still we were forced to listen to this unbalanced woman playing Saint-Saëns' frantic bizarre composition. She was a demon; I wanted to rush over to the piano and shake her by the shoulders as hard as I could.

Finally it was over, the crowing of the cock signaling the time for the ghouls to return to their graves, their uproarious frolic on All Hallows Eve at an end.

But the silence that followed was even worse.

"Really, Gwendolyn, that was perfectly dreadful," said Olive Chandler. "You are really the most unnatural girl."

"Not perhaps in the best of taste, my dear," said her father lamely. He was plainly embarrassed. "Could we have some — some Chopin?"

With a slight smile Gwendolyn began to play again, and gradually some of the tension in the room subsided.

"Shall we go into the dining room?" asked Drew when she had finished. "It doesn't look as though anyone else will be joining us." His voice was cool.

"Oh, what shall I say to people when next I see them!" cried Isadora indignantly.

"I understand your feelings completely, my dear," said Dr. Chandler, "but people are unsure of how to react to a situation such as this."

"You're wrong, Prescott," said Aunt Hermione bluntly. "They know just how to react."

We went into the dining room, taking our seats at the table. There was no more talk of the murder or the police. Dr. Chandler talked about some necessary improvements for the town, and asked Drew's opinion on certain things. The rest of us ate mechanically, and shortly after luncheon the Chandlers took their leave.

Dr. Chandler had found it difficult to believe that a lady of wealth and consequence could be murdered in such a place as Newport. Newport, the Valhalla above the sea, chosen paradise of the rich and powerful. On the surface that was what it was. But I now realized that the elegance, the luxury, the splendor were merely a veneer. And in the time I had been there, I had observed many cracks in that veneer, dazzling and crystalline though it was. Underneath it raged the same turmoil and desperation as in any other location where people lived. Camille de la Salle's blissful dreams had been crushed by her mother and the foreign count; William Everett lay in a bed it was doubted he would ever leave; Maisie Leander had sought death rather than face the scandal of bearing a servant's child; her lover, the coachman, had joined her. And, in Copper Beeches, a man and wife had lived as enemies; one child had died and another was plagued by incomprehensible anxieties.

To those who did not belong, the Newport of the summer colonists was a glittering opulent world of lavish spectacle and luxury. But beneath that facade lurked something quite different. The millionaires preyed on one another, probing for vulnerabilities and transgressions, always in desperate attempts to verify their own superiority over the rest of humanity and over one another. Beneath the alluring facade of wealth and magnificence, the undercurrents ran like a tainted underground river, foul-smelling and malevolent.

That night after Isadora and Aunt Hermione had retired, I went to the library where I knew Drew was working. As I paused on the threshold of the room, I saw him fling down his fountain pen and push aside the papers. Then he caught sight of me standing in the doorway and shrugged.

"One of our agents in Shanghai has sent me all this to approve," he said, gesturing to the papers, "and I can't make head or tail of it. Damnation!"

"Oh, Drew . . ."

"I'm worried, Ariel. I'd be a fool not to be. About Blythe, about you, Isadora—everyone I care about and who relies on me. I've made an infernal mess of everything. I should have suspected that Cordelia had some devilish scheme in mind—all that about the 'unveiling,' the presenting of you to her guests. I could have stopped this before it ever began."

"You couldn't have known what she planned to do, Drew. If anyone has made a mess of things, I have. I never should have agreed to stay here, to paint her portrait. Besides, none of that may have prevented what happened afterwards—her murder."

"Don't blame yourself, Ariel, for God's sake," he said roughly. "You *should* be painting portraits. Now I know to what extent the feeling in the town is against me—the fact that none of Cordelia's friends attended the funeral luncheon. I've never cared before what they thought, but now they are the witnesses."

"To the dinner party, yes, but not to the crime! No one saw you kill Cordelia. What did you think of Dr. Chandler's theory of a vagrant, a thief caught in the act?"

"It seems a bit far-fetched. Nothing taken, no signs of a struggle. Why go to the trouble of strangling someone and then not take anything?" He shook his head. "But I can't think beyond that. Who in the world would someone want to murder Cordelia? If I'm arrested—"

"Hush," I said, putting my fingers over his mouth. "Don't say it, don't even think it. For just a while . . . let us forget everything else."

In the privacy of my room we kissed hungrily, our clothes falling swiftly to the floor as we ardently released what was fierce and splendid between us, eager to seize, eager to surrender.

It was our last night together.

Shortly before noon on the next day, Lieutenant

Pierce and his sergeant returned to the house. But this time they had no questions to ask. This time they carried a warrant for Drew's arrest.

I was in the upstairs sitting room with Isadora. There was no melodramatic scene. It was Merriman who came upstairs and informed us, once the three men had already left the house.

"Now?" cried Isadora. "Al—already? I didn't hear a carriage."

"Did he take some things with him?" I asked, my voice shaking.

"Yes, Miss Morrow. Earlier this morning he had evidently packed a bag for himself. It was with him in the library."

Drew had been that certain, then, of the outcome. Merriman looked terribly distressed; I realized he had probably known Drew as a boy. He went away, his shoulders stooping.

"Oh, Ariel, what are we to do?" cried Isadora.

I sat stiffly down. "We must wait for the trial. Then we will say what we can to help him. There is nothing else for us to do."

She lifted her tear-stained face. "But I'm so frightened of the trial! The police are so certain he did it. Does he even have a chance?"

"It's all my fault," I said. "None of this might ever have happened but for me."

Mrs. Perkins had warned me; she had sensed some approaching horror. But I had not heeded her.

Isadora took a sobbing breath and wiped her face with her handkerchief. "I must go to Blythe. I must tell Miss McCready what has happened."

"I'll go with you."

Drew was the largest part of Blythe's world. I was terrified that somehow she might learn that people believed her father had killed her mother and he had been taken away.

We found Blythe and Miss McCready on the terrace having an alfresco luncheon of egg salad sandwiches and blackberry jam cake.

"Blythe chose the menu and I am her guest," explained Miss McCready. Wisps of pale red hair flew about her head.

"What a lovely idea," I said mechanically.

"Darling, I must speak to Miss McCready," said Isadora. "Perhaps Ariel may sit down with you for a few minutes."

Blythe cocked her head. "All right. Would you like a sandwich, Ariel?"

"No, thank you, Blythe. I'm not hungry just now. You like Miss McCready very much, don't you?" I asked her after the two women had gone down the terrace steps to the lawn.

Blythe nodded, a streak of egg salad across her cheek. "I like the stories she tells me. And we play counting games, and look at different places on my globe. She showed me Scotland. All the people there talk like Miss McCready." She paused. "Daddy has gone away."

"Yes, I know," I said gently. "But how did you know?"

"He came to my room this morning while I was having breakfast. He said he had to go away for a while, and that everyone here would take care of me, and that I must mind Miss McCready."

"Daddy will be very proud of you . . . when he gets back," I said.

The days passed. Some of them I went about in a sort of numbness, and those were the good days. On other days I could not sit still, overwhelmed with panic and anxiety. The waiting, the feeling of helplessness, of futility, was almost intolerable.

Drew's attorney, Mr. Oliver Bredbeck, came to Copper Beeches to see Isadora. He was a friend of the

320

family, and a shrewd and competent defense lawyer from Boston, she told me. Not that any of the family had ever required the use of his services previously.

"He says there's no proof at all," declared Isadora almost jubilantly. "The evidence is all circumstantial—whatever that means."

"It means that Drew happened to do the wrong thing at the wrong time," said Aunt Hermione heavily. "The newspapers are the worst. And you can be certain that every summer resident is pouring over them gloatingly."

"Mr. Bredbeck says the district attorney is eager to go to trial as soon as possible. He's as revolted by the newspaper headlines as Mr. Bredbeck is. Of course, with the summer people here it's that much more notorious. 'Foul Murder in Society's Playground,' and all that sort of thing. But Mr. Bredbeck considers the prosecution's case to be very weak."

"We can only pray he is right," said Aunt Hermione grimly.

There was an altogether different atmosphere in the house now. Some of the servants were avidly curious, some wary and fearful, others bold and just short of disrespectful. Merriman kept them in line, but even he could not control the expressions on their faces as they regarded me.

Isadora, Aunt Hermione, and I had been summoned to testify by the prosecutor as had a few of the servants. I dreaded the ordeal because I feared that somehow my words would be twisted and would work against Drew rather than support him. I knew only too well how I would be viewed by the jury—"a bohemian of loose morals and depraved inclinations" one newspaper had labeled me. My life in New York, sharing my father's studio and acting as hostess to his friends, had been blown out of proportion so that the readers were left with the impression of a woman who had rejected all suitable feminine behavior, a woman who doubtless advocated "free love," who, though left with some of her father's fortune, had nevertheless chosen to intrude on the male-dominated world of art, a world where no "proper" woman had a place. I was unnatural and immoral.

Cordelia was seen as the wronged wife, deceived in her own house by her husband and the shameless young woman who had lured him into infidelity and murder.

Those were the Boston and New York papers. The Newport paper handled the story differently; they did not condemn Drew, and there were editorials demanding that the case not go to trial due to lack of conclusive evidence. But *Town Topics* seethed with righteous indignation at the loathesome behavior indulged in by the wealthy and influential, going so far as to intimate that if Drew were not found guilty that would prove to America that the laws were different for the privileged class.

The reporters hung about the grounds, hoping to catch sight of us and hurl their questions and accusations. But we remained inside the house, careful to avoid being seen. A few of the servants must have slipped down to the entrance to the drive from time to time; the articles reporting vicious arguments between Drew and Cordelia had to come from some source within the house.

Isadora went to visit Drew in jail, but Oliver Bredbeck had said in no uncertain terms that I was not to do so. My presence would merely fuel the fire.

We had no visitors except Dr. Chandler. He was concerned about the state of Aunt Hermione's health, he explained, and so he came over several times to see how she did. But I believed he was just as worried about the rest of us, and so on several evenings we sat in the drawing room drinking tea and discussing the upcoming trial. Dr. Chandler was going to speak as a character witness for the defense, as he had promised.

"The police are apparently so convinced that he did it that they've stopped the investigation," he said, shaking his head. "But I'm afraid that one can hardly expect more than that. They are basically good men, but they can see only the obvious. They doubtless do not possess the necessary intelligence to solve such a complex case as this one. They immediately assumed that Drew was to blame and they looked no further."

"I wish there might be some way we could figure out who killed her," said Isadora. "The only person I can think of who had a motive would have been Bartholomew Reed's wife. But the police are certain a woman couldn't have done it because of the strength it would have taken. Ugh, I can't bear to think of it."

"Could she have—I don't know—got someone to do it for her?" I asked wildly. "Or why not Bartholomew Reed himself? Why were the police so quick to assume he was innocent?"

"He must have a believable alibi," said Isadora.

"But so does—" I broke off, reddening. Drew's alibi was *not* believable, because it was known we were lovers. And the very fact that we had spent that night together condemned us in the eyes of the world.

One morning shortly before the trial was to begin, Isadora said to me, "I really cannot stand it being cooped up in this house any longer! We can never go farther than the gatehouse or behind to the rose arbor—not even to the Cliff Walk because we're so afraid of being accosted by a reporter! I've had enough. Ariel, I must get out!"

I regarded her in some dismay. "Where do you wish to go?"

"Oh, I don't know. For a drive perhaps or . . . I know, let's go to the Casino. We can sit and listen to some music and feel a part of the world again."

323

"I wouldn't advise it, Dora," said Aunt Hermione flatly. "Perhaps a drive out to Middletown in a covered carriage would be best."

"I simply will not continue to act as though I've done something—if *any* of us have done something to be ashamed of! It's been wrong for us to hold up here as though we were under siege. They may think the worst of Drew, and my staying closeted in here hasn't helped matters. I'm not afraid to show my face. Perhaps—perhaps I can persuade public opinion to change."

"How could you do that, Dora?" asked Aunt Hermione wearily. "You're talking like a child."

"Well, at least it's preferable to acting as though we're all criminals, too awful to mix in decent society."

"Well, do what you wish, Dora. You will anyway, I daresay," said her great-aunt.

"I'm going to the Casino this morning, and Ariel is coming with me," she announced.

"Oh, no, Isadora—I couldn't possibly!"

"Dora, you're a fool if you drag Miss Morrow there."

"Why? She wasn't the cause of Cordelia's death. Why does she have to act as though she were? I'm not going to stand for it any longer. Ariel, put on your prettiest gown. We'll show them we have nothing to hide!" Her cheeks were scarlet, her eyes feverish.

"You're in mourning, Isadora," I reminded her.

"Don't be so old-fashioned, Ariel. It hardly suits you."

I flushed and she quickly said, "Oh, I didn't mean it that way. I'm just so miserable with everything that's been happening. I just have to get out. If you won't go with me, I'll go alone."

"I'll come, Isadora," I said unhappily.

"I'm doing this as much for Drew as for myself. We simply must not hide away as though we are evil

324

people. And as for being in mourning, do you think that Cordelia would have curtailed any of her activities in the weeks following *my* death?"

"But the reporters . . ."

"I already sent a man down to check. There aren't any out there now."

So I went upstairs and changed my gown, and the two of us climbed into the wicker phaeton with its red wheels and rode down the graveled drive, turning onto Bellevue Avenue. It was a gorgeous day in late August with just a hint of fall in the air—the sky a vibrant blue, the air fresh and crisp.

In front of the Casino, we climbed down from the phaeton and passed under the long entranceway to the lush open area framed by the shingled wings of the building. The orchestra was playing; the gay crowd was assembled to listen and exchange pleasantries.

Isadora was smiling in anticipation of greeting her friends, but I could not repress the unease I was feeling. I gripped my parasol tightly. I should not have come here; I should have let her go alone after all. She was blameless in the whole affair, but I was viewed as the scheming adulteress who had somehow convinced Drew to rid himself of his wife. Isadora, by insisting I join her today, was bravely showing Society that she did not believe me guilty of such treachery.

We were making our way to the Rockwell family's box when I noticed the people were beginning to turn and stare. At first it was merely a few heads, a few gazes, a few whispers and nudges, but gradually a ripple moved over the crowd, until it seemed that there was no one not looking in our direction.

And then a few ladies here and there rose from their seats, and I felt a surge of relief. They were going to receive her, to welcome her, to show their support. If she had to be the one to seek it out, then so be it. They were willing to give it, to rally round her.

We had nearly reached the box. Isadora was openly smiling, even waving. Only the music now filled the air; all rustling, buzzing, and chattering had ceased. More and more of them stood up until the entire gathering seemed to be on its feet.

Isadora leaned forward eagerly to call out something. But before she actually spoke, the crowd of summer colonists moved in one collective, deliberate action. They turned their backs on us. We had been cut dead.

Isadora stood rooted to the ground, her lips white. Very gently I took her arm and led her away, underneath the bell-shaped clock tower, underneath the elaborate iron lantern, through the passageway, and out into the street. Isadora moved like a sleepwalker, stiff and unaware of her limbs.

"Take us home," I said to the driver.

There was nowhere else to go.

"Mark my words," said Aunt Hermione later after I had put Isadora to bed. "They may have turned their backs on you today, but in court they won't dare glance away for a moment for fear they should miss something. They would normally be leaving Newport now, closing up the cottages, but very few of them will leave with this going on. There'll be nothing quite this exciting in New York this fall," she added sardonically.

On the morning of the day the trial was to begin, I awoke before dawn with a dull headache and fear writhing like a snake in my stomach. When it was finally time to get dressed, I got out of bed and put on my black watch suit. Mr. Bredbeck had tactfully suggested that I wear something as modest and severe as possible. He wanted me to appear as prim as possible to the jury: a victim of circumstances, not a bold adventuress.

In the dining room I joined Isadora and Aunt Hermione for a breakfast I could scarcely eat. Isadora ate

326

rapidly and nervously. Aunt Hermione wore her favorite purple and one of her enormous tea-tray bonnets covered with plumes and silk flowers.

At half past nine the three of us got into the closed carriage. On the sidewalk of Bellevue Avenue, a small group of reporters had gathered, those that were not already at the courthouse. They called out to us as we turned onto Bellevue, joining the throng of other vehicles also headed to the courthouse.

"Vultures," said Aunt Hermione.

At least I would see Drew today. These past weeks I had longed to be with him, yearned for even a glimpse, but I had had to be content with Isadora's reports of her visits to the jailhouse. For days now I had been desperately waiting for the trial to begin. Anything was preferable to the terrible impotent waiting.

A huge crowd waited outside the courthouse, filling the square. When we climbed out of the carriage, I pretended not to notice the pointing fingers, the avid gazes from the ordinary people, and the hostile, censuring stares from the elegantly dressed millionaires. Aunt Hermione clasped one of my arms and one of Isadora's, and together we went through the crowd and up the steps of the Colonial brick structure. The policemen had cleared a path for us.

We took our seats in the courtroom. The heat had returned and the room was very warm even that early in the morning.

When Drew was brought in I had to press my lips together and dig my nails into my palms to keep from crying out. He was pale, but he seemed composed and he met the faces of the jurors squarely. Then I realized that what I was feeling was written all over my face, and so I looked down. When I glanced up again, he was seated beside Mr. Bredbeck. But for an instant our gazes had locked and my heart had gone out to him.

The judge entered, and Mr. James, the prosecuting attorney, an older man with thick white hair, presented the case as he saw it: Drew had strangled his wife soon after a dinner party in which she had denounced him as an adulterer and me as his mistress.

Mr. Bredbeck stood up slowly, pushing back his chair. Then he turned to face the men of the jury. "My learned colleague would have you believe that my client, Mr. Drew Rockwell, an outstanding member of the community who has done much for his beloved city, strangled his wife in a fit of uncontrollable rage. But this crime, as we shall see, was committed sometime between two and four in the morning, several hours after the party, when Mr. Rockwell's undeniable anger had had time to cool. You will see that the prosecution has no solid evidence to convict my client, except that he argued with his wife in front of their guests. Well, as you know, my friends, many men argue with their wives, but most do not kill them. You will hear from several sources that Mr. and Mrs. Rockwell had discussed a divorce on several occasions, and had she lived, their marriage undoubtedly would have ended in that way. But Mrs. Rockwell was murdered before such proceedings could begin. Gentlemen, there is no doubt here that a horrible crime has been committed, but Mr. Rockwell has been arrested for this crime simply because the police have been unable to produce any evidence except an argument at a dinner party. But we cannot in this courtroom commit another crime as well—to convict this man of his wife's murder."

"Mr. Bredbeck makes it sound good," Isadora whispered.

Shortly after, the state called its first witness, Molly McIntyre. She looked frightened as she climbed into the witness box.

328

"Your name, please."

"Molly McIntyre," she said tremulously, darting a glance at the jurors.

"Where are you employed, Miss McIntyre?"

"At Copper Beeches, sir."

"The house that belongs to whom?"

"To—to Mr. Rockwell."

"Is he in the courtroom?"

She nodded, glancing swiftly across at Drew. "He's seated—just there."

"Miss McIntyre, I must ask you to speak up," said the judge.

"What is your position at that household, Miss McIntyre?"

"Parlormaid," she said more distinctly.

"And how long have you been employed there?"

"Since May of this year."

"Miss McIntyre, how would you describe the relationship between your master and former mistress?"

"Relationship?" she repeated. "They were married."

There were a few laughs.

"How did Mr. and Mrs. Rockwell get along?" asked Mr. James with a trace of irritation.

"Sir, I don't think it's my place to—"

"Answer the question, please."

"Well, I didn't often see them together. Mrs. Rockwell was always going off to luncheons and parties, and Mr. Rockwell might be in the library or upstairs in the nursery with Miss Blythe—"

"—Simply answer the question, Miss McIntyre."

"I'm trying to, sir."

"When you did see them together, were they affectionate, friendly?"

Molly cast a troubled look at Drew.

"I ask you, Miss McIntyre," continued the prosecutor, "did your master and mistress argue frequently?"

"Yes," she said softly.

329

"Did they behave as though they were fond of one another?"

"Not—not exactly."

"Did you ever hear your master make any threatening statements to his wife?"

Molly said nothing, her eyes darting over to the jury and back to Mr. James.

"Miss McIntyre, you told the police that Drew Rockwell threatened to kill his wife."

"No!" she cried, shaking her head. "It wasn't that way at all. He was angry—she'd upset the little girl, slapped her—"

"Just answer the question, Miss McIntyre. Did or did you not hear Drew Rockwell say that he would kill his wife in order to protect their only child?"

Molly looked close to tears; she bent her head. "Yes."

"That is all, Miss McIntyre, you may step down."

More members of the staff were questioned about arguments they had witnessed or overheard between Drew and Cordelia. The prosecutor was painting a picture of a couple who loathed one another, who were always on the brink of anger when they were together. Which had, in reality, been the case. Even Drew could not blame his household staff for stating the truth.

That afternoon the prosecution called Gideon Lawrence to the stand. Drew sat calmly, handsome despite his pallor, his eyes fixed intently on the witness box.

"Mr. Lawrence, how are you related to the deceased, Mrs. Cordelia Rockwell?"

"She was my sister," said Gideon solemnly.

"Mr. Lawrence, do you agree with the testimony we heard in court this morning about the frequent arguments that took place between the defendant and your late sister?"

"Objection, Your Honor," said Mr. Bredbeck. "We'd

like to hear what this gentleman has observed first-hand, not whether he agrees or disagrees with one of the state's so-called 'witnesses.' "

"I think Mr. Lawrence can be trusted to speak his own mind," the judge said sternly, not appreciating Mr. Bredbeck's tone. "Overruled."

"Please answer the question, Mr. Lawrence," said Mr. James.

"Yes, I do," said Gideon, looking over at Drew.

"Did Mrs. Rockwell ever discuss her feelings toward her husband with you?"

"Yes, she did. My sister wanted a divorce. She had asked him for one a number of times."

A muscle jerked in Drew's cheek as his face hardened.

"And what was his answer, to your knowledge?"

"He refused. He would not agree to the terms."

"And what were those terms, Mr. Lawrence?"

Mr. Bredbeck was on his feet again. "Objection, Your Honor. The defense is willing to give the state a reasonable amount of latitude, but we're wandering into an irrelevant area here of a highly personal nature."

"Response, Mr. James?" said the judge.

"Your Honor, this matter is admittedly very personal, but it is quite pertinent. The state is endeavoring to show motive for this heinous crime."

"Very well. Overruled."

"Cordelia wanted Copper Beeches, the house," said Gideon smugly. "She also wanted custody of Blythe, her only child and daughter."

"And did your brother-in-law object to that?"

"He did. He refused to allow her to have the house. And he insisted that the child was to stay with him."

"And what was Mrs. Rockwell's response?"

"That there would be no divorce except on those terms."

There were whisperings and murmurings in the crowd.

"They did not come to an agreement, as far as you are aware?" said Mr. James to Gideon.

"What do you expect? A mother wouldn't give up her child," said Gideon righteously. "It was rotten of him to ask it of her."

"Objection," said Mr. Bredbeck softly.

"Mr. Lawrence, we are not interested in any personal remarks, just the facts," admonished Judge Harrison.

"I have no more questions, Your Honor," said Mr. James.

Mr. Bredbeck rose and went toward Gideon. "What is your present address, Mr. Lawrence?"

"Objection, Your Honor," said Mr. James.

"I will rephrase the question, Your Honor," said Mr. Bredbeck. "Where were you residing in the earlier part of the summer?"

"What does that have to do with anything?" asked Gideon sullenly.

"Let's let the jury decide that, shall we? You were living at Copper Beeches, weren't you?"

"Yes, I was."

"Why did you leave, Mr. Lawrence?"

"Well, I decided it was for the best," said Gideon breezily. "To tell you the truth I got tired of all the bickering. Many times I'd be in the middle and I didn't like it. I thought I'd be better off elsewhere."

"Liar!" hissed Isadora.

Mr. Bredbeck nodded, looked down, and then glanced back up at Gideon as though he had just thought of something. "And there was a governess at Copper Beeches when you were living there, isn't that correct, Mr. Lawrence?"

Gideon flushed; he had not expected this. I felt a stab of satisfaction. "A—a governess? Yes."

332

"A Miss Jennifer Simmons?"

"I believe that was her name," said Gideon, moving restlessly in his chair.

Suddenly Mr. Bredbeck dropped his easy manner. "And weren't you found in a compromising situation with her, Mr. Lawrence?"

"I don't know what you're trying to imply, Bredbeck!"

"Then I will be more specific. Did not Mr. Rockwell come upon the two of you in her bedroom in the middle of the day?"

"Of course not! What a tale!" blustered Gideon, but his voice lacked conviction.

"I can call witnesses who can testify to it, Mr. Lawrence. I put it to you that Mr. Rockwell discovered you and his child's governess engaged in what was obviously a seduction, and he ordered you to leave the house. Isn't that the real reason you left Copper Beeches, Mr. Lawrence?"

"I object to this badgering, Your Honor," said Mr. James. "Mr. Lawrence is not on trial here."

"Sit down, Mr. James. I want to—I want the jury to hear this."

"Thank you, Your Honor," said Mr. Bredbeck. He turned to Gideon. "You don't like your brother-in-law very much, do you, Mr. Lawrence? In fact, you hate him for finding you with the governess and throwing you out of a comfortable house where you had every luxury."

Gideon's face was red; he leaped to his feet, sputtering, "What about him? What about him and Miss Morrow?"

"Silence!" said the judge.

"I have no more questions, Your Honor," said Mr. Bredbeck smoothly.

"Step down, Mr. Lawrence," said the judge.

Mr. Bredbeck remained standing. "Your Honor, the

defense would like to express our gratitude for permitting us to call to the stand Dr. Prescott Chandler out of order to accommodate his schedule."

"The court is willing to be flexible," said the judge dryly.

Dr. Chandler took his place on the stand.

"Dr. Chandler, how long have you known the defendant?" asked Mr. Bredbeck.

"Ever since I purchased the house closest to his eight years ago."

"And what sort of man is he, to your knowledge?"

"He is a good man, one of the best. He has donated money to the city to be used for the public good and for the restoration of some of the buildings. His money has even been used to repair the building in which we now sit."

The jurors stirred uncomfortably. "I had forgotten that!" said Isadora.

"He is a loving father and, as far as I could tell, a considerate husband."

"Do you believe it possible that he could have murdered his wife?"

"Certainly not. There is not a doubt in my mind."

"Thank you, Dr. Chandler."

"That has to help," whispered Isadora. "Dr. Chandler is well-respected."

"Dr. Chandler," said Mr. James, "you are a personal friend of the defendant, are you not?"

"I have said I am," said the doctor almost curtly.

"He has dined with you and you with him?"

"Yes."

"On numerous occasions?"

"Yes."

"And as a close personal friend and frequent guest of the defendant, you don't want to see anything bad happen to him, do you?"

"Well, I certainly would not lie on his behalf, if that

334

is what you are trying to suggest," said the doctor indignantly.

"I put it to you again, doctor, you don't want to see anything unpleasant happen to Mr. Rockwell, do you?"

"No."

"I understand that you undertook the care of Mr. Rockwell's two children when they were ill with scarlet fever two years ago."

"That is so."

"What happened?"

"Objection, Your Honor. This has no possible bearing on the case," said Mr. Bredbeck.

"Overruled."

"What happened, Dr. Chandler?"

"Nathan, the little boy, died."

"Despite your efforts."

"Yes, I'm afraid so."

"You must have felt great remorse — as a doctor and a personal friend."

"A doctor always feels it deeply when one of his patients dies, sir. Especially a child." Dr. Chandler was obviously exasperated.

"And so you felt sorrow. And perhaps a little guilt."

"Objection, Your Honor!"

"Sustained. Mr. James, you must be more direct in your questions. We are not here to listen to your musings."

"I am merely trying to show, Your Honor, that when Nathan Rockwell died, Dr. Chandler was helpless. He was unable to save him, or to help his grieving parents. So it is quite understandable that now Dr. Chandler seeks to do what he can for Mr. Rockwell."

"No, I consider that line of questioning highly inappropriate. Dr. Chandler is a distinguished member of the medical profession. The jury is instructed to disregard those remarks."

Dr. Chandler stepped down, and the prosecution called Isadora to the witness box.

"Miss Rockwell," began Mr. James, "I want you to tell the court what happened on the last night of Mrs. Rockwell's life. The night of the ill-fated dinner party."

"Very well." She spoke clearly. "My brother and sister-in-law hosted a dinner party which was in honor of a presentation Mrs. Rockwell was going to make following dinner."

"And what was this presentation?"

"Miss Morrow had painted her portrait and she was to show it to the guests."

"Miss Morrow. Is she now in the courtroom?"

"Yes."

"Point her out, if you please."

"There she is." I felt, rather than saw, all heads turn to me.

"Did Mrs. Rockwell show this portrait to the guests?"

"Yes. And it had been destroyed, ruined."

"How so?"

"The paint had all run together."

"And then?"

"My brother accused Cordelia of destroying the portrait herself. At first she denied it, but then she admitted that she had. It was all done to disgrace Ariel—Miss Morrow. Cordelia cried that she would not keep a portrait of herself painted by—by Drew's mistress."

There was another stirring in the crowd.

"Drew told her it wasn't true, that Miss Morrow was not his mistress. Cordelia slapped his face and left the room. And the party broke up after that."

"I should think that it did," said Mr. James, glancing meaningfully at the jury. "And then?"

"Drew went after Cordelia. They were talking about a divorce. I didn't hear all that they said. I stayed behind with my aunt."

"Did you see your brother later that night, Miss Rockwell?"

"No, I went to bed."

"Did you see Miss Morrow?"

"No."

"One more question, Miss Rockwell. Is Miss Morrow your brother's mistress?"

"Objection!" growled Mr. Bredbeck.

"Overruled," said Judge Harrison. "Answer the question, Miss Rockwell."

"I don't know and I don't care!" snapped Isadora.

"It is not your duty to care or not to care, Miss Rockwell," said Mr. James coldly. "Is your brother in love with Miss Morrow and she with him?"

Isadora glanced from Drew to me and to the men of the jury. "I—they have never told me so. To my knowledge, my brother and Miss Morrow have never behaved wrongly. Miss Morrow was planning to leave Copper Beeches right after Cordelia's portrait was completed. She only agreed to stay for the dinner party because Cordelia insisted that she should. Whatever her feelings for my brother and his for her, she was returning to New York. My brother did not kill his wife, Mr. James, no matter what you get people to say on this stand."

"Your witness, Mr. Bredbeck."

Oliver Bredbeck rose, placing one hand on his hip to draw aside his jacket. "Miss Rockwell, your sister-in-law's body was found in the summerhouse, was it not?"

"Yes."

"Did that surprise you?"

"That she was dead? Of course it surprised me!"

There was some nervous laughter. Even Mr. Bredbeck smiled. "No, Miss Rockwell. I mean, were you surprised that she had apparently gone to the summerhouse that night?"

"No. She often went there at night."

"Why did she do that, Miss Rockwell? Why leave her house at night?"

"Because it was there that Cordelia entertained her lovers."

Exclamations sounded from one end of the courtroom to the other. The judge rapped on his gavel not once, but several times.

"Objection, Your Honor," Mr. James stammered, instantly on his feet.

"Response?" asked the judge.

"The sauce for the gander ought to apply to the goose as well, Your Honor," said Mr. Bredbeck smoothly.

"Your Honor, Mrs. Rockwell is dead. The difference is plain, as well my learned colleague knows," said Mr. James severely.

"We can understand why the prosecutor wants the jury to have but half the story. We trust Your Honor will not permit such an injustice," declared Mr. Bredbeck.

"Please stop your bickering," said the judge. "I'll allow the question."

"Tell the court exactly what you mean, Miss Rockwell," said Mr. Bredbeck.

"Cordelia used the summerhouse for rendezvous with her current lover. We all knew about it—Drew, Gideon, my great-aunt, the servants as well, I suppose."

"So you are saying that Mrs. Rockwell made a habit of being unfaithful to her husband."

"Yes, she did. For the past two or three years. Cordelia knew better than to be seen with the man in public, but he would come to the house, and at night they would meet in the summerhouse."

"Miss Rockwell, do you know the identity of Mrs.

338

Rockwell's latest lover—the man with which she was most recently involved?" asked Mr. Bredbeck intently.

"Yes, I do," stated Isadora deliberately. "His name is Bartholomew Reed."

Chapter Seventeen

Isadora's defiant response caused such an uproar that Judge Harrison declared an adjournment for the rest of the day. I had not seen Bartholomew Reed in the courtroom so far, but many of those present were well-acquainted with both him and his wife. Hands pressed to ponderous bosoms, tongues wagging feverishly, the agitated matrons were escorted from the courtroom by their silent husbands. When the voices and scraping of chairs had lessened considerably, Isadora, Aunt Hermione, and I stood up to go.

Drew was being led away; I got a glimpse of his face. His square jaw was clenched; there were tight lines about his mouth. How humiliating this must be for him, to have his family's dirty linen flapping in the breeze for all to scrutinize.

"Should I have said it, do you think?" asked Isadora. "I mean, will it help Drew—or make things worse?"

"Mr. Bredbeck evidently wanted you to tell the court what you knew," I assured her.

Bartholomew Reed was called to the stand the following morning. He had an arrogant, almost contemptuous air for the proceedings which, I hoped, could not but set the judge against him. The large diamond ring he wore flashed across the room.

"State your name for the court, please," said Mr. James.

"Bartholomew Anthony Reed."

"Mr. Reed, what was the exact nature of your relationship with the deceased?"

"Mrs. Rockwell was a friend of mine, and of my wife."

"You say that Mrs. Rockwell was your wife's friend?"

"Yes, most certainly. My wife and I had known her for years."

"Was your wife fond of Mrs. Rockwell?"

"I have said so, haven't I?"

"Was she your mistress, Mr. Reed?" asked Mr. James bluntly.

"Certainly not."

"So you claim there is no truth to Miss Rockwell's allegation."

"As much as I hate to contradict a charming young lady such as Miss Rockwell, none whatever. I was often in her company, yes, but so am I often in a number of other people's company as well."

Beside me Isadora was fuming.

"Where were you on the night of Mrs. Rockwell's death?"

"I attended the dinner party. Then, when it rather disastrously broke up, I escorted my wife home."

"And after that?"

"I remained at home, going to bed about one o'clock."

"Thank you, Mr. Reed. That is all."

He smiled easily, too easily. Isadora was still seething; he had made her appear to be a malicious liar who would say anything to protect her brother, even to the point of inventing Cordelia's infidelities.

Drew stared hard at Bartholomew Reed from under bent brows. I bit my lip, hoping desperately that Mr. Bredbeck could pierce Mr. Reed's cool arrogance.

341

"Mr. Reed, isn't it true that you visited the deceased at her home often, and not in the company of your wife?"

Bartholomew Reed waved his hand slightly, the large diamond ring sparkling. "I may have done so from time to time."

"Are you in the habit of calling on married ladies in their homes, Mr. Reed?" asked Mr. Bredbeck smoothly.

"Objection, Your Honor," said Mr. James. "Mr. Reed's habits are immaterial."

"Sustained," pronounced the judge.

"Very well, Your Honor. I will withdraw the question," said Mr. Bredbeck. "Did Mr. Rockwell join you when you called on Mrs. Rockwell?"

"Not usually, no," admitted Bartholomew Reed.

"Never!" hissed Isadora.

"Then you saw Cordelia Rockwell alone."

"Not alone, no, Miss Morrow was there."

My eyes met his; unmistakably he smiled. Around me the crowd stirred.

"Miss Morrow?" repeated Mr. Bredbeck.

"Yes. As you know, sir, she was painting Mrs. Rockwell's portrait. Mrs. Rockwell would get bored and restless during the long sittings and she asked me to keep her company in the drawing room."

"Should that not have been her husband's job?" asked Mr. Bredbeck sternly.

It was a mistake. Mr. Reed shrugged his shoulders. "I would have thought so. But Mr. Rockwell was very often occupied with business affairs."

Mr. Reed was making Cordelia sound like a neglected wife that he had befriended. And with me there to chaperone.

"Did Mrs. Reed accompany you on these visits to Copper Beeches when the portrait was being painted?" asked Mr. Bredbeck.

"No. Cordelia invited her, naturally; she invited the

342

both of us. But my wife had other things to attend to on those mornings."

Mr. Bredbeck straightened, gazing coolly across at the man in the witness stand. "Mr. Reed, did you ever visit Cordelia Rockwell at night in the summerhouse behind Copper Beeches? I must remind you that you are under oath."

"Of course not. We met at parties and balls at night, but never alone."

Stone-faced, Mr. Bredbeck dismissed him. Then, to our amazement, the prosecutor called Mrs. Reed to the witness box.

I had never seen her before; all necks craned to watch her make her way to the stand. She was thin and used-up-looking, with rather limp hair of a non-descript brown. Her frightened rabbits' eyes lifted to her husband as he passed by her. He took her hand and patted it, saying in a voice loud enough for all to hear, "Don't be afraid, my dear. Do not allow him to badger you. Merely tell the truth."

She stepped up to the stand, and Mr. James said, "You are Mrs. Helen Reed?"

"Yes," she said softly, her hands fluttering in her lap.

"Well, Mrs. Reed, let me assure you that neither I nor my learned colleague, I'm sure, have any intention of badgering you. I wish merely to ask you a few simple questions."

"It's common knowledge she's scared to death of her husband," moaned Isadora. "This will only make things worse for Drew."

"Mrs. Reed, are you happily married?"

"Oh—oh, yes," murmured Mrs. Reed.

"Your husband, of course, loves you?"

"Y—yes."

"Has he been a good husband, Mrs. Reed?" asked Mr. James.

"He—he is kind and thoughtful," rattled off Mrs. Reed in an agitated fashion.

343

"And he is a faithful husband?"

"Why—why, of course." Her thin face was scarlet.

"To your knowledge, Mrs. Reed, and I am sorry to have to ask this of you, was he conducting a love affair with Mrs. Cordelia Rockwell?"

"N-no. Cer—certainly not."

"Was Mrs. Rockwell a friend of yours?"

"Yes, we were close friends," came the almost whisper.

"Cordelia despised her!" snapped Isadora.

"Thank you, Mrs. Reed. I have no more questions, Your Honor," said Mr. James.

In great relief Mrs. Reed stood up.

"Just a minute, Mrs. Reed. Mr. Bredbeck, the defense attorney, may wish you to answer some questions."

Mrs. Reed glanced wildly about before sitting down again.

"What happened, Mrs. Reed, when you and your husband went home after the dinner party at Copper Beeches?"

"Why—I—we retired for the night."

"Your husband did not go out?"

"Certainly not."

"Mrs. Reed, where is your home?"

"On Ocean Drive."

"It must have a beautiful view of the ocean."

Mrs. Reed smiled faintly, acknowledging his supposition.

"And is your bedroom situated where you can take advantage of this view?" asked Mr. Bredbeck sweetly.

"Really, Your Honor. The location of Mrs. Reed's bedroom is hardly relevant," said Mr. James testily.

"Your Honor, I am prepared to show that it is indeed relevant."

"Overruled. Proceed, Mr. Bredbeck. Please answer the question, Mrs. Reed."

She looked from the judge to the defense attorney,

rather like an animal caught in a cage. "I—I don't seem to recall . . ."

"I asked you, Mrs. Reed, whether you can see the sea from your bedroom."

"Yes. My bedroom faces the sea." She seemed relieved the question was one she could easily answer.

"And what floor is it on?"

"The second floor."

"And your husband's bedroom? Can he also see the sea?"

Mrs. Reed appeared confused; her hands fluttered in her lap.

"Surely that is not a difficult question, Mrs. Reed. Does your husband's bedroom face the ocean?"

"N-no. His room is . . . at the rear of the house," she admitted, her face flushed.

"On the same floor?" continued Mr. Bredbeck gently.

"His room is—is on the floor above mine," she said, not meeting his gaze.

"So you enjoy a room on the second floor at the front of the house while your husband sleeps on the third floor at the rear of the house."

Mrs. Reed's cheeks were scarlet; she glanced about the courtroom. Her husband had obviously not coached her in what she was to say if questioned about the arrangement of their bedrooms.

"Y-yes," she murmured reluctantly.

"Is that not rather far apart for a couple who claims to be happily married?" asked Mr. Bredbeck, smiling slightly.

"Objection!" cried Mr. James, leaping to his feet.

"I withdraw the question, Your Honor," said Mr. Bredbeck genially. "I put it to you, Mrs. Reed, that in so large a house and with your bedrooms situated where they are, you cannot be certain of your husband's whereabouts, and whether, in fact, he has retired for the night."

Isadora squeezed my hand. "Finally a point for our side!"

Mrs. Reed drew herself up, straightening her thin shoulders. "I—I am certain. Because—because Bartholomew was with me that night."

Mr. Bredbeck looked skeptical. "All night, Mrs. Reed?"

"Yes, all night," she said tremulously.

Far better for her to pretend a recent intimacy with her husband than to reveal that she hadn't the slightest notion of whether he had actually retired for the night or gone out again.

"No more questions, Your Honor," said Mr. Bredbeck testily.

"I don't think the jury believed her," whispered Isadora. "She wasn't very convincing, was she?"

"Stupid woman," growled Aunt Hermione. "But her husband will no doubt be pleased with her. She ought to get a diamond necklace out of today's work."

"The prosecution calls Mrs. Olive Chandler."

"What!" gasped Isadora. "The prosecution! What on earth can she have to say?"

I felt a sinking in my stomach. If the prosecutor was calling her, it was not a good sign. I looked about for Dr. Chandler but did not see him anywhere. Olive Chandler, all in gray like a plump bird, went up to the box.

"Mrs. Chandler, kindly tell the court what you observed on one occasion from your window."

"I looked out the window of my sitting room on the second floor and saw Mr. Rockwell with a young woman," she stated flatly.

"And is this young woman in the courtroom today?"

"Yes, she is. Miss Ariel Morrow," announced Mrs. Chandler.

So Gwendolyn Chandler was not the only one who had observed us from the turret at Oaklawn. I tried to keep my face expressionless. Above all, I

346

would not look *guilty*.

"And what time of day was this?"

"It was night."

"Before or after midnight?"

"Before. About ten o'clock."

"And just what did you see?"

"I distinctly saw Mr. Rockwell and Miss Morrow engaging in what I can only call improper behavior, improper considering that he was a married man and she was an employee in his house."

"Just what did you see, Mrs. Chandler?"

"They were kissing, embracing."

I shut my eyes; there were gasps and exclamations from every direction. The judge rapped irritably with his gavel.

"If only she had bothered to look through the window of the summerhouse," said Aunt Hermione.

"Your witness, Mr. Bredbeck," said Mr. James with satisfaction.

Olive Chandler was no Helen Reed. She faced Mr. Bredbeck belligerently, her eyes narrowed.

"You say that on one occasion you observed the defendant and Miss Morrow kissing."

"Yes," she said, sitting there snug and plump like a hen on a nest.

"And where were they standing?"

"By the Chinese Moongate at the wall of Copper Beeches."

"You have stated that it was ten o'clock at night, or thereabouts. You could see them that clearly in the dark?"

"There are street lights on Shepard Avenue, Mr. Bredbeck," said Mrs. Chandler. "I know what I saw."

"I wonder if Dr. Chandler knows she is here," whispered Isadora. "I don't see him. He would be very upset if he knew she were testifying against Drew."

"It's not Drew, really, it's I. She has never approved of me, not from the first," I said heavily. "She doubt-

347

less imagines I have spent years drawing male nudes and then a great deal more."

That night I could not sleep; it was my turn to take the stand the next day, and I was terrified. All night I silently called out to Drew, knowing that my testimony could damn him forever. Mr. Bredbeck had taken dinner with us earlier that evening and he did not seem to be as optomistic as he had been before the trial began. I saw the pit yawning blacker and deeper than ever before.

There was silence the following morning as I took my place in the box. I did not dare look at Drew. I wore a plain dark skirt and jacket with a high-collared white blouse, my hair scraped back in a prim knot. In my mirror I had looked haggard, violet smudges under my eyes. I scarcely resembled a temptress who could come between a man and his beautiful wife. Well, so much the better, I thought defiantly.

"Miss Morrow," Mr. James began, "Mrs. Chandler has testified that she observed you and Mr. Rockwell embracing at the Chinese Moongate on the grounds of Copper Beeches. Is this true?"

"Yes," I admitted.

"And did you once drive out of town with Mr. Rockwell?"

"Yes."

"Where did you go?"

"Only for a drive."

"Miss Morrow, do you often go out driving with married men?"

"Certainly not!" I said fiercely.

"Then Mr. Rockwell was an exception," said Mr. James coolly. He let that sink in.

"You are an artist, Miss Morrow?"

"Yes."

"An unusual occupation for a woman."

"Perhaps."

"Your father was the portrait painter Lancelot Morrow?"

"He was."

"And, before his death, where did you live?"

"With him in New York City."

"Just the two of you alone?"

"He had a servant."

"But no lady lived with you. No relative to undertake your moral upbringing?"

I was becoming very warm; it was another hot humid day, unusual for September. "I did not need anyone but my father," I said shortly.

Mr. James did not say anything more; he did not need to. He had made his point. I had been raised by a father who had never taught me morals or proper behavior.

"On the night of August first, Miss Morrow, did you attend a masquerade ball at Hedgerow, the home of Mr. John Evans?"

I could feel beads of perspiration on my upper lip. "Yes."

Judge Harrison rapped his gavel twice for silence.

"Were you invited by the hostess, Mrs. Evans?"

I flushed. "I was given an invitation."

"Did Mrs. Evans realize the invitation was going to you, the artist at Copper Beeches?"

"Objection, Your Honor," said Mr. Bredbeck.

"I am only trying to demonstrate, Your Honor, that Mrs. Evans was deceived into welcoming Miss Morrow into her home."

"Proceed."

"Who procured the invitation for you?"

I said nothing.

"It was Mr. Rockwell, was it not?"

"No, it was Miss Rockwell," I said defiantly. "It was her idea that I attend. We told no one else."

"Mr. Rockwell did not know that you would be attending?"

"He did not."

"Very well, Miss Morrow. And whom did you dance with on that night?"

"I had several partners," I said stiffly.

"I am certain of that. But was Mr. Rockwell one of those partners?"

"Yes."

"Was he surprised to see you there?"

"Yes."

"Why did you attend the ball, Miss Morrow?"

"Why?" I repeated nervously. If only I could fan my hot moist face. The collar was too tight about my neck.

"Yes. Why did you go to the trouble of having a costume made—I assume you ordered a costume—and attend a ball you knew you had no right to attend in the first place?"

"I told you, Miss Rockwell suggested—"

"But why did you agree, Miss Morrow? Why did you go along with the idea? Did not the deception worry you at all, the trickery?"

"Well, I—"

"How many times did you dance with Mr. Rockwell that night, Miss Morrow?"

"I don't know."

"More than once? More than twice? More than three times?"

"Yes," I said desperately.

"And did you leave the ball in his company?"

"Yes."

"Why, after going to all the trouble of securing an invitation and ordering a costume, did you leave so much earlier than the rest of the guests, Miss Morrow?"

I felt the dampness of my camisole underneath my clothes. Drawing my handkerchief across my heated brow, I said, "I had not planned to stay long. Mr. Rockwell was kind enough to escort me back to Copper Beeches."

350

"But you had arrived in a carriage, had you not? Surely it was waiting for you."

"I—I did not think of that."

"You preferred Mr. Rockwell to take you home."

I said nothing.

"Mr. Rockwell, had, I believe, escorted his wife and sister there, but he did not take them home. He left them at the ball and took you back to Copper Beeches. Why did he do that, Miss Morrow?"

"I—I wanted to leave the ball before midnight."

"And why was that? So you could be alone with Mr. Rockwell while his wife was occupied?"

"No."

"Then why?"

"I—I had to leave the ball before the unmasking."

"Why?"

He knew; he had said it himself. Why did he keep harping on the ball? Why did Mr. Bredbeck not object? Why was there no breeze coming through the open windows of the courtroom? Why this hostile, accusing sea of faces glaring at me?

"I didn't want anyone to know who I was," I said feebly.

"And why was that? I'll tell you why, Miss Morrow. It was because you had gained admittance to that affair under false pretenses, by trickery and fraud. You had gone to the ball to be with Mr. Rockwell, but under the discretion of a mask. You and Mr. Rockwell could spend the evening in full view of everyone because no one knew your identity or his. Then, before you could be identified, you left together to return to Copper Beeches so that you could be alone without Mrs. Rockwell knowing."

"No! It wasn't like that. We went back to the house and found Miss Blythe Rockwell nearly overcome by gas fumes. She almost died! Mr. Rockwell sent for Dr. Chandler. It wasn't at all the way you are implying!"

"But when you left Hedgerow for Copper Beeches,

you had no way of knowing you would find Miss Blythe Rockwell in such a state. You did not plan for your evening to end in that way. Answer me, Miss Morrow. You did not know then that Miss Rockwell was in any danger, did you?"

In an agony I said, "No."

"Miss Morrow, did Mr. Rockwell ever discuss divorcing his wife so that the two of you could marry?"

I glanced over at Drew and hastily glanced away. "Yes, but he did not wish to because of his daughter."

"What do you mean, Miss Morrow?"

"He did not want her touched by any scandal."

There were a few ugly snickers.

"But he later changed his mind?"

"Yes."

"You told the police that after the dinner party he and Mrs. Rockwell were involved in an argument concerning a divorce. What was the basis for their argument?"

"The basis?" I asked, bemused.

"Miss Morrow, were they not arguing over which parent would get custody of their daughter?"

"Yes."

"But it is not likely that Mr. Rockwell would have been granted custody. Courts do not take children away from their mothers. Are you aware of that, Miss Morrow?"

"Your Honor, I object to my colleague's speculations concerning what a court would or would not do," said Mr. Bredbeck.

"Sustained. Confine yourself to direct questions, Mr. James," said Judge Harrison.

"Mr. Rockwell was very angry with his wife, was he not?"

"Yes."

"Because he had disgraced you before all the company."

Again I dabbed at my face with the moist handker-

352

chief. "It was untrue what she accused us of. I was not his mistress. And I was planning to leave Newport the next day."

"But surely you were planning to meet Mr. Rockwell at a later date."

"We had not discussed it." Not specifically.

"When Mr. Rockwell told his wife he wanted a divorce, what was her reaction?"

"That she would divorce him on grounds of adultery, naming me."

"And what of Miss Blythe Rockwell, the child?"

"She cared nothing for Blythe. She only wanted her because she didn't want Drew—" I bit my lip, "Mr. Rockwell—to have her."

"So you are telling the court, Miss Morrow, that Mr. Rockwell feared losing the custody of his daughter were Mrs. Rockwell to sue him on grounds of adultery."

"It was not true. We were not lovers."

"Did or did not Mr. Rockwell stay in your room on the night of the murder, Miss Morrow?"

There was a film before my eyes; blinking rapidly, I passed my hand across my brow.

"Stop it! Stop this at once! Can't you see she's ill?" Drew was on his feet, shouting.

There was a general uproar. The judge rapped his gavel and said harshly, "Mr. Bredbeck, if you are unable to restrain your client, then I will be forced to hold him in contempt of court. Mr. Rockwell, you are not on the stand, sir. Sit down! Proceed, Mr. James."

"Thank you, Your Honor," said Mr. James suavely. "You cannot have it both ways, Miss Morrow. You have told the police that Mr. Rockwell stayed the night in your room. So how can you expect the court to believe you were not lovers?"

"We were not lovers . . . until that night," I said, and then I toppled over into blackness.

Within a few moments I opened my eyes to the

nightmare again. My jacket had been removed and a cool cloth was pressed to my forehead.

"If you feel you are unable to continue, Miss Morrow," said the judge, "we will adjourn until later."

And have this drag on indefinitely? I shook my head. "I am recovered, Your Honor." My head swam dizzily when I sat up, but I was determined to complete my testimony.

So I answered the questions Mr. Bredbeck put to me about Drew not leaving my room until after five in the morning, an hour or so after Cordelia's death, but I could show no proof. If Mrs. Reed had lied for her husband, as I supposed the jury suspected, then just as easily could I be lying to protect Drew. And why shouldn't I? I had hated Cordelia as much as he had; hadn't she destroyed my chances of painting Society portraits? Finally, drained and battered, I limped back to my seat. The judge rapped out, "The court will resume at nine o'clock tomorrow morning."

Drew was already being led away, a man holding each of his arms. He stopped as I came near.

I could not look at him. Biting my lip, I felt the tears spilling down my cheeks.

"It's all right, Ariel," he said softly, but then they were taking him from the room.

Isadora and Aunt Hermione came toward me and then somehow we were outside in the crowd and then I was being bundled into a carriage. Collapsing on the leather seat, I sobbed uncontrollably. I had failed Drew completely.

When we reached the house I went up to my room alone. I did not want anyone with me. They had tried their best to soothe me, and I was calmer now, but I needed to be alone.

The first thing I did once I had shut the door was remove my hot sticky clothing. In the bathroom I ran a cold bath and climbed in, lying down in the water until the cold temperature became too much for me.

But I was revived. Teeth chattering, goose bumps on my skin, I got out of the tub, dried off, and put on clean fresh underclothes. Then I went into my bedroom.

There was something lying on the floor that I had not noticed before. Something that looked strangely familiar there. Something starkly white that sent nausea surging up to my throat.

An envelope, just like the others. This time it was not the cold water which brought the chills.

NOW YOU'VE GOT WHAT YOU DESERVE, YOU FILTHY SLUT. IF YOUR MOTHER AND FATHER COULD ONLY SEE YOU NOW! YOUR LOVER WILL HANG AND YOU ARE RUINED.

My mother and father . . . what in God's name had they to do with any of this? Why always the mention of my mother? Who was writing these horrible notes?

My heart hammering, I rushed downstairs and knocked violently at Isadora's door. When she opened it, I thrust the letter in front of her.

"What is it, Ariel? What's this?" She looked exhausted; she had changed her courtroom attire for a simple gown.

"Read it, Isadora. I've been getting these notes periodically since I came here."

She took the letter from me. "Oh, no, this is vicious, sickening! You say you've had others?"

I nodded grimly. "I thought Miss Simmons was writing them, but then I got one on the night of the dinner party. I had forgotten all about it, with everything that happened afterwards."

"You suspected Miss Simmons?"

"Yes, she was in love with Drew. And she realized that he and I—Someone has been writing these monstrous things and leaving them in my room. I have to find out who! It may be important."

"Important? What do you mean? This note may have something to do with the case, Cordelia's death?"

"I don't know. But there is one thing of which I am dead certain. I have an enemy somewhere close by, and that person does not want Drew and me to be together. Perhaps—perhaps that person killed Cordelia, just to implicate Drew, so that we would both be destroyed. Oh, I know it's a wild thought, but I feel certain now that somehow these anonymous notes are connected in some way to Cordelia's murder. Here, this is the last one I got. I tore up the first two."

"Oh, this is vile," she said, scanning it. "And why this constant mention of your mother? It's almost as if the person writing the letters knew your mother . . . and wasn't too fond of her. Didn't you tell me your mother is dead?"

"Yes, she died when I was a very small child. I have no memory of her at all, and my father rarely spoke of her. She and my father lived in London; I was born there. Before meeting my father in Paris a year or so before, she attended school in New York City. Then she went abroad with friends."

"Well, I know what I can do. I'm going to go downstairs and question all the servants. We have to get to the bottom of this. You should have told me about these letters before. Perhaps one of them knows something, saw someone enter your room sometime. Or perhaps one of them has been bribed to deliver these. If that is the case, I shall find out."

I left her, returning to my room. Perhaps some progress would be made now. Why had I not thought to show these notes to Lieutenant Pierce? He might have drawn some conclusion I could not.

A few moments later there came the sound of high-pitched, terrified shrieks. Blythe's cries were unmistakable. They did not cease as I waited. Oh, no, what else would happen today?

Without another thought I dashed down the hallway to the nursery wing. The cries grew louder and more piercing as I approached, horrified shrieks which stripped me to the bone. Never had I heard her sound this distressed.

But what I saw in Blythe's room was undeniably worse. The child was backed into a corner, her arms flailing about, her eyes like a wild animal's, her mouth open to emit those ghastly screams.

Miss McCready was on the floor beside her, struggling to take the little girl in her arms. Blythe was fighting and kicking, past hearing, past understanding.

"Child, child, it's just Miss McCready," she said over and over.

"What has happened?" I gasped.

"I don't know," she cried over the child's shrieks. "I turned my back for a few minutes and when I looked back at her she had left the room. I found her in a room down the hall. She wasna screaming then; she was just sitting in a rocking chair."

"Her brother's things are in that room," I said.

"So I realized. I talked to her while I looked about. I took up that lovely mobile of the wee boats and told her to come back to the nursery. I went ahead and she followed me. When we got back I hung up the mobile." She gestured to it suspended from a hook in the ceiling. "I thought how nice it would look in here, something for Blythe to watch. There was even a hook for it. And then the child noticed it—ah, sweetie, don't. It's only Janet McCready." Gripping the little girl, she clasped her to her breast, wincing as Blythe's head knocked against her jaw.

"She's been so much better," I wailed. "What is it about that mobile? It was her brother's—I suppose it reminds her of him. Still, that shouldn't—"

The mobile, the moving shadows on the wall, the swaying chandelier, the jostling branches . . .

"Nathan! Nathan!" shouted Blythe.

"I'll take it down, it's all right! I'll take it down," I said to her.

"No, Miss Morrow," said Miss McCready firmly.

"Wha—what?"

"I want Blythe to see it. I want her to remember. Look, Blythe, look, my wee one." She took Blythe's head in her hands and held it up toward the mobile of sailboats.

"Miss McCready, for God's sake! What are you—"

She silenced me with a quick movement of her hand. All her attention was focused on the terrified little girl. "What do you see, Blythe? Do you see the pretty boats?"

"Make them stop! Make them stop!"

"Stop what? They aren't moving, my love. They're verra verra still."

"They were dancing, dancing!" screamed the child. "He came through the wall—he came through the wall. And then the sailboats were dancing! And Nathan—he wouldn't wake up! He wouldn't wake up!"

She collapsed suddenly into sobs, the savagery and tension leaving her little frame. Miss McCready folded her in her arms. Appalled, I could only stare at the two of them, and up at the sailboat mobile.

"So he came through the wall, did he, my wee one?"

"The wall? What wall? Who is *he?*" I gasped.

"It had to be a wall she could see from her bed that night," said Miss McCready softly, as though to herself. "Blythe's bed is there, and Nathan's—*Nathan's bed must have been directly beneath the mobile.*"

"From her bed she can see out into the hall," I said. "But I don't understand."

"She has just remembered what happened the night her brother died," said Miss McCready. "There, my precious one, it's all right. You are safe now. And no one can hurt you." Miss McCready looked at me. "The mobile brought it back to her, something she'd forgotten, but not forgotten altogether. Something that frightened her and made her feel so miserable that she kept it deep inside. She had always looked after him, as much as she was able. She had protected him. But that night she could not."

"But what? What wall? And who came out of it?" I paused, gasping. "Are you saying that someone came through a wall and—and into the nursery on the night Nathan died of scarlet fever? But why?"

"Why?" repeated Miss McCready. "To kill Nathan Rockwell. Why else?"

Chapter Eighteen

Horror stricken, I gazed at the matter-of-fact Miss McCready. Her color was high but she was calm and composed.

"No!" I finally managed to say. "What—what are you saying? It can't be! Nathan . . . murdered?"

"For two years Blythe has been suffering from fears that no one, not even her father, has understood," said the little governess. "Mr. Rockwell told me that she has never recovered fully from the scarlet fever that struck two summers ago. But what if her frailty is not due to the scarlet fever, the illness, but to something verra verra different—*something which occurred while she was ill?* Something she has forgotten, but which prevents her from being a healthy child?"

She looked down at the child in her arms. Blythe had stopped crying and lay peacefully, the frenzy drained from her. Her lashes were dark crescents against her flushed cheeks; her dusky curls were wildly tousled.

"Miss McCready," I said tremulously, "I don't understand any of this."

"Blythe said she saw the wall open and someone come through. She said 'he,' but we canna take that too seriously as she was but four years old. And then the sailboats in the mobile began to move, to toss and spin. What does that mean to you, Miss Morrow?"

My stomach gave a sudden tight lurch. "If—if someone was bending over the bed, he—or she—might have knocked against the mobile," I said softly.

"And that was the verra same thing I was thinking," she said grimly.

"But Miss McCready—who? And *why*, for God's sake? Why should anyone wish to do such a terrible thing?"

"Everyone believed that it was the scarlet fever that took him," mused Miss McCready. "Just as, no doubt, they were meant to. There's no understanding the 'why' of it now. But Miss Morrow, there's something verra odd going on—verra evil. And it began two years ago."

"Miss McCready, do you think that Cordelia's death could be somehow connected to this? If only I might find some way to prove Drew innocent!"

"You must find that panel in the wall, Miss Morrow," said Miss McCready. "Because somehow I think it all starts there."

"I believe you're right." Going out of the nursery I went across the corridor to the far wall. The paneling was tongue-and-groove work; frantically I ran my hands up and down, pressing at random, desperate to locate the mechanism which would open the panel. But the wood remained static and intact; my fingers were useless.

"I can't find anything!" I wailed. "Perhaps—perhaps she dreamed it."

Miss McCready came to the door without Blythe. "Take a deep breath, Miss Morrow, and go over it verra slowly. In the state you're in you won't find anything at all, and then where will poor Mr. Rockwell be? Still in jail as he is this verra minute. Begin again, Miss Morrow, there—just between the area there and there that one can see from the child's bed. Knock on it. See if it is hollow."

I did as she suggested. The wood did have a faintly

hollow sound. But the panel, if there were one, was obviously thick.

This is ridiculous, I thought to myself, as I began to methodically press and push. Blythe was a very disturbed little girl. Gradually she had been coming out of her shell, but still she was plagued with strange fears and notions. Was a hole in the wall merely another bizarre fancy of hers? And Nathan—hadn't he died of scarlet fever as everyone, even the doctor, had assumed? He had been very ill. What in the world had his death, and Blythe's fears, to do with Cordelia's murder and Drew's trial? And did the poison-pen letters I had received fit into any of this?

Drew. My heart and body ached for him. I thought of him brooding in the jail cell, forced to sit in the courtroom and listen to his most intimate thoughts and hopes aired before an enthralled audience. He had hated to see me interrogated; he had lost his temper and shouted at the prosecuting attorney, with no thought for himself and the impression he made on the judge and jury.

I had not helped him with my testimony; the speculations concerning my reputation had likely prejudiced his case even more. Slowly, despite the valiant efforts of Mr. Bredbeck, the evidence was circling Drew, circling and looming like a python, until he would be strangled by it. So far I had had no leads to follow, nothing except a vague suspicion of Bartholomew Reed. But vague suspicions could not aid Drew. It was vitally important that somehow some piece of evidence be uncovered which could sway the trial. And until now I had seen no way to seek out such evidence. But because Miss McCready had brought out Nathan's mobile, quite innocently, Blythe, terror-stricken, had recalled the night the mobile had tossed and swayed, the sailboats dancing, as the shadows and the leaves and the chandelier had danced. Perhaps by patiently investigating the child's memories and searching diligently for an opening in the wall, I might uncover something tangible which would override the evidence against Drew.

"It was the *movement* she remembered," I said. "From stillness to sudden motion, swaying. Drew said that when a flock of birds had abruptly taken off from a tree, filling the air, she had become hysterical. Her little brother died while she was watching the mobile tossing back and forth. She must have realized very soon after that he was dead—perhaps she got out of bed once the murderer had left the room, not realizing she was awake and had seen him or her. Miss McCready, I must find that panel!"

"Go lower. Kneel down and feel down there. You'll find it, Miss Morrow. I feel sure of it. Why else did Blythe remember today of all days? Why else did I decide to take the mobile and hang it in here? There must be a *reason*."

A wild eager hope surged, leaving me breathless. Kneeling, I slowly moved my fingers along the groove work. And then I felt it. As my fingers advanced along the wooden plank, a portion suddenly depressed.

"I—I think I've found something!" I cried. "But nothing's happening," I added in agony.

"Push now, as hard as you can," said the little governess urgently. "That same part."

There came a click, and a faint scraping sound. The wall had moved in a little but then stopped. "Oh no! I thought I had it!" I was nearly beside myself with frustration.

"Press again."

I leaned into the portion of the wall with all my might, and this time the scraping sound was louder. The top portion of the panel began swinging outward and the bottom portion inward. I was staring into an opening bisected by the now-horizontal moveable panel. There was a strong musty smell issuing from the utter darkness.

"Miss McCready—look! Someone could have hidden in here!"

"I dinna think the wee one was dreaming," she said. "I'll fetch a lamp."

When she returned and handed it to me, I held it in the opening and was astonished to see a flight of stairs leading down. "It's not a room! It's a staircase—a winding staircase! But where does it lead—to a room on the ground floor?"

"It's narrow and winding so it could easily be concealed behind the central chimney," said Miss McCready.

"But what is its purpose? Why was it built?"

"It's odd, Mr. Rockwell himself not knowing of it. How old is the house? Not old at all by Scottish standards."

"Well, nearly half a century," I said. "It was built by Mr. Rockwell's grandfather in the decade before the Civil War. Oh, Miss McCready, I must go down those stairs. I have felt so paralyzed, so horribly helpless. Now perhaps I can uncover something that will clear Drew—Mr. Rockwell!"

Miss McCready looked troubled. "Yes, but shouldn't you go and find Miss Rockwell? Tell her about the staircase?"

"No. You don't understand. I must do this—now. I don't know what I'll find, if anything. But the trial will be over very soon, as soon as Drew testifies himself. I've done nothing but bring Drew misfortune. Miss Rockwell is with all the servants now. I can't wait for her. I must go down here now."

"Take one of the men with you then, Miss Morrow."

I shook my head stubbornly. "No, I can't wait. I must do this myself. Perhaps—perhaps it leads to the summerhouse, to an underground passage connecting the house and the summerhouse. Cordelia—Mrs. Rockwell wouldn't have known of it either. Or perhaps she did. Perhaps, oh, I don't know. But I'm not bringing one of the servants with me. It will be better if I go alone. I'm not at all frightened. Just—just don't shut the panel."

"Verra well, Miss Morrow. I won't touch the opening. But you must be verra careful. There's not only Blythe and Mr. Rockwell. You must think of yourself as well."

"I will. I am." Possessed of a feverish but determined excitement, I was convinced that this was the only way to help Drew. The police had found no leads; nothing had come up in court which had pointed the finger away from Drew, although Mr. Bredbeck had tried to do just that when he stated that Mrs. Reed would have had no way of knowing whether her husband was in the house due to the distance between their respective bedrooms. But she had shot down even that flimsy hope with her insistence that Bartholomew Reed had stayed the night in her room.

If Blythe had actually awoke and observed someone emerging from the corridor wall—someone she could not recognize in the darkness—then the case of Nathan's death was no longer clearcut. And if Nathan Rockwell had been murdered, and two years later his mother was also murdered, could not the two deaths be related? Perhaps Cordelia herself had discovered something unsettling or dire about Nathan's death. Perhaps she had learned, or suspected, that something other than scarlet fever had been responsible for her little boy's death. And she had been silenced before she could make her discovery known.

"Well, here I go," I said, pressing my lips together. "I'll be back as soon as I can. But I must see where the stairs lead. Don't—don't tell anyone yet, Miss Mc-Cready. Not that I'm in any danger from someone in the house, but . . ." A slight chill rippled over me.

She nodded grimly. "It's better that I keep it to myself now. We don't know who uses this staircase, do we?"

Picking up my skirts in one hand, holding the lamp in the other, I crouched down and scooted into the opening at the top of the winding staircase. Taking a deep breath, I stood up — for I found I could stand at full height — and began to descend the stone staircase.

I was surprised at how quickly the darkness swallowed up the light from the corridor. The stairs were steep and the ledges narrow. I moved slowly, deliberately, determined not to stumble. It was chilly and damp and the air was poor. When I looked behind and above I could not see any light from the open panel. I went on for what seemed to be a very long time, surely long enough to have descended two flights to the first floor, or even three to the kitchen below ground level, but still the narrow staircase spiraled downward.

At last I came to the bottom. Holding the lamp above my head, I looked about the round stone chamber for a door or another possibly concealed opening.

And then I saw to my amazement that there *was* an opening, but not the type I had envisioned. Before me was the yawning blackness of a narrow tunnel.

I hesitated, wondering what to do. Should I retrace my steps to the third-floor nursery and tell Miss McCready I had found a tunnel? But then what? Come back down again? I did not want to waste time. The tunnel had to be explored; I had to learn where it led. I felt certain now that I was on the right track in discovering the truth about Nathan's death, and hopefully Cordelia's murder as well.

I felt an overwhelming, compelling urge to proceed, to find the answers that I believed the tunnel held. All the odd, sinister events in the past must somehow be linked, and, in determining how, I might be able to stop the trial, veering suspicion, finally and irrefutably, away from Drew.

After all, I could turn back at any time; there would be no chance of my getting lost. One could only go forward or reverse. There was only one tunnel, only one staircase. I must be somewhere under the house, perhaps near to the cellars. So far I had heard nothing; the stone walls of the staircase were thick. Had the stairway and tunnel been constructed by Drew's grandfather to link the house with one or more of the outbuildings? And had he never bothered to show it to Drew's father before his death? Or had Drew's father been aware of its existence but never thought it necessary to inform his son, who, after all, had been away at school for many years? Many houses had been built with secret rooms and passages. In some cases there was no reason except a whim of the owner. Belcourt Castle, I had heard, had a tunnel which went from the house to Bailey's Beach.

Entering the tunnel, I began to walk swiftly with the light from the lamp wavering before me. I would not lose my nerve; everything depended on what I might find, the lives of people I loved—Blythe, Isadora, and Drew. And my own. I had a fondness for Aunt Hermione as well; she had stood by me in the trial and never uttered a critical or hurtful word.

If I had thought the staircase damp, the tunnel was much worse. The walls gleamed with drenched moss and green stains. The air was musty, even fetid. I was terrified that I would see a rat, or more than one. That thought frightened me far more than the tunnel itself. I had no idea in what direction I was moving; the winding stairway had caused me to lose all sense of direction. I might be headed anywhere—toward Bellevue Avenue, toward the stables, the summerhouse, anywhere.

The lamp lit up just the immediate area and those slime-ridden walls. Always there was that cavernous opening before me—and behind me. I walked as quietly as I could, anxious for my black boots to make as little sound as possible on the stone floor.

What if the tunnel had caved in up ahead? What if

a pack of rats suddenly rushed at me? What if there was no outlet up ahead—or no end to the tunnel? But that was absurd, irrational, I chided myself. Every tunnel connected one place with another; that was its purpose. And this tunnel could not be any exception. It had to lead somewhere.

I continued to walk on. When the cloying smell of mildew and decay grew too much for me, I would breathe through my mouth. It was cold in the tunnel, and I was chilled. But I was determined to go on. I had no notion of how long I had been walking, but the tunnel could not be that long. It must lead to a place not far from the house, a place on the Copper Beeches estate. Drew's grandfather would scarcely have built it to a place not on his own property. Behind me and before me was gaping blackness, but there was plenty of oil in the lamp. Shuddering a little, I forced myself to go on.

I would count to one hundred, I decided. Thinking of the numbers would occupy my mind and distract it from uncomfortable thoughts about what lurked in the tunnel. Counting, I was gradually steadied by the listing of the numbers in my head. I would not say them aloud.

Nineteen, twenty . . . thirty-one . . . forty-four . . . I would not look at the walls of the tunnel . . . fifty-six . . . I would not think of rats—Don't think of rats! Fifty-seven . . . sixty-nine . . . eighty-three . . . ninety. My breathing came more evenly. If I had not reached my destination by the time I counted to one hundred, I would turn around. I would get a couple of menservants to come with me and start again, it would be all right. Ninety-three, ninety-four, ninety-five, ninety-six.

And I stopped. Ahead of me was a small wooden door. I had reached the end of the tunnel. The hinges of the door were rusty, the wood spotted and partly rotted with damp, but it was a door all the same. And it opened into . . . somewhere. My heart hammering, I paused and listened. What could be on the other side of the door? Where in the world was I?

Drew. Think of Drew. You must save him. You *will* save him. Lift the latch and pull open the door. It's too late to have second thoughts now. *Open the door.*

Chewing on my lip, my ears pressed to the door, still I heard nothing. Go ahead. Open it!

So I did. To my surprise it opened easily, with barely a sound. And I no longer needed a lamp. I was standing on the threshold of a large room lit by glowing gaslights. In the silence I heard the faint whoosh they made.

In the center of the room was a rectangular table covered with a white cloth. Against the walls were small tables and bureaus covered with instruments — knives, bowls, some things I did not recognize. On another wall stood a large wardrobe. What *was* this place? I wandered about, completely baffled. The knives, the tablecloth — but this was no butler's pantry, no dining room. I shivered in the cool air. Wherever I was, it was still below ground. There was a strange quality to this room, the things in it . . . it was almost medicinal, like a room at a hospital.

A hospital. My blood slowed, creeping sluggishly, thickly through my veins. That was what this place resembled — an operating room. The long table covered in the stark white sheet, the sharp steel instruments, the bowls in which to wash bloodied hands . . .

But that was ridiculous. It couldn't be. What was an operating room doing underground, at the end of a tunnel, a tunnel leading from Copper Beeches? My head swam a bit in dazed shock. This couldn't be *real*.

My baffled fear turned to frustrated anger. This was no lead. There was no evidence here to clear Drew. It was fortunate that I had not come here with several servants. We would likely have been overheard and arrested for trespassing. Whatever this place was, it was none of my business. But then I remembered Nathan, and the fear returned. Someone had come from here through the tunnel and up the staircase to the panel in the corridor wall.

Suddenly I bit back a scream. Someone was coming. I could hear footsteps, and they were growing louder. What was I to do? I hadn't the time to rush to the door and close it behind me without being seen. Wildly I glanced about the room, wondering where I could hide. Under the table? No, the sheet wasn't long enough to shield me from sight. On the other side of the wardrobe, or behind the door on the opposite wall? No, I would be seen for sure.

In the wardrobe. It was the only place.

Hastily I pulled open the doors, stepped up into the wardrobe, turned around and drew the doors as closely as I could toward me. There were clothes inside — men's clothes. And white coats. Gently I set down the lamp at the back, careful to keep the hanging garments and my skirt away from it.

Holding my breath, I peered through the crack between the two doors to see who was entering the room. I nearly cried out, biting my lip savagely.

It was Gwendolyn Chandler. And then I knew. I was in Oaklawn, the house across Shepard Avenue from Copper Beeches, the house near the Chinese Moongate in the stone wall. The house belonging to Dr. Prescott Chandler.

Doctor Chandler. I felt a horrible surge of nausea. This, then, was his room, his *operating* room. Why did he have one in his house? What was the need for one *here?* He had told me that he had given up surgery years before. Was it known that he had an operating room in the cellar of Oaklawn? These white coats brushing my hair, the knives laid out on the small tables, the instruments I could not identify which gleamed evilly on the snowy white linen, the long table, the bright gaslights overhead .

370

Scarcely aware of what I was doing, I bent down, picked up the lamp, and pushed open the doors of the wardrobe. Gwendolyn's back was to me, but when I stepped onto the stone floor she whirled around.

Her pale eyes bulged; rapidly the color drained from her face as from a sieve. "Miss Morrow! What are you doing? You must get out—you mustn't stay here!"

"I came through the tunnel," I replied, vaguely surprised by how calm I sounded. "Gwendolyn, what is this place?"

"Don't you know? Can't you tell?" she asked scornfully. "It's a chamber of horrors.

"What do you mean? It's like a—a hospital. What does he *do* here?" I was filled with terrible dread, waiting for her answer.

But she merely said, "Get out, Miss Morrow. Get out of here. Right now. He could be back any time."

"I came through the tunnel, Gwendolyn. Miss McCready and I found a staircase in the nursery wing. A secret staircase, concealed in the wall behind the paneling. She knows I've come. She's back there waiting for me, on the other side of the tunnel."

"So someone at Copper Beeches has finally discovered the tunnel! Rather late, I must say. I told you—I told all of them that night at Copper Beeches that the houses were connected. Mr. Rockwell's grandfather built both houses, remember? This one was built for his sister. But she was old, like he was, and died soon after. It then had several owners until my father bought it. And he found the old tunnel. The tunnel even Drew Rockwell had no idea of." She began to laugh wildly.

She's mad, I thought. She's not just odd. She's really and truly mad. Those knives—would she use one on me? But I was closer to the knives than she was.

"Stop it, Gwendolyn! Stop it! I must know—has someone at Oaklawn used the tunnel to get into Copper Beeches, unobserved? You must tell me!"

Abruptly she stopped laughing, like a faucet being turned off. And the horrible amusement in her face was replaced with pitiable terror. "You must leave here now, Miss Morrow! Go the way you came—through the tunnel! He's away from home now, but it won't be long before he returns. And he'll probably come down here. He usually keeps it locked, but every once in a while he forgets."

"Who's away? Your father? Why should I fear him? Why do *you* fear him?"

Something very like a sneer distorted her features. "You like him, don't you? You think he's kind and charming. He's even taken the stand as a character witness for Drew Rockwell. Of course, after what my mother said, his testimony was a bit diminished."

"Your mother hates me."

"My father tried to talk her out of testifying that she had seen the two of you together, just as I had. Isn't that amusing? He told her he didn't want to see Drew's name blackened any further. She doesn't know, you see. She didn't see the humor of it."

"She doesn't know what, Gwendolyn?" I felt like shaking her. "I came here because Blythe Rockwell suddenly remembered that the wall in the corridor outside her room opened up on the night her little brother died."

"He was sickly, you see. He was a cripple. There was no reason for him to live. He was weak. He would not enhance the species."

"What are you talking about?" I whispered, appalled.

"Nathan Rockwell did not die of scarlet fever, Miss Morrow. Did you know that my father was his doctor? He said it was the scarlet fever that killed him. But it wasn't. My father killed that little boy."

"Oh, my God."

"He keeps a journal, you see. He writes about his

372

thoughts and what he's accomplished in the 'Pursuit of a Greater Humanity.' I've seen it, although he doesn't know I have. He even wrote about me in it." She gave a stifled cry and covered her face with her hands.

"Gwendolyn," I said urgently, "what about Cordelia Rockwell? They all think Drew did it. He'll be convicted if I don't find something to help him. Do you know anything about her death? Did she discover your father had killed Nathan?"

"It wasn't anything to do with Nathan," she said slowly. "He wrote that Mrs. Rockwell had figured out something about her friend, Mrs. Leander."

"Mrs. Leander? Maisie Leander?"

"He let everyone think he was out that night. But Cordelia learned at the dinner party that it wasn't true, that he had not gone out with my mother. He couldn't, you see. He had an appointment to keep with Mrs. Leander. Mrs. Rockwell realized that he had lied, that he was here all the time. He hadn't gone out sailing on the Evans' yacht as my mother had. He was here—and so was I. I saw—oh, my God, I saw!"

"What, Gwendolyn? You must tell me!" I insisted, although I was sick with terror.

"Maisie Leander lying on the table, the blood pouring out, soaking the sheets . . .

"Your father murdered her!"

"No, not really, something had gone wrong, you see. It wasn't like the others."

"The . . . others?"

"Yes, he couldn't stop the bleeding that night. When she was dead, he cleaned off the blood and dressed her. Then he threw her body over the cliff. He offered to examine her as a friend of the family so that nobody would learn that she'd had an abortion. The police were happy to allow him to. After all, he's a respected man. He told the police she had been pregnant when she committed suicide. Everyone believed him as he knew they would."

I stared at her, the nausea rising in me once again.

"Mrs. Rockwell knew that Mrs. Leander was going to see my father to get rid of the baby. He's been doing abortions for years, and Mrs. Leander found out and told Mrs. Rockwell. But Mrs. Rockwell thought that Mrs. Leander had never gone to my father, that she'd lost her nerve and committed suicide instead. It's all in his journal. It wasn't until Mrs. Rockwell learned that my father had lied about his whereabouts the night Mrs. Leander died that she began to suspect. She confronted him with it in the library at Copper Beeches — she said she'd tell my mother, that she would disgrace him, that she would tell everyone he had botched an operation, that he was a quack. My mother knows nothing of my father's . . . secret life. And she has all the money. If she found out, she would cut him off without a penny, and the scandal would kill him. If she dies during his lifetime, the money goes to me, not to him. So, you see, he must keep her content and well. That was the reason he gave up surgery, because she wanted him too. He couldn't let Mrs. Rockwell go to my mother."

I licked my dry lips. "So — so what did he do?"

"He went to the summerhouse. He suspected that she would go there. He knows things about people. He watches. And he reads *Town Topics*. He found out about Camille de la Salle and the schoolmaster."

"Camille de la Salle?" I repeated hoarsely.

"Camille was taken away by her mother. But the young man was still here. He had to be punished for daring to rise above his station, for threatening the pure lines of ancestry. And so . . . there was an accident, a carriage accident. And now he is crippled for life. He won't have the opportunity to fall in love with an heiress again. Just as Mrs. Leander's coachman won't have the opportunity to go to bed with someone like her again."

"Do you mean — are you saying that Dr. Chandler —

your father—is responsible for all those terrible tragedies? I can't believe it! Gwendolyn, we must go to the police. You must tell them everything you've told me. We must save Drew!"

She took a step back, her eyes like a terrified animal's. "No, no! He'll do something horrible to me. You don't know what he's done to me already!"

I gripped her arm. "He won't be able to do anything! He'll be arrested."

"No, it won't work. He's too smart for them. How do you think he's done all these things with never the slightest suspicion to himself? He'll tell them I'm mad! He knows people think me odd, peculiar. That's his protection. I know what he's done, but I'm also his protection!"

"Gwendolyn, you've got to help me! You are Drew's only hope!" I cried in anguish.

"It won't work," she repeated. "He'll say something to totally refute me. He'll say I'm mad, that I hate him. I do hate him. He told me if I ever said anything about Maisie Leander, he'd put me in a madhouse. He'd tell my mother it was the only place for me, that I had finally gone off the edge and it was for my own good. She would go along with him. No one would believe me—he wouldn't allow them to!"

"Yes, they will, Gwendolyn! Or at least your story would stop the trial and force the police to begin investigating again. They have only to see this room to become a little suspicious of your father. You saw Mrs. Leander here—you witnessed her death!"

"But they won't believe me! Even if he were arrested, his attorney would discredit my story. He's told me that. He's sure of me, that's why he talks to me, tells me things sometimes. He wants someone to appreciate all his work."

"Appreciate his work!"

"Yes. He truly believes what he is doing is for the good of mankind and society. Winnowing out the weak, punishing those who dare to tamper with the pure lines of ancestry of Society's fittest, the best families . . . This is only the beginning. He has great plans. For years he's been giving abortions to wealthy women — women who had never been married, widows, Society wives whose babies were not their husbands'. He considered it his duty to prevent those babies from being born. They were only the by-products of affairs with servants, the wrong men, the wrong fathers, not Society's fittest.

"Maisie Leander knew to go to him. But something went wrong. He didn't mean for her to die. He even felt sorry about it. But he didn't feel any remorse about the coachman, or the young man he ran down with the carriage. The little Rockwell boy was the first. Why permit someone like that to live — people such as he only impair the progression of the survival of the fittest. He's a judge — deciding who should live and who should die. He tried to kill the little girl, you know."

"What little girl?" I caught my breath in horror. "You — you don't mean *Blythe?* The gas fumes?"

He left the ball early, knowing you were all at the ball, that there was only a servant to look after her. He used the tunnel, of course. When Drew Rockwell sent someone to Oaklawn to get him, he knew it hadn't worked, she wasn't dead. Imagine the frustration he must have felt, having to listen to Drew Rockwell's gratitude for telling him his daughter would be all right!"

"Gwendolyn, you must go with me to the police. Or at least to Copper Beeches. They can come there to talk to you. You'll be safe there, I promise, now that we know about Dr. Chandler. I've simply got to save Drew!"

"You love him very much, don't you?" she asked solemnly.

"That's scarcely news to anyone," I said bitterly.

She seemed not to have heard me. "I was in love once," she murmured.

"Gwendolyn, please help me. You cannot allow him to go on destroying people. He must be stopped. Where does he keep this journal? He's a monster."

"I can't help you, Miss Morrow."

"Look, get the journal for me. I won't involve you at all, I promise. If I have the journal in my hands to show the police and the district attorney, then I'll say I found it in here, in this room. That I never saw you, I just came through the tunnel, found this room and found the journal."

She hesitated; I could tell she was wavering. "Please, Gwendolyn. I won't involve you. Perhaps you'll never have to speak to the police about him, not until he is under lock and key. He can't be responsible for another person's death—I've got to stop him!"

"Sometimes the journal is in that drawer there," she said softly.

I rushed over to the bureau and pulled open the drawer with shaking fingers. "It's not here!" I cried in almost physical pain.

"He must have it with him, or perhaps it's upstairs somewhere." She seemed relieved.

"Take me up there now!"

"I—I can't! You must be mad yourself!"

"You said he was gone, Gwendolyn. You've got to find it for me. I won't say anything to the police about you, but I have to get my hands on that journal! For God's sake, Drew will hang if I don't!"

Her pale green eyes glittered. "All right. But we must hurry. They only went to the Breakers. And remember your promise. If you break it and tell them I told you everything, I'll deny it. I'll say I never saw you today! Quick, put the lamp back in the tunnel."

We went through the door and up a staircase. "No one but you knows about that room?"

"My mother thinks he reads medical books down

there — that it's a sort of study for him. She's never shown any interest. The servants never go down there. It's usually locked, anyway."

"When did you learn what he did in that room — the abortions, I mean?"

"Six years ago."

"How — how did you find out?"

"He brought me down there himself. And — he told me."

I did not inquire further.

At the top of the staircase she opened a door and we stepped into a hallway. "My father's room is two floors above. But be quiet. I don't want any of the servants to hear us. The staircase is this way."

We walked down the corridor toward the front of the house. It was then that we heard the sound of voices, and a door closing heavily.

Gwendolyn whitened, the pupils in her pallid eyes dillating. "They're back! *He's* back!"

"What should I do?" I gasped, gripped by horror that made my skin crawl. "Should I go back down to the tunnel?"

"No, there isn't time! I'll say you came for a visit. To see *him*. He'll believe that. Say you wanted to talk to him about the trial, how worried you are, what he thinks Drew's chances are." Quickly she opened a door and pushed me inside. "Sit down! And act natural. What happens in the next few minutes is crucial to your getting out of this house alive."

Now the horror was within me, clutching and tearing like pincers. I could scarcely breathe.

And then a voice was calling, "Gwendolyn, where are you, my dear?" It was a voice which made me tremble with anxiety, a gentle, kind voice.

"In the sitting room, Father," she replied, sitting across from me.

Footsteps came down the corridor, stopping at the door of the sitting room. "Ah, there you are, my dear.

Why, Miss Morrow, how do you do?"

"Good evening, Dr. Chandler," I said shakily.

He put out his hand and I put mine into it, into the hand that had butchered Maisie Leander, that had pressed the gun to the coachman's temple, that had suffocated little Nathan Rockwell, that had turned up the gas in Blythe's room, that had held the reins of the horses bolting into William Everett, that had strangled Cordelia . . .

My hands were damp with sweat. But I turned my fear, my obvious agitation to advantage. "I—I had to come and see you, Dr. Chandler. I hope you don't mind that I waited. Gwendolyn was kind enough to receive me. I was in the witness box today, you see, and it—it didn't go well. I'm so discouraged, so afraid of what the outcome will be."

"I understand perfectly, my dear. You don't mind if I call you that, do you? You have become very like a daughter to me. I heard about the trial at the Breakers. I was going to call on you tonight after dinner."

"Drew is going on the stand tomorrow, Dr. Chandler. I'm terrified the jury won't believe him, that they'll assume he's lying."

"I'm certain he will be able to convince them of his innocence, my dear. You must calm yourself. Would you like me to give you a sedative to help you sleep?"

"No! I mean, I'll have some sherry before I go to bed. I just needed to get away from the house for a little while. Things are . . . difficult there just now."

"Mrs. Grant and Miss Rockwell resent you, you mean? I suppose they cannot help it. But I know they are fond of you, Miss Morrow. The jury members are local men, you must remember that. The Rockwell family has always been held in the highest esteem by the people of this city. They will believe him, I'm certain."

"Do you really think so? It's just that there has been so much damaging testimony—about Drew and myself."

"I want to tell you how sorry I am that my wife spoke as a witness for the prosecution. But she had to appear. I suppose the police reports . . .

"Yes, I understand," I said unsteadily.

"Miss Morrow, I want you to have faith that everything will turn out for the best. We both know that Drew did not kill Cordelia. I am convinced that the jury will reach that conclusion as well."

"You are right, of—of course. I had better be getting back now. It's nearly dinnertime."

Just then I glanced up and noticed an oil painting hanging on the wall. I stared at it, feeling the blood rush into my face, hearing Dr. Chandler's voice come from far off. "I'm glad you came; my dear. I hope I've allayed your fears somewhat. You must not give in to despair, that is the main thing."

"Yes," I murmured.

"I see you are looking at the portrait of my wife. It was painted many years ago when she was in Paris with her family. It is not signed by the artist, but it is very good, is it not?"

In a daze I forced my eyes away from the portrait. "Yes, it's very good." In God's name, didn't he *know*? Couldn't he tell? The dramatic brushstrokes, the luminous white skin against the dark background, the restless, agitated position of the hands . . . The style was undeveloped, not bold as it was in later works; he must have painted it as a very young man when he was still unsure of himself.

But my father, Lancelot Morrow, had painted that portrait of Olive Chandler. Or whatever her maiden name had been. She had been visiting Paris with her parents—and with a school friend. Millicent Van Horn. My mother.

Olive Chandler entered the room, her plump form encased in green taffeta. She scarcely resembled the young woman she had been. Her eyes narrowed when she saw me. "What are you doing here, Miss Morrow? You are not welcome in my house."

"Olive, my dear, please. Miss Morrow came to see me. She is worried about the outcome of the trial."

"She should have thought of that before she convinced her lover to kill his wife!"

"Olive—!" objected Dr. Chandler.

"I am just leaving, Mrs. Chandler," I said, standing up. "I was just admiring your portrait." My eyes met her hostile gaze steadily.

"I didn't know that you had a painting of my father's," I added deliberately.

"Your father?" asked the doctor, puzzled. "I don't believe I—"

Gwendolyn sat quietly, glancing from one of us to the others. She had not said a word; her face was expressionless. She doubtless had had years of practice in concealing her emotions.

"My father painted that portrait of your wife, Dr. Chandler. There can be no mistake. I'd know his style anywhere. And he studied and lived in Paris."

"Yes, he painted it!" spat out Olive Chandler. "And then he ran off with Millicent! She knew I . . . Oh, I hated them for it! I wrote her mother and father. I told them terrible things she—they—had done! I wished I could have done more—destroyed them both! She was a slut and you are no better!"

"You wrote my grandparents," I repeated. "You wrote them—lies. You—it's you who's been writing to me, those awful notes . . . You wrote them."

"What notes? Olive, Miss Morrow—Ariel—what is going on?"

"Yes, I wrote them," said Olive Chandler with an ugly twisted smile. "Matilda, my maid, is a visitor at Copper Beeches very often."

Yes, I had seen her in the kitchen myself.

"I—I must go home," I said. "It's nothing, Dr. Chandler."

"Allow me to take you in the carriage."

My heart leaped into my mouth; I had almost forgotten what I had learned today. "N-no, thank you. I need to walk—the fresh air. It's only a short distance. Good evening, Gwendolyn, good evening, Doctor."

I had to get out of this house. But I allowed the doctor to escort me to the front door, and to press my hand as he assured me everything would work out for the best. And then I was out the front door and hurrying across the lawn through the violet dusk to Shepard Avenue, and to the Moongate in the stone wall.

He's a monster, he's a monster, he must be stopped, he must be stopped, whispered the weeping beeches. And his wife was little better. Because of her jealousy—for it was obvious that she had been in love with my father herself—she had written malicious lies about my parents to my grandparents, damning them. I could just imagine what she had gloatingly related. And my grandparents, shocked, repelled by what Olive had written, had never wanted to see my mother again.

Dr. Chandler suspected nothing; I was certain of that. He would never know I had been in the tunnel; he would never guess that Gwendolyn had confided in me; he would not realize that I knew of the existence of his journal.

That is . . . unless Miss McCready had sent someone after me, someone who would discover the room at the end of the tunnel. And, in doing so, would alert Dr. Chandler so that he would destroy the journal and get rid of the white sheets, the knives, the long table, the white coats, altering the very nature of that room, discarding the horror from the chamber of horrors. And then Drew would be convicted, and it would have all been for nothing. And Gwendolyn—what would he do to her?

"Ariel! Thank God!" Isadora met me on the staircase. "We've been beside ourselves with worry! Miss

McCready said you'd gone down a secret staircase more than two hours ago! I was just about to go and get some of the men to go after you."

"I—I'm all right," I said shakily. "Thank heaven you didn't send anyone after me already."

"Miss McCready wouldn't let me; she didn't even want to tell me where you were, but I saw the open panel for myself. Ariel, none of the servants know anything about those notes. And I don't believe any of them are lying. Ariel, what is it? You're trembling. And you're white as a sheet. Where have you been all this time?"

I took a great shuddering breath. "We must close that opening in the wall. And two men must stand there all night, Isadora, to make certain that no one comes out of it. He—he may try again. Blythe and Miss McCready should take different rooms, perhaps on my corridor."

She gazed at me in consternation. "All right, Ariel. That's easily done. But who is 'he'? Tell me what's happened. Where did the staircase lead to?"

"To a chamber of horrors."

Chapter Nineteen

It was the next day, and we had again taken our seats in the courtroom. The unseasonable humidity had broken at last, rent by a cool wind that had come up in the night, blustering across the island.

Isadora and I had sat talking late into the night, trying to decide the best course to follow. Without Gwendolyn's own story, which she was adamantly against disclosing, without some evidence such as the journal linking Dr. Chandler with Cordelia's death, we knew that the police would never take us seriously. And it did sound fantastic, incredible, even to our own ears. The well-respected physician, a proponent of evil, with his hideous schemes to promote a better, stronger humanity, winnowing out the weak and, to his eyes, the immoral. Isadora had been just as incredulous when I had blurted out everything Gwendolyn had told me as I was when I first learned the truth.

We had agreed that the least we could do was show the police the secret panel and staircase which led to the tunnel linking Copper Beeches with Oaklawn, but I placed no reliance on their using that as a determining factor to stop the trial. Cordelia had been murdered in the summerhouse, so the doctor had not used the tunnel that night. There was really nothing linking Cordelia's death with the other ghastly acts Dr. Chandler had committed, not without Gwendolyn's testimony or the journal. Still, we had resolved to confide all we knew to Mr. Bredbeck following the day's trial, and hope that he might be able to come up with some way to convince the police to reopen the investigation.

The courtroom was no longer hot and airless, but I was warm and flushed with agitation and a new desperate sort of anticipation. On entering the courtroom I had searched the crowd for Gwendolyn, praying that she had changed her mind and would testify against her father. But she was not there. Sick with disappointment, I sat down, noticing, as I did so, that Dr. Chandler and his wife were seated across the room. So again he had come ostensibly to support Drew, but in reality to watch as the noose drew tighter about his neck. I wanted to stand up and accuse him myself, to point my finger and shout before everyone his list of infamous crimes. But I would be dragged from the room as a hysterical woman who was willing to invent any preposterous story to save her lover. Even now I trembled to think that Mr. Bredbeck himself would be loath to believe me.

The courtroom was crowded, the summer colonists present in full force. This was the most important day of the trial, and they were all eager to hear what Drew Rockwell would have to say for himself.

Mr. Bredbeck was asking him about the various philanthropic concerns in which he had participated; I was scarcely listening. I could only think of the horrible discoveries I had made yesterday, and I knew that Isadora and Aunt Hermione were as frantically restless as I was. If only I could get the journal from Gwendolyn; that way her story would not have to be the crucial factor, and she would not have to testify against her own father. I wondered whether she could be forced to appear in court and submit to interrogation about what she knew. Was there a law which forbade a person having to testify against his or her mother or father, the way a wife did not have to testify against her husband? But even if she were placed in the witness box, she still might refuse to tell the truth. She was terrified of her father and feared what he might do to her if he were not convicted. If I was unable to get hold of the journal, then Gwendolyn's willing compliance was Drew's only hope. I doubted whether my insistence of Dr. Chandler's guilt would be enough to make the police exhume Maisie Leander's body and examine it for signs of a recent abortion, or to inspect the doctor's carriages for indications that one of them had been involved in an accident.

Mr. Bredbeck had now got to the night of the dinner party. Yes, he had been furious with Cordelia; yes, he had demanded a divorce. He was determined to end their marriage. But that decision did not make him a murderer. At the time of Cordelia's death, he had been in Miss Ariel Morrow's room, and he had not left it. He and Cordelia had agreed to a divorce; they were going to discuss the details the next day. It simply did not make sense that he had gone to the summerhouse and strangled her, leaving the body to be found. The very least he would have done would have been to make it look like an accident.

Studying the faces of the jurors, I could see they were uncertain. They knew of Drew and respected him, but the circumstances were so damaging. Drew had hated his wife; she had been repeatedly unfaithful to him (if they were to believe Isadora); she had publicly humiliated his mistress (for she was *now* whatever she had been before) and left her career in tatters; she had threatened to take his beloved daughter away from him; and now she was dead.

It was all the same, over and over. When would Mr. Bredbeck finish? None of this was important; none of it mattered. I sat there twisting my gloves in my lap, trying to think of ways I could get a message to Gwendolyn without her father's knowledge, urging her to find the journal and somehow get it to me.

And then the prosecutor, Mr. James, stood up. Drew met his gaze squarely, hard lines about his mouth, his face pale. He had answered Mr. Bredbeck's questions clearly and calmly, but Mr. Bredbeck was his own attorney. I gnawed on my lip, wondering how much more of this I could endure.

All the while the kind-faced Dr. Chandler sat across the room, playing so well the role of concerned friend. And why not? He had had years of practice, pretending to be so saddened at the death of Nathan Rockwell and worried about his frail sister.

"Mr. Rockwell," Mr. James was saying, "how long were you married to your wife?"

"Almost nine years."

"And how did you decide, nearly nine years ago, to marry her? Did you fall in love in the conventional way and ask her to be your bride?"

"Not exactly."

"Tell us exactly."

"I agreed to my father's wishes."

"In other words, your father chose her as a suitable bride for you. How old were you then, Mr. Rockwell."

"I was twenty-two, she nineteen."

"Did you want to marry her, Mr. Rockwell?"

"Objection," said Mr. Bredbeck.

Mr. James glanced over his shoulder at the indignant Mr. Bredbeck, and then turned to the judge. "I am attempting to show, Your Honor, that Mr. Rockwell was forced into a marriage at a young age when he conceivably did not know his own mind."

"Overruled," said Judge Harrison.

"Were you and Mrs. Rockwell happily married?"

Drew did not answer; a muscle jerked in his taut cheek.

"Answer the question, Mr. Rockwell," said Judge Harrison sternly.

"No, we were not."

"You did not wish to marry Mrs. Rockwell and the marriage became increasingly repugnant to you over the years, is that not true?"

"Yes," he said curtly.

"I understand, Mr. Rockwell, that you had a son. What happened to him?"

Briefly a look of pain crossed Drew's features; then he straightened. "He died two years ago of scarlet fever."

No! I wanted to shout. It's not true! Oh God, when would this fruitless ordeal be over?

"You were greatly distressed by this. What about Mrs. Rockwell? How did she react to this tragedy?"

"She—she was not particularly overwrought."

"Isn't it true that she continued to take part in social events while the rest of the family was still in mourning?"

"Yes."

"And did you consider that the behavior of loving mother, the mother you wanted for your children?"

"No, I did not." His voice was cold.

"Is it true that your wife rarely saw her own children?"

"Yes."

"I understand that Miss Morrow helped out in looking after your daughter between governesses. Is this true?"

"Yes, along with a few of the maids and my sister."

"But not your wife. Miss Morrow has a way with the child, doesn't she? She is caring and gentle and patient—just the sort of mother a child should have. Is this not so, Mr. Rockwell?"

"I suppose so."

"You suppose so. Come, Mr. Rockwell, have you

388

not envisioned Miss Morrow as the new mother of your daughter, the little girl that her own mother avoided and ignored whenever possible? It was Miss Morrow and Miss Rockwell who took the child home when she became frightened in the carriage, was it not, while her own mother continued on Ocean Drive?"

"Yes."

"You were very angry with your wife, weren't you?"

"Yes."

"Because she had struck your daughter across the face. You threatened to kill her on that day. Your own servants testified to that."

Drew said nothing.

"Isn't it true, Mr. Rockwell, that your daughter wakes up frequently in the night and cries out?"

Yes, she does—and I know why! I wanted to shout.

"Yes," said Drew.

"Who goes to her to comfort her when this happens?"

"I do, generally."

"What about Mrs. Rockwell? Did she ever go up to soothe her daughter?"

"No."

"And Miss Morrow—did she?"

"Once or twice, yes. Her room is on the same floor as my daughter's."

"So again Miss Morrow did things for the little girl that her own mother refused to do. Miss Morrow was beginning to take the place of the child's mother soon after her arrival. Not deliberately, not purposely perhaps, but nonetheless she was nurturing the child."

Why did Mr. James keep on referring to Blythe as "the child"? She had a name, for God's sake.

"You must have thought many times over the last three months, Mr. Rockwell," continued Mr. James, "how much better suited Miss Morrow was to be the

389

child's mother than your own wife."

"Objection!" cried Mr. Bredbeck, leaping to his feet.

"Sustained. Mr. James, keep your speculations to a minimum."

"I apologize, Your Honor. You claim, Mr. Rockwell, that you and your wife discussed a divorce just after the break-up of the dinner party."

"Yes."

"What was your wife's reaction?"

"She was just as determined as I to end our marriage."

"And why was that?"

"She claimed I had giving her grounds which she was going to bring up in court."

"And what were those grounds?"

"What she believed to be my affair with Miss Morrow."

"What she *believed*." Mr. James raised his brows. "Do you deny that Miss Morrow is your mistress?"

Oh, no, this was far worse even than the interrogation I had received. Mr. James was making Drew look blacker and blacker.

"What I told Cordelia that night was the truth — Miss Morrow and I had not committed adultery."

"Your forbearance, if it to be believed, is remarkable, Mr. Rockwell."

"Objection, Your Honor. My colleague's sarcasm is quite unprofessional," said Mr. Bredbeck.

"Sustained. I do not wish to warn you again, Mr. James. We are not in this court to provide your opinions with a podium."

Mr. James regarded Drew with narrowed eyes. "Mr. Rockwell, did you engage in sexual relations with your wife?"

There were gasps and murmurs from all directions; the judge rapped on his desk.

"No," said Drew.

"Not ever? How long had it been since you and Mrs. Rockwell had engaged in such relations?"

Drew's face was tinged with color; his voice was cold. "Not since she was pregnant with our second child."

"And so you had a marriage in name only for the last five years?"

"Yes."

These questions were too much for one woman who had collapsed in a presumed faint and had then to be carried out of the courtroom. I fought an hysterical urge to laugh uproariously in an effort to release the stifling tension.

"You claim that your wife was repeatedly unfaithful to you. You have admitted that for five years you did not enjoy the normal pleasures of a husband. Why then, Mr. Rockwell, did you not seek a divorce years ago? You had grounds yourself, if we are to believe you and Miss Isadora Rockwell."

"I did not want my children — my daughter — to be affected by the scandal which I feared would result were I to divorce my wife on grounds of infidelity."

"So you sacrificed your own happiness for the sake of your child. You are a very noble character, Mr. Rockwell." Mr James's voice was silky. "That is, noble when you had no other temptation. But then this past June something happened. Miss Ariel Morrow came to Copper Beeches. And you began to revise your thinking about divorce, did you not?"

"No, I did not," said Drew. "I was still thinking of Blythe, my daughter. She — she has not been well since her brother's death. I felt that the scandal of a messy divorce could do irreparable damage to her future. I did not want her growing up in the shadow of all that."

"But you did wish to marry Miss Morrow, did you not?"

"Miss Morrow . . . understood the way things

were."

Oh yes, I had understood. We had both been prepared to be noble, as Mr. James had said, yet still everything had gone drastically wrong, I thought bitterly.

"Let us proceed to the night of the dinner party, Mr. Rockwell. Let's assume that, as you say, you had been opposed to a divorce from a selfish, unfaithful woman you loathed, and were resisting your very natural desire of taking a lovely, talented young woman as your mistress—let's assume that is indeed true for the time being. On the night of the dinner party, your wife revealed a portrait painted by Miss Morrow that she had ruined with turpentine. Then Mrs. Rockwell accused you and Miss Morrow of being lovers in front of fifty guests. Suddenly your wife has gone too far; at this point it is obvious that you and she can no longer live under the same roof. Suddenly your daughter's future is pushed into the background; you demand a divorce. What were your grounds going to be?"

"That she had been unfaithful to me," said Drew shortly.

"In other words, the grounds you had refused to use before."

"Yes."

"And your wife—she also wanted this divorce. Was she going to stand by and allow you to divorce her?"

"She—"

"Didn't she threaten, Mr. Rockwell, to name Miss Morrow as corespondent in what would, in the light of Miss Morrow's famous father and your and Mrs. Rockwell's positions in Newport Society—where all eyes of the country are drawn—be a notorious divorce case?"

"I no longer cared about that. Cordelia had already created a scandal."

"Mrs. Rockwell threatened to take your daughter,

392

did she not?"

"Yes."

"And what was your response?"

His face hardened. "I was prepared to fight for custody of my daughter."

"Isn't it true, Mr. Rockwell, that you said you would see your wife dead before she took your daughter from you?"

"I did say so, but it was said in the heat of anger."

"Just answer the question, Mr. Rockwell," said Mr. James crisply. "You love your daughter very much. She is a sensitive child, is she not? Fearful? Sickly?"

"Yes," said Drew through his teeth.

"You had the argument with your wife on the second-story landing, and most of what was said was overheard by Miss Morrow and a few of your servants in the dining room. Each of you was determined to win custody of Blythe Rockwell."

"She would have destroyed Blythe's life," said Drew, trying hard to keep his control. "I would never have given her up willingly."

"So you were prepared to go through an ugly custody case — the kind, in fact, you had resolved to steer clear of heretofore."

Drew said nothing.

This was a nightmare; in agony I whispered to Isadora, "I can't stand it! If I have to listen to this any longer, knowing what I know now, I'll scream!"

She squeezed my hand. "We'll go straight to Mr. Bredbeck once court is adjourned. You must be as calm as you can, Ariel. Mr. Bredbeck will put no stock in what you say if you aren't. This can't go on much longer. Just try to be patient. Do you want to go outside? I'll go out with you."

Distractedly I shook my head. Leaving the courtroom would be even worse. I had to know what was happening.

393

Mr. James was saying, "At the time you were discussing a divorce with your wife on the second-story landing at Copper Beeches, did you believe that you would be granted custody of your daughter?"

"Yes. I was the better parent," said Drew forcibly.

"So in the heat of the moment you considered it plausible that you would win a custody battle, marry Miss Morrow, and take your daughter to live with the two of you."

"That was my plan. And it never altered," Drew said.

"But I put it to you that it did indeed alter, Mr. Rockwell. I put it to you that sometime after leaving your wife on the second-story landing, after going to Miss Morrow's room to consummate your relationship for what you claim to be the first time, you began to view the matter in a serious light. That you realized that your chances of winning custody of your daughter were slim, and that you had better take matters into your own hands, once and for all. You did not want to leave your daughter's life, her future — something you admit to being most concerned about — to the whims of a judge. Pardon me, Your Honor."

"That's ridiculous!" cried Drew. "If I had wanted to kill her, I certainly wouldn't have implicated myself, choosing strangulation as the method, making it so obviously murder. I have more intelligence than that, Mr. James!" Drew was now openly furious.

So did Dr. Chandler normally have more intelligence than to obviously murder his victims, except that on this occasion he knew there would be a prime suspect.

"I would say that you have a great deal of intelligence, Mr. Rockwell," answered Mr. James smoothly. "So much of it that you purposely chose that method, as you refer to it, to rid yourself of your wife, simply because it would look as though only a fool would kill his wife in that way. And you were no fool, Mr. Rockwell. You were a man goaded beyond endurance, who calculated the best way to end your marriage and send your wife out of your life forever where her influence could never touch your child. By killing her and leaving her to be found dead in the summerhouse, you hoped that it would be viewed as the act of a roving maniac, or of a burglar, and not the husband who had actually done it."

"That's a lie!" shouted Drew, his knuckles white as he gripped the wall of the stand in front of him. "I never saw my wife again after our argument on the landing. I was going to fight and win custody of Blythe and leave Copper Beeches to Cordelia."

"Oh, God, Isadora—" I got out hoarsely. "I don't know if I can—"

"I have no doubt that you were confident of that coming to pass *then*," said Mr. James to Drew. "But it was later that the calm light of reason took over and you realized the future could not be as you wished were your wife still alive."

"No, that is not true. I am *not* a murderer!"

"Ariel, look!" said Isadora, gripping my arm. "It's Gwendolyn!"

"What?" I gasped out, searching the room wildly.

"Over by the door, at the back. This *must* mean she is willing to talk!"

"But that's impossible! She was so adamant! What could have made her change her mind?"

"What does that matter? We've got to get a message to Mr. Bredbeck to call her to the stand. Quick—before the court adjourns!"

Hastily I scratched a note to the defense attorney imploring him to call Gwendolyn Chandler as a witness for the defense. Isadora snatched it and moved over to hand it to a bailiff.

Mr. James was saying a few more things, but I

could not absorb them. My nails dug into my palms as I watched the man give the note to Mr. Bredbeck. What if he refused to call her? What if she suddenly lost her courage and refused to speak? What if her father did something to prevent her being heard? What if she collapsed on the stand, failing to convince the jury of her father's complicity?

Frantically glancing back and forth between Mr. Bredbeck and Gwendolyn, I thought I was going to be sick. Mr. Bredbeck frowned, staring down at the note. Then he turned round to look at us searchingly.

"Please, please," I mouthed, gesturing back to where Gwendolyn stood.

Mr. Bredbeck rose. "The defense would like to call one remaining witness, Your Honor. Some new facts have apparently come to light, and I ask the court's permission to hear them." His voice was hard; it was obvious that he was reluctant to question Gwendolyn in court before having had the chance to speak with her privately. His reputation was at stake, but so was Drew's life. And he realized this. Still, he looked very uneasy.

Judge Harrison's face was impassive, but I imagined that he was as surprised as the rest of the court. Mr. James was regarding Mr. Bredbeck with narrowed eyes; even Drew looked wary.

The judge said, "Very well, Mr. Bredbeck. But these facts had better be relevant to the case. I had assumed that we had heard the testimony of all the witnesses."

"Thank you, Your Honor. The defense calls Miss Gwendolyn Chandler to the stand."

"Gwendolyn Chandler!" I heard again and again. There were startled cries; Dr. Chandler had leaped to his feet, his expression thunderstruck. But just as swiftly he had resumed his seat, assuming a worried look. Oh dear, Gwendolyn was acting very oddly.

396

Everyone knew how concerned he was about his brilliant but peculiar daughter. She stayed at home much of the time so her father could look after her. What had she to say that would have any bearing on the case? She would show that she was even more disturbed than people had imagined. So disturbed, in fact, that she might have to be put away . . .

Gwendolyn walked forward, her gaze leveled straight ahead. She wore a plain brown suit. The incredible tension I felt was just as evident in her face, in her frame. All eyes were on her, some exasperated, some perplexed, some even repelled. But the noisy confusion had been replaced by a tangible silence as everyone waited breathlessly to hear what she would say.

Drew was looking as startled and baffled as all the others. He had been dismissed from the stand earlier and had resumed his seat.

Gwendolyn stood in the stand, facing Mr. Bredbeck and all the court.

"State your name for the Court, please."

"Miss Gwendolyn Chandler."

It was obvious that Mr. Bredbeck was uncertain of how to proceed. He was not in control and he did not like it. "Miss Chandler, have you any information to tell the court that is relevant to this case? Remember, this man, Drew Rockwell, is on trial for the murder of his wife, Cordelia Rockwell." His voice was grave.

Gwendolyn hesitated; I was nearly biting my lip in two. Isadora's forehead was damp with perspiration.

"Come on, girl," said Aunt Hermione softly, "Don't lose heart now."

Gwendolyn spoke. "Drew Rockwell did not kill his wife." Her voice did not waver.

"How do you know this, Miss Chandler?" asked Mr. Bredbeck.

"Because I know who killed her," she said harshly.

There was more commotion; the judge barked out, "There will be silence in this courtroom!"

"Just—tell us what you know, please, Miss Chandler."

"Drew Rockwell did not kill his wife," repeated Gwendolyn. "Mrs. Rockwell was murdered by . . . my father, Dr. Prescott Chandler."

All hell broke loose. The judge was pounding with his gavel; Drew was staring at Gwendolyn, shocked beyond belief; the spectators were twittering and exclaiming, ignoring the appeals for silence.

Dr. Chandler was on his feet, crying out, "Your Honor, please allow me to take my daughter home. She is not well. Last night she suffered a breakdown of the nervous system. As her father and physician, I ask that she be sent home where my wife and I can see that she is cared for, before she makes a mockery of this court of justice."

He spoke convincingly, his voice filled with concern for the well-being of the daughter he loved, despite her unbalanced mind.

The judge looked as though he didn't know what to do. I was terrified that he would send Gwendolyn down from the stand. But then her voice rang out clearly and coldly.

"I ask that the court listen to what I have to say. If, after you have heard everything, you doubt both my sanity and my sincerity, I will step down."

This was a new Gwendolyn, I realized. There was a determination, a purpose to her that had been missing last night. What had happened to make her change her mind?

"Very well," said the judge, reassured by her calm demeanor. "Please go ahead, Miss Chandler."

"My father went to the summerhouse behind Copper Beeches and strangled Cordelia Rockwell."

"Did you see this happen, Miss Chandler?" asked

Mr. Bredbeck.

"No."

Mr. Bredbeck frowned. "Then how do you know?"

"I know. He told me."

"Why would your father kill Mrs. Rockwell?"

"Because she was going to tell my mother that Mrs. Leander had not killed herself by jumping off the cliff, but had died following an operation my father had performed."

There wasn't a sound in the courtroom; even the reporters had ceased their endless sketching and scratching on their tablets.

"What sort of operation, Miss Chandler?"

"An abortion."

Dr. Chandler stood up again. But there was nothing on his face but evident distress for his daughter's precarious state of mind and health. "Your Honor, I implore you. My daughter is very obviously unwell. I must take her home. She suffers from these . . . delusions from time to time. Her mother and I are very worried about her as her condition is seemingly deteriorating. We have tried to help her live a normal life, but that is becoming increasingly impossible. She is very ill, Your Honor."

He was so convincing. I almost believed him myself. The judge glanced from Dr. Chandler to Gwendolyn who had begun to tremble. Unable to stand it any longer, I jumped up from my chair.

"Please, Your Honor! Let Miss Chandler speak! It is imperative. She is *not* unwell—just frightened!"

From across the room Dr. Chandler gazed at me, aghast.

"Miss Morrow, sit down! The court does not recognize you. I will no longer endure interruptions of any kind. You may take your daughter away, Dr. Chandler, when I say so, and not until then. Go ahead, Miss Chandler. There is nothing to be afraid of."

"How do you know that your father performed an abortion on Mrs. Leander?" asked Mr. Bredbeck.

"Because I saw it. I saw with my own eyes her body on my father's table in the basement. The sheet she was lying on had been white. When I saw it, it was soaked in blood, and on the floor . . . horrible . . . horrible . . ." She bent her head, shuddering.

Mr. Bredbeck's face was horror-stricken, as were the faces of those around me.

"And—and Mrs. Rockwell found out about this atrocity?" asked Mr. Bredbeck, trying to recover himself.

"Yes. She had told him she would go to my mother and tell her that he had been performing abortions for years. And she was going to let it be known among Society members that my father was nothing but a hack. My father would have been shunned by the people he most admired—Society's best and fittest." Her voice was heavily sardonic.

"You see, Your Honor, my father believes that it is his mission in life to weed out those people who, according to him, do not deserve to live—the sickly, the crippled, the ones who stray from their class and threaten the strength of the elite. Aside from Mrs. Leander and Mrs. Rockwell, he has killed several others—Thomas Bateman, a coachman employed by Mrs. Leander. He shot him and made it appear to be suicide. He also drove a carriage which struck down a young man, William Everett. And two years ago, he suffocated two-year-old Nathan Rockwell by pressing a pillow to his face."

Drew bolted out of his chair, his face livid, his eyes wild. Out of his mouth came a terrible strangled cry, ghastly to hear. He would have lunged across the room at Dr. Chandler had not two men restrained him.

Dr. Chandler had also stood up in the midst of the

400

resulting confusion. "This is ridiculous! I demand that you allow me to take my daughter away! She is mad—isn't it obvious? Many of you know her fragile mental state. Isn't what she is saying proof that she has gone over the edge?" He glanced around, appealing to his friends and acquaintances.

"Sit down, Dr. Chandler, or I will hold you in contempt of court. And you won't be able to take your daughter anywhere!" shouted the judge. He turned to Gwendolyn. "Miss Chandler," he said severely, "you have made some very serious allegations. Do you have any proof that they are true?"

"Yes. I have this." From inside her jacket she drew out a small black book.

"The journal—she has it!" I gripped Isadora's arm.

"Look at Dr. Chandler's face!" she hissed back.

"What is that?" the judge was asking.

"It is a journal my father keeps. In it you will find all that I say is true. He wrote about each person I have mentioned. He wrote that he knew Drew Rockwell would be suspected and arrested. He had plans for his daughter, Blythe, as well. He tried to kill her once, by turning on the gas in her room while she and the maid slept. He knew it would be assumed the maid had been careless. What did it matter? She was only an ignorant Irish girl—and there are far too many of them for his liking. It's all in there, in the journal.

"My father will try to convince you that I wrote the journal myself. But I can show the police his operating room in the cellar of our house, Oaklawn. And Miss Morrow and I can show you the tunnel connecting our home with Copper Beeches, the tunnel that was built years ago by Mr. Rockwell's grandfather who had built both houses, one for himself and the other for his sister. My father discovered it himself. It had been sealed up when Oaklawn was first sold and it became unnecessary—and likely unsafe. My father, though, used that tunnel to go to Copper Beeches and murder the little Rockwell boy. The tunnel leads to a panel in the wall of the nursery wing—Miss Morrow found it herself yesterday. If I am delusionary, then so is she. But I do not believe the police will be delusionary as well. And if the body of Maisie Leander is exhumed, the real cause of her death can be determined."

Drew's face was stricken; I longed to go to him and comfort him. It was heartbreaking to watch him learn the truth about his son's death, that he had not died from scarlet fever, but had been murdered in his sleep.

Suddenly it was Olive Chandler who stood up. "Your Honor, I beg that you will allow me a few words."

"Who are you, madam?" asked Judge Harrison sharply.

"I am Mrs. Prescott Chandler. This disturbed girl is my daughter. Her father is right—she cannot be held accountable for what she is saying. I beg you to allow us to take her home. It isn't her fault, however. Miss Morrow has put her up to this!" I gasped; Mrs. Chandler glared at me with hatred from across the room. "Miss Morrow has poisoned my poor daughter against her own father, so that her lover will go free. She came to our house last night to see Gwendolyn, although she pretended it was to see my husband. She is wickedly using my daughter for her own purposes! I know nothing of this so-called operating room, this tunnel. Don't you think that if my husband had truly done these dreadful things that I would have some inkling of it?"

Gwendolyn fixed her pale, luminous eyes on the judge. She was trembling again. "It's true, Your Honor. My mother knows nothing of the operating room or of anything else. She cares for nothing but her position in Society. Six years ago my father discovered I had fallen in love with my piano instructor and was planning to run away with him. He was a very talented young man, but poor, hardly someone my parents would have allowed me to marry. I was . . . pregnant. My father sent my lover away and then told me I must get rid of the baby, that I wasn't to have it. I refused. I threatened to run away, to search for my lover. He . . . drugged me and performed an abortion." She paused, swallowing hard.

"Why did you never tell anyone of this before, Miss Chandler?" asked Mr. Bredbeck, almost dazed.

"I—I couldn't. I was afraid. My father said he would have me locked away. But then late last night, I spoke with my father alone. I told him that I was leaving his house, that I could not sleep another night under his roof. I was not going to stand by and watch him destroy more lives. I told him I was going to look for . . . the young man I had once loved."

She gazed steadily across the room at her father. "He—he told me that I would never find him. Because he was dead. My father told me that six years ago he had beaten him, breaking his hands so that he could never take his joy from the piano again. And then—then he had drowned himself." She took a great sobbing breath. "My father had known this all along. He was certain that I would never leave, that I would never betray him. When he and my mother came to court this morning, I searched for and found his journal."

Mr. James rose. "Your Honor, this is a very affecting story, but very strange as well. Miss Chandler, by her own words, has great reason to hate her father. But this hardly excuses the wild accusations that she is expecting the court to swallow."

"Do you desire further proof of the infamy of my father, Mr. James?" cried Gwendolyn harshly. "Then let me disclose one more thing. I have told you that my father drugged me and performed an abortion. But that was not the only operation he performed on me. Do you know what a clitoridectomy is, Mr. James? I believe that they are still legal in France. My father saw to it that . . ." She began to weep, tears coursing down her cheeks. "My father made certain that I would never again be able to take pleasure from lying with a man. He . . . maimed . . . me for the rest of my life, six years ago. And if you still refuse to believe me, Mr. James, I will submit to an examination."

There were outraged, revolted exclamations from all about the courtroom. Mr. James was stunned; the judge was regarding the silently weeping Gwendolyn with terrible pity. Olive Chandler had fainted. Dr. Chandler pushed through the crowd and rushed to the back of the room in an attempt to flee. But before he reached the doors, he was seized by a court guard and two male spectactors, and held fast.

"Your Honor," said Mr. Bredbeck shakily over the noise of the crowd, "I ask that the charge be dropped against Drew Rockwell for the murder of his wife, Cordelia Rockwell."

"Granted," said Judge Harrison, suddenly looking old and weary. "I now issue a warrant for the arrest of Dr. Prescott Chandler."

Pandemonium filled the court as it was dismissed, but I paid no heed to the hue and cry or the appalled gazes of the spectators and reporters. I surged forward to meet Drew and fell into his embrace, rejoicing in the feel of his arms about me, his kisses on my cheeks and mouth. And then Isadora and Aunt Hermione were beside us, and Mr. Bredbeck was asking what should be done about Gwendolyn who was still weeping in the witness box.

"We'll take her home with us," said Drew.

* * *

That was nearly ten years ago. Dr. Chandler never went to trial for his crimes. He hanged himself in jail while the prosecution was building a case against him. Olive Chandler sold Oaklawn and returned to New York where we understood she lived as a total recluse until her death three years ago.

Gwendolyn stayed with us at Copper Beeches for several weeks, but after her father's death she announced she was leaving the country for good. She lives in Geneva, Switzerland now where she give piano concerts to benefit the poor and ill, the people her father despised and deemed unfit to live. I see now that in her earlier bizarre behavior and remarks, she was desperately hinting at the wickedness of her father.

Drew and I were married in October in John La Farge's Byzantine-style Congregational Church, less than six weeks following his trial for murder. We had no guests except for the family; Blythe was my flower girl. That winter we remained in Newport, relishing the raw wind and bleak sky which gave us the privacy we so cherished and which was vital to our building a new life together.

When the summer came and I knew I was pregnant with our first child, we sailed to England with Isadora, Blythe, and Miss McCready. And so it has been every year since. In early June we leave Newport to its orchestrated gaiety, and, in the fall, when the other mansions are boarded up and left useless, we return to open Copper Beeches to the bracing temperatures, the salt-laced breezes, the views of fading hydrangea and hedges of scarlet rosehips.

We roam the Cliff Walk where far below the surf pounds against ocher rocks, where the water gleams azure or teal or a dusky bayberry. And the other mansions stare out gloomily to sea, cold and sterile.

Drew and I have four children of our own, three boys and a girl, and Miss McCready is still with us, beloved by them all. Blythe is now sixteen. She understands everything that has happened, but her intense fears of early childhood did not vanish overnight. The night Nathan died she had sensed that something was taking place when the mobile began to sway. It was that image which remained with her, although she could not remember what it signified. It was guilt over her brother's death which kept her plagued by anxieties; she had always been protective of him while he lived, and blamed herself for her helplessness in preventing his death. We have helped her see that she was in no way responsible, and, although it has taken years, I believe that she is finally free of her fears.

Drew ordered the tunnel sealed up completely at our end. The movable wall panel was taken out and new paneling put up to conceal the bricked-up entrance to the staircase. For months Drew was haunted by thoughts of the diabolical man Dr. Chandler stealing through the tunnel, entering the nursery and bending over Nathan's bed. While Drew was cleared of Cordelia's murder and set free, the relevations made by Gwendolyn in the courtroom left agonizing scars that took a long time to heal.

I wrote to my grandparents, a long, difficult letter informing them of my marriage and explaining what Olive Chandler had done, turning them against my mother because of her own thwarted desires. The letter was returned to me and I made inquiries, learning that they had both passed away. The house, Starlings, and its contents had been left to a distant connection of my grandfather's. What saddened me most when I learned the news was that they would never know that whatever Olive Chandler had written to them many years before had been vicious lies. But they had chosen to believe Olive and had repudiated their own daughter themselves; Olive had not done it for them.

I have continued to paint, though not for commissions, and have exhibited some of my works — portraits of my children and friends and one of Isadora — at both the Royal Academy in London and the National Academy of Design in New York.

Isadora is married to a Harvard professor whom she met on one of the first summers we spent in England. She has a full, happy life and children of her own; we see her family often when we are in Newport. Aunt Hermione lives with them, still a peppery old lady at eighty-two.

Drew and I have known great joy together while we have dealt with the pain of the past. And we feel blessed that we have been granted a life together, despite the terrible ordeals which came before.

In the autumn evenings as the lavender dusk deepens to plum, as the surface of the fish pond dulls like the colors in the Dawn stained-glass window, we walk arm in arm over the grounds of Copper Beeches. It is the weeping beeches I miss most when we are away, their dense hanging branches like the long heavy locks of enormous dryads. And each September when we return, I hurry down to the Moongate, listening for the whispering.

It is then that I know I am home.